Maggie Furey was born in North East England. She is a qualified teacher, but has also reviewed books on BBC Radio Newcastle, been an advisor in the Durham Reading Resources Centre and organized children's book fairs. She now lives in County Wicklow, Ireland, with her husband and six cats.

ALSO BY MAGGIE FUREY

Aurian
Harp of Winds
Dhiammara

THE SWORD OF
FLAME

Maggie Furey

For Jean, whose indomitable character was a
match for any Mage.

An *Orbit* Book

First published in Great Britain by Legend Books 1995
Reprinted by Orbit 1998

A CIP catalogue record for this book
is available from the British Library.

ISBN 1 85723 653 X

Printed and bound in Great Britain by
Mackays of Chatham PLC, Chatham, Kent

Orbit
A Division of
Little, Brown and Company (UK)
Brettenham House
Lancaster Place
London WC2E 7EN

1

The Miracle of Spring

Parric would never forget that sunrise – that momentous dawn when winter's evil grip had been loosed at last, and glorious spring had spread her gentle wings across the world. The cavalry master had been standing through the long hours of darkness on the high parapet of Incondor's tower, chilled to the bone despite his cloak and an extra blanket thrown loosely around his shoulders. The unaccustomed burdens of leadership had chased away all hope of sleep so he had volunteered to stand watch while the others rested, and had climbed up here to be alone with his thoughts.

Parric had much to plan concerning his journey back to the Xandim lands, and the cavalry master from Nexis, who had risen to become Herdlord of the Xandim, had an additional responsibility now in Aurian's strange new companions from the south. But Parric found it hard to concentrate on mundane details this morning. Instead, he found his gaze turning repeatedly to the northwest, towards the towering mountain peaks beyond which lay lofty Aerillia, the Skyfolk citadel. Aurian, the headstrong young Mage whom the cavalry master had followed halfway across the world, had gone there in haste the previous day, borne aloft by winged warriors. She had left Parric again, with barely a word of explanation, though he had travelled through so many perils in search of her and had only just found her.

The cavalry master's thoughts had been dark with dismay as he stood looking out across the bleak expanse of snowfields that were slowly emerging beneath a sky growing pale behind its gloomy overcast, as the wan light of another shrouded sunrise seeped reluctantly across the bleak, stark landscape. What the blazes was Aurian up to now? What was so important that she had left her newborn son behind at the

Tower of Incondor? Parric only knew she had gone to find Anvar, the servant who had fled with her from Nexis on the night of Forral's death. Parric frowned. What was Anvar to her, that she had gone rushing off in such frantic haste? True, she'd always been fond of the lad, but ... 'Oh, don't be bloody stupid, Parric,' he told himself. It was a waste of time to worry about Aurian. She'd had little time to tell him much about her adventures, but from the fragments he had managed to glean, it was obvious that the Mage was capable of coping with far more than a bunch of flying freaks such as the Skyfolk of Aerillia.

Somewhat cheered, Parric decided to go in search of something to drink that would take the chill from his bones. As he turned away from the parapet he was startled by a movement above him, on the very edge of his vision. His warrior's reflexes had him crouched in a defensive corner, sword in hand, before he even realized what was happening. When his thoughts had time to catch up with his instincts, the cavalry master emerged somewhat sheepishly from his refuge, sheathing his sword with a rueful curse. It was a good thing no one had been about to see him, he thought. A right fool he'd have looked!

Parric scowled up at the changing sky. Clouds. Nothing but bloody clouds, that's what had alarmed him. 'I must be getting old,' he muttered to himself – then suddenly he stopped and looked again, his eyes narrowing as they squinted up into the growing brightness. Something un-natural was happening. The clouds were moving faster and faster; racing, hurtling across the sky towards the north. Towering banks of dark vapour rolled ponderously across the heavens, disintegrating, even as Parric looked on in awe, into smoking, streaming shreds, as though they were being ripped apart by the jaws of some mighty wind – yet on the ground, where the cavalry master stood, not even the breath of a breeze was stirring. Patches of high, clear sky began to appear as the cloud cover thinned and was whisked away. Parric looked up into a breathtaking blueness, such as he had not seen for a long and dismal age. He let out a low whistle

2

of surprise, and lingered to watch the clearing sky. The unexpected beauty of the sight lifted his spirits far better than any liquor could have done.

As the last of the vanquished clouds fled the eastern horizon, the sun burst forth in all its glory, spreading a blaze of golden warmth like a benison across the world. Before Parric's disbelieving eyes, the snow that had locked the land in chains for so long began to melt, dissolving and shrinking away with uncanny speed. On the walls of the tower, icicles formed and dripped, and the nearby thicket was filled with the patter of falling droplets as boughs and twigs shed their coating of snow. Within minutes, it seemed to Parric, the chill white blanket that had covered the mountains for so long had vanished completely, leaving great pools and lakes of standing water that were already beginning to seep away – and a familiar sound that the cavalry master had not heard in many months: the joyous, rippling song of rushing water as the icebound streams were freed at last.

This miracle had to be Aurian's work! The untried young woman who had fled the northern city of Nexis so many months ago was older and wiser now, and hardened by sorrow and struggle. And somehow – Parric felt the certainty deep within his bones, and shuddered in awe – she had managed to find the power to break the paralysing spell of winter that the evil Weather-Mage Eliseth had cast across the world. At long last, Aurian had started to turn the tide of evil wrought by the foes who were her own kin and blood, and soon would be bringing the battle home to those who had slain her beloved Forral and enslaved the free Mortals of Nexis.

Parric would have rushed down into the tower to share the good news – but there was more to come. Spreading like a verdant tide across the brown, frost-blasted hillsides came a haze of varied green as the earth awakened, and the plantlife, dormant for so long in corm and seed, began to stir and stretch. Heather and juniper, grass and moss and fern, put forth foliage and fronds in an explosion of new life. In the thicket below the tower new leaves began to sprout, like tiny banners of celebration, while snowdrops dotted the grour

3

between the outspread roots. The air was moist and fragrant, and tingling with new life. Spring had come to the mountains in a single bound, erasing every trace of winter as though it had never been. Somewhere in the depths of the thicket, a lone bird – one tiny, valiant survivor of the iron cold – began to sing.

Parric's joyful yells aroused the sleepers in the tower. One by one, they stumbled out through the narrow doorway, rubbing sleepy eyes, then stopping to stare and gape in astonishment as they registered the changes that had taken place in their world while they slumbered. Out came the swarthy Khazalim soldiers from the far south, leaderless now that their prince, the misguided and treacherous Harihn, had been slain. Out came Parric's own troops, the little band of Xandim warriors he had brought with him to help in the rescue of Aurian. In their midst were the two Xandim exiles, Schiannath and his sister Iscalda, who had befriended Aurian during her imprisonment in the tower. They had been redeemed now, and reunited with their people, and such joy shone in their faces that Parric found himself smiling in response to their happiness.

Following somewhat more hesitantly, as though they were still in fear of their traditional foes the Xandim, came the companions that Aurian had picked up on her southern travels – what were their names? Parric frowned, trying to remember. Eliizar – that was it. The bald, rangy, one-eyed man was the swordmaster Eliizar, and the small, plump woman who followed in the wake was his wife Nereni, chattering, to Parric's amusement, non-stop as usual as she voiced her astonishment at the sudden spring. The cavalry master didn't have to understand her language to know just what she was saying.

Behind Eliizar and Nereni came Bohan, towering above the others. Cradled tenderly in the eunuch's huge arms was the tiny form of Wolf, Aurian's son, born amid a storm of violence and bloodshed only two days (could it only be two ~~uld~~ scarcely believe it) before. The child had ~~ed~~, he reflected with a shudder. The poor in~~cursed~~ before his birth by the evil Archmage

Miathan so that he would take the shape of the first beast Aurian saw after bearing him. When Aurian had called the wild wolves from the surrounding area to help her escape from the tower, little Wolf's fate had been sealed. Parric looked down sadly at the tiny cub in Bohan's arms. It was as well that the child had such a staunch protector. The poor mite had not had much of a start in life. And when was his mother coming back for him? Why had she left so precipitately? Just what, in short, was Aurian doing in the lands of the Skyfolk?

Spring had come to Nexis. Sunlight washed over the city in a honeyed tide, gilding the tips of towers and spires, pouring its healing warmth over sagging thatch and flaking limewash, and mellowing the harsh old fascias of crumbling brick and venerable stone. The trees that screened the merchants' mansions on the southern bank of the river were misted over with a haze of new leaves that mingled every possible shade of green. Across the river on the northern bank, delicate threads of smoke, soon whisked away by the fragrant breeze, rose from every chimney – a sure sign of coppers aboil in the kitchens below, where the householders were indulging in an orgy of spring cleaning. New-washed clothing, strung up across every inch of space in backyards and on balconies, wreathed the city in a rainbow patchwork of celebration banners.

The air was vibrant with birdsong, and from scores of shutters, flung wide to admit dry air and sunshine, came the rasp of saws and the rhythmic tapping of hammers as the citizens of Nexis set to work with a will to repair the ravages of winter. Women sang as they wielded scrubbing-brush, bucket and broom; children, half-wild with the heady thrill of liberation from endless days spent in dark, damp rooms, ran shrieking with excitement through the drying mud of the alleys.

Only in two hearts was the joy of spring conspicuously absent. Miathan, Archmage of Nexis, stood looking out over the parapet that guarded the lofty, open temple crowning the roof of the Mages' Tower. Beside him was Eliseth, the

5

Weather-Mage, whose plans had been so cruelly thwarted by the death of the unnatural winter she had summoned. The endless, ice-locked season had been her own creation and charge, and now, as she looked out across the city, a scowl of angry disgust distorted her flawless features, while her cold grey eyes held the expression of a hawk that had struck at – and missed – its prey. The Archmage suppressed an ironic smile. Though his own plans were currently in tatters, he was old and cunning enough to know that such setbacks could be reversed, given time. Meanwhile, he could take some small consolation from this irresistible opportunity to feel smug at Eliseth's expense, despite the fact that he himself had not emerged unscathed from his latest encounter with his rene-gade, runaway apprentice – Aurian.

Miathan had clearly not been paying sufficient attention to the screening of his thoughts – or Eliseth's mind had been running along a similar track. Turning to the Archmage, she scorched him with a scathing glance. 'Well?' she snapped. 'Proud of your pupil, are you? Just look at this – and all because you let Aurian and her paramour Anvar escape you!' She glared at the sunlit panorama below her as though it was a personal affront. 'What in the name of all the gods do we do now?'

'I have no idea.' With an abrupt motion of his hand, Miathan quelled the protest that was forming on the Mage-woman's lips. 'I have no idea – yet,' he continued, 'but rest assured, Eliseth, this battle is not over – not by a long road. Now, of all times, we must stay calm, and think, and plan – and, as a matter of priority, complete our defences.' Striding across the flat rooftop, he crossed to the other side and turned the glittering gaze of the gems that were his eyes towards the south, as though to pierce the long miles that separated him from Aurian. 'One thing is certain,' he mut-tered. 'Suppose we do nothing at all, it is only a matter of time, now, before Aurian comes to us.'

Aurian was cleaning the rust from her sword.

'Must you do that in bed?' Anvar protested sleepily.

'I was waiting for you to wake. Now that you have, I'm sure I can think of a better alternative.' Aurian's eyes twinkled as she looked across at her fellow-Mage. Winning the Harp of Winds had changed him, much as she herself had been altered when she had recreated the Staff of Earth and claimed it as her own. Anvar was *more*, somehow, than he had been before. His blue eyes sparkled with a greater intensity; his hair was a brighter shade of gold. An aura of vibrant power surrounded him, transforming his entire being into something that appeared more than merely human. Aurian, however, had undergone a similar transfiguration, and knew that appearances could be deceptive. In his heart, where it mattered, her fellow-Mage was the same as he had ever been.

Anvar stretched and smothered a yawn. 'What time is it?'

Aurian shrugged. 'Haven't a clue.' She glanced out of the window. 'It's dark again, though, so we must have slept all day.' She sighed. 'I suppose they'll be coming to fetch us soon, for Raven's celebration banquet – not that it'll be much of a feast. This winter has left the Skyfolk on short rations indeed.'

'It won't be so bad,' Anvar replied. 'While you were talking with Shia this morning, Raven remembered all the food we left cached in the forest on the edge of the Jewelled Desert. She went off at once with a squadron of Winged Folk to collect it. *And* to try out her newly recovered powers of flight,' he added with a frown.

'Blast her! I just healed those wings of hers – and it was anything but easy,' Aurian said. 'She had no business putting such a strain on them so soon!'

Anvar was still frowning. 'I don't understand why you did it at all,' he burst out angrily. 'After betraying us as she did, she didn't deserve . . .'

'Hush, love.' Aurian laid a gentle hand on his arm. 'You were still in trouble, here in Aerillia, and Shia was trapped here too, remember? I knew you both were in danger, and I had to get here quickly – I needed Raven's cooperation.' She looked down at Shia, who was curled up fast asleep, taking up the remaining space in the odd-looking circular scoop

7

that the Winged Folk called a bed. The great cat was still exhausted from her heroic, near-impossible climb up the sheer cliffs to Aerillia, to bring Anvar the Staff of Earth – and her part in the battle that had taken place in the Temple of Yinze, that had resulted in the death of Blacktalon, the vile and corrupt High Priest of the Winged Folk. Shia was also worn out by her grief over the fate of Hreeza, the gallant, valiant, sharp-tongued old cat who had been her friend, and who had been brutally slain in the temple, at the hands of a blood-crazed Skyfolk mob. Aurian sighed. Poor Hreeza's body still had not been found.

'I'm sorry.' Anvar's voice pulled the Mage away from her sad thoughts. 'I know you had good reasons for healing Raven. It just – well, it galls me, that's all. After everything we suffered, because *she* betrayed us . . .' With an effort, he dismissed the subject. 'Anyway, Raven can wait. What were those alternatives that you were mentioning when I woke up?' Now he was grinning, and there was a wicked twinkle in his eyes.

'Allow me to demonstrate.' Aurian was consumed by a surge of pure happiness as she slipped the now-gleaming Coronach, her precious and long-disused sword that she had rescued from the Tower of Incondor, back into its scabbard, and reached out to her lover. She slid her fingers through the silken gold of Anvar's hair; lost herself in the blue depths of his eyes. Her arms encircled him, his skin smooth to her touch, his body hardened to spare bone and muscle and sinew by the privations of their quest. His embrace welcomed her . . .

And at that moment they heard the whirring of great wings on the landing platform outside their tower lodgings, followed by a thunderous knocking on the door, and the ring of steel as Yazour and Chiamh drew their weapons in the adjoining room where they had been sleeping with Khanu, Shia's other feline companion.

Aurian cursed, and groped beyond the edge of the bed for her scattered clothing. 'Now what?' she muttered sourly.

The winged messenger, when they let him in, was in a state of considerable agitation. 'Come quickly, come quickly,' he cried. 'Something dreadful is happening in the ruins of the temple. We heard screams . . .'

'It's not fair!' Linnet muttered. Scowling, the winged child glowered around the now-deserted ruins of the Yinze's temple, and kicked a loose stone from the top of a tottering pile. The stone went bouncing away, dislodging a small cascade of other rubble that slid after it with a staccato rattle. Linnet jumped back, startled, her wings spread for flight. She half-expected to hear a grownup voice raised in reprimand – the Father of Skies only knew, the temple was wrecked enough without her adding her own contribution – but nothing stirred save the sharp, dying echoes of the clatter of stone on stone. Nobody was there to scold Linnet – no one, in fact, had even noticed that she was missing, the fledgeling thought, with a sniff of self-pity. The grownups were all across at the palace, celebrating the unexpected coming of spring to their lands, the accession of the new queen, and the rediscovery of the Harp of Winds by some strange, alien, wingless Wizard. Linnet's small but vital part in these miraculous events appeared to have been forgotten.

'It's just not fair!' Linnet muttered again. 'By Yinze – *I* was supposed to be the hero!' Had Cygnus, the white-winged Skyman, not promised her as much? Why, had she not single-handedly carried the news that the queen was being held captive by Blacktalon, the evil High Priest? *And* at the risk of dire retribution from her mother for having been playing where she had no business to be in the first place! Linnet sat down on a fallen beam and dropped her chin disconsolately into her hands. 'That Cygnus promised me a reward, too,' she sighed. 'But what with all the fuss and excitement about everything else, I don't suppose he'll remember.'

A lot of things had been forgotten since the strange, wingless Wizard with eyes the colour of the sky had appeared out of nowhere in the ruined temple, carrying the Harp of Winds. Linnet couldn't understand what all the fuss was about. A harp – so what? Why, old Martin, the instrument-maker, could turn out harps by the dozen! Oh, the thing looked pretty, for sure, twinkling and glowing as though it

9

had been wrought of purest moonlight and the glimmer of stars – at least, it had seemed that way in the quick glimpse that Linnet had been able to snatch before Louette, her mother, had whisked her away to take care of her little brother Lark while Louette went off to the palace with everyone else.

'And now they're all having fun except me,' the winged child grumbled, aggrieved. She huddled down, shivering, and wrapped her wings tightly about herself. Spring it might be, but the glittering starcrazed night still held a lingering chill, as if winter, though defeated by the power of the Harp, was loath to slink away. Linnet tried to warm herself with the fire of righteous indignation. 'I should be there, at the palace! I should be getting my reward for saving the queen – not sitting at home with that little brat!' But in truth her conscience was nagging her – for, of course, she was *not* at home taking care of Lark. Once her brother had fallen asleep, Linnet had crept out and headed for the palace, hoping that she would be able to sneak up close as she had done on the fateful day (could it really only be yesterday?) when she'd found the captive queen – and catch a glimpse of the festivities through some window. And if only she could attract the attention of Queen Raven's white-winged companion, without her mother catching her first, then she might get her reward after all.

Linnet's plans, however, had come to nought. Halfway to the palace, her courage had failed her. It had been different last time, when the gigantic edifice had been virtually deserted while the Winged Folk mourned the passing of Queen Flamewing. Tonight the towers and spires had been aglow with a blaze of torchlight that outrivalled the red-gold glory of the sunset, while clamorous swarms of excited Skyfolk circled the turrets and went zipping in and out of every doorway, preparing the best possible feast that could be managed from the meagre stock of remaining supplies. The winged child could not get anywhere near the building without being spotted – and if her mother should catch her, it wouldn't be a reward that she'd be getting! A bitterly disappointed Linnet had been turning away to head back home

10

when her eye had caught the black and shattered shell of Yinze's temple.

The fledgeling's thwarted, rebellious spirit had guided her towards the menacing hulk of the temple ruins. She had so desperately wanted to be distinguished by the important folk at the palace – already, she had unwisely bragged to her friends about her adventures, and the reward she'd been promised. Linnet couldn't bear to think of the teasing she'd receive on the morrow when the other children discovered that she'd been left tamely at home to sit with Lark. At least the ruins held out the hope of another adventure – or at least, if she used her imagination, an incredible and thrilling tale with which she could impress the others, and hopefully avert their taunts.

Now, however, the rush of indignant disappointment had begun to cool, and Linnet was having second thoughts. While the blush of sunset had still bathed the sky with rose and amber light, the ruins had just looked like some old, harmless heap of stones; but now that night had laid a shadowy caul across its scarred and shattered face, the temple had taken on a far more sinister aspect.

A shiver ran down the winged child's spine. In the deceptive gloom, eerie transformations were taking place all around her. An upstanding sliver of stone, all that remained of one of the decorative archways, had become a tall, cloaked figure, its features hidden within the fathomless depths of a cowl of deepest black. Twisted pieces of votive silver took on the eerie gleam of ghosts, while a scattered drift of broken crystal from the massive stained-glass window depicting the Fall of Incondor had become the glitter of many unknown eyes. A pile of fallen stone had turned into the lithe, sinister contours of a crouching beast. Everywhere, shadows were advancing in the stillness: obscure shapes of deeper black against the thickening darkness. They seemed to be reaching out for Linnet – and what did they conceal? Was the ghost of Blacktalon stirring amid the desolate ruin of his stronghold? Would he come creeping forth out of the darkness, clutching the ghastly trophy of his severed head?

'Oh, for Yinze's sake, don't be stupid!' the winged child

11

told herself sharply, speaking aloud to boost her faltering courage. 'There's no such thing as ghosts – they don't exist!' Nevertheless, a tactical retreat at this point seemed a very good idea. After all, she told herself, Lark just might awake, and be afraid to find himself alone . . . Linnet only needed to find a souvenir – some distinctive item, to prove to her friends that she had actually been here . . .

Linnet stooped, peering narrow-eyed into the gathering gloaming and wishing she'd had the sense to bring a torch. Then, as she scrabbled amongst the cold, rough, sharp-edged stones, a blood-chilling sound came tingling into her ears. A low, bubbling moan that reverberated through the very rocks below her feet and rose in an eerie, wailing crescendo. With a breathless squeak of terror, the fledgeling spread her wings to flee – and went sprawling to her hands and knees as her left foot slipped between two loose chunks of masonry and twisted, unbalancing her and pulling her down. Though Linnet, oblivious in her panic to the pain, tugged with the strength of terror, the foot remained obstinately jammed. She was trapped.

Linnet bit her lip to stop herself from crying aloud; a fleeting glimmer of common sense told her that the last thing she needed was to draw attention to herself. The wailing came again – softer this time, as though whatever creature was making the anguished sound had gone beyond the limits of its strength. Linnet wet herself. The warm, spreading dampness was an utter humiliation, noted in some deep, buried place at the back of her mind – the part of her brain that dealt with normal, everyday occurrences. But the terrified core of herself had taken control now. The fledgeling wrenched again at her unyielding foot, too scared to even cry out as another white-hot lance of pain pierced her leg. All at once, time seemed to slow, as her mind began to work with the speed of desperation. Linnet analysed her predicament in a lucid flash of inspiration born of extremity. She saw that the two great chunks of stone trapping her foot were too heavy for her childish strength to shift – but they were bedded on a base of loose rubble. If she could dig that out, she might unbalance one of the blocks, and free herself . . .

Sobbing with fear, Linnet clawed frantically at the loose, surrounding stone until her fingers bled, hoping to shift the balance of the larger blocks. Then, as she cleared a space, her stinging, abraded fingers met with something warm, soft and yielding. Something that moved. Into the fledgeling's mind came the faintest whisper of a harsh old voice: *'Help me . . . You can hear me – help me . . .'*

One of the palace revellers, having slipped briefly outside to clear the wine fumes from his head, heard a scream of terror ripping through the night. The unnerving sound came from the vicinity of the temple. Grey with shock, he swooped back inside on shaky wings, to raise the alarm.

'Well, I'll be damned.' Aurian, kneeling in the shallow pit from which the rubble had been hurriedly flung aside, laid a fleeting hand on Shia's broad head. 'So this is your old friend Hreeza who you thought was dead!' She laid her hands on the cold, battered, recumbent body that lay before her, and shook her head in amazement. 'She's incredibly lucky to be alive, that's all I can say!'

'That remains to be seen.' Shia, with Khanu peering anxiously over her shoulder, poked Hreeza's body with an anxious muzzle. 'Will she survive, do you think?'

Aurian caught the underlying thread of anxiety in the great cat's tone. The *caring* was different, she mused. Shia, though speaking in extremity, and in tones of deepest concern, had never spoken of the Mage, or Anvar, or any of their party in that way. But this time, the casualty was one of her own folk. Aurian wished she had a comforting answer, but she could never bring herself to lie to Shia. Their relationship went too deep.

Aurian probed Hreeza with her healer's senses, but the response of the old cat was not encouraging. None the less, she tried to remain positive. 'If the stubborn old fighter has such a stranglehold on life, I'd say she has every chance, so long as we act quickly.' The Mage shook her head in amazement and dismay. 'Broken bones – the lot!' she muttered. 'She must have been unconscious all the time, or you'd have

13

heard her, Shia. I would guess that the child disturbed her – brought her out of it in some manner. Somehow, in the depths of her being, she must have realized it was her only chance of rescue – but that one last, desperate struggle to seek help was almost enough to finish her . . .'

Even as she spoke, Aurian was summoning her healing powers, augmented by the might of the Staff, to pull the old cat back from the brink of death. Swiftly she worked at knitting fragile bones and restoring the sundered tissue; losing herself in the complexity of the task, yet half-aware, after a time, that Anvar was by her side, his hand on the Staff, steadily feeding her with energy to supplement her own so that she would not be too depleted at the end of her work. Chiamh knelt by the great cat's head, using his own spells to force air in and out of Hreeza's lungs, keeping her breathing while Aurian worked. The winged physicians Elster and Cygnus hovered behind the Mage, peering rapt with fascination over her shoulders and marvelling at her healing powers.

Aurian's repair work was basic, and carried out as swiftly as possible to minimize the threats of cold and shock to her fragile old patient. After a time, she rose swiftly to her feet. 'Very well,' she said briskly, 'that'll hold her for now, but we must get her quickly to warmth and shelter without disturbing the remainder of her injuries or jeopardizing these delicate new repairs.' Aurian turned to her fellow-Mage. 'Anvar – I'll need you to back me up. Will you hold the Staff with me, as you did in the desert, and boost my power? I want to take Hreeza out of time for a few minutes, and use my mother's old apport spell to send her safely to our quarters.'

Anvar's eyes widened. 'What – simultaneously? Isn't that a little drastic?'

Aurian shook her head. 'Not really. It'll be tiring, though – I'm somewhat out of practice, having recovered my powers so recently. That's why I'd appreciate your help.'

Anvar made her a sweeping bow. 'For my Lady – anything.'

'Get on with it!' Shia growled, and the Mages, sensing her anxiety, turned quickly back to their patient.

14

The time spell was simple enough, and Aurian sent a brief prayer of thanks to the spirit of her old friend Finbarr, who had taught her that particular piece of magic while she was still a girl. Once Hreeza was safely immobilized, Aurian prepared herself for the apport spell. She grasped the Staff firmly, feeling Anvar's hands, warm and steady, beside her as she opened herself to the power of the Artefact. Concentrating hard, she wrapped the web of her power around the old cat, cradling Hreeza in a sheath of magic that shimmered with the Staff's unearthly green light. Then, visualizing the desired destination – her own tower rooms – Aurian gathered her will and *pushed*.

In a flash of emerald radiance, Hreeza vanished. Air rushed in with a thunderclap to fill the space the cat had occupied, and the watching Skyfolk leapt back with oaths and cries of startlement, rubbing the dazzle from their streaming eyes. Aurian sagged against Anvar, feeling, despite his assistance, as though she had carried Hreeza every inch of the way on her own back. That was the trouble with apport spells, the Mage reflected ruefully. They might move objects quickly, but their range was very limited, and they took every bit as much energy as more conventional methods.

Chiamh, the Xandim Windeye, was leaning limply against a pile of broken masonry, his eyes unfocused and blank with their sheen of silver, and Aurian realized that he was using his particular talent of riding the wind to check whether the old cat had reached her destination. Even as Aurian watched, he shook himself abruptly and pulled himself upright, the reflective glimmer draining from his eyes to restore them to their usual warm amber. 'She got there safely,' he informed the Mage in awestruck tones. 'Light of the goddess, Lady – what a spell! Can you move yourself like that, also?'

Aurian smiled and shook her head. 'Can you pick yourself up by your own boots?' she countered, and turned back to Anvar. 'Come on – let's go and finish healing Hreeza.' Frowning in sudden recollection, she looked around. 'By the way, what happened to the little girl who found her? In all the excitement, we forgot to thank her . . .'

'I would leave that for now, if I were you.' Anvar gestured

15

over his shoulder, and Aurian, gathering her wits after the draining apport spell, became aware of a commotion taking place in the shadows some distance away. A scolding voice and a flurry of slaps followed by a rising wail told the Mage that the winged child's mother had passed the point of relief and had reached the stage of anger. Aurian winced sympathetically. 'Poor mite,' she murmured.

'Wait until it's your turn,' Shia interjected slyly. 'You have all these joys of motherhood still to come.'

Aurian raised her eyes to the heavens. 'May the gods help me,' she muttered.

As Aurian approached the young physician-priest, calling for her winged bearers to take her back to her tower, Cygnus turned hastily away from her, unwilling to show the Mage his face, lest she divine his most secret thoughts. In a blaze of bitterness and envy, he had watched her healing powers at work, knowing in his heart that he was wrong to resent such miraculous gifts, but unable to help himself. How could the gods be so unjust? the white-winged physician wondered, as his mind went back to the depredations of the dread, uncanny winter, and his own inability to help his suffering people. Why should these freakish wingless ones possess such powers while his own race, once Magefolk in their own right, remained impotent and bereft?

Across the shadows, Cygnus looked at Anvar, who was clambering into a net to be transported across to his tower. As the Mage pushed a hampering fold of his cloak aside, the Skyman glimpsed the eldritch glimmer of the Harp of Winds, strapped securely to Anvar's back. The physician clenched his teeth, seething with resentment. Why should this alien, this interloper, possess the most precious heirloom of the Winged Folk? What right had he to keep it, when it truly belonged to its creators? Perhaps – just possibly – the precious Artefact would be able to return the lost and stolen powers of the Skyfolk ... 'And if I possessed the Harp,' Cygnus murmured to himself, 'I might become a true healer at last ...'

Eliizar stood in the open doorway of the Tower of Incondor, blind to the beauty of the rich spring landscape that spread out before him like a colourful tapestry, and deaf to the song of the returning birdlife and the cheerful calls and chatter of the warriors who brushed past him as they bustled in and out of the tower, preparing to set out for their various destinations. It seemed to the one-eyed swordmaster that he was the only one who wasn't busy, on this second day of the miraculous spring; and with the possible exception of Parric, the leader of the Xandim band, who, by his demeanour, appeared to have a weight of worries on his mind, Eliizar was certainly the only one who wasn't cheerful.

The swordmaster sighed, feeling low in spirits and very much alone. Nereni had gone off, some time before, towards a nearby stream, carrying a tottering pile of dirty laundry and singing cheerfully to herself. Bohan was sitting in a sheltered patch of sunlight in an angle of the tower wall, with the two great wolves that Aurian had selected to be foster-parents to her son in her absence stretched out beside him, for all the world like shaggy grey hounds. In the eunuch's lap, on a blanket, lay the tiny cub that was the Mage's child. Eliizar shuddered, nauseated by the sight of the accursed creature. How could Aurian bear it? he wondered. How could she possibly love such an abomination? How could she be so calm about the whole dreadful business?

If only Yazbur would return from Aerillia! Apart from the practical difficulties that Eliizar's little group had been encountering because their translators were all away in the lands of the Skyfolk, the one-eyed warrior desperately needed to talk to someone who might understand. He had lain awake all night, wrestling with the dilemma that beset him, and in the bleak and solitary watches of the night he had reached his decision at last – the only decision, he had decided grimly, that made any sense. The problem was that Aurian would not be very happy about it – and Nereni wasn't going to like it at all. None the less, the matter must be addressed – and there was no point in putting it off. Squaring his shoulders, the former swordmaster of the Khazalim arena set off in search of his wife.

Guided by a drift of fragrant woodsmoke on the breeze and the sound of distant singing, he soon found her where the stream ran out of the thicket below the tower. A large old cauldron, which had hung from a hook in the tower hearth, was now scrubbed free of its rust and dirt, and was steaming gently over a crackling fire. Blankets and various items of clothing had been spread to dry on the bushes. Nereni was kneeling on a folded cloak at the water's edge, beating a linen tunic against the rocks that edged the stream and singing softly to herself as she worked.

Eliizar hesitated for a moment at the edge of the coppice, screened from his wife's view by a patched grey blanket and a curtain of fresh green leaves. It had been a long time since he had seen Nereni happy like this – and now he must be the ruin of her newfound contentment. As he stepped out reluctantly to greet her, she scrambled to her feet, the dripping tunic still clutched in her hands, and her face beamed with additional joy at the sight of him. 'Eliizar! I was wondering where you could be. I . . .' As her voice faltered, the sword-master knew that his expression must have given him away.

'Why, Eliizar, whatever ails you?' Nereni was frowning now. 'How can you seem so gloomy on such a wonderful day?'

'I must speak with you.' Eliizar was hoping, praying, that she would forgive what he was about to say to her. 'Nereni, our kinfolk are leaving tomorrow,' he plunged on quickly. 'They are returning to the forest at the desert's edge, to build homes and make new lives for themselves, away from cruel kings and magical battles, and I – I firmly believe that we should go with them.'

'What?' Nereni's expression was growing stormier by the second. 'Leave Aurian? Leave Anvar? Absolutely not, Eliizar! How in the Reaper's name could you even suggest such a dreadful thing?' As if to emphasize her words she hurled down the tunic that she had been washing. It hit the surface of the stream with a resounding slap and began to float away on the current as the little woman rounded on her husband, her water-wrinkled fingers clenched into fists.

Eliizar took a hasty step backwards. He had never seen his

gentle spouse so angry. 'My dearest – only listen for a moment . . .' he begged.

'*Only listen?* Why should I sully my ears with such treacherous, ungrateful talk?' Nereni shouted. 'Aurian is our friend, Eliizar! How could you even think of leaving her? Who will care for her if I do not? These Magefolk may be powerful, but *practical?* Why, neither one of them can so much as boil a pot of water without burning it . . .'

Eliizar sighed. He had known that this was going to be difficult. 'They have other powers that will more than compensate,' he insisted, 'and other companions who can help them, far better than we can, on their northward journey. Hear me out, Nereni, please. It is not our business to involve ourselves in this unnatural sorcery, and this is our last chance to leave – before we become hopelessly embroiled in their fight against these other Magefolk.'

Eliizar was talking quickly, not giving his wife a chance to interrupt. 'We cannot pass through the mountains alone,' he went on. 'We either leave now, with our own folk – our own kind, Nereni – or embark on a road that has no turning back. And what will the future hold for us, as strangers in a foreign land – a land beset by blackest sorcery?'

There was a new coldness, unnerving and unfamiliar, in Nereni's eyes. 'You're afraid,' she said softly.

Shamefaced, unable to meet her gaze, the swordmaster dropped his face into his hands. 'Yes,' he whispered. 'In the face of this sorcery, I *am* afraid – afraid as I have never been before.'

'And so you ask me to choose, now, between you and Aurian, who became our friend, and forgave us for putting her through the ordeal of the arena, and freed us from the power of the tyrant Xiang . . .'

'Nereni, stop! This is more than I can bear!' Her words had pierced Eliizar's heart like a spear of ice, turning him cold with horror. Nereni thought he was asking her to *choose?* The notion had never occurred to him – it was not the way of Khazalim. It was a man's place to decide the comings and goings, and a woman's place to go, or stay, as he dictated. For the first time in all their wanderings, he understood how greatly matters had changed between himself and Nereni. And yet . . .

Eliizar looked at his once-timid, placid, unadventurous little wife, and saw the newfound spark and spirit in her eyes. He suddenly realized that her courage and common sense had become more pronounced – and appreciated by the other companions – as their journey had progressed. Why had he been so blind for so long? Indeed, Nereni had coped far better with many of the shocks and surprises of their adventures than Eliizar, swordmaster and seasoned warrior, had done!

Even as these thoughts were racing through Eliizar's mind, he was aware of Nereni's unrelenting gaze fixed upon his face as she waited for an answer. He had been humbled and outdone by the courage of his wife, and it was not a pleasant feeling. The swordmaster felt his face grow hot with anger. 'No, wife,' he growled. 'I am not asking you to choose. I have decided that we will return to the forest with our people, and I am telling you that you are coming with me.' With that, he turned on his heel and strode away, back up the hill in search of Jharav, the veteran officer who was now in charge of the Khazalim contingent. Eliizar did not look back, and it was his own misfortune that he did not. The expression of anger and disgust on Nereni's face might well have persuaded him to reconsider.

2

Journey's Beginning

In the moonlight, the lichened grey stones of the Tower of Incondor looked as though they had been dipped in silver. On the slope between the ancient, crumbling pile of stone and the reaching shadow-fingers of the thicket, every blade of the blossom-starred turf was sharply outlined in a chiaroscuro of sharp-cut shadows and frosty light, almost as though winter had stolen back again on stealthy feet. But the air was alive with the tingling fragrance of spring: a reassuring promise that the days of endless cold were gone at last, although the night breeze was still cool enough, and the two winged couriers were grateful for the warmth of their close-wrapped wings.

The Skyfolk messengers, stationed here at the behest of Queen Raven and the groundling Mages, sat perched like a pair of gargoyles on a high projection of worn stonework at the rear of the tower, as far away as possible from the presence of the wingless aliens with whom they had been forced to associate. Following their refusal to sleep with the foreigners inside the tower, they had been allotted a place on the roof, where a crude lean-to shelter had been constructed for them against the warm stones of the chimney; but the constant circuits of the rooftop sentry had disturbed their slumbers, and the brilliance of the night – for the dazzling moon was just past its full – had made them restless. Eventually they had been driven to this dizzy perch between sky and ground, where they could think in peace, and talk softly and privately about the momentous changes that had taken place in their city over the previous two days.

Apart from the monotonous footfalls of the sentry as he made his rounds on the rooftop above the Winged Folk, nothing stirred in the moondrenched stillness. After a time

21

the quiet speech of the couriers grew fitful, and faltered into silence. Then, breaking into the profound peace of the night, came the tiniest of sounds – a faint, high-pitched creak as the tower door eased open.

The two Skyfolk stiffened, instantly alert, and glanced at one another in wide-eyed alarm. They did not completely trust these groundling strangers, and anyone skulking about in the middle of the night must surely be up to no good. An unspoken signal flashed between the two winged figures. Silently, stealthily, long knives were eased from sheaths, and the couriers tensed their wings for flight. Soft footfalls could be heard ... Someone was creeping round the side of the tower.

It was fortunate for the prowler that the moonlight was so bright. As soon as the Skyfolk saw the silhouetted figure of their stalker, they sheathed their weapons and relaxed their combative stance, their expressions changing from alarm to amused astonishment. Why, it was the little woman who seemed to feel the need to mother everyone in the en-campment – the one who kept plying them with such delicious food. The one groundling among the lot of them that the Skyfolk trusted to pose them no threat.

'What in the name of Yinze can she be doing?' one of the winged messengers hissed to his companion. At the sound of his whisper, the groundling looked up, placed a finger to her lips in signal silence, and beckoned them down. 'Aerillia, Aerillia,' she whispered urgently, tugging at the arm of the nearest Skyman and pointing first to herself, and then to the dark heap of meshes that was their cargo net, left safely at the foot of the tower wall. For a few moments, the winged couriers had difficulty believing what they thought she meant by her urgent gestures. At last, however, one looked at the other. 'She wants us to fetch the net and take her to Aerillia?'

His companion shrugged. 'She can mean nothing else.'

The first winged messenger looked ruefully at Nereni's plump form and flexed his wiry arms. 'Why her?' he sighed. 'Couldn't they have sent one of the others, for Yinze's sake?'

Aurian, narrowing her eyes in concentration, peered into the

22

deceptive, shadowed gloom of the cramped tunnel, and blessed the gods once again for the gift of her Mage's night vision. 'Shift that torch a little, would you please?' she muttered over her shoulder to Cygnus. 'I'm working in my own shadow here.'

Beside her, the Mage felt Anvar's shoulder brush against her own as he wormed his way forward to take a closer look into the narrow gap between the fallen stones. 'That's the place we want,' he said. 'There – can you see it? Where that big slab of rock has slipped at an angle. If we can just wedge it upright somehow, it should prop the others . . .'

'Look out!' Aurian's sharp cry was all but drowned by the ominous grinding noise overhead. As her soulmate had leaned forward to point, even that small movement had disturbed the delicate balance of the stones. As one, the two Magefolk flung their magical shields outward and upward, extending the fields of force to support the shifting slabs. After an endless moment, the grating rasp of stone on stone wore down into silence, leaving only the liquid patter of a stream of grit and dust that sifted through the cracks.

The last spark of fitful torchlight vanished. The Mages leaned against each other in a darkness that only their eyes could pierce, panting slightly from the effort of holding the sagging roof in place. 'Bugger!' Anvar muttered. 'That was a bad one.'

'*He* obviously thought so.' With a tilt of her head, Aurian indicted the deserted stretch of clear tunnel behind them, down which their winged companion had, unsurprisingly, fled.

'Skyfolk!' Anvar grimaced in disgust, although the Mage knew that he blamed their frightened companion no more than she did. Or did she? Aurian frowned. This mad notion to explore the ruins of the priestly archives below the Temple of Yinze in search of clues that might lead them to the Sword of Flame had been suggested by Cygnus. It had seemed a good idea the night before, when discussed at length with the winged physician over a flagon of wine, but the reality of burrowing through these unstable tunnels had proved to be a perilous undertaking indeed. Surely Cygnus must have known of the dangers involved? He had certainly wasted no time in saving his own skin when the roof began to crumble. Aurian shook her head. I'm too suspicious these days, she thought. Why should Cygnus harm us after we freed him from Blacktalon and saved his queen? It could only have been honest fear. Though she and her partner had been shielding the group from the start, she knew it was hard for the Skyfolk to put their trust in something they couldn't even see.

The strain of holding up the sagging roof forestalled any further reflection. Aurian looked across at her partner, and the two Mages shared a wry grin. 'Think we can do it on our own?' Anvar's words were a challenge.

'Why not!' Aurian shrugged. 'Besides, the Skyfolk will be back shortly – if only to erect a memorial!'

Anvar chuckled. 'Come on, then. Which would you prefer? Keeping the shield up, or heaving stones?'

'The shield,' Aurian said decisively. 'Because I have the Staff of Earth, I'll have more power to take the weight of these rocks above us.' She glanced up doubtfully at the tons of stones balanced precariously over their heads. 'The last thing we want is the whole bloody mountain coming down on top of us. What's wrong?' She had caught a glimpse of Anvar's stricken expression.

'Nothing,' Anvar muttered. 'I was just remembering the last time I was down here . . .' He shuddered. 'It's a good thing for us that the Moldan's dead.'

'Hold on . . . Just a moment more . . .' Anvar's voice was harsh with strain, and Aurian, feeling as though she bore the entire weight of the mountain on her trembling shoulders, knew exactly how he felt. The great slab of tilted rock that Anvar had worked loose from its surroundings teetered on its base and began to rise slowly upright, impelled by the force of the Mage's will. As Aurian watched, her partner began the tricky part of the operation, manoeuvring the massive stone snugly into position to support the sagging tunnel roof. Almost there, and . . .

'Lord! Lady!' The sound of hurrying feet echoed down

24

the tunnel, shearing like a blade through Aurian's tight-stretched concentration and scattering the delicate balance of opposing forces that Anvar was using to move the rock. The great slab went crashing over, and in the split second before the roof came down on top of them, Aurian snatched the faltering shield back into place and felt Anvar throw the weight of his power behind her own. With one quick look at one another, they fled back down the tunnel that they had opened with such labour, crashing into the messenger, whoever it was, as they went. Aurian grabbed at a flailing arm and pulled the Skyman along behind her, and all three burst out into the daylight together. Behind them, there was a thunderous crash within the tunnel and loose stones toppled from the temple's ruined walls as the ground shuddered beneath them. Then there was nothing to hear but silence – and nothing to see but the cloud of dust that came drifting from the tunnel's dark maw and eclipsed the pale light of early day.

'You bloody fool!' Aurian snarled, rounding on the hapless, quaking messenger. 'You nearly got us all killed.' Ignoring the Skyman's stammered apologies, she looked around for Cygnus, who ought to have had more sense than to let stray wanderers into the tunnel when there was magic at work. She was sure she'd caught a glimpse of him as she emerged, but he had vanished now – presumably until she and Anvar had managed to get over the worst of their rage.

Anvar, his blue eyes icy with anger, was looking down into the tunnel mouth and scalding the air with curses. He put his arm around her shoulders and sighed bitterly. 'That's done it,' he muttered. 'We won't find anything down there now without excavating the entire peak.'

Aurian's heart sank. 'Well, it was a slender hope in any case, that we'd actually discover something down there that might lead us to the Sword. We'll manage somehow, love.'

'We'll just have to,' Anvar agreed grimly. 'We don't have any choice.'

The two of them stood, hand in hand, gazing gloomily down into the dark mouth of the collapsed tunnel. After a moment, Aurian noticed the winged messenger, still lurking nervously in the vicinity and clearly trying to pluck up enough courage to attract the attention (and possibly the ire) of herself and Anvar. She turned to the Skyman with a sigh. 'Well?' she snapped. 'Spit it out, man! What was so desperately important that you had to risk all our lives for it?'

The messenger turned pale beneath her withering glare. 'Lady,' he blurted. 'A visitor has arrived for you, from Incondor's tower. She demands to see you at once.'

'She?' Anvar was frowning, perplexed. 'There's only one she at the tower just now, if you don't count the Xandim, and that's Nereni. But she would never dream of – '

'It has to be Nereni,' Aurian interrupted. 'Who else could it be? It could be one of the Xandim, I suppose – but I doubt if Parric would send a stranger when the courier could bring a message just as well alone. But if it is Nereni, and she has actually flown all this way alone, her errand must be urgent indeed. We'd better go and see what she wants.'

Nereni wrapped numb fingers around the thin metal of the goblet and took another sip of the warm spiced wine, in the hope that it would stop her hands from shaking. The desperate courage that had brought her so far was threatening to slip away from her now. The airborne journey in the fragile, swinging net had been a nightmare beyond her worst imaginings. It hadn't seemed so bad at first, while darkness hid her surroundings and her thoughts had been wrapped up in anger with her unreasonable, mule-headed husband and the cold, sinking fear that Eliizar would, indeed, force her to make a choice between himself and Aurian – the two people she loved most in all the world. Eventually, however, at that freezing altitude, sheer discomfort had taken her mind off her worries. Then the sunrise had caught up with her winged escort, and Nereni, unwisely glancing down, had been treated to a dizzying view of the jagged peaks, so far – so terrifyingly far – below. At that point, she had forgotten both discomfort and concerns, and had simply shut her eyes tight and started to pray.

The nightmare had ended abruptly as she was dumped

unceremoniously on to an unyielding surface. Nereni, muttering imprecations, opened her eyes to find herself upon a narrow balcony without any railings. On one side of her was a mass of ornately carved stonework that proved to be the wall of a tower. On the other ... Nereni stifled a gasp and quickly tore her eyes away from the seemingly endless drop.

A tall, arched door of beaten copper led from the balcony into the tower. Nereni was puzzled for a moment by its unusual construction, for metal doors must surely be heavy, inconvenient and cold, but then she realized that wood must be very scarce among these barren peaks, while metal could probably be mined from the mountains' bones. One of her winged escort gave her a mocking bow and gestured towards the doorway, with a grin that Nereni wanted to strike from his smug face. She was annoyed that she had let him see how badly the flight had terrified her. The other Skyman, however, proved more considerate. He patted her arm comfortingly and, standing between Nereni and the edge of the chasm, disentangled her from the meshes of the net and helped her to climb unsteadily to frozen feet that had as much feeling in them as two blocks of ice. Leaning heavily on his arm for support, she hobbled as quickly as she could into the chamber beyond the landing platform – and staggered, as her guide dropped her arm and bolted at the sight of the massive black shape that came arrowing out of the shadows.

'Shia!' Nereni cried delightedly. It seemed so long since she had seen the great cat – not since that dreadful night when Prince Harihn, his mind controlled by the evil sorcerer who was Aurian's enemy, had turned his troops loose on the Tower of Incondor. Frankly, when Shia had escaped from the tower bearing the precious Staff of Earth to safety, Nereni had despaired of ever seeing the cat again. Now she was ashamed of her doubts and bent to hug Shia as the cat rubbed a huge head against her, almost knocking the little woman from her feet.

'You did it!' Nereni cried. 'You wonderful, brave creature – however did you manage it? To come all these leagues through cold and hunger and hardship with the Staff...'

Her voice tailed away as she suddenly took in her surroundings – and the two other great cats who seemed, to her shocked eyes, to take up most of the space within the chamber. One was curled, asleep, in the down-lined circular scoop that must pass for a Skyfolk bed, while the other sat nearby, watching her, its blazing golden eyes round with curiosity.

The little woman froze, her heart hammering wildly – then Shia gave her a quizzical, somewhat disgusted look and went to rub heads with the other cat. Nereni realized, rather sheepishly, that if these awe-inspiring beasts were friendly with Shia she would have nought to fear from them. None the less, she felt safer keeping her distance. Shia, an old, familiar companion, was one thing; these strange, wild and unpredictable beasts could be another matter entirely – and she was all alone in the chamber with them. Of Aurian and Anvar there was no sign.

Nereni, suddenly at a loss, wondered what her next step should be. Her winged bearers, obviously terrified of the cats, had beaten a hasty retreat, and there was no one to help her – nor, supposing one of the Skyfolk had been nearby, could she speak their language. Nereni's rash courage had been enough to bring her thus far, but it would get her no further. She looked helplessly at Shia, wishing that she could communicate with the cat as Aurian and Anvar could. 'Now what am I going to do?' she muttered.

She did not have long to wait for an answer – only long enough to mull herself some wine from the ingredients she found near the brazier that was the only source of heat in the chamber. While she sat there, trying to recapture her fleeing courage, Nereni heard the thrumming of wings outside, and the thud of someone landing on the platform. Shia snarled, loud and long, her eyes kindling with a menacing light as the door swung open and Raven entered.

The winged girl looked very different from the waif in the patched tunic, half woman, half child, that Nereni remembered. Now Raven was dressed in sumptuous crimson robes, cunningly designed to leave her wings and limbs free for flight, and a coronet of beaten gold gleamed richly amid her clouds of dark hair. Lines of sorrow gave an unexpected maturity to her face, and behind her eyes lurked the shadow of a bitter sadness that would never go away.

For an instant, the motherly woman felt her heart clench with pity for the suffering in the young girl's face. Then she remembered Eliizar, hurt and imprisoned in the dark, dank dungeon beneath Incondor's tower. She remembered the suffering Bohan, chained to the wall, each wrist a festering mass of sores beneath his manacles. She thought of poor Aurian, forced to give birth amid terror and turmoil, and shuddered at the memory of that moment of utter horror when reality had twisted and the Mage's child had changed shape within her hands. Nereni's mouth tightened. As Raven stepped forward hesitantly, plainly unsure of her welcome, she lifted her hand and slapped the winged girl as hard as she could across the face.

Raven took the blow without flinching, though her huge, dark eyes brimmed with tears. 'Would that you'd strike me a hundred times, Nereni, rather than stare at me with such contempt in your eyes.' The winged girl's voice was shaking with such anguish that Nereni's heart was almost softened – save that the events of the preceding months had changed the little woman so that she barely recognized herself.

'Do you think you deserve anything other than contempt?' she retorted bluntly. 'I loved you like a daughter, Raven, but you betrayed me to die without a thought – and Eliizar and Bohan with me.'

'No!' Raven gasped. 'Harihn promised! I didn't realize . . .'

'Yes you did,' Nereni went on inexorably. 'You should have known better – you *did* know better, in your heart – than to set the word of Harihn – the word of a stranger – against the safety of those who had loved you and cared for you when you were alone and afraid. Had the prince not had a use for Bohan, Eliizar and myself, we'd have been slaughtered out of hand – and even were that not the case, you had no right to betray the Magefolk to their enemies. Well you knew the fate that lay in store for *them*!'

Raven squirmed beneath Nereni's accusing gaze. 'But my people were suffering, and the Mages wouldn't help me . . .'

29

'You stupid girl!' Nereni snorted. 'Of course they would have helped you – eventually, once Aurian's powers had returned. You were not the only one to be in difficulties at the time, remember? If you had used your common sense, instead of behaving like a spoilt, pampered little . . .' She got no further, for her words were drowned in the storm of Raven's weeping.

'Forgive me . . .' the winged girl sobbed.

'Why should I?' Nereni snapped.

Raven took a ragged breath. 'Because you are the only mother I have left . . .'

As she heard Raven's anguished, pleading words, the woman realized, with a pang of guilt, that she had let the pain and terror of the last few months get the better of her. She remembered, belatedly, that Raven had been made to suffer the consequences of her folly, for not only had the girl been dreadfully, horribly injured by the evil High Priest, but she had lost her mother besides.

Nereni's motherly instincts finally triumphed over her anger – and, she thought ruefully, probably her common sense as well. She sighed, and went to put her arms around the weeping girl. 'There, there,' she muttered roughly. 'We can't have the Queen of the Winged Folk bawling like a lost calf! Come, dry your tears, child. Just remember, however, that you weren't the only one to suffer as a result of your folly! Strive to atone for your mistakes, and you'll find that folk will forgive you in due course – and then, in the end, you might be able to forgive yourself.'

'Fine words, Nereni – if somewhat optimistic!' With a start, Nereni recognized Anvar's voice. The Mages had arrived, unnoticed, and were standing in the doorway. The woman saw Raven flinch away from Anvar's stony gaze, and shivered. Here was one, at any rate, who would not forgive the winged girl in a hurry! Raven, sensing Anvar's hostility, made her hasty farewells and left the chamber.

'Nereni!' The coldness fled from Anvar's eyes as he came forward to embrace her. Nereni heaved a sigh of relief at the reappearance of his old, broad grin. She was so glad to see him safe and well! And at least the Mage's ordeal had not embittered him completely. No, Nereni thought, it's only Raven he hates – and more, I'll wager, because of what was done to Aurian and her child than what happened to himself.

'But what in the world has brought you here like this?' Aurian asked anxiously, as she embraced the little woman in her turn. Remembering the gravity of her mission, Nereni felt obscurely comforted by the Mage's staunch presence.

'It's Eliizar,' she blurted. 'Aurian – he wants us to leave you!'

Bit by bit, the whole story came out. Aurian, sitting hand in hand with a grave-faced Anvar, frowned. 'What? He wanted to leave today? Without even letting you say goodbye to us?'

Nereni nodded. 'Jharav and his folk were preparing to leave for the forest this morning. Already they will be searching for me . . .' She tried to keep the rising note of panic out of her voice. Seeing the glint of anger in Aurian's eyes, she shifted uncomfortably on the flimsy Skyfolk stool and struggled with her feelings of disloyalty towards her husband. 'Eliizar is terrified,' she tried to explain. 'Battle and privation he can deal with, in any amount, but the sorcery . . .' She shook her head sadly. 'Something about your magic unmans him – especially after what happened to the child – so he must hide his fear in angry bluster. What am I to do, Aurian? I love Eliizar – I cannot leave him, not for all the world – yet how can I leave you and Anvar, whom I have come to love so deeply? I feel so torn . . .'

Aurian knelt beside her and took Nereni's hands in her own. 'What do you want to do?' she asked.

'I want us all to stay together,' Nereni replied simply. 'I want you to come back with me and talk Eliizar out of this nonsense.'

Anvar has been listening to the conversation with increasing dismay. He didn't want to lose Eliizar and Nereni as companions, but the more he thought about the alternatives . . . 'Nereni, are you sure?' He frowned. 'In some respects, Eliizar is right. You'd be far safer returning to the forest with your countrymen. There's bound to be fighting where we're

31

going – and knowing Eliizar, he'll be in the thick of it. Do you want to take that risk? If anything should happen to him, what would become of you, stranded in a foreign land?'

'Why, we would take care of her, of course!' Aurian's voice was sharp with indignation.

'So long as we're in a position to do it,' Anvar said sombrely. 'There's no guarantee that we'll survive ourselves. And what about Eliizar's fear of magic? Once we return to Nexis, that's what this fight will be all about.'

'Are you saying you want us to go?' Nereni asked in a small voice that trembled on the edge of tears, and Anvar hated himself for killing the hope that his soulmate had put into the little woman's eyes. But it was for the best.

'Yes,' he told her brutally. 'That's exactly what I want.'

'Anvar – why?' Beyond that one pained gasp, Nereni, for once, was shocked into speechlessness, though Anvar recoiled from the look of hurt on her face. Aurian was glaring at him in a way that, if the look could be solidified, would have flayed the flesh from his bones.

'Anvar, what the bloody blazes are you doing?' Her mental voice resounded sharply in his mind.

Anvar sighed. 'The right thing for Eliizar and Nereni.' His own mental tones were hushed with sorrow. 'It may not be what you or I or Nereni want – but think about the alternatives, Aurian. It's by far the best option for their survival.'

Aurian bit her lip. Anvar could see how much she wanted to deny his logic, but . . . 'Curse it, you're right,' she told him softly, and turned away, but not before he had glimpsed the sheen of tears in her eyes. When she turned back to Nereni, however, she had her emotions back under control. 'Anvar and Eliizar are right,' she told the woman firmly. 'I'll miss you so much, dear friend, but we must think of your future. Once our quest is over . . .'

'Don't lie to me, Aurian!' Nereni snapped. 'We'll never see you again.' Her eyes flashed angrily. 'Reaper curse you – I came to you for support, not this! Don't you care about us any more? Eliizar and I were good enough to help you through the desert, and the mountains beyond – and in the forest you had a use for us, while supplies needed gathering and there was clothing to be made.' Nereni's voice was harsh with bitterness. 'But now that your other friends have arrived from the north, you no longer want us!' She burst into tears.

'Nereni, that's not true!' Aurian cried.

'It certainly isn't.' Anvar leapt to his feet and went to put an arm around the little woman's shoulders, persisting even though she tried to shrug him away. 'Nereni – listen to me. Aurian and I will be travelling far to the north, across the ocean, and we'll be going into peril far greater than anything we've experienced so far. Frankly, if it were up to me . . .' He smiled ruefully. 'Well, if there was any way we could do it, Aurian and I would be going back to the forest with you right now, to make a new life for ourselves in peace. But that's just not possible. We have to go on, into more hardship and danger – but it would help us to know that some of our companions, at least, will be safe.'

'But you need me,' Nereni protested. 'Who will look after you? I'll be sick with worry and what about the babe?'

'Wolf is another reason why you ought to go,' Aurian told her gently. 'You know that Eliizar has a horror of the poor child.' Her eyes smouldered at the idea, but she controlled herself with a deep breath. 'It's not Eliizar's fault, really. *You* know that Wolf was born as a human child – you were there – but Eliizar never saw him as he was before. He doesn't want you to have anything to do with the babe, and I don't want that to come between you. Besides,' the Mage went on persuasively, 'you'll have enough folk to take care of without worrying unduly about Anvar and me. As well as his surviving soldiers, Harihn's household folk were left behind in the forest. There'll be enough people to start a thriving little colony, and it will need leaders, Nereni. If Anvar and I can win through, and bring peace back to the world, it will be an enormous help in the future to have allies in the south.' She smiled. 'Why the next time we see you, we'll be coming back to visit the king and queen of the forest!'

'Aye – if we all survive that long,' Nereni said sourly, but the anger had fled from her voice, and Anvar began to hope that she was coming round to the idea of staying behind.

'So you'll do it?' he cajoled. 'For us?'

'Do I have a choice?' Nereni snapped.

Aurian put a hand on her shoulder. 'Of course you have a choice,' she said. 'If you really want to come with us, that's fine by me – but I have a feeling that you'll be doing it without Eliizar. Is that what you really want?'

Nereni, defeated, lowered her face into her hands. 'No,' she whispered in a muffled voice. Anvar saw a single tear trickle out between her fingers. Aurian, with tears in her own eyes, knelt to embrace the woman who had been such a staunch friend to her through so many hardships.

'It'll be all right,' she murmured. 'It's for the best – you'll see. And the next time we meet, all this trouble will be over, and Wolf will be a human boy again.' She turned to Anvar. 'Would you mind leaving us for a little while, Anvar? If you would send for Raven to say farewell, we can make arrangements to take Nereni back.'

'I'll organize that,' Anvar agreed. 'We'd better hurry. Eliizar will –'

'Eliizar won't say anything,' Aurian said shortly. 'Not after I've spoken to him, he won't!'

'You're going too?'

'Yes – to talk to Parric. And I'd like to say goodbye to Eliizar and bring Wolf back with me. Want to come?'

'Indeed I do.' As the Mage left the room, he took pains to screen his thoughts from his soulmate. He didn't want to worry Aurian unduly, but Anvar also needed to speak with Eliizar – to pass on a warning.

Possession of the Harp of Winds had left Anvar with a preternatural awareness of the weather patterns over a very wide distance. When the Mages had brought spring back to the world, there had been one unfortunate effect of which Aurian had not been aware. The lethal sandstorms over the Jewelled Desert had ceased completely. With a shudder, Anvar remembered Xiang, the cruel tyrant king of the Khazalim. When the Mages had escaped his clutches, along with his son Harihn, Aurian had managed to terrify the king into letting them go. By now, however, Anvar had a feeling that the fear would be wearing off. Xiang was a vengeful man – it seemed impossible that he would not try to pursue them sooner or later. And now that the desert was safe once more, the way to the north lay wide open – and passed directly through the great forested valley that Eliizar wanted to colonize. If Xiang should come ... Anvar shuddered. Eliizar must be warned.

Soft curls of morning mist drifted around the feet of Incondor's tower. The jingle of bits and the impatient stamp of horses' hooves carried clearly through the cool, damp air, while cloaked and hooded figures, their voices hushed and low in the pre-dawn stillness, hurried to and fro from the tower to complete their last-minute preparations for departure. Others, such as Jharav, the veteran Khazalim captain, had been more efficiently organized than their tardy companions, and were already mounted and waiting impatiently to leave. At the edge of the thicket, away from the bustle in the tower, sorrowful farewells were taking place.

'I'm sorry you can't go with us, but I understand your reasons.' Anvar clasped Eliizar's hand. 'Go well, my friend. Take good care of yourself – and Nereni.' He glanced across at the little woman, who stood nearby, deep in conversation with Aurian. 'You have a very special lady there, Eliizar. If you find, in the days to come, that she's full of surprises, try to understand how much she has been growing in these last hard months.' The Mage grinned wryly. 'It's strange, but travelling with Aurian tends to have that effect on people.'

Eliizar shook his head ruefully. 'Her changes will take a good deal of getting used to. The way she went off like that, alone to Aerillia – my timid Nereni, of all people! But how could I be angry with her?' He spread his hands helplessly. 'I was so afraid that something dreadful had happened to her, or . . .' Anvar could see the struggle in his face, as he tried to form his next words. 'Or that she had left me, because of my cowardice,' the swordmaster finished softly.

Anvar laid a hand on his shoulder. 'You're not a coward, Eliizar,' he reassured the older man. 'It takes a great deal of courage to face up to your fears as you did. And unfortunately, I'm convinced that you'll still have a part to play in the struggle to come.' At the earliest opportunity, he had taken Eliizar aside and told the swordmaster of his fears of an attack by the vengeful Khazalim king.

Now, Eliizar nodded gravely – but there was a twinkle in his one good eye, and Anvar was certain that the ageing warrior was looking forward to the prospect of a battle. 'Your warning has been well taken,' he assured the Mage. 'In coming from the desert, Xiang must bring his army through our valley – a narrow place indeed.' He bared his teeth in a mirthless grin. 'We may be outnumbered, but our forest is the ideal place for an ambush – indeed, for any number of them! When Xiang comes, he will find a welcome he will not forget!'

'Good man, Eliizar!' Anvar clapped him on the back. 'Remember, though, that two winged messengers are going with you. If you do find yourself in difficulties, send for help to Aerillia.'

'We will need no assistance from those winged traitors,' the swordmaster snapped proudly. Like Anvar, he was finding Raven's treachery very hard to forgive – but the Mage did not want Eliizar's antagonism to cost him his life.

'Now listen,' Anvar began firmly. 'You will be very badly outnumbered, Eliizar. Don't let pride deceive you into – ' He broke off abruptly as Aurian approached. The last thing he wanted was to start worrying her with this business. Luckily, Nereni was issuing a stream of last-minute instructions that had drowned his words.

'And don't let the little mite get wet,' she was saying, 'and remember to keep him warm, Aurian – tell that Bohan to make sure to keep him out of draughts – and . . .'

'Don't worry, Nereni,' Aurian protested with a smile. 'He's a wolf, remember – a tough little thing! But never fear – we'll take the best possible care of him.' She turned to Eliizar. 'All ready to go?'

The swordmaster nodded. The farewell was brief and awkward, with Nereni hugging first Anvar, then Aurian as if she would never let them go, and weeping bitter tears. Then she tore herself away with the first curse that Anvar had ever heard her utter, and ran off towards the waiting group of riders, closely followed by Eliizar.

36

As the couple reached their horses, Anvar saw a lean figure, still with the slightest trace of a limp, detach itself from the knot of onlookers and put his hands on Eliizar's shoulders in a warrior's embrace. At his side, the Mage heard Aurian sigh with relief. 'Yazour unbent, then, in the end,' she murmured. 'I'm so glad he did.'

Anvar, too, was pleased. Yazour had been appalled by what he had seen as Eliizar's defection from their group. He had always held the older warrior in the greatest esteem, and the swordmaster's weakness, therefore, had disappointed him all the more. As the group of Khazalim made their way down the hillside, the young warrior came over to join the Mages. 'That's that, then,' he muttered.

'Yazour, are you sure you won't be too lonely without them?' Aurian asked. 'Now that Eliizar and Nereni have gone, you've lost all of your countrymen save Bohan. If you want to change your mind and go with them – well, Anvar and I would hate to lose you, but we'd understand.'

'Lady, do you take me for a skulking coward?' Yazour looked affronted. 'You are my companions – where you go, I go!' With that, he walked stiffly away.

Aurian sighed, and laid her head on Anvar's shoulder. 'I had to go and say it, didn't I?'

'Actually,' Anvar comforted her, 'I think you did.' He tightened his arms around her, enjoying the feeling of closeness. 'Yazour is only feeling prickly because Eliizar has gone. He'll get over it.' Suddenly troubled by a vague sense of unease, he looked up, over Aurian's shoulder. A short distance away, at the edge of the thicket, Parric stood watching them. The little cavalry master's expression was cold and bleak as stone. Meeting Anvar's eyes, he turned away sharply and melted into the undergrowth. A shiver, like a finger of ice, ran down the Mage's spine.

Three days after her miraculous rescue, Hreeza demanded, much to the surprise of Aurian and Shia, to see the child who had saved her life.

'Are you sure?' the Mage asked doubtfully as she sat with Shia beside the old cat's bed. Hreeza's words had captured

37

her attention with a jolt, for Aurian had been paying scant attention to the mental murmur of conversation between the two cats. She had been brooding over the events of the previous day, when she and Anvar had returned with Nereni by net, courtesy of Raven's winged bearers, to the Tower of Incondor.

A great many matters had been arranged among the companions in a very short time. The Mage had returned Chiamh and Yazour, both protesting bitterly, to Parric's forces, for the little cavalry master was desperately in need of translators for the widely assorted group who would be under his care during the ride back to the Xandim fastness. Aurian chuckled wryly. Trust Parric! Only he could find himself suddenly ruling a race whose language he couldn't even speak!

After bidding a sorrowful farewell to Eliizar and Nereni, the Magefolk had seen them off on the first leg of their journey back through the mountains, and had arranged for a pair of winged couriers to accompany them in case of emergencies. Only then had Aurian been free to collect her child and its lupine foster-parents – and to placate Bohan, who had been determined not to leave the wolfling, even for a little while. The matter was taken out of his hands, however, for the winged bearers were unable to transport one of his vast size, and wisely refused even to make the attempt. Instead, the eunuch was to go with Parric, on the sturdy, stolid horse that had borne him all the way across the desert. He would meet the Magefolk again at the Xandim fastness.

While the cavalry master made the slower journey by horseback to the Xandim lands, the Mage planned to return to Aerillia and use her mother's Earth-magic to speed the growth of the new crops that the Skyfolk were currently planting – and she still had a great many matters to resolve with Raven. There was also the matter of Anvar's continuing hostility towards the newly crowned Queen of the Skyfolk – but she would resolve that too, given time. In the meantime, Aurian's immediate concern had been to persuade her child's foster-parents to leave their pack and make the journey by net to Aerillia; and, even more difficult, to persuade the winged bearers to take them. By the time that everything had been arranged, and the Mages were ready to return to the Skyfolk city, Aurian had been ready to tear her hair out and scream.

Hreeza's words, however, drove all of these matters to the back of the Mage's mind. The old cat, though she still slept for much of the time, seemed well on the road to recovery, but perhaps the experience had turned her mind. Aurian raised a questioning eyebrow at Shia, who returned the mental equivalent of a shrug.

'I would have thought,' the Mage suggested cautiously, 'that you'd have had enough of the Skyfolk for the time being.' Following the cat's ordeal at the hands of her people's ancient foes, Hreeza had acted with undisguised hostility towards any of the Winged Folk who had entered her chamber.

Shia, in her usual style, was much more forthright. 'What do you want with the cub?' she demanded. 'Be still, you old fool; rest. Have you forgotten how close we came to losing you?'

'No, I have not forgotten.' Hreeza's mental voice, though faint and weary, still held a spark of her old acerbic spirit. 'That is why I wish to see my rescuer. Had it not been for that cub of the Skyfolk, I would have perished indeed, and it is against my nature to let a debt go unpaid, as well you know, Shia. I must thank the little one – and as it galls me to be beholden to any of these skyborne scum, I wish to get the unpleasant business over with as soon as possible.'

'Pah! You don't fool me!' Shia retorted. 'I know you too well, Hreeza. You are keeping something from us, or I'm a chunk of Xandim horsemeat! Come on – spit it out!' When Hreeza remained obstinately silent, the younger cat continued: 'I won't let Aurian send for the child until you do.'

Hreeza grumbled through her whiskers, but she knew when she was beaten. 'Very well,' she conceded grudgingly, 'but you won't believe me.' She shot Shia a challenging glare. 'The Skyfolk can hear us, Shia – they have the potential to understand our mindspeech just as Mages can!'

Aurian, listening in on this conversation, uttered a startled exclamation, but Shia was silent, too stunned for speech.

After a moment, she collected herself. 'Nonsense!' she snapped. 'Delirium – that's all it was! You imagined it!'

'I did not!' Hreeza snarled. 'I called out for help, I tell you – and that winged cub *heard* me!'

Aurian, lacking Shia's background of inborn hatred and resentment of the Winged Folk, was quicker than her friend to grasp at the possibilities. 'But if the two races can communicate, then surely there must be a way of making peace between you,' she suggested cautiously.

'Never!' Shia spat. She turned on Aurian, eyes blazing. 'What of our slaughtered people? Have you forgotten so quickly the skins that the Skyfolk gave to you and Anvar to warm yourselves? Have you forgotten how Raven betrayed us, and almost cost us all our lives – including your child? The Winged Folk are not to be trusted! They are base, treacherous, murderous . . .'

'Hush.' Hreeza's voice cut firmly through the snarling tirade. She looked sympathetically at the dumbfounded Shia, and sighed. 'In my heart I agree with you, my friend – but my head tells me this war between our people and the Skyfolk must cease. The slaughter of our race has gone on long enough – and I would never wish another cat to suffer as I did. Someone must call a halt to these senseless hostilities – and if the winged cub holds out a hope for the future, then let us take advantage of it!' Her head drooped with exhaustion, and she laid it down on her outstretched paws. 'Enough, Shia – I am weary. While I sleep you must consider my words – find Khanu, too, and discuss it with him. Then, when I awaken, you must send for the little one.'

3

Strange Havens

Emmie was almost walking in her sleep as she entered the kitchen cavern. The empty chamber was wrapped in shadows, for most of the lamps in the smugglers' complex network of caves had been extinguished long ago. Emmie didn't mind. The slumberous red glow from the banked fires provided enough illumination for her needs. She crossed to the long, knife-scarred table, pulled out one end of the sturdy bench that was tucked beneath it, and sat down heavily. She was ravenously hungry, but lacked the energy to find herself something to eat. It was well after nightfall, and the kitchen helpers had long since gone to their beds. Everyone had worked so hard without rest these last two days that Emmie didn't want to wake them now. It wouldn't be fair. She propped her elbows on the table, ran her fingers through the tangles in her dishevelled blonde curls, and lost herself in worried thought.

As though it could sense her weariness, the white dog, now christened Storm, laid its head on her lap and whined, looking up at her trustingly with an uncannily intelligent expression in its dark eyes. Emmie swallowed hard as her vision blurred with unexpected tears. She muttered a curse, and brushed an impatient hand across her face. My, but you've sunk low, she chided herself. Bawling like a babe over sympathy from a dog!

'Gracious, girl – you look worn to a shadow! Here – get some of this inside you.' Emmie jumped. She must truly have been lost in her thoughts, for she'd heard no one come in. A rough, sturdy, work-reddened hand appeared, bearing a mug of soup that was plunked down unceremoniously on the table in front of Emmie. She looked up to see Remana, the mother of Yanis, the Nightrunner leader. The woman pulled out the

41

opposite bench and lowered herself wearily on to the hard wooden seat. Though she must also have been ready to drop from fatigue, she still managed a bracing smile for the younger girl. 'Did you get it sorted, then?' she asked, taking a cautious sip from her own steaming mug. 'And why wasn't Jarvas dealing with it?'

Emmie shrugged. 'It was just another squabble over accommodation,' she sighed. 'Jarvas was asleep – I finally found him in a corner but it looked as though he had just fallen over where he sat. I hadn't the heart to wake him – the loss of his sanctuary has hit him very hard. I managed to settle the ungrateful fools myself, without further bloodshed.' From somewhere, she found the ghost of a smile. 'Luckily, they are all very much in awe of Storm here.'

Hearing its name, the dog whined, and Remana reached out to stroke the broad white head. The dog looked up sharply at the touch of a strange hand, but she had already decided that, as a friend to her mistress, the Nightrunner woman was acceptable. Slowly, the white-plumed tail began to wag – then a large black nose came up over the edge of the table to sniff hopefully at Remana's mug. 'You'll be lucky,' Remana chuckled, removing her soup to a safe distance. 'This is the first thing I've had to eat all day!' She turned back to Emmie. 'My word, she's going to be a beauty! All she needs is fattening up . . .'

Emmie saw the shadow of a frown cross Remana's broad forehead. 'The problem is, there won't be enough food to go round, will there?' she prompted the Nightrunner woman.

'Oh, we'll manage – don't you worry.' Remana's cheerful front did not fool Emmie in the least.

'How?' she asked bluntly. Since the arrival, two nights ago, of the ragged band of fugitives from Nexis, matters had been going from bad to worse in the smugglers' lair. The secret network of caverns had seemed such a haven at first to the hungry, exhausted refugees, after the horror of the attack on their compound, the hellish journey to freedom through the sewers beneath the city, and the cold, cramped, perilous voyage back to the Nightrunner hideout on a ship so overloaded that the gunwales threatened to dip beneath the surface with every passing wave. For the Nexians, however, relief at their salvation had been short-lived.

Some sixty folk had escaped the city with their lives, and the smugglers' caverns were far from capable of accommodating such an influx. The result had been chaos. Emmie, Remana and Jarvas, the leader of the refugees, had been hard-pressed indeed to find sufficient space to cram the Nexians into, while the smuggler families had been aghast at the invasion. To be honest, Emmie could hardly blame them. The fugitives had nothing but the rags they stood up in, and each and every one of them reeked from their journey through the sewers. Arrangements had to be made for bathing and feeding them, and the overworked sanitation arrangements in the cavern network, which depended on the twice daily rise of the tide through channels beneath the stone, were fast becoming unbearable. Worst of all was the disease.

Emmie sighed, regretting for the thousandth time that they had been forced to make their escape through the sewers. It had been inevitable, she supposed, given their chilled, half-famished state, that her people would fall easy prey to the diseases that proliferated in those narrow, stinking tunnels beneath the ground. Most of the Nexians were already worn down with grief and hardship, for there was not a family present who had not lost loved ones to the dreadful slaughter that the city guards had carried out in their compound. And many of Jarvas's refugees were among the vulnerable groups who had been unable to support themselves in the city: the old, the very young, those who were crippled or unfit to work – and those already suffering from illness in the first place.

'Damn it!' Emmie hit the table with her fist and bit her lip to keep from shedding tears of weariness and frustration. Since the loss of the physician, Benziorn, in the attack on the refugees' sanctuary, Emmie had been the only remaining Nexian with any knowledge of healing. All the responsibility rested on her shoulders now. Assisted by Remana's herb-wives, she had been on her feet for the last thirty-six hours, tending the sick, advising the others on what few precautions they could take to prevent the further spread of disease, and

43

arranging for the disposal of the dead. The fourteen corpses, three of them pathetically small, that had been shipped out that evening for burial at sea were the ultimate evidence of her failure – and that was what hurt Emmie the most.

'Don't.' Remana's strong hand closed over her own. 'You can't take everyone's burdens on your shoulders, lass. We'll get through this crisis in the end.'

'The ones that survive it.' Emmie barely recognized the dull, defeated voice as her own.

'And most of them will, you'll see,' Remana retorted briskly. 'Most of those that died were old, lovey, and already near the end of their days. And the little ones – well, what chance would they have had to grow up in Nexis, the way things are these days? At least you'd given them that chance in the first place, Emmie – you and Jarvas. As for the rest – well, it looks as though they've turned the corner now, thanks to your nursing. Don't dwell on the few you lost. Think instead of the many you've saved.'

'Thank you, Remana.' Emmie squeezed the older woman's hand gratefully. 'That helps – but what are we going to do for the survivors? You'll never manage to feed and clothe them all, and I know your own people are giving you trouble about the allocation of living space . . .'

'I've dealt with my own people already, thank you,' Remana said darkly, 'and that's the last we'll hear on that subject, I expect! I have extra fishing boats going out to help ease the food shortage – ' For a moment, her face brightened. 'What a blessing this sudden change in the weather is! By the gods, but it put new heart into me, to see the sun again!'

'Weather?' Emmie frowned, perplexed.

'What? You mean you haven't even put your nose outside for the last two days? You haven't seen it?' Remana cried. 'Why, a miracle has happened, lass. It's spring again!'

Emmie shook her head in disbelief. It had seemed so long . . . After so many months of snow, and cold, and dismal darkness, she could barely remember what spring was like.

'Just wait until tomorrow,' Remana told her. 'Wait until you see it for yourself. I'll take you out for a sail – it'll do you good.'

'But I can't!' Emmie cried. 'I have to –'

'You have to do nothing of the sort!' Remana snorted. 'Tomorrow you'll rest, my girl! Everything's under control,' she went on in quieter tones, 'or it soon will be. You leave it to me. Tomorrow I'm sending messengers to my sister Dulsina, who is with the rebels in Lady Eilin's Valley. They are much better supplied there than we are; they can help us out with extra food. I had thought to send your able-bodied Nexians – those still capable of wielding a weapon, and anyone else who wants to go – to join them. That should give us enough space here to cope with the remainder. What do you think?'

'Oh, Remana – thank you!' Emmie cried. The sudden lifting of the weight of worry from her shoulders made her feel light-headed. 'What would we have done without you?'

'I don't know what you'd have done without me – but I know what you're going to do for me,' the Nightrunner woman replied briskly. 'First of all, you're going to have something more solid to eat than soup, then you're going to bathe – and then you're going to my room, where you'll sleep, undisturbed, until you've slept yourself out. Is that clear?'

Emmie nodded gratefully. 'Yes – I think I could sleep now,' she said. But despite her words, she found that sleep was hard to come by, once she was settled beneath thick quilts in Remana's warm bed, with her white dog curled by her side. Now that her mind was no longer preoccupied with the practicalities of settling her folk, she found her thoughts straying helplessly to those who had not survived the attack. So many had been lost – people she had known and cared about. Poor Benziorn, her mentor and teacher in the healing skills, was missing, and unlikely to be alive. And poor Tilda . . . With a shudder Emmie remembered the sword that had pierced the streetwalker's belly, spilling her guts out on to the bloodstained ground. And what of Tilda's young son Grince? He had rushed back into the burning warehouse, to rescue Storm's litter, not knowing that the pups were already dead . . . Emmie choked back a sob. In a short time, she had become fond of the boy, but there seemed little hope that he

45

was still alive. Even if he had survived the inferno in the warehouse, it seemed unlikely that a ten-year-old child would come unscathed through the carnage outside.

Emmie had lost so many loved ones already – her husband and her own two children had been slain months ago, during the depredations of the Archmage. By now, she should have no more tears left to shed. But as she lay alone in the darkness, Emmie clung to the white dog for comfort, and wept for the ragged young boy who had never stood a chance. Not for one minute did she believe that she would ever see him alive again.

After nightfall, the Grand Arcade in Nexis was an eerie place. The vast pillared halls, once the beating heart of Nexian commerce, now held barely an echo of their former glory. Many of the myriad shops and stalls were shuttered and empty in the black days of Miathan's reign; the endless rows of crystal globes that had once been filled with golden light were guttering or already dark. The aisles and alleyways, trodden in happier times by a multitude of feet, were silent now, and shadow-stalked. Spiders spun their silken tapestries undisturbed, and the stillness was broken only by the pattering, rustling footfalls of cockroach and rat, who had pursued their nightly rounds without competition or hindrance – until now. A new scavenger had begun to haunt the Grand Arcade. A new form, silent as the shadows, flitted through the deserted aisles, rattling a shutter here, trying a doorlatch there, alarming the vermin with its human scent, and human noise. They scattered for cover as the newcomer approached, unable to understand that the disturbance of their existence was far less of a threat than it seemed – for their competitor was only a child.

The puppy must be saved – this was the only thought that had kept Grince going throughout the last day, or two, or three – he couldn't remember how long he had been running and hiding, in fear of his life, cradling the small dog that was tucked into the scorched tatters of his shirt. He had fled in terror after the soldiers had stormed the sanctuary owned by gruff, ugly Jarvas – searching for Emmie, his best friend in the world, who had given him all five of the puppies from her huge white dog to be his very own. Four of those little scraps of life now lay dead in the burnt-out shell of the warehouse that had been a home for so many poor families. Grince was desperate to save this one remaining survivor – for as far as he was aware, the puppy was the only living creature that he still knew. Emmie, if still she lived, was nowhere to be found.

The boy's first clear memory after the swords and the blood and the flames was daylight, an open kitchen doorway, a small loaf cooling on a table – and hunger: terrible, gnawing hunger and thirst. He had been in and out of that house before the goodwife had time to turn round from the fire she was tending, with his booty clutched tightly in one dirty fist. The woman had been too stout to catch him, though the sound of her wails and curses pursued him all the way down the street, until he rounded a corner and found a chink of an opening in a cellar grating through which his skinny form could slide.

Grince remembered how difficult it had been to feed his dog, that first time. The little creature was scarcely ready to progress beyond its mother's milk, and already it was limp and weak with hunger, showing no interest in the morsel of bread that he held up to its mouth. The boy shuddered, remembering how close he had come to losing his precious pet. If he hadn't remembered what Emmie had told him about mother dogs chewing up the food for their youngsters ... When he tried it Grince's mouth had been almost too dry with apprehension to chew the bread, but somehow he had managed. Once he had forced one or two of the resulting pellets between its tiny jaws, the puppy seemed to get the idea. Like the child, it was a survivor.

The evening in the cellar marked the turning point for both of them. Grince, though still deep in shock after seeing his mother's disembowelled corpse in the ruins of Jarvas's compound, found new purpose to his life in caring for the tiny dog. Puppies ought to have milk, he knew, but milk was scarce indeed in Nexis, and though he searched long and desperately he could find none. Then he thought of cheese – would that do instead? By now, his search was taking him towards the less poverty-stricken homes in the north of the city. Cheese he found in an unguarded pantry, having slipped like a shadow through an open kitchen window. There was also a pot of porridge, simmering at the edge of the fire, ready for the morning. Grince stole that too, wrapping the hot handle in a scrap of rag before picking it up. He had been astonished at how easy it was.

Seeking a lair to enjoy his spoils, the boy had discovered a high window at the rear of the arcade which had its wooden shutter swinging slightly ajar. It had been difficult to climb with the puppy still tucked into the scorched rags of his shirt, and even more difficult to get the porridge pot up there without spilling the contents, but Grince, goaded by his need, had managed it in the end and, grunting and swearing, had pulled himself up over the sill. The opening was protected by a row of metal bars, but the spaces between were just wide enough for a small and skinny boy to squeeze between.

Grince had dropped down hard on the other side of the wall, falling awkwardly because he was trying to protect both his precious dog and the contents of the porridge pot. Luckily, the floor's stone flags were covered in a layer of dusty prickly straw which cushioned the bump a bit. For all his care, though, the landing still knocked the breath from his body and slopped a bit of the congealing cereal over the edge of the pot. Grince swore, and with a grubby finger scooped up a lump of porridge which was still clinging to the rim. He popped it into his mouth, and it suddenly made him realize how hungry he was. He could have eaten the lot, but restrained himself with difficulty. The porridge would have to be saved for his puppy.

The puppy! Was it all right after his fall? With shaking hands, Grince opened his shirt and checked on the little creature, facing into the faint glimmer of light that came through the window above, and squinting his eyes in an attempt to pierce the shadowy gloom that filled the interior of the building. The little dog whimpered plaintively as it felt the cold air against its body, but apart from that it seemed fine. Grince was willing to bet that it was hungry, too. He must find somewhere safe for the two of them to hide out . . .

The boy had already heard the small rustlings and scrabblings in the straw that betrayed the presence of lurking rats. Grince could imagine their shiny little eyes in the darkness, watching him. He was not afraid of them, he told himself stoutly. After all, there had always been rats at home. But the puppy was in deadly danger, and they would make short work of his meagre supply of food. Grince abandoned his plans to leave the porridge pot in a corner while he explored. Awkward as it was, he would have to take it with him. What he really needed to find, to start with, would be a stub of candle – and a good, stout stick wouldn't go amiss! 'Come on, puppy,' the boy told his small companion. Taking a firm grip on the handle of the porridge pot, he set off into the darkness.

The inside of the building was too dark for exploring. Grince had not taken three steps before he ran bang up against a wooden wall. Moving to his left, he came near to tripping over the pile of casks and crates that had been stored beneath. Grince bit down on a curse, and then suddenly brightened as an idea came to him. Stooping down, he began to burrow his way into the haphazard pile. And there, right in the centre, he found his lair at last, in an old flour barrel, where the rats could only come at him from one direction – and be deterred by a slat of wood he had pulled from a broken crate. For the first time in ages, Grince had a shelter in which he could almost feel safe and secure – somewhere from which he could begin to make his plans for survival.

Once his initial relief wore off, however, the boy's new-found feeling of security did not last long. He was exhausted and hungry; he was all alone in the cold and dark of this strange, enormous, creepy building, and there was no one left in the whole of his small world to whom he could turn for help.

They were all dead. Grince closed his eyes and shuddered. His mind still tried desperately to writhe away from the brutal truth. Once more, he wanted to run – to run as he had been running ever since his young life had fallen apart in blood and flames. But the boy had been running away from the truth for too long. He had found a good hiding-place

49

now and he had enough sense to know he ought to stay here. The arcade was a haven away from the dangers and violence of the squalid dockside area. It would shield him from the weather and hide him from the brutal guardsmen whose swords had drunk the blood of his protectors. Here, with luck, there might be a little food to scavenge, and comparative peace in which to take care of his only companion.

Grince decided that the best way to fight off his encroaching tears was by tending to his puppy, which was shivering beneath his shirt and whimpering with hunger. It was a terrible business, trying to get porridge into the tiny mouth in the darkness, and by the time he had finished the boy felt that most of the sticky stuff was all over himself, and matted into the little dog's white fur. Still, at least the puppy seemed satisfied now. Grince could hear the soft, even sigh of its breathing as it fell asleep. He tucked it back into his shirt, right at the back of the barrel where the rats couldn't reach it without getting through him first. Remembering his own hunger now, he fished a squashed and battered morsel of cheese out of his pocket, to keep himself going. Then, squirming awkwardly to find a comfortable position within the cramped, curving space of the barrel, he took his stick in hand, curled himself protectively round the furry little body of his puppy, and told himself to go to sleep. This was as safe a place as any, and in the morning, once it was daylight, he'd be able to explore a little . . .

Grince woke, screaming, from a nightmare. The compound gate had been broken down and the warehouse was consumed by a roaring wall of fire. Folk were running, screaming . . . The soldiers were everywhere, their long, sharp blades gleaming crimson in the light of the flames, drinking thirstily of more blood. Bodies were everywhere, littering the mud like broken toys. And Grince's mother lay sprawled where she had fallen, sliced open like a slaughtered animal, while the grim-faced soldiers with their swords swept on and on . . . Grince whimpered, tears running down his face, his inner eye filled with swords and fire and death . . . He scrunched up within his barrel, as if to hide from the guardsmen with their sharp blades – and from inside his shirt the puppy yelped sharply, in pain.

50

The sound brought Grince out of his nightmare with a jerk. The puppy – he had almost hurt it! Cursing himself for a fool, the boy slipped a trembling hand into his shirt. A soft, furry shape wriggled beneath his fingers with a joyful whine, and a tiny tongue licked his hand. Deep within him, Grince felt a warm glow of pleasure that helped dispel the last chilling dregs of his nightmare. Why, it knew him! Really, he thought, it ought to have a name . . . Crouched in the darkness, his hand still stroking the warm, comforting fur of the little dog, Grince considered the possibilities. It had to be a special name, somehow. This was his dog, and it deserved no less. Huddled alone in the darkness, the boy racked his brains for a suitable name – a perfect name – but without success. One possibility after another he discarded as not being quite good enough. Still, it helped take his mind off the cold, and his hunger and loneliness and midnight terrors . . .

Deep in thought, Grince stroked the wiry body of the pup. It wasn't really so very small, he reflected. It only seemed that way when he compared it to its mother's vast size. It had been the biggest of the litter, too, he thought proudly, and it had enormous ears and feet. Emmie had told him that they were big so that the puppy could grow into them. One day, she had said, it would be as big as her own white dog. Where was Emmie now? Without realizing what was happening, the boy slipped back into the hideous visions from the compound. The soldiers were there again, with their brutal swords – only this time, Grince was not alone. At his side was an enormous white dog – *his* white dog, all grown up. With a snarl, it leapt at the soldiers, tearing at them with its great teeth, which were more than a match for any sword. Shrieking with terror, the soldiers ran away . . .

And Grince came back to himself, curled uncomfortably in the musty barrel, the great white dog a tiny helpless puppy snuggled into his ragged shirt. But he won't stay small for ever, the boy thought delightedly. If I take care of him now, he'll grow up to be big like his mother, then he'll look after me! And he'll be a better fighter than any of those rotten soldiers . . .

Grince shot bolt upright, banging his head on the curving top of the barrel. The pain of the bump did nothing to quench his delighted grin. Of course. That was it! It was perfect! The small boy hugged his puppy. 'Guess what?' he told it. 'I'm going to call you Warrior.' Still smiling, Grince fell asleep at last, secure in the knowledge that his own white dog would protect him from his dreams.

Far above sleeping Nexis, high on the promontory that overlooked the remains of that once fair city, the white walls of the Academy trapped the moonlight in an eerie glow. From a distance, had anyone been looking up from the lesser dwellings of the city, the home of the Magefolk still seemed unsullied and perfect, save where the massive weather-dome had been shattered into shards like a broken eggshell. From within the walls, however, things looked very different.

Is it always so? Miathan wondered, as he shuffled carefully across the stained, cracked flagstones of the courtyard. Is everything different, when viewed from the other side? The Archmage still wearied easily, from the strain of spending so long, lately, in the occupation of another body, not to mention the superhuman effort it had taken to wrench himself back to his own form when his pawn Harihn, whose shape he had borrowed, had been slain. Partway across the moon-silvered courtyard he stopped to rest, seating himself on the cold stone rim of the central fountain, whose springing waters and laughing, bubbling song had long since been stilled. A bitter laugh sprang to Miathan's lips. This was a fitting throne indeed! At last he had achieved his ambition – his rule over the city's Mortals was absolute, as he had always wished it to be – and his victory was as hollow, empty and ruined as the cracked shell of the once-mighty weather-dome.

It used to be so beautiful here, the Archmage thought. Then the Academy had been filled with life and movement, as Magefolk hurried to and fro, their minds bent on perfecting the use of their powers. Servants had bustled about, cleaning and repairing under Elewin's stern gaze, maintaining the place in all its splendour ... There had been a sense of pride and purpose in those days, Miathan reflected. Not just the purpose and pride of one ambitious Mage, but of many folk, all going about their allotted business ... All of the work, the personalities, the hopes and dreams of those folk had combined to give the Academy a life and a spirit that was unique – and in reaching out to possess the greater world, he, the Archmage, had destroyed the place that he had rightfully ruled. It was as though he had reached out towards a rainbow and come back with a handful of rain, which trickled through his fingers and vanished without trace.

The Archmage scanned the Academy courtyard with the multiple, prismatic vision of the gems that had replaced his eyes. The pearl-white buildings that had once been so pristine and spotless were now mottled with dark patches of moss and slimy mould. The glass and iron lacework structure of the plantroom had melted and buckled in the heat of the exploding weather-dome, and coarse weeds had sprung up between the cracks in the courtyard's flags. The windows of the Great Hall and the Mages' Tower were cracked and smeared with grime, and tiles had slipped from the library roof, leaving gaping holes that exposed the priceless works within to all the depredations of dirt and damp.

Miathan shuddered. 'I never meant it to turn out like this,' he whispered. Then his expression hardened. He had sacrificed so much for the sake of power that now he must keep it, whatever the cost. None the less, he was unable to bear the sight of the desolate, memory-haunted courtyard a moment longer. Pulling the hood of his cloak about his face as if to hide the sight, he stood abruptly and headed for the sanctuary of his garden.

From her window in the Mages' Tower, Eliseth watched the stooped figure hobble across the courtyard like the old man he was, and smiled. Miathan's grip on the reins of power was weakening at last. Soon – very soon now – it would be her turn, and it was time to put some of her plans into action. As soon as Miathan had vanished into his garden, she turned back into her chambers and took up her scrying crystal. This new, diminished Miathan the Weather-Mage could deal with. Aurian had done most of her work for her. First and foremost, however, Eliseth wanted to know what her true enemy was up to.

Eliseth paused in the centre of the room, balancing the glittering crystal on her palm, her brows creased in thought. Scrying was not among her natural skills, and it would therefore require a great amount of concentration and effort on her part if she was to succeed in spying on Aurian without the other Mage – not to mention that meddling Anvar – detecting her presence. Also, there was the matter of her own safety. Miathan had already lost his eyes when Aurian had struck back at him through a scrying crystal, and the Weather-Mage had taken that lesson to heart. 'I need more power,' Eliseth muttered to herself. 'Sufficient power to find and reach Aurian in the first place – and sufficient power to protect myself when I do.' Her lips stretched back in a feral smile. 'How very fortunate that there is just such a source of magical energy right here in the Mages' Tower.' Striding briskly, she left her lair and headed upstairs, towards Vannor's chambers.

4

A Burnt-Out Shell

'This is hopeless,' Yanis grumbled. 'At this rate, I don't think we're ever going to find Vannor.' He took a sip of his ale and spluttered as he swallowed. 'Gods – this stuff tastes as if it came out of a privy!'

'It probably did. There are so many shortages in this city now, nothing would surprise me,' Tarnal replied uneasily, hoping to deflect the leader of the Nightrunners from his original complaint to the lesser one. Though he was accustomed by now to his companion's grumbling, lately he'd become increasingly worried by Yanis's frequent comments about the hopelessness of the task they had set themselves. He doubted that the Nightrunner leader knew the extent of his devotion to Zanna, but as far as Tarnal was concerned there was no possibility of going home before he had found her.

The fair-haired young smuggler sighed, and looked with disgust around the taproom of the Invisible Unicorn. It was not a place that encouraged optimism, he admitted to himself, wrinkling his nose at the stench of the filthy, verminous straw on the floor and grimacing at the sight of the once-white walls that were now stained with smears of soot, grease, and rusty spatters that looked suspiciously like dried blood. 'When Parric stayed with us in Wyvernesse, he said that this was his favourite tavern,' he commented. 'It's a good thing he can't see it now.'

'Hush, you fool!' Yanis peered around suspiciously, but only a handful of the other drinkers seemed to be within earshot. 'Don't go mentioning names like that! This place is full of bloody mercenaries in the pay of you-know-who, and you go shouting your mouth off . . .'

Tarnal felt his face burning red with embarrassment.

'Well, you were the one who wanted to come here in the first place. I told you it was an idiotic idea. And you started it, too, mentioning Va – '

'Will you be quiet!'

'But you did . . .'

'Yes, all right. I was careless. I'm sorry,' Yanis said hastily. Tarnal noticed several heads turning in their direction, and shivered.

'Come on, let's get out of here. Whatever you think, Yanis, it was a stupid idea to come to this particular tavern.'

The two Nightrunners slunk through the dark streets, heading towards the north of the city. They followed a roundabout route among the back alleys, scrambling over yard walls and fences and cutting through abandoned buildings until they were quite certain they had not been followed. At last the streets around them turned from the labyrinthine clusters of crumbling buildings of ancient, soot-stained stone to neat rows of newer houses faced in limewash and brick.

'These streets all look the bloody same to me,' Yanis groaned, but the younger lad, at least, had memorized what few landmarks there were, and was sure of his route.

'This way.' Tarnal took a sharp turning to his right, heading towards the city's northern gates, and then cut through a smaller alley to his left. Another sharp turn brought them to the neatly scrubbed doorstep of Hebba's house.

'I don't know how you do it,' Yanis marvelled, shaking his head. As Tarnal pushed open the wooden door, he bit back a short reply. He only thanked the gods that the young leader of the smugglers was more at home on the sea than in a city – otherwise the Nightrunners would have been in desperate straits indeed. At least Yanis had the idea of coming to Hebba for sanctuary, Tarnal reminded himself, anxious to give credit where it was due. Had it not been for her, who knows how we'd have managed!

When the two young men had come to Nexis, it had taken several days of discreet inquiries to find Vannor's old cook. They had started with a surreptitious midnight visit to the servants' quarters of the merchant's former mansion, and had been horrified to discover that it was now occupied by the corrupt and money-grabbing Guildsman Pendral, who, so the gossip went, was in the Archmage's pocket and was already styling himself head of the Merchants' Guild. Most of Vannor's former servants had already left, but the gardener's lad remembered Hebba, and thought that one of the young kitchen-maids – a good friend of his, he assured them with a lewd wink – might know of her whereabouts. The girl was serving in a tavern now, and would be there tomorrow, and if she didn't know she was sure to know of someone who would . . . From person to person the trail had led, until they had finally discovered the former cook living in the northern part of the city, in the house of her sister, who had been slaughtered along with her husband and children on the Night of the Wraiths.

Hebba remembered Yanis as the nephew of Vannor's housekeeper Dulsina, but fortunately for her nervous disposition she had no idea of their connection with the legendary smugglers. When they told her that they had come in search of her beloved Zanna she had been more than ready to give them sanctuary, and besides, she was afraid of living alone now in these violent times, and pathetically desperate to have someone to take care of again. She had welcomed the two young men with open arms, and though she had little, she shared it without reservation.

Though Hebba had already gone to bed when Yanis and Tarnal returned, they found that she had left a welcome for them in her cosy, spotless little kitchen with its colourful rag rugs on the floor, shining copper pots twinkling among the low ceiling beams, and shelves of brightly glazed mugs and plates that had been unofficially removed by Hebba from Vannor's house when the mansion had changed ownership. A pot of thin broth was keeping warm by the edge of the fire – the final remains of a scrawny chicken they had stolen three days ago on an unauthorized foraging expedition among Pendral's outbuildings.

The Nightrunners took off their cloaks and swords, and sat down gratefully by the fireside with brimming bowls. A short time passed in a hungry and appreciative silence. Though it was not exactly filling, the broth was warming and,

57

thanks to Hebba's skilful touch, delicious. Thoughts of having foiled the fowl's previous owner added extra spice to the meal.

Finally Yanis scraped the bottom of the bowl with his spoon, and set it aside. For a time he sat frowning and fidgeting, looking into the fire. 'Look here,' he burst out suddenly, 'to go on with what I was saying back in the tavern: I've been thinking a lot about it lately, and I don't believe we should stay here any longer. I should be back at home, Tarnal. As Nightrunner leader I have responsibilities to my own folk – and besides, what's the point in staying? We're never going to find Vannor – or Zanna. We've been combing the city for days now, without a word or a trace of either. I reckon they must have escaped already, or . . .' Suddenly he couldn't meet his companion's eyes. 'Or they must be dead.'

Horror gripped Tarnal's heart, swiftly followed by a blaze of outrage. He leapt to his feet, tipping his chair over with a crash. 'You bastard! Zanna is not dead!' he yelled. 'You miserable bloody coward – you're afraid of getting caught. And you're desperate to get back so you can bed the fair-haired wench we rescued, the one you fancy so much. You don't care about Zanna at all. Call yourself a leader? If it wasn't for your mother, you'd be – ' His vision exploded into sparkling blackness as a fist smashed into his face.

Tarnal staggered to his feet and Yanis hit him again, but this time the younger man was ready. Reeling backwards, he rebounded off the wall, using it as a springboard to launch himself forward. His blow brought a leaping fountain of red from Yanis's nose, and the Nightrunner countered with a vicious kick to Tarnal's knee. The fight went to and fro across the kitchen in a cacophony of clattering pots and pans and splintering crockery, until Tarnal saw an opening and butted his opponent in the stomach. Yanis fell backwards on to the rickety table, which collapsed with a crash into matchwood, taking the smuggler down with it. Tarnal dived on top of him, fists flailing, and got in three or four telling blows before Yanis recovered both wind and wits, and brought a knee up into his balls. Tarnal curled up gasping in helpless agony – and choked as a deluge of cold water hit him in the face. He looked up through streaming eyes to see Hebba standing over them with a wooden bucket in her hands. Her plump, round face was crimson with anger.

'What do you mean by this brawling, you ungrateful, good-for-nothing ruffians? Just look what you've done to my lovely kitchen!' Abandoning the bucket for her besom, she began to hit the two young men about the head and shoulders, belabouring them until they howled for mercy, and giving them the rough edge of her tongue all the while.

'I don't know . . . Is this your gratitude for my kindness in taking you in, out of the goodness of my heart? What your poor aunt Dulsina would say . . . You'd have had the city guards down on us with your ruckus . . . My poor table a pile of kindling and all the good crocks smashed to smithereens . . . It comes to something, when two healthy young lads who should know better treat a poor helpless widow-woman in such a heartless way . . .'

On and on Hebba went, even after she had exhausted her anger and her voice had turned querulous with tears. She kept up her scolding commentary even as she rummaged in her cupboard for witch-hazel and willowbark for the chastened men, and bathed their hurts in cold water. Tarnal had almost preferred it when she was hitting him with the broom, although when he cast his rapidly swelling eyes over the wreck he and Yanis had made of her home he was ashamed, and sick to his stomach with guilt.

'Oh, shut up, woman, for goodness sake!' Yanis roared.

Tarnal looked up, horrified, in the ensuing silence and saw Hebba's mouth hanging open in shocked indignation. The leader of the smugglers was scowling blackly. 'I'm sorry about your kitchen, Hebba,' he muttered indistinctly, through puffed-up lips. 'I'll make amends to you one day, I promise. I'm leaving now,' he flung at Tarnal. 'You can stay here if you want – or go to perdition for all I care. As far as I'm concerned, you're a Nightrunner no longer!' With that he snatched up his sword and went stamping out of the house.

The slamming of the door seemed to echo for an age in the wreckage of the kitchen. To Tarnal, still in a state of shock following Yanis's announcement, it was the death knell of the only life he had ever known. It was Hebba who finally broke the silence that followed the smuggler's departure. 'Did he say *Nightrunner*?' she demanded.

That tore it. Tarnal could only nod miserably.

'And Dulsina *knew* about this?' Hebba's eyes were wide with astonishment. 'Well!' she said indignantly. 'Whatever next?'

Tarnal only wished he knew.

It had started to rain. The streaming, leaden skies were a perfect match for Yanis's spirits as he sloshed, shivering and already hopelessly lost, through the confusing maze of empty, muddy streets. Already his anger was melting, as though doused by the pounding rain. Guilt, however, was enough to keep him going. He couldn't go back and face Hebba again after what he had done, and as for his former companion . . .

Yanis gingerly fingered the throbbing bruises on his face and felt a flash of his former anger. 'Damn Tarnal!' he muttered. 'This is all his fault. How dared he question my authority like that?' Yanis's pride supplied the final goad. What? Go back now and apologize to the little turd? Why should I? he thought. I wasn't in the wrong. I am the Nightrunner leader. I should be at home with my people – especially in these hard and dangerous times. *And*, prompted a nasty little voice from within, *there are plenty of folk besides Tarnal back home who doubt your fitness to lead. If you want to keep your authority, you'd better be there to defend it.*

'The trouble is, my ma is going to skin me when I come back without Zanna,' Yanis groaned. There was nothing he could do about it, though, he assured himself. Had he not searched for her all over? What more could anyone expect of him? 'No – I'm going home, and that's final.' Saying it aloud somehow helped to strengthen his flagging resolve. Now all he had to do was find his way.

For the first time since leaving Hebba's home, Yanis began to pay attention to his surroundings. The buildings in the narrow street were still those accursed brick and plaster

60

structures, though it struck him with some force that after all this time he should have been in the older part of the town. 'Damn these bloody houses,' he muttered in disgust. 'I must have been wandering round in circles.' He stopped for a moment and looked around, trying, without success, to find a familiar landmark, and his heart sank as it occurred to him that right now the long journey home was the least of his concerns. In his fit of temper, he'd stormed out without so much as a cloak to his back, and he was already chilled so that his teeth were chattering. He desperately needed warmth and shelter, but since he had so thoroughly lost himself, returning to Hebba was not even a possibility. The locked doors and firmly shuttered windows of the nearby houses turned blank, indifferent faces towards him. With so much lawlessness in Nexis nowadays, folk wouldn't open their doors to a stranger after dark. Yanis muttered an oath. There was no point in just standing here getting wetter – not that he *could* get any wetter, he thought sourly. With a shrug, he set off to walk again. He had no other option.

In a little while, however, hope returned to the Nightrunner as he emerged from the end of a street to find another road leading steeply downhill to his left. Thank the gods for that! Yanis exhaled on a sigh of relief. All he had to do now was keep heading downwards, and he was certain to come to the older part of the city. Maybe then he'd be able to get his bearings, and down among the deserted warehouses and derelict buildings near the docks he'd be sure to find a place to shelter.

Yanis hurried along the lonely streets, his head down, his eyes fixed on the treacherously muddy cobblestones, wary of keeping his footing as the steep downhill gradient gave impetus to his jolting strides. The only illumination filtered through the chinks in shuttered windows or shone weakly from the occasional lantern slung above a doorway, and the rain-dimmed lamps that hung on the corners of buildings to mark the intersections of the streets. The smuggler was distracted by discomfort from being soaked through and, more particularly, from the damage inflicted upon him by Tarnal's fists and feet when they had brawled. Because his mind was

61

befuddled by cold, fatigue, and unpleasant thoughts, he was not really concentrating on self-preservation.

The smuggler was trying to give the appearance of a normal citizen, caught out in the deluge whilst going about his rightful business, and heading for home as quickly as he could go. He had forgotten that he was not the only criminal to be out and about on the streets of Nexis after dark. He was alone and off his guard, and the further down into the labyrinths of the old town he went, the greater was his chance of being set upon by the desperate relics of humanity that haunted the night-dark streets. And the nearer to the docks he ventured, the more the risk increased. As he hurried on his way, he was unaware of the eyes that watched him from the shadows. The sheets of rain obscured swift forms that slipped in and out of concealment behind him, and the pounding of the deluge drowned the scuff of stealthy feet.

One minute Yanis was striding along, his eyes and thoughts turned inwards; the next, something hard and heavy struck him and he stumbled, fetching up hard against a wall and falling face-down on the oozing ground with his head ringing and mouth full of mud. Instinct took over and he rolled, choking, but a bolt of cold fire in his right arm told him he'd moved too late. The knife had gone right through the muscle of his forearm before its point hit the cobbles beneath. Yanis yelled, and jerked his arm away, and the blade came with it, jarred from his assailant's hand. Even as the agony hit him, the smuggler glimpsed a shadow stooping over him, a darker silhouette against the glimmer of a lantern in a nearby doorway. Two other shapes lurked beyond, closing in on him like wolves.

With his left hand, Yanis scooped up a fistful of mud and flung it into his attacker's face. The man yelled an obscenity and reeled back, clawing at his eyes. Yanis struggled to his knees and grabbed the knife, his muddy fingers fighting for a grip on the blood-slick haft. He yanked it from his arm in a spray of blood as his assailant came at him again and plunged it into the robber's belly, ripping the blade upwards and out. The man fell screaming, tripping one of his fellows as he went down. Using the wall for support, Yanis staggered to his feet and kicked the sprawling fellow solidly in the face.

The third footpad, a scrawny little man who so far had shown little stomach for the fight, was closing in now, wielding a long and sturdy cudgel. Yanis saw him glance down at his fallen companion and hesitate, and marked the little rat as a coward. He flipped the bloodstained knife and threw it, clumsily and left-handed. Though the blade was not designed for such work, the closeness of the target made up for the deficiency. The small man shrieked and dropped his weapon as the knife hit him in the chest, though Yanis knew the throw had lacked sufficient force to inflict much more than a scratch. He groped awkwardly for his sword, and at the sight of the gleaming steel the scrawny robber took to his heels and fled. The Nightrunner, his arm still dripping blood, staggered away in the opposite direction, only wanting to put as much distance between himself and his attackers as he could.

Luckily, he had already come close enough to the river to be able to see the high roofs of the warehouses looming over the lesser buildings. Though his left hand was still firmly clenched around his sword hilt, Yanis used his forearm to brush the rain and his muddy, tangled hair out of his eyes. He set his teeth against the white-hot agony in the useless right arm that dangled at his side, and his mind against the knowledge that even if he could find the shelter he so desperately needed, he stood little chance of being able to bind the injury effectively left-handed. But there was no sense in worrying about that now. He was losing too much blood, and the wet and cold were weakening him further. Added to that, the longer he roamed the open streets, the greater was the risk of encountering another gang of footpads. Unless he could quickly find a safe haven out of the rain where he could light a fire, the problem of treating his injury would never arise. Yanis looked around and, seeing no one, laid his sword reluctantly against a wall for a moment. Clenching his jaw against the pain, he worried loose a rag from the torn sleeve of his shirt and bound it as tightly as he could above his leaking wound, tying a clumsy knot with his teeth and the cold-numbed fingers of his left hand. Then, picking up the sword again, he struggled onward.

As the dim light of a leaden dawn began to crawl across the sky, the rain finally slowed to a dismal drizzle before stopping altogether. The Nightrunner tottered down the last twisting alleyway towards the flat, sprawling, semi-derelict area of the waterfront in a darkening dream of pain and exhaustion. He was past the stage of worrying now. The single thought of shelter that he had fixed in his mind's eye was all that kept him going. Beneath the blurring of his conscious thoughts, however, the instinctive part of his mind was still at work, taking note of familiar landmarks. He was much more at home in his area than the upper parts of Nexis. In better times, his people had done much of their surreptitious business on the wharves, and lately he and Tarnal had spent a good deal of time here, searching among the warehouses and derelict buildings for any trace of Vannor. The overwhelming need for sanctuary that was uppermost in the young man's mind automatically led his steps towards the place that he remembered as a haven for so many of the city's desperate and wretched folk.

Yanis blinked with astonishment as he caught sight of a familiar silhouette of crumbling, soot-scarred stone rearing against the slate-grey sky. How did I get here, he thought blearily. Am I dreaming? Memories came flooding back to him, of the night when he and his mother Remana had come with Tarnal to Nexis in search of Zanna, and had emerged from their secret underground route through the sewers into a nightmare of blood and fire, and the tearing sound of screams. He remembered the big old warehouse, its roof collapsing inward in a fountain of sparks and flame, and Pendral's soldiers with their thirsty swords that drank the blood of women, children, and infirm old folk with brutal impartiality. He remembered Remana's desperate attempt to get the survivors down to safety in the old drain that ran below the fulling mill, while Jarvas, the unlikely founder of this sanctuary for the destitute, had witnessed the destruction of his dream with tears of anguish running down his ugly face. And most of all, Yanis remembered Emmie, the blonde-haired girl who combined an ethereal loveliness that

64

had turned his heart over in his breast with a relentless practicality that had thoroughly daunted him and left him tongue-tied.

With reluctance, Yanis shook himself back to the present. What was he thinking of, standing here gawping and daydreaming like a moonstruck fool when shelter was so close? There was no longer any need to find the gate of the stockade – the scorched timbers of the once-high fence had been pulled down in ruins. Though the warehouse was a burntout shell, the fulling mill was still intact – and it also contained a water supply and a safe escape route. Blessing the gods for his good fortune, Yanis staggered with weaving steps towards the tall old building.

The wan light of the grey morning did not pass beyond the doors of rotting wood that sagged ajar. It was so dark within the mill that Yanis wondered, with a chill of fear, if his vision was starting to fail him as he succumbed to bloodloss at last. As his eyes grew accustomed to the gloom, however, he thought he could discern a faint glimmer of brightness like the warm amber flicker of firelight, far down the length of the dusty, echoing chamber. If his mind was not playing tricks on him, the light seemed to be coming from behind the row of great dye vats at the further end. As he was about to start forward, the Nightrunner found himself hesitating. If that *was* a fire, then who had made it? And would they prove to be friend or foe? At that moment, a slurred and wavering voice broke into song, and Yanis made his mind up to go on. Whoever was down there, they sounded far too drunk to do him any harm. Indeed, if they had wine or strong spirits with them, he only hoped they would be in a mood to share. None the less, a certain amount of caution seemed a good idea. Creeping down the long, narrow chamber as quietly as he could on uncertain feet, Yanis slunk around the edge of the dye vat and peered round the corner.

The singer, clad in a disreputable collection of filthy rags with a threadbare, tattered old blanket draped around his shoulders, sat with the curving wall of the massive stone vat at his back, and a small fire before him. He seemed oblivious of his surroundings, beating time to his song with the near-

empty flask clutched tightly in his hand. He was a man of indeterminate years, and to Yanis the deeply graven lines on
his gaunt face seemed to owe more to sorrow than the depredations of age, though glints of silver frosted the dulled gold
of his lank and greasy hair. His face seemed vaguely and
annoyingly familiar, but Yanis had no chance to pursue the
thought further. Having reached the end of his endurance at
last, he swayed dizzily, clutched vainly at the smooth stone
side of the vat, and toppled like a felled tree, almost landing
in the stranger's fire.

'Though she could have been younger, I had to admit, I only
had eyes for the size of her –' Benziorn's song broke off
abruptly as someone fell into his fireplace. 'What in perdition . . .' He scrambled to his feet, his heart pounding wildly,
and stood swaying uncertainly, squinting down at the apparition that had suddenly plummeted out of the sky. 'But there
is no sky, Benziorn, you fool,' he muttered to himself with
impeccable drunken logic. 'Only a roof . . . So he couldn't
have fallen out of it . . .' This was all getting too complicated.
Anyway, he decided, I suppose I'd better help him before he
starts to singe . . .

Benziorn pulled the inert figure further away from the
threatening flames and squatted down beside his mysterious
visitant. As he turned the body over, he let out a muttered
oath of surprise. Why, wasn't this the smuggler lad? And in
dire trouble, by the looks of it. Someone had made a fair old
mess of his face, but more worrying was the wounded arm,
where a knife had slashed down through flesh and muscle,
and torn its way out of the other side. Frowning, the physician picked with unsteady fingers at the knot in the makeshift
tourniquet that had been tied above the wound. That would
have to come off for a start. It had been left on far too long –
the arm below it was already white, with an unhealthy bluish
tinge, and the flesh had swollen up around the strip of rag,
tightening it and making it hard to untie with stumbling,
drunken fingers.

'Emmie?' Benziorn cried instinctively, as he continued to
worry at the stubborn knot. 'Come and help me here – and

66

bring my...' His voice trailed away into silence as the memories that he had been drowning in wine came thrusting back like a knife-blade twisted in his heart. Emmie was gone. Jarvas was gone, and all the old folk, and the little children ... For a moment his vision was obscured by the sight of the burned and dismembered corpses that had littered the bloodstained yard outside.

'Damn you,' Benziorn muttered savagely at the unconscious man. 'Why did you have to come back here, reminding me? I'm not a physician any more – what's the point? I've given up healing, I tell you ...'

'Well you'd better take it up again – and fast.'

Benziorn whirled to find himself face to face with the point of a sword. His eyes tracked the blade up its gleaming length – up and up, until he met the cold gaze of the other young smuggler – the shorter, blond one whom he also remembered from that dreadful night when Pendral had attacked.

Tarnal looked down at the physician's swaying figure and owlish gaze with mounting irritation. What the blazes was wrong with the man? Then he smelled the alcohol on Benziorn's breath, and his annoyance turned to alarm. 'Don't just sit there gaping, you drunken fool. Do something. Help him.' The sharpness of his voice also stemmed from guilt, he knew.

The young smuggler had been awake all night, regretting his fight with Yanis and worrying about the Nightrunner leader wandering the town alone in the storm and darkness, without even his cloak. Besides, if only he had tried to persuade his companion to stay, instead of losing his temper like that ... And Tarnal couldn't bear the memory of Yanis's last angry words. Surely, now that his temper had had time to cool, he would see things differently? As soon as it was light Tarnal had set off to find him, suspecting, rightly, that his erstwhile friend would have made his way down to the wharves, and shelter. Once he'd reached the waterfront, he had soon discovered the distinctive prints of the soft-soled boots that smugglers wore to keep their footing on slippery decks, and a trail of darker blood in the drying mud, which had sent his heart into his mouth and had finally led him to this place.

'All right, all right.' Benziorn's voice snapped Tarnal back to the present. 'Put that blasted lump of steel away then, young man, and get down here and help me.'

Tarnal hastily sheathed his sword and dropped to his knees at the physician's side. 'What do you want me to do?'

'See this?' Benziorn pointed to the bloodstained strip of rag. The smuggler felt nausea rise in his throat at the sight of the gaping knife wound, surrounded by red and swollen flesh. He swallowed hard and tore his eyes away from the ghastly sight. He had never been too good with that kind of thing.

'Yes,' he said faintly.

'Well, get your knife out and cut it off.'

'What – the arm?'

'No, you dimwit! The tourniquet!' roared the physician.

'Oh. Well, how was I to know?' Tarnal muttered sheepishly. He was blushing as he fumbled for his blade.

'Did you actually think you could saw the poor bugger's arm off with a belt knife? Melisanda save us!' Benziorn cast his eyes skywards. 'Hurry it up, there. Now – just slide the blade very carefully under the binding – and don't cut him in the process! I'd do it myself if my hands were more steady. A touch of ague, I think . . .'

Ague my behind, thought Tarnal sourly. Gripping the tip of his tongue between his teeth, he manoeuvred his knife-point beneath the bloodstained rag, trying not to look at the torn flesh beyond. Holding his breath, he turned the blade very slightly to angle the sharp edge upwards, and gasped with relief as the fabric parted and the tourniquet fell away.

'Thank you so much,' Benziorn said sarcastically. Tarnal reminded himself that this obnoxious, acid-tongued sot was the only one who could help Yanis, and reluctantly unclenched his fists.

'Put more wood on the fire – I can't see what I'm doing.' The physician stooped low over the inert form of the Night-runner, peering at the injury, from which a trickle of blood had begun to seep. 'Well, it looks as though we still have cir-culation,' he murmured. 'Your friend is fortunate in that

68

respect – though he'll have to be extremely lucky to avoid infection. There's mud and all sorts of other muck inside the wound. You'll find a pot of water over there by my blanket, lad – just put it on the fire, would you? And pass me the leather satchel that you'll also find there. I'll try to clean this up as best I can, but . . .'

As Tarnal hurried to do his bidding, Benziorn continued to probe Yanis's wound and voice his thoughts aloud. 'Wouldn't do much good to stitch at this point – the flesh is too swollen now, and besides, I suspect the wound will need to drain before much longer.' He looked up at the young smuggler with such a grave expression on his face that Tarnal felt his heart turn to lead.

'I'll do my best of course, lad, but you must prepare yourself.' The physician shook his head. 'Your friend is going to be a very sick man for some time. If we can't control the infection, we may have to remove his arm to save his life.'

5

Words of Warning

'Majesty, do you not think you've wasted enough time on these groundling Wizards?' Elster winced and inwardly cursed her own temerity as the queen's dark eyes kindled with a flash of anger. I would have to go and open my mouth, she thought.

'How dare you even suggest such a thing, after all that Aurian and Anvar have done for us?' Raven leapt up from her seat and began to pace up and down the richly appointed chamber, her expression dark with a furious scowl. 'You may be old enough to be my grandmother, Elster, and you may have saved my life, but that does not give you the right to tell me how to run my kingdom!'

Elster hesitated, then decided that she had already gone so far that she might as well go all the way. 'If I do not, then who will?' she countered. 'You are right, Majesty, I know little of ruling, but I have spent many years in the world. Because I am a physician, folk confide in me, and I know how to keep my eyes and ears open besides. You are young, and for all your mother's training you have little more experience than I. Because of the royal isolation in which you were reared, you have few or no friends within the palace. Queen Flamewing's counsellors all perished in Blacktalon's reign, and you have not appointed any of your own. That is only one of the many essential tasks you have put off while the groundlings have taken up all your attention and time. Why, you aren't even officially crowned yet, and will not be until a new High Priest is appointed; another task you have neglected. But be warned: if you don't take a hand in the selection, then the priesthood will do it for you – and their choice may not be the same as your own, or necessarily to your good.'

70

'Curse you – give me a chance!' the queen snapped.

'I may – but you have enemies in Aerillia who will not.' Seeing storm clouds gathering on Raven's face, the winged physician tempered her reproof with a smile. 'Will you not listen, at least, to one who would be your friend? I am only offering information and advice. You could use the information, you know, even if you decide to discard the advice.'

'What information? And what do you mean by enemies? Who dares to oppose me?' the queen demanded.

The healer, relieved that the girl seemed to be coming to her senses at last, settled herself more comfortably on her spindly chair with a rustle of her black and white wings. She glanced around Raven's comfortable, lamplit room with its gold-stitched hangings on the wall, and longed for the peace and anonymity of her own cramped, draughty quarters on the lower spur of the pinnacle. But it was no good wishing – the little hanging turret had been smashed to rubble, along with the entire area of Aerillia, in the fall of Blacktalon's tower. The queen, in gratitude for Elster's having saved her life, had given her the title of Royal Physician and moved her into the palace – much to the healer's dismay. Her quarters were far more sumptuous and comfortable now, but it sat ill with her that Raven should have a hold over her comings and goings and a monopoly on her skills; and in her experience, such close proximity to a reigning monarch was neither comfortable, peaceful, nor safe.

'Well?' Raven's sharp voice cut through her thoughts. 'You seem very slow with your answers, for one who only a moment ago was so full of advice. Or were you just trying to frighten me?'

Elster sighed. 'I only wish I did know the names of your foes,' she admitted. 'But I would advise vigilance, Majesty. Blacktalon left many secret supporters in this city. Be wary of those in whom you place your trust.'

'You have told me nothing, you useless old crone! If the identity of Blacktalon's supporters is such a secret, then who in Yinze's name should I decide to trust?' Raven replied sulkily. Elster took a deep breath, and reminded herself that

71

in spite of all her trappings of power, the queen was still little more than a child.

'Usually – though I say so myself,' she answered wryly, 'you can trust those who are prepared to risk your wrath by telling you the painful truth.'

'How very convenient. In that case, I suppose I should make you my chief counsellor,' the winged girl sneered.

'You could do worse. At least I am not saying it was Blacktalon who ended the winter, and not the Magefolk. Nor am I spreading rumours that, for any number of reasons, you are unfit to rule.'

Raven's mouth fell open. 'What reasons?' she managed to say, in a small, choked voice.

For the first time since the start of their conversation, Elster felt that she had the queen's complete attention. She began to count off the points she made on her fingers.

'For one thing, they are saying that Aurian's healing spells are a trick, and that the injuries to your wings will come back as soon as she leaves, leaving you crippled once more . . .'

'Preposterous!' Raven snapped. 'That will be revealed as a falsehood the minute the Mages depart.'

'True – but to guard their falsehoods, they are also saying that you are in league with the natural enemies of the Winged Folk: Wizards, Mortals and the great cats. Because of what happened with the Khazalim prince who was Blacktalon's ally . . .' Elster nodded her head in mute apology at the sight of Raven's stricken face. 'I am sorry, Majesty, to distress you, but somehow word of that regrettable business has got out, and it is best you know. The talk is that you have been duped by outlanders, and that you will betray us to our foes. The queen, they say, is too young and inexperienced to rule the Skyfolk.'

'Yinze blast them – how can they spread such lies!' Raven struck the wall with her fist, but the force of her blow was smothered by the heavy tapestries. 'It's not true – none of it!'

The healer felt a desperate urge to comfort the beleaguered girl, but cosseting the queen would not solve anything. It has hard, but she would have to learn to deal with crises such as these – and fast. 'Then what are you going to do about it?' Elster asked levelly.

72

'I don't know,' Raven wailed. 'I would have them arrested as traitors, but we don't know who they are . . . And how can I counter their vile calumnies? If I make any public protest, it will just add fuel to the rumours and make matters worse.' She twisted her hands together. 'I never realized that being queen would prove so difficult . . .'

'It isn't, necessarily,' Elster told her wryly. 'All you need is the backing of the military and the priesthood – and, as a secondary consideration, the rest of the populace.' She smiled at the distraught girl and patted the seat beside her. 'Here, child – sit down and stop panicking. Have some wine. Now, let's think this through together, shall we?'

Meekly, Raven sat, and accepted the goblet that the other thrust into her hands. Elster let her take a long draught before saying: 'Firstly, I suggest you employ a taster. As a physician, I have extensive knowledge of poisons . . .'

The colour drained from the queen's face. She began to choke.

'It's all right – I haven't done anything of the kind,' Elster shouted over her splutters, hoping that the lesson had hit home. 'But I very easily might have done.'

Raven's face went from chalk to crimson in an instant. 'Hag! Harpy!' she shrieked, launching herself at the physician with her taloned claws extended. Elster's old bones rediscovered a nimbleness they had lacked for years as she grabbed the girl's wrists in her strong, gnarled hands and hung on grimly until Raven's struggles ceased.

'Enough!' the physician panted. 'Forgive me, Majesty – but it was a lesson that you had to learn.'

Raven glared at her, speechless with rage. After a long moment, she found her voice. 'If you ever do that to me again,' she growled, 'you'd best make sure you poison me in truth, for otherwise I will have your head!'

'If you give me a chance to do that again,' Elster countered bluntly, 'then I suggest you tell the guards to take your own head. It will save time in the end.'

The queen bit her lip, as if to hold back an angry retort. Then she suddenly burst out laughing. 'Do you know, Elster, sometimes you remind me of the Lady Aurian. She is as plain-spoken and impatient with fools as yourself.' Her face suddenly sobered. 'And I have been a fool, have I not? Bearing in mind my mother's fate, I should be more wary . . .' She frowned. 'But tell me: who would undertake the perilous position of queen's taster? How can I condemn a friend to constant danger? Yet how could I trust an enemy? Who would I choose for such a task?'

'Cygnus.' The name was out of her mouth before Elster knew it.

Raven's eyes opened wide in surprise. 'But why? You trained him yourself. He helped you to save me. Cygnus is a friend, is he not?'

How can I tell her? Elster thought. The queen has no idea that Cygnus was responsible for the poison that killed her mother. And besides, he has repented and reformed – or has he? It was no good. The physician could call herself a foolish old woman and chide herself for being overly suspicious, but she could not shake off a lingering feeling of mistrust. Whoever had spread those rumours knew entirely too much – and who knew more than herself and Cygnus? Yet she could scarcely accuse him with no proof. No, probably the best place to keep the young healer from further mischief would be at the queen's side – where I can keep my eye on him, Elster thought. And I'll be watching him like a hawk.

'You must be patient with the queen, my friends – she is little more than a child as yet.' Cygnus looked from one to the other of the three figures seated with him at the table. Aguila, Captain of the Royal Guard, would be hardest to sway. The young physician would be very careful with regard to him, for his sworn duty was to protect the queen. The other two posed less of a problem: Skua, acting High Priest following Blacktalon's demise, was also the head of the Temple Guard, and would do anything to have his temporary position officially confirmed; and as for the leader of the Syntagma, Aerillia's warrior elite – well, Sunfeather had been Cygnus's closest friend ever since the two were fledglings. After the accident that had almost claimed the life of the handsome, brilliant young warrior and led to Cygnus

74

eschewing the way of the sword for the way of healing, Sunfeather's rise through the ranks of the Syntagma had been meteoric. The healer often reflected that his friend's close brush with death had led him to seize upon everything that life could offer with greedy hands. When the existing Wing-marshal had met with a mysterious but fatal accident after crossing Blacktalon, Sunfeather had been all too ready to step into the role.

It was good, Cygnus mused, to have friends in high places. After his first attempt to get rid of Aurian and Anvar and claim the Harp of Winds from the fallen tunnels below the temple had failed, he had been racking his brains for an alternative. Though no plan had suggested itself as yet, he had decided that the first step lay in driving a wedge between Queen Raven and the Mages. Divide and conquer, as his old military tutor always used to tell him. And today he would begin. Clearing his throat and fighting down the hollow feeling of nervousness in his stomach, he addressed the others. 'I have called this gathering so that we four may consider what must be done for the good of our people – and the good of the queen, of course,' he added hastily, with a sidelong glance at Aguila.

The weatherbeaten, tawny-haired captain looked unimpressed. 'I hope so,' he said bluntly. 'Queen Flamewing's tragic fate is a disgrace from which the Royal Guard will not easily recover, and I have sworn a solemn oath that it won't happen to her successor. Your clandestine meeting stinks of treason, Cygnus – and for your sake, you'd better convince me otherwise.'

Cygnus cursed inwardly. When Blacktalon had perished, many fortunes had been reversed overnight, and the leadership of all Aerillia's military forces had undergone a rapid change. Trust this loyal, conscientious lowborn bonehead to have wrested control of the Royal Guard.

'You wrong me, Captain,' the physician said in injured tones. 'You should know that I, of all people, am loyal to the queen. Why, did I not labour with Elster to save her life after the High Priest's reprehensible attack upon her person? Did Blacktalon not intend to take my life too? Each day I thank

75

Yinze that her Majesty is safe now, and upon her rightful throne at last.' He looked at the faces of his companions to judge the effect of his words and, encouraged, continued: 'I merely speak now for the good of both the queen and her subjects. Can it truly benefit Aerillia that its ruler has become enamoured of foreign groundling Wizards? Have you all forgotten the bitter lessons of the Cataclysm?'

'I don't know about that, but it seems that you have conveniently forgotten a fact or two,' Aguila growled. 'For one thing, we have the foreigners to thank for ridding us of Blacktalon and putting the queen on her throne. They have laboured long and hard since they came here to get our crops growing again, and save Aerillia from starvation.' He leaned over the table and fixed the bristling Cygnus with his gaze. 'And also,' he went on, 'if my memory does not deceive me it was Incondor, one of the Winged Folk, who set in train the catastrophe of the Cataclysm. He was every bit as much to blame as the groundling Wizard Chiannala.'

'Come, come, friend Aguila,' Sunfeather put in smoothly. 'No one would dispute your words, but I think you misunderstood our companion. He has only the best interests of everyone at heart. The groundlings have played their part, true – but what will be the price of their aid? Now they are causing her Majesty to neglect her most essential duties. She talks of depleting our forces at a time when we can least afford it, to send our people off to fight in some foreign war of magic.'

'Exactly,' Skua interrupted. 'Are we now to forget what befell us in the Cataclysm? After we lost our magic, the Winged Folk swore never again to consort with Wizards.' Laying his palms flat upon the table, he looked gravely at them all. 'My friends, I believe that Cygnus is right. The queen is but a young girl, vulnerable and gravely in need of guidance. It is our duty and responsibility to advise her – and we must start by wooing her away from her groundling friends and purging our land of this foreign infection.'

'I agree.' Sunfeather nodded. 'Aguila, you are needlessly suspicious. Blacktalon no longer reigns here, and – '

'Aye – and there may be some who still miss him.'

At the captain's words, Sunfeather half-raised his coppery wings and put his hand upon his sword. 'I suggest that you explain yourself and apologize,' he hissed, 'or prepare to defend your vile slanders in the arena of the skies!'

Aguila looked unperturbed, but his hand had also gone to his weapon. 'It occurs to me,' he answered with deceptive mildness, 'that the High Priest was responsible for your rise to your present exalted position. I would simply like to establish, once and for all, the extent of your loyalty to the queen.'

Cygnus, realizing too late that control of the meeting had slipped from his grasp, tried to dissipate the tension. 'Please, my friends, there is no need for such suspicion between us. Aguila, you have misjudged the Wingmarshal. As you all know, Sunfeather was my childhood companion, and we have remained close over the years. I know his reasons for accepting his position from the hand of Blacktalon, for he confided in me at the outset. It was I who advised him to take promotion, for at least then he would have sufficient authority to help our people clandestinely, and counteract the worst of the High Priest's depredations. He acted from the best of intentions – as do we all.'

'I see. Well, if that is truly the case, then I beg his pardon,' Aguila answered, though Cygnus suspected that he spoke more from caution than true conviction. 'You must understand, however, that as guardian of the queen's person, it is my duty to ask these questions,' the captain went on. 'However, I admit that there is sense in what you say. I see no gain in sending our warriors off to some foreign war when we should be consolidating our position here in Aerillia, and I will join with you in advising Queen Raven to that effect.'

It was only through rigid control that Cygnus managed to suppress his sigh of relief.

'Good,' he answered. 'I am grateful to you all for your cooperation. I suggest that we present our case to the queen on the morrow.'

It couldn't possibly last, thought Raven – but by Yinze, while it did, it was a marvel to behold! The winged girl, now Queen of the Skyfolk, dropped out of the thermal in which she'd been circling, and swooped down towards the lower slopes of Aerillia Peak. Let them say what they like, she thought – at least I've already achieved a miracle in my short reign.

There, on the hand-hewn terraces below the Citadel of the Winged Folk, a great work of cultivation was in progress, and everyone capable of such labour, from ragged-plumed elders down to the smallest of fledgelings, had been mobilized to assist. Raven looked down with pride upon her people, all engaged in the work of clearing, tilling, and planting, and felt her raptor's vision blur with tears of gratitude and relief. I have the Mages to thank for this, she thought. Aurian and Anvar. Even though I betrayed them, they have still come to my aid in this great-hearted way.

Raven cringed inwardly at the memory of her recent folly. How close she had come to bringing ruin upon them all. How could I have let myself be duped by Aurian's enemies, and my own? she wondered. How gullible I was. Aurian might have forgiven her, but the young Queen of the Skyfolk would never be able to forgive herself – and that made her feel even more guilty about the news that she must now impart to the Mages.

'Ho, Raven!'

The winged girl banked sharply in the direction of the cry from below, and saw Aurian, with Anvar at her side, waving from a bank of earth at the end of a row of grapevines. Raven bit her lip as her stomach clenched in trepidation. They weren't going to be at all happy with the word she brought them, but she would have to get it over with. Furling her wings, she landed beside the Magefolk, apologizing hastily as her final backsweep whirled a cloud of dust into their faces.

Aurian coughed grit from her throat and wiped her streaming eyes on her sleeve. 'I see your whirlwind landings haven't altered,' she said drily.

'You're right,' Raven acknowledged. 'My mother always used to say . . .' Her features twisted in a grimace of pain.

'Don't dwell on it.' Aurian laid her hands on the winged girl's shoulders. 'Raven, you can't change the past. You've repented, and what's more, you've learned from your mistakes. Now you're doing your best to set matters to rights.

You have promised to help us in our fight, and your winged warriors will make all the difference, though I know how difficult it is for you to spare them just now, when you have so much to do here in your own kingdom.'

Raven could not meet the Mages's eyes. 'That's just it,' she muttered. 'I . . .' There was no way that she could break this news gently. 'Aurian, they won't come,' she blurted. 'I spent the morning closeted with what remains of the Temple Guard and the officers of both the Royal Guard and our fighting force, the Syntagma. They all say the same thing: that it's insane to leave our land unprotected when we are at our most vulnerable, and that since the time of the Cataclysm the groundling Wizards have earned nothing but our enmity.'

'They said what?' Anvar shouted, his blue eyes icy with anger. His hand swept out to embrace the verdant terraces on the mountainside. 'They call this nothing?' he snapped. 'All the work that Aurian has done to keep the ungrateful bastards from starvation? And what about Blacktalon? If it weren't for me, you wouldn't even have a kingdom . . .'

'Without the backing of the warriors, I do not!' Raven cried. 'They have already made that perfectly clear,' she added in a smaller voice, into the shocked silence that followed. 'It was Elster who warned me. Despite his cruelty, Blacktalon had many followers, especially among the military, because they believed that he was trying to restore the ancient self-respect and supremacy of the Winged Folk. How else do you think he could have succeeded as he did?' Her voice took on a brittle edge of bitterness. 'His only mistake was murdering my mother. Even for those who were loyal to him, that was going too far – yet even now, there are those in Aerillia who are saying that the coming of spring had nought to do with Anvar. That it was Blacktalon who ended the winter as he had promised – and at the cost of his own life.'

'But that's outrageous!' Aurian was scowling.'You know, I thought I was sensing hostility from some folk while I was working on the terraces. I simply put it down to suspicion of an outland Wizard. But who started these ridiculous rumours? How can people believe them?'

'I wish I knew who was responsible,' Raven sighed. 'Because of what happened with Harihn, my rule over the Skyfolk is tenuous at best, and to have a secret enemy spreading such poison behind my back makes me very uneasy. Your selfless work upon our crops has strengthened my position, but . . .'

'But it's not enough.' There was grim finality in Aurian's words.

Raven nodded. 'Not only that, but . . .' She looked up at Anvar, tacitly pleading for his understanding. 'The finding of the Harp has caused a good deal of resentment. People believe that Anvar had no right to claim it. Only today, Sunfeather, the Wingmarshal of the Syntagma, was saying that it should be returned to its rightful keepers: the Winged Folk. The hope of regaining our long-lost powers of magic is a powerful and dangerous lure. With the resentment that is building, it may no longer be safe for you to stay here . . .'

'Damn it, Raven – the only reason we did stay here so long was to help your people,' Anvar began hotly. Aurian silenced him with a shake of her head.

'It's time we were leaving, anyway,' she said calmly. Only the cold grey glint in her eye betrayed her true feelings. 'Far from helping you establish your authority, Raven, I think our presence is making matters worse – and besides, we ought to be heading back north. Can you still arrange to have us transported to the Xandim fastness?'

'I owe you that – and so much more.' Raven's vision blurred with tears. 'You gave me back the gift of flight . . .' She took a deep breath, fighting to control her emotion. 'My people have shamed me, Aurian, but I will make amends for betraying you, I promise. I'll do whatever I can to put things right. There are some still loyal to me, who will act as bearers and couriers for you until you cross the ocean. I will make the arrangements at once.' Too ashamed to say more, she took wing again, heading back towards the sunlit spires of the Citadel.

Anvar's eyes were bleak and cold as he watched Raven fly off. The anger in his guts was too great to be contained any longer. Aurian, catching his expression, raised a questioning brow. 'Does she still trouble you so much? After all, you can hardly blame her for this.'

Anvar took a deep breath. 'I never understood how you could forgive her.' His tone was flat and uncompromising. 'After what she did to us – after what became of Wolf – how can you just act as though nothing had happened? How can you be so calm about it?' The Harp of Winds, strapped, as always, to his back, began to thrum discordantly in tune with his anger, and Anvar silenced it hastily, though not without an effort. Like Aurian in the early days of her stewardship of the Staff of Earth, he had not yet perfected his control of the powerful Artefact.

Aurian, who had been leaning, chin in hands, with her elbows resting on the crumbling drystone wall of a terrace, turned to look at him. 'Anvar, don't be too quick to judge. At least Raven didn't kill anyone. Oh, she precipitated situations in which there were deaths, but that was because she was manipulated. Her chief crime lay in being too young and un-tried, and trusting in the wrong people.'

Anvar shook his head in denial. 'So she was deceived. But that doesn't alter the fact that she betrayed us!'

'True.' Aurian looked away from him. 'But I remember, not so long ago, a young girl who trusted in the Archmage, and –'

'Aurian, that's not the same!'

'Oh, isn't it?' Aurian's mouth had thinned to a tight line. 'Seeing the way he despised the Mortals of Nexis, should I not have realized what he was like? After the way he treated you, should I not have known that he was evil? When he tried to have his way with me, should I not have faced the truth?'

Anvar, in his mind, added the words she had left unsaid: *And if I had, then Forral need not have died . . .*

'That wasn't your fault,' he told her stubbornly.

'Exactly!' Aurian's voice rang with triumph. 'It took you to teach me that, yet there's little difference between Raven's situation and mine – not to mention your own.'

'What?' Anvar gasped.

Aurian took his hand. 'Think back, my love. Back to the

young man who once loved a girl so much that he would sacrifice anything for her – though she plotted his death and abandoned him to marry, first a rich merchant, then a powerful king.'

Anvar recoiled as though she had slapped him. The blind folly of his love for Sara was not a subject he cared to dwell on. 'I . . .' he began in protest, but there was no answer to Aurian's charge. Anvar felt his face turn hot. She was right, much as it pained him to admit it. Suddenly, he began to see the winged girl in a new light.

Aurian squeezed his hand apologetically. 'Raven changed,' she said softly. 'She grew up – just as we did. She knows better now. She learned the hard way, as did you and I. Does she not deserve a chance to redeem herself?'

Anvar sighed. 'I take your point. But, Aurian – can you trust her? How can you be sure that she didn't start these rumours herself, to get rid of us? Have you ever wondered if *she* wants the Harp?'

Aurian shrugged. 'I don't trust her entirely – I'd be foolish if I did. But for now I'm prepared to give her the benefit of the doubt. If the situation is as precarious as she claims, then Raven has more than enough troubles of her own.'

Anvar dug the toe of his boot into the new-turned earth. 'Well, she's welcome to them. As far as I'm concerned, the Skyfolk have proved themselves to be as arrogant, ungrateful and untrustworthy as all the legends claim. They can stay up here and squabble amongst themselves until the sun turns cold for all I care, but . . .' His eyes flashed fire. 'If any of them try to take the Harp from me, they'll be sorry they were ever born.'

Aurian hugged him. 'If they are stupid enough to try that, they'll have both of us to reckon with!' Frowning, she dismissed the Winged Folk with a shrug. 'We've done all we can for the citizens of Aerillia. It's time we turned our thoughts towards heading northward once more. Our allies must be nearing the Xandim fastness by now.'

Raven, revelling in the strong beats of her newly healed wings, approached her pinnacle-palace and looked down upon the shimmering forest of towers, domes and spires with mingled pride and sorrow. She was queen now; all of this was hers – as were the burdens and responsibilities that went with it, she reminded herself sharply, feeling another stab of shame for the behaviour of her people. The evil reign of Blacktalon was ended, and the fell winter that had slain so many of her folk had been banished – but at what cost? Sadly she looked up at the shattered shell of Yinze's temple – a hideous structure it had been, but how much irreplaceable knowledge had been lost beneath that mound of fallen stone?

The winged girl turned her eyes downward, towards the great scar on the moutainside where the High Priest's tower had crashed down in ruin, taking so many lesser dwellings, and lives, down into darkness with it. She looked across at the Queen's Tower, her destination – and the place where her mother had died in agony and torment. The legacy of Blacktalon still lingered, and it would be long indeed, if ever, before his evil influence could be eradicated. Raven sighed, and then, taking her example from the dauntless Aurian, lifted her chin proudly. Well, so be it. Nothing could undo those sacrifices – and Flamewing, her mother, had often told her that any sacrifice would not be in vain, if the good of the people had ultimately been served. As queen, Raven knew that it was her responsibility, and hers alone, to make sure that it was so. And, by Yinze, she meant to do it.

'Your Majesty – your Majesty! Please . . !'

The shrill, piping voice that had startled the Queen of the Winged Folk from her royal thoughts ended in a squeak of fright, and the enraged bellow of a guard. Raven stalled, spilling wind from her wings, and sideslipped to turn and look for the cause of the commotion. Her eyes widened in surprise as she took in the balcony of a nearby tower and the slight, brown-winged child held firmly in the grasp of the scowling guard. The fledgeling was struggling and swearing, shrieking out curses that no child should know. Raven's lips twitched in an involuntary smile at the recollection of her own rebellious childhood. Putting her own troubles aside for the moment and composing her face into a semblance of royal dignity, she flew across to question the little intruder.

'Let me go! You filthy carrion-scavenger, fit for nothing but to pick flesh off a rotting corpse! Let me –' The words were cut off in a wail as the guard cuffed his captive.

'Gracious – who taught you such language?' Raven thought it best to interrupt at that point, before matters could deteriorate further.

The child, who had been too busy yelling to notice the queen's approach, turned her head sharply, her mouth dropping open in an O of surprise that changed swiftly to horror. 'Your Majesty!' she gasped, and writhed in her captor's grasp in a desperate attempt to dip her wings in obeisance.

Raven fought off the tender urge to straighten the girl's tousled brown curls, and said sternly: 'How comes this? Why are you trespassing in the precincts of the palace?'

'I caught her earlier, your Majesty,' the guard interrupted. 'The little wretch was trying to sneak into the throne room. Tried to give me a lot of nonsense about an urgent message for you. I sent her off then, but she must have sneaked back . . .'

'Be quiet!' Raven told him. 'Are we still in the hands of a tyrant, that you must bully children? And let the girl go, for Yinze's sake. If she has a message for me, she's hardly likely to go flitting off.' She turned back to the fledgeling. 'Now, little one, what is your name? And what word do you bring for the Queen?'

The child, released from the grip of the scowling guard, straightened her tunic in a pathetic attempt at dignity, and dipped her wings once more to her queen. 'Thank you, your Majesty,' she piped. 'If you please, my name is Linnet. And I do have a message – an important one – from the cat Hreeza.'

'So you are the brave child who rescued her!' Raven said. She had been astonished when Aurian had brought her word of one of her folk – and a fledgeling at that – who could accomplish the mind-speech of the great cats. She had been meaning to look into the matter further, but . . . Raven put her thoughts aside with an impatient shrug. The child was here now, at least. 'And what was your message?' she asked.

Linnet looked blackly at the guard. 'She said it was private.'

The queen laughed. 'Come then, little one. We will adjourn to my chambers, and see if we can find any refreshment there that is fit for a messenger.'

'She said *what?*'

Linnet flinched from the forcefulness of the queen's tone. Had that dratted cat got her into trouble again? Was she to be thrown out of these cosy royal chambers in disgrace? I told Hreeza that this idea was crazy, she thought resentfully. Linnet took an enormous bite out of the sweet cake in her hand – it tasted so good, and if she was to be thrown out, she might as well – and that was as far as she got, for, not unnaturally, it went down the wrong way.

By the time the queen had finished thumping her on the back and giving her a drink of water, Linnet had forgotten the original question. She flushed with embarrassment as Queen Raven repeated: 'Now then, tell me again, Linnet, exactly what Hreeza said.'

'She said that she had an urgent request.' Linnet scowled in concentration, doing her best to remember the exact wording. 'She asks if you will wait until the others leave, the Mages and the cats, and then provide bearers to return her to the land of her people.'

'But in Yinze's name, why?' The queen was frowning. In her consternation, she seemed to have forgotten that she was speaking to a child. 'Shia said that she and her friend were outlawed in their own land, and could not return on pain of death . . .'

'That's why it has to be a secret,' Linnet told her. 'Because if the others find out they'll worry, and they won't let her go. Hreeza says that her queen is bad – not like you,' the child added hastily, blushing for the slip, 'and if she isn't dealt with, she will always be an enemy at Aurian's back. But Hreeza has a plan – a wonderful plan – and if she can just get back quickly . . .'

'Wait, wait!' Frowning, the queen held up her hand for silence. 'Linnet, you had better come with me and talk to Hreeza. If you can translate, I would hear this plan for myself. What the Mages would say, if they knew of this . . .'

Linnet felt a weight of responsibility lift from her shoulders. Forgetting, in her relief, the exalted rank of her companion, she darted round the table and took hold of Raven's hand. 'Let's go now,' she said excitedly. 'I didn't understand it myself, but you will. And Hreeza is very wise, so it's sure to be a very good plan . . .'

As the excited child pulled her from the room, Raven lifted her eyes heavenwards. 'It had better be,' she muttered to herself, 'or Aurian and Shia will have my hide.'

6

The Storm Breaks

The little band of Xandim cavalry were but a scant handful of days from their destination, and excitement was growing within them as they neared their homeland. They had climbed high, now, into the great mountain range, and were looking forward to the day when they could look out across the roof of the world and see the familiar shape of their own sacred Wyndveil Peak, glimmering in the distance like a promise.

Spirits were high around the fire that night, and the talk and laughter were loud as the flask was passed round again and again, from hand to hand. The Xandim maiden crept away from the crowd of warriors who had crammed themselves into the bright circle of the campfire's glow. After so many months of near solitude, Iscalda still found herself overwhelmed, on occasion, by such a press of people, and she wanted to be alone for a time; at peace with the immense stillness of the night. On quiet feet she crept past the sentries and ventured a little further beyond the glare of the flames, until the soft hum of voices had receded and the stars above her were bright once more.

Iscalda unbraided the rippled flaxen banner of her hair and pushed her cloak back from her shoulders, letting the wind that swirled down from the snowpeaks stroke her arms with fingers of ice, raising tingling gooseflesh along the bare skin. She shivered pleasurably, luxuriating in the sensation of being clothed in human flesh once more. For her, this trek back through the mountains to her homeland had turned into a wondrous voyage of discovery. She had been trapped in her equine form for so long that she had almost forgotten simple, ordinary sensations such as the smooth slide of linen and the rough drag of wool against her skin; the savour of hot food in

87

her mouth and the supple weight of a leather cloak around her shoulders; the heartlifting, all-enfolding warmth of strong arms pulling her into an embrace, and the delight of shared laughter with a friend. Sights, sounds, scents, emotions – they had all seemed like thrilling new experiences, tasted for the very first time. In these last few days, Iscalda had felt like a child again, running out, full of excited expectation, into the morning of the world.

'Lady, do you not feel cold?'

Iscalda jumped at the sound of the soft voice that came from behind her. Whirling, she came face to face with Yazour. He was the last person she had expected to hear addressing her in her own language. During the journey, she had been chiefly occupied with renewing old friendships among her own people, and had forgotten that Chiamh the Windeye had extended a spell of tongues around the strangers so that they could be understood. With a startled exclamation, she took a hasty step backwards, and pulled her cloak around her shoulders once more.

The young warrior inclined his head in apology. 'I did not mean to startle you.'

'No?' Iscalda inquired softly. 'You creep up soft-footed as a Black Ghost of the mountains, and suddenly speak from out of the darkness. What, then, did you expect?'

Yazour laughed. 'You have me there. What I meant to say was that I did not come out here with that intention. In fact, I left the fireside to satisfy a much more mundane and pressing need, but as I was returning I saw you standing there, alone in the darkness.' He hesitated. 'Lady, I must confess that I was driven to approach you by curiosity. Since our rescue, we have had no chance to speak privately with one another, and . . .'

'And?' There was an edge to Iscalda's tone. Already she knew where this must be leading. When he did not reply, she went on for him. 'And you remembered what I was when you first met me, and wanted to know whether, as a woman, I had retained the instincts of a lowly beast – to be at the beck and call of any passing man . . .'

'No!' Yazour's protest interrupted her. 'Lady, you misjudge me. I simply wondered how it could be, that the most

88

magnificent horse I had ever seen could have been changed, as if by magic, into the most beautiful woman. I wished to understand the nature of your race, but as your warriors talk with one another around the campfire something – a fear of giving offence, perhaps – has held me back from asking, especially since my people and yours have been foes for so long. Yet I felt, because of the long days of captivity we spent together in the cave, that you and I might share some fellow-feeling. Your thoughts then, I know, cannot have been those of a mere beast. The night you took me to the tower you understood my need, and when I saw you tonight I thought that you, of all people, might understand again, and forgive any offence that an outsider and former enemy might convey with his prying questions.'

Iscalda was mollified, if not a little surprised, by his words. 'In a sense, you were wise not to ask the warriors,' she mused. 'Once, your questions – your very presence in our lands – would have meant instant execution. Yet you do not seem like an enemy to me, Yazour. And if what I hear from Chiamh is true, that our people soon will go to war, then the secret of our dual nature, which the Xandim have guarded so jealously for so long, may soon be out in any case.' She smiled at him. 'Ask, then, Yazour, and I will try to satisfy your curiosity.'

The young warrior spread his hands helplessly. 'I scarcely know where to begin,' he confessed. 'I – well, there was one thing that puzzled me . . .'

Iscalda laughed. 'You want to know where the clothes go?' Even in the dim light, she could see his blushes. To rescue them both from his embarrassment, she went on quickly. 'The garments just seem to be part of us, and change as we do – into horsehair perhaps – who knows? You might try asking the Windeye. Leather, wool, flax – fastenings of thong or carven horn or bone – anything that once was living matter changes with us. Weapons, buckles, personal adornments of metal or polished stone do not change, however. If we wish to take such items with us, they must be carried by another, in human shape. It's sometimes inconvenient, but at least the clothes are always there when we change back to our human form, and that's the most important thing.'

Yazour smiled. 'Given the barbaric climate of these mountains, Lady, I cannot fail to agree with you.'

Iscalda had noticed that the young man always seemed to require more garments than her own folk, and yet he appeared to be forever shivering. Chiamh had told her that the sun burned hotter where Yazour came from, but she found that impossible to imagine. She was robbed of her chance to question him, however, for he was already speaking again. 'How came your people to be as they are, Lady? What is their history?'

Now it was Iscalda's turn to shrug. 'That I cannot answer. No one knows where we came from, or how we came to be – not even the Windeye. It seems that we were always here, and always as we are.'

'And yet you knew that you differed from other races,' Yazour said thoughtfully.

'I believe so.' Iscalda nodded. 'That is why we have kept secret our ability to change our shapes. Forgive me, Yazour, but your own people, the Khazalim, have always been notorious for enslaving other races – imagine what useful slaves we Xandim would make, if the truth were known!'

'No one shall enslave you, Lady!' The vehemence of Yazour's reply startled Iscalda. 'The secret of the Xandim will always be safe with me,' he assured her. 'Even were it otherwise, I am an exile from the lands of the Khazalim, and may not return on pain of death. I owe no allegiance to the Khisu whatsoever.'

Iscalda felt her heart clench with pity for the young warrior. She too had been an exile, and she knew the bitterness and sense of loss that he must be feeling. She bit her lip. 'You know, do you not,' she said quietly, 'that even if you wished to do so, you would never be allowed to return to your lands alive, now that you know our secret?'

Yazour nodded gravely. 'I had guessed as much. But it makes no difference. My way lies northwards now. Where Aurian and Anvar go, I will go also – and if I survive the approaching conflict, then . . .' He shrugged. 'Well, then we will see. But one thing I can promise you. I will never return to the land of my birth.'

'Never?' Iscalda sighed in sympathy with the young warrior. 'That seems too harsh a fate . . .'

'Iscalda! What are you doing out here beyond the sentries?' Iscalda recognized the familiar outline of Schiannath, walking towards them, silhouetted against the glow of the distant flames. 'At least you had the good sense not to wander off alone,' he added, but as he drew nearer, and discovered the identity of her companion, Iscalda heard a note of doubt creep into his voice. She was stung into a swift defence of her companion.

'Don't treat me like a child, Schiannath.' The words came out sharper than Iscalda had intended, and she strove to reach a more conciliatory tone. 'I know that no one should stay out alone, unguarded, my dear – but after our long period of isolation, so many people overwhelm me at times. I crept away to be alone with the night, but Yazour discovered me, and thought much the same as you. When he found me here, he kindly stayed to bear me company.'

'Indeed,' Yazour concurred. 'But in truth, Schiannath, I was also glad of the opportunity to make the acquaintance of your sister in her human form at last.'

Schiannath came up between them and put an arm around each of their shoulders. The honeyed scent of mead was on his breath, and as he rested his weight upon her Iscalda realized that he must have been drinking heavily from the flasks that each Xandim warrior carried – ostensibly – in case of emergencies. 'You mistake me, my sister,' he told her, his voice slightly slurred. 'Yazour, as far as I am concerned you are not an enemy. You may be an outlander – but did the goddess herself not instruct me to befriend you?'

'What?' It was the first time that Iscalda had heard of this. She had a vague, equine memory of meeting the great cat in the pass – a recollection of terror and blood, and rage – the buried, instinctive urge to defend her beloved brother at all costs from the predator. She also remembered Yazour – a still, dark huddle, with his lifeblood sinking into the chilling snow.

Her brother went on to explain how, in the pass beyond the Tower of Incondor, the goddess Iriana herself, in the form of one of the great Black Ghosts of Schiannath's home mountains, had given him instructions to befriend and succour the wounded warrior. Iscalda listened, incredulous, as his tale unfolded – until, out of the corner of her eye, she saw Yazour's mouth quirk in suppressed amusement. Goddess indeed! The young warrior knew, or suspected, more about this matter than he was revealing, and Iscalda intended to get to the bottom of it – but not now.

'So you see,' Schiannath was saying, 'I trust you in the company of Yazour. I befriended him at first because I was told to, but later he earned my true respect. The rest of Xandim, however, are another matter.'

At that, Iscalda switched her attention back to her brother's words. 'What have they to do with it?' she demanded.

'They view me as an outlander, and suspect me accordingly,' Yazour put in, his voice sharp with hostility. He was right, Iscalda realized.

'Exactly, Yazour.' Schiannath nodded. 'They have no idea of what lies behind your inclusion in our party – and what reason have they to trust the word of my sister and myself, who have only lately been accepted, on sufferance and through the most unusual circumstances, back into the Xandim?'

Iscalda looked at her brother through narrowed eyes. Clearly, he was not as drunk as she had thought. Despite the absence of light, he turned to look deep into her eyes. 'There is, however, another complication, Iscalda – one that you have not considered.'

'And what is that?' The Xandim maid felt the first true stirrings of alarm.

Schiannath sighed. 'Your betrothal to Phalihas.'

'Nonsense!' Iscalda snapped. Her anger, however, was not directed at her beloved brother. It stemmed from a sudden, sinking fear. 'The Herdlord is defeated now,' she protested. 'Schiannath, you know I only agreed to the betrothal in the hope that I might have sufficient influence to protect you – and much good it did either of us, in the end. But Phalihas is defeated now. His reign, and his power, are ended. The Windeye would not permit him –'

'The Windeye cannot prevent him,' Schiannath said heavily. 'I have just been talking to Chiamh. This is the heavy news that I had come to break. Iscalda, under Xandim law you were betrothed to Phalihas. While you were exiled, the betrothal was void – but now that you have been accepted back into your tribe, the agreement still stands. Should the Windeye ever allow Phalihas to revert to his human form – and how can Chiamh refuse? – you, of all people, should know the alternative – then you will belong to our former Herdlord, as you did before.'

Will he never come? Basileus muttered irritably. Restless within the great mountain peak that comprised his body, the Moldan kept his vigil; awaiting the return of Chiamh, the Xandim Windeye. For the first time in all the endless aeons of his existence, the giant Earth-Elemental was finding it difficult to resign himself to patience, for these were the most momentous times he had known in many centuries.

The world was changing: the course of history was turning relentlessly towards a newborn age. The ancient Artefacts of Power were waking, and three of the four Great Weapons had already been loosed upon the world. The Mageborn were at war once more, and the fate of the future hung trembling in the balance, awaiting the discovery of the final Artefact – the Sword of Flame, the great master-weapon designed long ago by the farseeing and powerful Dragonfolk, to be their legacy of hope for the future. Into whose hands, the Moldan wondered, was the Sword destined to fall at last? The answer could either spell hope of freedom for Basileus and all his Elemental kind, or herald the onset of slavery, annihilation and the start of a new Age of Darkness.

Magefolk! Basileus felt the slow burn of anger deep within his core. Long ages ago, the ancient Wizards had imprisoned himself and all his kind in these immobile shells of stone to prevent them from using their vast, arcane and unpredictable powers of the Old Magic to influence the fate of the world. Any future hope of freedom for the Moldai and the other Elemental races, such as the Phaerie, depended upon the Artefacts of Power – or, more precisely, upon the intentions of those who wielded them.

93

High up on the slopes of the Wyndveil, rocks ground together and the flanks of the mountain trembled as the
Moldan expressed his frustration. There was so much at
stake, yet he could do so little to influence the outcome of
the approaching conflict. It was scarcely surprising, Basileus
reflected sourly, that he could find no rest.

The Moldan was not the only watcher on the Wyndveil. Had
Basileus been paying less attention to his inner thoughts, and
more to what was taking place upon his outer skin, he might
have noticed the lurker on his peak. Night after night, while
the moon went through its changes, the madwoman had lain
in wait, spying upon the Xandim fastness from her hiding
place among the rocks above. She knew they would return,
the ones she sought – and from this vantage point she would
have early warning of their coming.

Wild-eyed, wasted with hunger and pierced through and
through with cold, Meiriel kept her lonely vigil, concealed in
a hollow in the frost-cracked rocks well away from prying
Xandim eyes, and feeding on little more than the hatred and
desire for revenge that had sustained her for so long. Soon,
now, her wait would be over. She had found friends – new
and powerful friends who would help her wreak her ven-
geance. The one who had caused the death of her beloved
soulmate Finbarr would soon be here, along with that
accursed monster, the half-Mortal abomination that she had
borne. Aurian was coming, and when she arrived . . . Meiriel
ran her tongue across the sharp points of broken teeth. 'I will
rip out her heart, and drink her blood,' she whispered.

Parric struggled with warring feelings as his tight-knit band
of Xandim warriors picked their way through softly falling
rain, across the final projecting ridge of the Wyndveil to
strike the trail that led towards their fastness. 'What in the
world is wrong with me?' the little cavalry master wondered.
He ought to feel happy and triumphant after his achieve-
ments. Had he not done what he'd set out to do? His journey
to the sprawling hostile Southern Kingdoms had been a

nigh-impossible gamble, yet against all the odds he had succeeded in finding Aurian ... 'And what's more, I *will* bring
her home with me, to join our fight against the Archmage,'
he muttered.

At the sound of the cavalry master's voice, the powerful
black stallion he rode flattened his ears and turned his head
to roll a wicked, white-rimmed eye at his conqueror and foe.
Resentment burned behind that gaze: hatred (not unjustified,
Parric admitted) for the one who had consigned this once-
proud king to the humiliation of captivity and servitude. The
cavalry master must never forget for a moment that his
mount was Phalihas, one of the shape-shifting Xandim, who
had not only occupied a human form, but had once been
Herdlord, the Xandim leader – before Parric had challenged
and defeated him, and Chiamh had trapped him in his
equine shape.

Phalihas, sensing his rider's distraction, tried to dislodge
Parric with a series of jolting bucks. Swearing, the cavalry
master tightened his seat in response, and rashly urged the
beast to a faster pace. While the horse was preoccupied with
picking a footsure way through the treacherous terrain, the
creature would have little opportunity to be causing trouble.

Trouble. It always came back to that. 'Why must everything be so bloody complicated?' Parric fretted. Back in his
old role as cavalry master of the Nexis garrison, Parric had
been equal to anything. When it came to soldiering, his skills
could scarcely be bettered, but ever since Forral, his friend
and commander, had been murdered by the corrupt Archmage, the foundations of Parric's world had been slipping.
Even Aurian, whom he had come so far to rescue, had
seemed so altered ...

The cavalry master shook his head in dismay, then chided
himself for being unfair. You fool, he told himself. Of course
she's changed. After what that poor lass had been through
... At this point, his imagination failed him. Treachery,
battle and death Parric could understand, but when it came
to magic he was utterly lost. Even now, he could scarcely
bring himself to contemplate the fate of Aurian's firstborn –
Forral's son. Cursed by the Archmage to take the form of the

first beast his mother saw after bearing him, the child had been transformed into the shape of a wolf cub.

Parric gritted his teeth against a surge of anger, and wished that he could have Miathan at his swordpoint, to make him pay for the atrocity he had committed upon a helpless child – especially since the boy was all that was left of Forral. In his secret heart, the cavalry master had been hatching a plan to care for Aurian. It would have been a pleasure, not a duty, to raise the son of his friend and commander, and though he could never really hope to take Forral's place as a father to the lad he was determined to do his best. The boy would have taken the place of the son that he, Parric, had never (knowingly at least) fathered. But how, in the name of all the gods, could a man be a father to a wolf cub? Besides, one look at Aurian had disabused the cavalry master of such unrealistic notions.

Parric sighed. It was his own fault, he acknowledged ruefully. He had always thought of Aurian as an untried young girl, when she was in the presence of Forral. The swordsman had always been so confident and capable that those around him seemed diminished by comparison. But the steel-eyed, grimly resolute Aurian that Parric had found in the Tower of Incondor had stunned the cavalry master, and shaken him to the core. She had matured, true, but that was only to be expected. What Parric had not anticipated was the aura of power that surrounded her, wrapping her about in a cloak of numinous force. He had not expected the hardness in her eyes, the chiselling of bitter experience on her face, and the flat practicality that led her to leave her newborn son in the care of others while she went off in pursuit of other, more urgent goals. It wasn't right, somehow, though he acknowledged that her actions had been necessary.

Parric cursed himself for entertaining such unjust thoughts. Had he not served and fought with pragmatic female warriors such as Sangra and Maya? Was Aurian not a better swordswoman than either of them – and a Mage besides? So why was he swamped by this irrational protectiveness towards her? It was almost as though the shade of Forral haunted him. But that was ridiculous, Parric told himself, as he tried to shake himself free of his doubts. Soon he would be back at the Xandim fastness, and would have more urgent matters to consider. There, too, he would see Aurian again – and surely, once they had spent more time together, he would recover his former sense of ease with her?

Aurian and Anvar arrived at the Xandim fastness with their escort of Winged Folk, and landed, damp and shivering in their nets, in a mist of fine spring drizzle that was becoming heavier by the moment.

'Ugh!' Aurian stepped carefully from the tangle of meshes and tried to pull the clinging folds of her wet cloak more closely around her shoulders with her free hand. The attempt was made awkward by the fact that Wolf was cradled in the other arm, snugly asleep against the warmth of his mother's body. Above the Mage, more Skyfolk circled, waiting their turn to land, bearing the net that contained the cub's lupine foster-parents within its enclosing meshes. They looked a bedraggled sight, with their wet fur clinging spikily to their bodies, and Aurian could sense from their thoughts that both of them would be infinitely relieved to get their feet back on to good solid earth once more. The Mage never ceased to be amazed and humbled by the extent of their forbearance and their loyalty to herself and her child.

Anvar, aware of the restless mutterings of his winged escort, was squinting through the drifting veils of rain. 'Where the bloody blazes is everybody?' he muttered irritably. 'Even if they haven't posted guards, they should at least be keeping some sort of watch. According to our winged scouts, Parric and his lot should certainly have arrived by now.'

'What useless humans,' rumbled Shia, shaking a spray of moisture from her fur. 'Anvar, will you help us, please?' The cat sounded thoroughly disgruntled. She and Khanu had been landed quickly – due, Anvar suspected, to a good deal of nervousness on the part of their squadron of winged porters. The Skyfolk had dropped the net all in a tangle and retreated to a safe distance, and Shia and Khanu, without hands to unwind the mare's nest of knotted rope, were securely enmeshed. Anvar, wiping rain out of his eyes, went to disentangle his friends.

'I've just spoken to Chiamh,' Aurian reassured them. 'He was asleep – they all were. They didn't expect us so soon. He says that the last part of the journey over the Wyndveil was gruelling – they were exhausted by the time they reached the fastness. He's rousing them now and they're sending out an escort.'

'About time,' Shia muttered. 'Lazy two-legged – ' Her head swung sharply. 'What was that?'

'What?' Anvar frowned. All his concentration had been centred on unravelling the snarled net.

'I thought I heard somethi – '

None of them had any more warning than that as a black shape streaked out of the darkness towards Aurian. Hampered by the child in her arms, the Mage had neither the time nor the opportunity to react. Even as he leapt to his feet, Anvar saw the dark form close upon her, saw her crumple, heard a terrified squeal from the cub. Then the shape was gone.

'Follow it!' Anvar bellowed at the Skyfolk, who were still standing nearby, paralysed with shock. Two of them took off in pursuit. Shia and Khanu burst free of the tangled net and went bounding after them, with the two wolves, who had been landed too late to help the Mage, close upon their heels.

'Aurian!' Anvar bent over the limp form that lay, motionless, face-down on the waterlogged turf. Sliding his arms beneath her, he turned her gently, but was unable to make out any details in the gloom. Her skin was dreadfully cold. Somewhere in the background, he heard the sound of running feet. Then he was surrounded by Xandim who milled uselessly about him, unable to keep torches alight in the rain, and blocking what little light was available even to Anvar's night vision. Frantic, Anvar gathered all his rage and fear and threw the energy into a brief, bright flare of Magelight that sent the Xandim reeling backwards, covering their eyes and screaming in panic.

'What in Chathak's name is happening here? Get out of the way, you fools! Let me through!' To his relief, Anvar recognized the voice of the cavalry master.

'Aurian was attacked,' the Mage cried. 'Quick, Parric – help me get her inside.' He heard the cavalry master curse, and then the little man was at his side.

'Is she badly hurt, Anvar?'

'I think so.' He lifted Aurian from the rain-soaked ground, and followed Parric quickly as the little man cleared a path through the milling crowd. How badly she was hurt he didn't dare think – but in that brief flare of Magelight, Anvar had seen that her tunic was soaked through with dark blood that was welling around the blade of a jagged knife, sunk deep into her chest.

7

The Mountain King

Aurian was drifting, somewhere out beyond her body. From above, she could see the pale, still form that was laid out on a bed of cloaks in the great entrance hall of the Xandim fastness. Is that me? she wondered. Can it be, really? She felt dreamlike, oddly detached. She knew that she had been badly hurt; she knew her son had been stolen. Curiously, none of that mattered now. She viewed everything from outside, from above, from beyond . . .

From her high vantage point, the Mage could see Parric, one of her oldest Mortal friends, kneeling over her body, his face contorted with grief. She could see Chiamh, the Xandim seer, propped against the wall in a nearby corner, his face blank and expressionless as he rode the winds to track her lost child. His whole attention was not given to his task, she knew. Always, a shred of consciousness remained with her, in the great hall, worrying about her recovery. And there, most painful of all – if anything in this soothing limbo could cause her pain – was Anvar. Her lover had wasted no time in weeping. Instead, he was hunched over her lifeless form, trying with every shred of his power and his love to pull her fleeing spirit back into her body.

Poor Anvar. What chance did he have? Now Aurian understood what Forral must have felt, when he was slain by the Wraiths, and had seen her, much younger then and much more innocent, trying to forestall the inevitable. Gods! How much it would have spared her, then, if she could only have understood the reality. This farewell to mortality was so easy! You only had to let go, and . . .

A fleeting glimpse of a memory passed through Aurian's mind. A small boat, a moonlit river and white foam glimmering on the churning waters of a lethal weir . . . An icy plunge, and a thought: *It would be so easy, just to let go and leave all this behind* . . .

It was enough to shock the Mage out of her drifting dream. What the blazes are you thinking of? Aurian scalded her drifting spirit with angry thought. You can't die now! Yet could she prevent it? She felt terror twist her heart within her. A vision of Forral stood before her, veiled by drifting mists – but even beyond the obscuring veils, she could see the pain on his face, and the glimmer of tears in his eyes. Resolutely, Aurian turned away from the shade, stifling the longing within her. 'Go away,' she gritted. 'I can't give up now!'

'He may not go – not this time. He has come for you – to meet you, and escort you to my realm.' The ghastly voice pierced Aurian to the core with an ever-deepening grasp like talons of ice. The Mage shuddered. She had heard that voice before – once, long ago, in a dusty, sun-hammered courtyard in the lands of Khazalim.

'What do you want with me?' she whispered.

Death laughed. 'What could I want, little fool? You have overplayed your gamble; overstayed your welcome in your world. Once before, you defied me – but this time you are mine!'

The massive, shrouded figure loomed huge and dark in Aurian's vision, but with a strength born of desperation, and a howl of agony that was wrenched from her lacerated soul, she ripped herself free from the grasp of his icy claws and eluded him. *'No!'* She shrieked her defiance in his face. 'I hold the power of the Staff of Earth now. Wrought as it is with the High Magic, it gives me sufficient power to resist you, even in your realm. If you want me, you'll have to fight me every step of the way!' Aurian strove to hide her astonishment at her own words. She hadn't known that about the Staff. How did she know it now?

Death hissed a chilling curse. Turning to Forral, he beckoned the warrior with a snarl. 'Defiant as always,' he muttered. 'She was your love, swordsman – *you* take her! Do this, and she will be yours for all eternity.'

Forral looked sadly at the Spectre, and shook his head. 'Not now – not like this. Not unless she wants me.'

'Of course I want you, you great fool!' Aurian took refuge in sharpness to keep back her tears. 'But remember what you once told me, about living my life out in the mundane world? And what about our child?' Though guilt smote Aurian – a physical force in this unearthly world, like a spear through her heart – she forced herself to continue. 'I love Wolf, too,' she said softly. 'And I must get back now to save him. He is all that remains of you and me.'

Forral smiled sadly. 'Not all,' he told her. 'Never believe that. But he is a child – lost, threatened and afraid. If I could protect him, and you, I would, but I can't. You're right, love. You should go back.'

'Can I?'

Forral forced a smile, and the Mage understood the measure of the great man's courage. 'I always said you could do anything you wanted to,' he told her, and turned back to the looming figure of Death. 'You heard her. If you want her, you can bloody well get her yourself.'

There it was – that same old flashing, unquenchable grin that Aurian had always loved. She grinned back at him, sharing one last instant of communion – then tore herself away and went spiralling back down towards her body. She had almost reached it when, to her horror, she felt her momentum slow. Death was pulling her back – back into the mist.

'It is not up to you – either of you.' The Spectre's voice was implacable, like the slamming of the lid on a tomb. 'Your time is over, Aurian. You must pass Beyond . . .'

'You can do nothing to force me.' The Mage was sure of it now. 'I must go back to Anvar, fight the Archmage, and, especially, save my child . . .'

'Can I not?' Death hissed. Again, Aurian's soul was torn by the grasp of icy claws, as the Spectre's voice grated: 'You may possess the Staff, O Mage, but one thing you have forgotten. We made a bargain once, and you still owe me a life. That debt must be repaid . . .' The words ended in a startled shriek, and once more the Mage felt herself released.

'Wizard, go back to your body!' The voice had no business here – it was alien – this was none of its concern. In the limbo that enfolded her, Aurian felt fear, and found herself reaching for a nonexistent swordhilt.

Death seemed equally startled. 'This is not your concern!' the Spectre snapped furiously.

'It is no business of mine – except that I can see what is import-ant and what is not,' the voice retorted. *'This is not the time for you to be reclaiming your debt, O Grey One, and well you know it. Your concerns may differ from those of the living, but your greed for this one bright soul would prove to be all our undoing. It cannot be permitted at this time. Why must you take her now? Sooner or later she must come to you in any case.'*

In the shadows of her consciousness, Aurian could see a massive shape, unspeakably old – powerful, and utterly alien – hovering between herself and the Reaper of Souls. For a terrifying instant Death seemed to hesitate, then: 'Very well,' he snarled. 'I will spare her – for now.' The grim Spectre vanished, leaving Aurian alone in the void with the alien presence.

'I am Basileus,' the shadow said. *'I am the body and soul of this fastness. I will speak with you later, but now you must return. Flee, little Wizard, towards the one you love – he will help you!'*

What, back to Forral? For an instant, Aurian was con-fused; then all became clear to her. 'Anvar!' she cried joyously, and arrowed her spirit towards his seeking mind. Searching, searching for him in the grey nothingness of Beyond. And suddenly, to her joyful astonishment, a brilliant green light shone before her: a clear and powerful beacon to guide her through the veils that kept her from her love.

'Damn it, I'm losing her!' Anvar cried in anguish. Aurian's face was grey-white. Blood and froth bubbled horribly from her wound with every gasping, shallow breath she tried to take. Her heart was faltering and stumbling like a runner at the very end of a race, and only his stubborn will – and that of Aurian, perhaps – was keeping it going at all.

As if through a haze, he became aware of someone at his shoulder – Chiamh.

'I'll look for the child later,' the Windeye said. 'Now, you need me here.' His eyes still silver with Othersight, he bent over Aurian's still form, his hands moving, knotting, mould-ing the air above her. 'This is bad,' he muttered. 'I can keep her breathing a little while, but . . .' He looked up at Anvar, his silver gaze sharp and piercing. 'Do you go forth and seek her with your mind, beyond the Veil,' he commanded. 'Use her Staff, that once you carved and she imbued with power. It may link you. I – I will get us some help, if I can.' So saying, he sank down, head bowed, deep in trance. Even as Anvar reached across to find the Staff among Aurian's scattered belongings, he heard the Windeye whisper a single word: *'Basileus.'*

Anvar clasped Aurian's cold, limp hands around the Staff and held them there with his own. He poured forth his mind, and his will, and his love into the Artefact, and his spirit went forth into the void, seeking his love with all his heart.

And he found her. Already, she was coming to him, hurtling back towards the light of the Staff, streaming tatters of grey. Her wraithlike form was hideously maimed, as though she had been scored again and again by the grip of giant talons. Anvar shrieked her name – felt his own name, cried in her voice, echo in his head. Hearing the joy and anguish in her cry, he held her tightly, and she clung to him as the emerald glow of the Staff fell about them like a benison.

There was no time for their reunion now; no time for love, or fear. 'Aurian,' he told her urgently, 'I need your help. Your healing is beyond me – I still lack the skill. You must come back now – join with me in the power of the Staff as we did in the desert, and give me your healing powers, so that I can help you.'

Her eyes grew wide. 'Is that possible?' she breathed. Then he saw her jaw tighten. 'It had better be,' she muttered. The world spun, and –

Anvar was back within his mundane form, kneeling over the Mage, but this time he felt her mind, in deep and intimate linkage with his own. He experienced her shock as she perceived the damage that Meiriel's treacherous knife had done to her chest, and heard her curse. Then her voice came again. 'We'd better hurry. I didn't realize there would be so much to do.'

Without the Staff of Earth, they would never have managed it. Without Aurian's skills, which had, with ultimate irony, been taught her by the very woman who had tried to take her life, the Mage would not have stood a chance. Anvar, trusting, simply gave his power into Aurian's hands, and his hands into her will, and let her do what she would with the combination of his strength and her knowledge. And after a dreadful, bloody, endlessly exhausting age spent rebuilding sliced muscle and damaged tissue, Anvar felt her mind slip free from his own. For an instant, he knew the clutch of panic round his heart – then Aurian opened her eyes. 'I love you,' she whispered. 'You did good work, my partner in healing – and in all things.'

From her nest of cloaks, the Mage saw Anvar grinning like a lunatic for the sheer joy of her safe return. Her heart went out to him.

'The skill was yours,' he told her, 'and I love you, too.' He clasped her hand tightly. 'But are you – will you be all right now?'

Briefly, Aurian's gaze became unfocused as she scanned inwardly with her powers, then she looked up and nodded, with a weary little smile. 'All mended. I'm just sore – and so very, very weary. I must sleep for a while, to regain my strength and let the healing settle – and then – ' Her grip on Anvar's hand grew fierce. 'Then we go after that bitch Meiriel – and my poor baby.'

Anvar was thunderstruck. 'It was Meiriel? But Parric thought she was dead . . .'

'I wish she was,' Aurian snarled. 'But it's a mistake that can be remedied. Is there any news? Has anything been done?'

Anvar squeezed her hand in comfort, and shook his head. 'But we'll – '

'You live!' Shia's voice echoed joyously in the Mage's mind as two great cats, their coats flattened and streaked with rain, came hurtling into the hall. Shia nuzzled her with care, her long black whiskers dripping icy drops on to the Mage's face as she purred her happiness.

Aurian, despite her worries, somehow managed to summon a smile for her friend. 'I live,' she agreed. 'Though the gods only know how. But . . .' Her mental voice was shadowed with fear. 'What happened to you, Shia? What news of my son?'

The great cat dropped her head. 'We failed,' she confessed miserably. 'Our foe threw up a barrier of magic through which we could not pass, and we lost her trail. The Skyfolk, too, seemed equally at a loss. I think the magic veiled her from their sight. Then we sensed that your life was in danger. Even from such a distance, we could feel your mind slipping away . . .' For an instant, Shia's mental voice trembled. 'Khanu and I returned, while the wolves began to quarter the mountain, to see if they could track Wolf's abductor.' She looked away from the Mage. 'Aurian – I believe our enemy had assistance. We could have been mistaken, but Khanu and I were convinced that we picked up a faint trace of strange cats, our own folk. I am ashamed . . .'

'Hush,' a voice interrupted. Looking around, Aurian saw the Xandim Windeye. 'Do not blame yourself,' he told Shia, including the Mages in his mental range. 'Things are not all bad. We do know which way the madwoman went. She may have been able to veil herself from normal vision, but with my Othersight I pursued her on the winds. I was forced to return to help Aurian when I sensed that her life was threatened. But when last I saw the witch, she had made no attempt to harm the child . . .'

His voice was soothing, reassuring. Much too reassuring, given the circumstances. Aurian's scalp prickled with suspicion. 'And the bad news?' she demanded. 'Come on, Chiamh – what aren't you telling us?'

Chiamh sighed. 'The madwoman took the babe up on to the high Wyndveil slopes, and headed towards the Dragon's Tail ridge. Shia was right – two strange cats were nearby, pacing her like shadows. She has taken your son to the dreaded Steelclaw Peak. Even if they trace her, the wolves will be unable to follow. None but the Black Ghosts may walk the slopes of Steelclaw and live.'

The stricken silence of the Mages was broken by Shia's growl. 'None but the Ghosts, you say? Chiamh, I *am* one of your Black Ghosts! Never fear, Aurian, Khanu and I will go to Steelclaw. I have unfinished business there, especially if

106

Gristheena and her people are aiding your foe. Be assured that I will bring Wolf back.'

Meiriel scrambled across the exposed Field of Stones towards the broken ledges of the Dragon's Tail ridge, alternately blessing her Mage's sight that allowed her to pass safely through the darkness, and cursing the wind that wrapped clinging tendrils of hair around her face and drove the rain stinging into her eyes to obscure the very night-vision that she needed so badly.

Despite the storm, despite the hardships of the climb, Meiriel's heart burned with a savage joy. At last, she had struck down her enemy, the slayer of her beloved soulmate! Her magical shield had foiled her pursuers. And now she had Aurian's child, that accursed, unnatural monster, to dispose of at her leisure. In the distance, Meiriel heard wolves howling, and dismissed the chilling sound with a shrug. Instead she looked down, her sharp eyes seeking the hidden way that led down from the plateau, to the shattered ridge. As soon as she reached Steelclaw, and was certain that she had shaken off pursuit, the child would be –

'Twisted serpent of a wizard – I think not!'

'Who's there?' Meiriel whirled, her voice shrill with panic. Though softly spoken, the words had been clearly audible above the whine of the storm.

'You are mistaken, mad one. Your treacherous attack was not as accurate as it seemed. Aurian will live – and if you have not lost the last shreds of wisdom you will keep her child alive, as hostage – or as bait.'

'Who are you?' Meiriel shrieked. Sobbing with terror, her joy extinguished, the Magewoman half-scrambled, half-fell down the sloping edge of the plateau, and crawled on to the broken ridge that led to Steelclaw. Once she had left the Wyndveil behind, the voice tormented her no more.

Crossing the Dragon's Tail was a nightmare. Meiriel was forced to creep inch by painful inch on hands and knees, her palms and shins lacerated by the razor edges of broken rock and leaving smears of blood behind to be washed away by the merciless downpour. The storm shrieked its derision at her, buffeting her frozen body on the exposed ridge and clutching at her with powerful fingers; threatening every moment to pluck her from her precarious perch and hurl her into the dark depths that plunged down on either side. Because of the energy and concentration needed to keep her balance she had been forced to abandon her magical shield, but that was of no consequence now.

Meiriel gritted her teeth and pressed doggedly onward, though her mind still reeled from the mysterious message she had received on the Wyndveil Peak. Whence had come that voice? Was it some kind of trick, and if so, from whom? What did it mean? Could it really be true that Aurian was still alive? Suddenly doubt assailed her, as she realized that she had not felt Aurian's passing. But surely, it could only be a matter of time, before the Mage succumbed to such a wound? Meiriel cried aloud in pain and rage, and spat upon the rain-slick stones of the ridge. She must assume that it was true. There was something in that voice that had convinced her – and besides, she dared not take the risk. The voice had been right about one thing. If Aurian was still alive, Meiriel would need that babe – one way or the other.

By the time she had reached the far side of the ridge, the Magewoman had managed to gather her wits once more. Even if Aurian should come here, Meiriel still had a trick or two to fall back on, not the least of which was her newfound friendship with the savage denizens of this shattered peak. When that fool Parric had left for the south with his make-shift army, Meiriel had headed for the sanctuary of Steelclaw, to be well out of the way of the Xandim and their keen-eyed scouts as they crossed the Wyndveil.

The Magewoman had had no idea of the Xandim legend that the Dragon's Tail was impassable, and besides, the unstable ridge was always shifting and being resculpted by wind and weather. She had, with difficulty, succeeded in making the crossing, and during her wanderings on the other side had met with the Black Ghosts of the mountain. There had been so many that she had been forced to use her powers to defend herself, and in the course of her magic had discovered the possibility of communication. On meeting their First Female, Meiriel had discovered that she and

Gristheena were of a like mind. The great cat was wounded, and still smarting from a recent defeat by some outlaw. Her position as leader was currently very tenuous, and she had been glad of the Magewoman's powers to back her authority. And Meiriel? She had needs of her own.

Tonight, the Magewoman could not have managed without Gristheena's assistance. Meiriel glanced across at the two great cats who were pacing her – one a guard, the other with a dangling cloth-wrapped bundle held delicately in its massive jaws. Meiriel smiled grimly at the sight. Thank all the gods that she had not been forced to bear that burden across the broken ridge! Without the use of her hands, as well as her feet, she would almost certainly have fallen.

Calling to the cat to stop, the Magewoman approached and poked the bundle with a bloodstained finger. A thin, protesting whine came muffled from within. Meiriel nodded to herself in satisfaction, and started tramping again, down the rough trail towards the broken core of Steelclaw. She must return to Gristheena as soon as possible, and then – well, then she would see.

'Curse this blasted rain – I can't see a thing!' Anvar muttered.

'Neither can we,' one of his winged bearers retorted bitterly, 'and we are the ones who must do the flying, and risk life, wing and limb along these treacherous peaks.'

'Oh, stop whining!' Anvar muttered, made ungracious by worry, but quicker, and louder, Chiamh said: 'Most courageous are the warriors of the Skyfolk who volunteered for this perilous mission. You have earned unending gratitude from us, the allies of your queen.'

Anvar felt the Windeye's elbow dig him sharply in the ribs, and he hastily added his thanks to Chiamh's. It had been a nice touch, he thought gratefully, for Chiamh to obliquely remind the Winged Folk that the Mages had rescued their monarch. He only wished the Windeye could have done something about this wretched storm. 'Have you any idea where we are?' he whispered.

There was a glimmer of silver from Chiamh's eyes as the Windeye turned to scan the darkened landscape with his

Othersight. 'We are perched on one of the shattered peaks overlooking the heart of Steelclaw,' he replied in mind-speech. 'The core is guarded, but not this high, for our winged friends have placed us where the great cats cannot climb. The noise of the storm will shield us from scent and sound, but keep silence in any case, as much as possible. And have a care for your footing in the dark. This will be a good vantage point – our foe, when last I looked, was headed this way. She must certainly come here if the cats are her allies. Once she arrives, the Skyfolk will take us quickly down – and our trap is sprung!'

'Then Gristheena is mine!' Even in mindspeech, Shia's voice was a savage growl.

'And mine!' Khanu echoed.

Anvar caught the odd little thought symbol that was Shia's equivalent to upcast eyes, and smiled to himself in the darkness.

'I would not smile if I were you,' Shia told him gruffly. 'Aurian is going to murder the pair of you when she wakes and discovers that Chiamh slipped that sleeping draught into her wine.'

'I don't care,' the Windeye protested. 'She would insist on coming with us, and she was in no condition to do it. Besides,' he added, 'if we bring Wolf back safely, she will be too glad to slaughter us.'

'You're right,' Anvar told him. 'Probably, she'll just damage us severely.' Though he was scarcely in the mood to jest, he welcomed the good-natured chaffing. It helped ease his nerves, which were strung tighter than a crossbow.

'Hush!' Khanu interrupted. 'I hear something!'

Anvar could see nothing in the thick brew of storm and darkness, but Chiamh, with his Othersight, saw it all. The dark, shelved, broken crater at Steelclaw's heart; the great projecting ridge of obsidian that glimmered here and there with clusters of firefly light as the life-forces of the cats gathered and shifted, moving here and there. And across from the blackly glittering tongue of the ridge, he saw the dark, featureless mouth of a tunnel. From its maw, a faint ghostlight emerged, red and roiling, half-veiled and shot through with spars of lurid darkness. The Mad One! Chiamh held his breath, watching as the sickly gleam of her unlight emerged from the tunnel and began to cross the ridge, coming right out into the open. Then: 'Now!' he whispered. The nets, on which the companions were still standing, were whipped up around them and pulled tight. The Skyfolk took wing and swept down into the crater.

Hreeza, shivering in the pouring rain, was beginning to wish that she had never come. This is no fit task for one old cat! She must have been thinking out loud, however, for a voice spoke scoldingly from nearby: 'For one old cat, perhaps – but we are many. You wanted this, Hreeza – this was your great vision, and you have given us life and purpose again. Have courage in the miracle that you have wrought!'

Hreeza chuckled drily. 'Some miracle – a bunch of skinny-ribbed, patch-coated old vagabonds!' she snorted. But warm courage flooded back into her veins, and her old heart soared with pride. 'Sentimental fool!' she told herself – but it felt good, none the less. Now, if only they could put their plans into action . . .

Back in Aerillia, Hreeza had thought the most difficult part of her mission would be persuading that little snippet of a queen to provide winged bearers, and to let her go in secret. Once that part of the plan had been accomplished, however, and Hreeza had found herself dangling above the clouds in a swinging net, she had abruptly changed her mind. Surviving this, the old cat was convinced, would be the really tricky part. She had been wrong, though. After several days spent sneaking about in the rain and cold, always hungry, living in constant terror of being caught, Hreeza would gladly have climbed straight back into that net, so long as there was the promise of a warm fire and a lavish meal at the end of the journey. Her convalescence in the Skyfolk citadel, the old cat thought disgustedly, had made her soft, as no cat should be.

Nevertheless, Hreeza had persevered. She had crossed and recrossed the areas on the outskirts of her people's lands, hunting the elusive Chuevah – the lonely outcasts who had been ejected from the clan because of age, or sickness, or unfitness to hunt. Since the brutal Gristheena had begun her rule, there were more than there had ever been before. One by one she had found them: timid, hunted, broken-down creatures, some barely holding on to the thread of life. She had cajoled them, persuaded them, tempted, badgered, nagged and browbeaten them. She had hunted for them, found them shelter, and at the last had gathered them together into the most unlikely army that had ever been. And now she had brought them back to the heart of Steelclaw – to challenge Gristheena's might, or die in the attempt.

At the time of gathering and persuading her bedraggled forces to assert themselves, the old cat had thought that this must definitely be the hardest part of her task. Now, as she looked down into Steelclaw's crater and saw the assembled masses of those who had once been her own people, she realized, with a chill of horror, just how wrong she had been.

'You old fool!' Hreeza muttered to herself. Whatever had possessed her? In the certain knowledge that she would not be able to hold her little band of Chuevah together for long – either they would be discovered, so many of them together, or they would lose their courage one by one, and slink ashamedly away – Hreeza had decided that she must strike as soon as possible. When she had heard from her spies that there would be a great meeting of cats in the crater, she had blessed her good fortune. But looking at her opponents now, all felines in their prime, well muscled and well fed, Hreeza's heart misgave her, and she began to think that the trip through the air in that net must have addled her wits. If she did this thing, she would be leading her wretched band of followers, who had come to depend on her, to certain death.

Hreeza sighed. Maybe those whom she had called cowards were in the right of it. Maybe it would be better to slink away, head bowed, and simply vanish into the night. Maybe she should take her followers and find them a new home, in another land. There was space in the mountains near Aerillia, and now that she could speak with the Winged Folk perhaps an accommodation could be reached . . .

Then into the arena below, escorted by two great cats, came a two-legged shape, shuffling and bowed, and reeking

112

of madness and evil. Hreeza twitched her whiskers forward in curiosity and opened her mouth to better scent the air. What in the world . . . Then her sharp ears caught the sound of a high, thin whimper, piteous and faint. The whiff of a scent reached her, so distinctive and redolent of memory that Hreeza felt her heart turn over. In Aerillia, she had played with Aurian's enchanted son; had even minded him, as she would the cub of another cat, when the Mage was otherwise occupied.

All thoughts of flight, of surrender, fled from Hreeza's mind. Leaping to her feet, the ancient warrior let out such a roar of outrage and challenge that the very mountain trembled. As though she were young and fleet again, she leaped down from the heights of her lurking-place – and like a great black river in spate, her Chuevah followed; hair bristling on their bony spines, eyes glowing bright in heads held high and proud, and voices uplifted in their song of battle.

8

The Mountain Queen

Anvar hurtled downwards through the darkness, clinging tightly with cold-numbed fingers to the rough meshes of the net that surrounded him, his skin tingling from the impact of the stinging rain. The keening of the storm grew louder in his ears, and suddenly became another sound. Anvar's belly tightened into a knot of fear for poor Wolf as he heard a crescendo of yowls rising above the wail of the wind. Below him the great cats were fighting.

Then, to his astonishment, the Mage heard a familiar, rasping old cat-voice in his mind, shrieking venom and defiance. He was not the only one to have heard it.

'Hreeza!' Shia's cry echoed in Anvar's mind. *'Don't be a fool!'* And then they were down, in the midst of a bloodbath. The Skyfolk, guided by Chiamh, had landed them near the tunnel-mouth at the edge of the crater, both to cut off Meiriel's retreat in that direction and to give them a chance of taking cover from the mass of fighting cats that covered the floor of the crater. To Anvar's fury, their winged escort took one startled look at the carnage around them and rocketed skywards again like a covey of startled birds. The Mage cursed savagely, and then thrust the matter from his mind, to be dealt with later. One problem at a time – and it seemed that he had troubles enough.

The rain was beginning to slacken, allowing Anvar's night-vision to function once more. He stared, aghast, at the bloody struggles taking place all around him, trying to make sense of it all – and, more important, wanting to catch a glimpse of Meiriel. Chiamh, however, had an advantage over the Mage. The Windeye, with his Othersight, could perceive the glow of life energy rather than the physical form, and the corpse-gleam of Meiriel's hideous, sickly aura was easy to pick out.

114

Shia, with her feline senses, had no difficulty in picking out her own foe. *'Gristheena!'* Her yowl rose in a blood-curdling crescendo, and she darted off into the mob of fighting cats, Khanu hot on her heels. Chiamh belatedly realized that her route was taking her in the same direction as he and Anvar wanted to go – towards the rearing obsidian spur, for which Meiriel was determinedly heading; picking her way through the warring felines as though they did not exist.

'Come on!' The Windeye tugged urgently at Anvar's arm. 'This way!'

Chiamh, his Othersight fixed firmly on his quarry, led the way, with Anvar close by him, guarding him with drawn sword from attack by the cats that packed the canyon floor. Shoulder to shoulder, Mage and Windeye forced a way forward together, taking advantage of the swathe that Shia and her companion were clearing with fang and claw through the ranks of battling felines. Anvar shuddered at the sight of so much mindless ferocity unleashed within the confines of Steelclaw's crater. It was difficult, at this moment, to remember that these were intelligent creatures, and not mere savage beasts. He could only pray that Shia's fellow cats would remain absorbed in their own bitter struggles, and continue to ignore the two frail humans who had invaded their realm.

Hreeza had already reached the spur. Ignoring the individual battles that raged all around her as her ragged band of Chuevah closed with the astounded great cats, she had taken with her a vanguard of close companions, selected for being in a less pitiful condition than the rest, and had clawed and bitten and slashed and fought her way in the straightest possible line towards the position of her deadly foe.

The blood-lust had taken possession of Hreeza. She was unaware of the many minor wounds that leaked blood into her tattered fur, and ignored the burning of the long gashes slashed by hostile claws into her flanks. The red fog of battle clouded her mind and glowed in her eyes, and her labouring old heart was swollen fit to burst with a fierce pride mixed with anger and grief for those of her poor valiant followers

115

who had already fallen in the onslaught, their death-cries ringing, as they would echo for ever, in her mind.

Had the old cat been human, and believed in such things, she would doubtless have said that the gods were with her that night. In fact, she owed her good fortune to her enemy. Brutal, swaggering, pitiless Gristheena may have been dominant, but she was not loved. Already, unknown to Hreeza, the tide of battle was turning in her favour. Many of the lesser cats, recognizing former companions and den mates in the returning Chuevah, had greeted them with joy, and abandoned the defence of their leader, whom they had only obeyed through fear of being cast out in their turn. On discovering that the much-respected Hreeza was First Female of the Chuevah, the canyon cats were changing sides with startling speed. Hreeza met with little resistance as she barged her way from ledge to ledge up the side of the massive ridge. Had her mind been fixed less on her quarry, and more on her surroundings, she would have noticed that many cats were falling back respectfully to let her pass.

Gristheena stood on the rising tip of the spur, surrounded by her coterie of bullying favourites. The burly cats stood snarling in a solid mass, blocking Hreeza's path. For one mad instant, the old female's blood-lust almost impelled her to charge right into them, carving a way to her enemy with teeth and claws. But she was wise and wily, and had not lived so many years for nothing. Cold sanity asserted itself just in time. She stopped, and lifted her cracked old voice in the discordant, blood-freezing yowl of the challenge: *'Come out, coward, and fight!'*

From the throne of her obsidian eminence, the First Female looked down upon her challenger and laughed. 'Fight with you, you toothless, crack-clawed, film-eyed bag of bones?' she sneered. 'Why should I soil my claws on your flea-ridden hide? My followers: rid me of this Chuevah vermin!'

'Wait!' Hreeza's answering snarl was soft and chilling, but it halted every cat in the crater in its tracks as her mental words were broadcast to them all. 'You had better fight me, you bloated bag of offal,' she hissed. 'If you do not, every cat

116

in the clan will know that the fire has gone out of Gristheena's belly. That their great First Female cannot even defend herself against one tottering, half-starved old Chuevah — because she is afraid!' Now it was Hreeza's turn to laugh, and her mockery raised the hackles of every cat who heard. 'Some First Female! Why, even the smallest purblind kitten will be lining up to challenge you after this!'

Gristheena's ears went down flat against her skull. Her tail lashed back and forth and foam dripped from her jaws as she bared her fangs in a terrifying snarl. Without further warning she leapt.

'This way!' Chiamh yelled. Had the Windeye not been reinforcing his voice with mental speech, it was doubtful whether Anvar would have heard him over the din of screeching, spitting felines. The Mage was relieved that Chiamh had succeeded, with his Othersight, in keeping track of Wolf's abductor, for Shia and Khanu, better able to insinuate themselves between the press of feline bodies, had already vanished, far ahead of the two men, and Anvar himself had lost sight of Meiriel in the confusion that raged all over the canyon floor.

'Over there!' The Windeye pointed, and Anvar caught a glimpse of the Magewoman, clothed in a tatterdemalion patchwork of rags and scraps of fur and hide, and clutching a bundle that must be Wolf. As they watched, she gained the bottom of the spur, and went scrambling like a spider up the side of the ridge.

'Come on!' Anvar tugged at Chiamh's arm, and with his free hand took a tighter grip on the hilt of his sword. Deeply reluctant as he was to harm any of Shia's kin, the Mage was so anxious for Wolf's safety that he was prepared to carve a way through them with his blade, if it became necessary. Fortunately, however, it did not. The cats seemed to be melting away before the two men, heading in the direction of the ridge. Anvar and Chiamh reached the foot of the escarpment unchallenged, and the Mage sprang quickly from ledge to ledge up the broken rocks, leaving the Windeye to grope his way up as best he might.

Gristheena sprang effortlessly over the heads of her followers to land all her vast crushing weight on top of the old cat – and discovered that Hreeza was no longer there. Gristheena's claws closed screeching on unyielding stone. Her jaws snapped shut on nothing save her own tongue. Blood spattered the froth around her muzzle as she howled her humiliation and rage – and howled again as a set of iron jaws crushed the fine bones in her tail. Gristheena whirled, screaming; her battle-cry drowning out the unbearable laughter of the watching cats. Hreeza gave one last agonizing jerk to the roots of Gristheena's tail before she twisted lightly away.

The battle raged back and forth across the top of the spur as the two cats whirled and twisted for position, striking out at one another with their great, curved claws. Again and again, the First Female tried to close with Hreeza, depending on her greater weight and strength to pull the old cat down. Again and again, Hreeza eluded her, occasionally getting a telling blow in on her enemy's nose or flank – but the elderly cat was tiring now; her movements were becoming less fluid, her sides were heaving, and her breath rasped harshly in her throat as she fought for breath.

Renewed hope goaded Gristheena into an unexpected burst of agility and speed. The great muscles in her haunches propelled her in an impossible leap – forward and sideways, catching the old cat by surprise. There was no escaping this time. Gristheena's weight bowled her over and over. Hreeza heard a rib crack; felt a red-hot agony in her side that strangled every breath she tried to take. Gristheena's heavy paws knocked and buffeted her across the ridge, hitting her again and again with a stunning force, the great claws raking slashes in Hreeza's sides.

Hreeza lashed out in blind desperation – connected – scented enemy blood. Gristheena's teeth met in her ear, ripping it to ribbons. Hreeza bit down on a cry of pain and tried to tear herself away, but her weary muscles lacked the strength to escape the other cat's claws. Another instant, and it was over. Gristheena had the old female pinned down flat against the rock, and was straining to push her over, on to

118

her back where she would be helpless against the great claws that would rip out her guts, and the lethal white fangs that would sink into her throat and drink her blood.

Meiriel was standing near the edge of the great black spur, and as she whirled to face him Anvar saw that her features were contorted with shock and dismay. The next second, he was almost knocked off his feet by a snarling black flurry of fur and muscle. On the top of the eminence, two great cats were fighting for their very lives.

Anvar caught his balance and leapt towards Meiriel but she eluded him, slipping like quicksilver out of reach of his blade. Lifting his sword he lunged at her again, but the Magewoman whirled away from him, to the very brink of the escarpment. 'Stop!' she cried. Anvar froze in horror as she lifted the wriggling, whimpering cub high above her head. 'Come one step nearer,' Meiriel hissed, 'and I'll throw him over the edge.'

Ice sheeted down Anvar's spine. Wolf's life was balanced on a knife-edge. Now what was he to do? And where the blazes was Chiamh?

'Back away, Anvar.' The Magewoman's voice was soft and menacing. 'Get away from me, you lowborn Mortal scum, or I'll make you sorry you ever dared meddle in the affairs of the Magefolk!'

It took a moment for the import of her words to sink in; then Anvar gasped. Meiriel didn't know! She still thought of him simply as Aurian's Mortal servant. She had no idea that he too possessed Mage blood – and its associated powers. Anvar smiled to himself, gathering the magical force deep within him, racking his brains for a spell – just the right spell – that would overcome Meiriel and also get Wolf out of danger. Maybe if he took them out of time . . .

From behind the Mage came the furious yowl of a great cat and the heavy thud of a falling body. Anvar jumped involuntarily, and in that split-second of his distraction Meiriel vanished. Anvar looked around wildly and spat out a vicious curse, but it was no good. The Magewoman had gone.

Hreeza, her claws anchored firmly in a small crevice, crouched low, but kept her ground, her limbs trembling with strain; a cold knot of dismay deep within her. Death did not hold many terrors for Hreeza now – this was the second time in as many months that she had come so close. But she was heartsick at having failed.

Gristheena's heart swelled with triumph. Already, she could taste the victory ahead. To gain a better leverage, she dug her sharp, wickedly curved claws deep into the black rock of the ridge, and pushed at the old cat with all her strength. The First Female snarled deep in her throat. She could scarcely believe that this stringy old bag of bones could have the strength to resist such an onslaught. It only needed time, however . . .

Something huge and heavy hit Gristheena from the side. The breath shot out of her lungs. She lost her grip on Hreeza and went crashing to the ground as the weight of another cat crushed her down against the cold black stone. Half-stunned, Gristheena shook her head, opened her eyes – and blinked in dismay and disbelief. Above her, silhouetted against the dawn-pale sky, loomed the shape of her oldest and most bitter enemy.

'I should have killed you when I had the chance!' Gristheena snarled.

'But you did not.' Shia's voice was chill and inexorable as a glacier. 'You failed, Gristheena – and now you have failed again. Your reign is over.'

The last thing that Gristheena saw was the burning gold of Shia's eyes as they caught the blaze of the sunrise. Then Shia's powerful jaws closed around her throat, and darkness fell.

Meiriel laughed softly in triumph as she slipped, unseen, down the far side of the spur. During the long, tedious wait for Aurian to return with Parric, the Magewoman had occupied herself in perfecting an illusion spell that bent the air around her, effectively concealing her where she stood in plain sight. And it had worked – better than she would ever have imagined.

The glow of satisfaction at the success of her ruse helped cushion the shock Meiriel had received when she had returned to Steelclaw to find her ally, Gristheena, and her subjects under attack. The Magewoman scowled. How could it have happened? Could this sudden assault on Gristheena have something to do with her own adversary? A chill crawled up Meiriel's spine. All this time, she had been thinking of Aurian merely as her impulsive, inexperienced pupil from the old days at the Academy. It seemed that she had underestimated the power of the younger Mage.

With an effort, Meiriel mastered the stab of panic and gathered her wits. While she had Aurian's child, its mother could do little to harm her. Meiriel tightened her grip on the misbegotten abomination that Aurian had birthed, though even touching the accursed creature was enough to sicken her. The wolf cub whimpered in protest. Its struggles were growing weaker now, but that was of no consequence. She only needed to keep it alive until she was certain that Aurian was dead – or had found a way to deal with her fellow-Mage once and for all.

The sky had paled from night's blackness to a rich, deep blue that was beginning to glow with dawn beyond Steelclaw's jagged peaks. The thin, cold wind that had finally banished the rainclouds snaked across the dark rock of the canyon floor. All the cats had vanished now; drawn to the rearing spur to witness the battle of the queens. Meiriel groped with her mind to catch Gristheena's thoughts, but only came up against a stark black void. Fear knotted the Magewoman's stomach. Gristheena dead? Impossible! But if her ally had been slain, then she had better get out of here – fast. Quickening her pace, Meiriel scuttled towards the dark maw of the tunnel that led out of the crater and rushed inside.

The uneven tunnel was narrow and so low that she had to stoop as she hurried along, and the darkness taxed even her Mage's sight. None the less, though she knew it was illusory, the darkness and secure stone walls on either side gave the Magewoman the feeling that she had attained a measure of safety at last, and she abandoned her illusion spell as an unnecessary drain on her energies. When a circle of pale daylight appeared ahead of her she approached it almost reluctantly, but she couldn't lurk in the darkness for ever. As she emerged cautiously from the entrance on to a wide, sloping ledge on the mountain's side, her ears were assaulted by a booming thunder of wings in the sky above her. A swirling gust of wind blew grit into her face and almost knocked her from her feet. Fighting for breath, Meiriel wiped the dust from her streaming eyes – and choked again, in terror at the sight of Aurian.

Cold shock drenched through the Magewoman's body. Time seemed to stretch and slow as she looked into the inexorable face of her adversary, while her mind screamed out in disbelieving protest. She had wished for Aurian's death so much that she had never truly believed the mysterious voice that she had heard upon the Wyndveil. She remembered plunging her knife towards Aurian's heart, and feeling the point catch and jar as it grated against a rib. She remembered the dark blood welling up around the deadly blade. Aurian should be *dead*!

Aurian kicked free of the tangled heap of meshes at her feet. With a slithering hiss, her sword slid from its scabbard – the same blade that Meiriel remembered from so long ago. In her other hand the Mage clutched a staff tipped with a great green jewel clasped between serpents' jaws. It thrummed with a power that shivered and twisted the air around it, flooding the wan dawnlight with a blaze of emerald radiance. At the sight of it, terror struck deep into Meiriel's heart. She took an involuntary step backwards, quaking, and automatically raised a magical shield about herself. She doubted that it would hold for long against the power of the staff, but it might buy her the time she needed.

'You look pale, Meiriel. Seen a ghost?' Aurian's voice cut like a whiplash. Her eyes burned silver with the icy flare of her wrath. *'Give me back my child.'*

Desperation gave Meiriel a measure of courage. She clutched Wolf even tighter to her chest, and put one hand around his throat. 'Make me give him back,' she sneered. 'Strike at me, and your brat dies with me. If you so much as call out with your mind to your companions, I will slay him.'

Aurian, still feeling weak and drained from the deadly

122

wound she had taken, and the energy expended in healing it, was shaking with the effort to suppress her rage. Now, of all times, her head must be clear, though the sight of her child with Meiriel's hand around his neck tore at her heart. Inwardly, she cursed the Skyfolk, who had been too cowardly to venture into the territory of their ancient feline enemies, and were unprepared to risk themselves by attacking a Mage. Their reluctance had lost her critical moments while she extricated herself from their net. Had she been in a position to strike at Meiriel while her foe was still blinded by dust, it would all have been over now, and Wolf would have been safe.

Possibilities flew through Aurian's mind, and were as quickly discarded. Even the option of taking both her enemy and Wolf out of time until she could get help was out of the question. Shielded as she was, Meiriel would still be able to kill the child before the spell could take effect. All the Mage could do was play for time, and hope that her companions would think of searching the tunnel before it was too late.

Aurian looked at the wild-eyed madwoman with the ravaged face and tangled hair, and remembered with sadness the neat, brisk, efficient healer who had saved her life and taught her the skills that had proved a blessing over and over again. 'Meiriel, why?' she pleaded. 'Where's the sense in this? Can't you see that your enemy should be Miathan, not me? And I can't believe that you, of all people, would want to harm an innocent child . . .'

'Child?' Meiriel shrieked. 'It's an abomination!'

Aurian gritted her teeth and reined back her temper, trying not to antagonize the madwoman further. 'Wolf is a normal child, Meiriel, save that Miathan cursed him. Surely, if you joined your skills with mine, you could help me to remove the curse.'

Meiriel's face contorted with hatred. 'Help you?' she snarled. 'Were it not for you and your filthy Mortal lover, and this half-breed freak you bore, my Finbarr would still be alive.'

So that was it. It had been a slender hope in any case, but Aurian knew for certain now that Meiriel could not be

123

reasoned with. 'Then it seems we have a stalemate,' she said tightly. 'I cannot attack you while you hold Wolf, but should you kill him, you'll have nothing left to bargain with – and death will be the most pleasant of your options.'

'That would be true – if you could keep me here,' Meiriel retorted. Aurian saw the Magewoman's brow crease in concentration. She made a sharp gesture with her free hand and the air around her shimmered as she began to fade. But Aurian, with the power of the Staff of Earth to draw on, could see through the illusion, and her racing mind seized upon the germ of a plan. While working her spell of invisibility, her enemy could not also maintain a magical shield. She cursed and looked around wildly, feigning consternation. And as Meiriel, confident that she could not be seen, turned to creep away, Aurian struck, dropping the Staff of Earth to get a two-handed grip on her blade. Coronach came whistling down in a glittering, deadly arc and embedded itself in Meiriel's neck. Without a sound, the madwoman crumpled, but even as her spirit fled Aurian's mind caught one last whispered, fading word.

'Finbarr . . .'

Then Aurian screamed and fell to her knees, blasted by Meiriel's death agony. Even so, she crawled forward over rocks that were slippery with warm blood, half-blinded by pain and with her head ringing. With a wrenching effort, she rolled Meiriel's limp body over. The head lolled, half-severed from the trunk, but the Mage had no eyes for the grisly sight. The pain of her opponent's death throes was ebbing now; she could see clearly once more. Wolf was caught beneath a fold of Meiriel's cloak, whining piteously in terror. Aurian tore at the heavy, soaked fabric, pulled it aside, and snatched up her bloodstained, whimpering child.

A quick scan with her healer's senses soon confirmed that Wolf had taken little physical harm except for cold and hunger and a bruise or two, but even though the mental link between them had weakened since his birth Aurian could feel his shock and acute distress. Since he shared her heritage, it seemed likely that the child, too, had been assaulted by his abductor's death pangs. Aurian fought to control her own roiling emotions so that she could calm and reassure him. Too limp with relief to even think of getting to her feet yet, she stayed kneeling in Meiriel's blood, rocking her son and thanking all the gods that he was safe.

Anvar, with Chiamh hot on his heels, burst out of the tunnel at a run. After a frantic fruitless search for Meiriel, he had been buffeted by her death throes and, through them, had located her at last. When he saw Aurian, with Wolf clasped in her arms, kneeling over the Magewoman's body, his heart almost stopped. As he ran to her, his mind whirled with conflicting anger, anxiety and relief, and as he sank to his knees beside her his questions tumbled over one another in his haste to get them out.

'Are you all right? Is Wolf? Are you *mad* to come out here and fight her so soon after she nearly killed you?'

For the first time, Aurian looked up from her child, a spark of anger flashing in her eyes as she looked from Anvar to the Windeye and back again. 'I had to come. Look what a mess you two were making of the business,' she snapped. Then her expression softened as she laid a hand on Anvar's arm. 'I'm sorry. I didn't mean that – though you deserve more than harsh words for trying to give me drugged wine. You idiots – did you really think I'd fall for that?'

Anvar looked at Chiamh, and saw his chagrin mirrored in the Windeye's face. Then, to his own astonishment, he burst out laughing. It was pure relief, he knew – and also a reaction to the events of the last few harrowing hours: Wolf's abduction, Aurian almost losing her life, the bloody battle of the cats and the physical and mental wrench of Meiriel's violent death. Aurian caught his eye, and suddenly she was laughing with him, as they had laughed away their shock and terror long ago, in the dark tunnels beneath Dhiammara, when both had been sure that Anvar's life had ended beneath a stonefall, but he had survived. Though the laughter was dangerously out of control for a time, Anvar felt the fears and turmoil of the night beginning to ease, as though a bowstring stretched taut within him was loosening at last.

Finally, Aurian's peals of laughter ended in something suspiciously like a sob, and she embraced him clumsily, with Wolf between them. Anvar, mindful of the cub, hugged her as hard as he dared before they broke apart reluctantly and scrambled to their feet to face the baffled Windeye. Aurian thumped him on the shoulder. 'Thank you, Chiamh my friend, for all your help this night – but next time, don't go slipping your peculiar Xandim concoctions into my wine.'

Chiamh smiled sheepishly. 'It seems there would be little point. But Lady, you must rest now, before you undo all the benefits of your healing.'

'You're right – I'm so tired I can barely stand.' Aurian sighed, and dragged her arm wearily across her eyes. She grimaced as the edge of her sleeve left a smear of blood across one cheek. 'Besides, we must get Wolf home. Where are Shia and Khanu?'

Anvar saw her expression change to a frown of concern. 'Back in the canyon. I don't know what happened to them. Chiamh and I lost them when we were searching for Meiriel . . .' His words tailed away. Aurian was not listening. Her expression turned vague as she called to the cats, then her eyes snapped open wide.

'Shia says that Hreeza is here – and she's hurt.'

'Hreeza?' Anvar gasped. 'How the blazes did she get here?'

Aurian shrugged. 'Let's find out. No – wait.' Thrusting Wolf into Anvar's arms, she turned back to Meiriel's body. Anvar could see the tension in her jaw as she stooped to the ghastly head, and closed the staring eyes. For a moment she lingered, her hand smoothing the Magewoman's tangle hair, and Anvar was amazed to see a glitter of tears in her eyes. 'I'm sorry, Meiriel,' she whispered.

'What?' Anvar could not contain himself. 'Why should you be sorry? She meant to murder Wolf, and she came too bloody close to killing you.'

Aurian shook her head. 'No,' she said softly. 'That was not Meiriel. I mourn the passing of the healer I once knew, who was a friend; who saved my life when I was a girl, and taught me the precious arts of healing.' Then her expression

126

hardened. 'As for the madwoman who tried to kill my son – she deserved what she got.'

Springing to her feet, she wiped her bloody hands on her cloak before raising them aloft. At her gesture a bolt of sizzling flame leapt from her fingers, consuming Meiriel's body where it lay on the bloodstained stones of Steelclaw.

'Now we can go.' Turning away from the pyre, Aurian reached down to pick up the Staff of Earth from the pool of blood in which it lay. Anvar, seeing the Artefact sullied with the lifeblood of a Mage, felt a shiver of unease crawl up his spine, and his thoughts were in tune with those of his soulmate.

'Damn,' Aurian muttered. 'Steeped in blood – this doesn't bode well.' Gingerly, she picked up the Staff – and cried out, almost dropping it again in astonishment. As her fingers had touched and lifted the Artefact, it blazed for an instant with a blinding emerald radiance – and when the effulgence faded, every trace of blood had vanished.

'Incredible!' Anvar breathed.

Aurian was holding the Staff as though the twin serpents might bite her. 'Yes,' she muttered, 'but why?'

Chiamh stepped forward to peer short-sightedly at the Staff, though he was careful not to touch it. Then he looked up at the Mage. 'Lady, why did you choose to kill the madwoman with your sword, and not this powerful tool of magic?'

'I . . .' Aurian frowned. 'Well, for one thing, there was too great a risk of harming Wolf, but mainly because it just wasn't right.' For a moment she faltered. 'This is one of the four Great Weapons that were fashioned to work against destruction. If I had used it for harm, then . . .' She shuddered. 'Something bad would have happened. Oh, it would have worked, I'm sure – but there would have been some kind of recoil, or backlash. I remembered what the Leviathan said, about a weapon having two edges . . .' She shrugged, unable to explain it any better.

Chiamh shuddered. 'Lady, you are very wise – and thank the goddess that it is so.'

Anvar looked at Aurian's pallor in concern. Though she

127

was trying to hide it, he could see that she was trembling with exhaustion. Shifting Wolf into the crook of one arm, he put the other around her shoulders. 'Come on – let's find Shia now, and then we can get back to the fastness.'

Aurian nodded. 'I could sleep for a month – not that we have one.' Almost as an afterthought, she ducked under his arm and gathered up Coronach from the ground, wiping the bloodstained blade on her cloak before sheathing it. Then, thrusting the Staff into her belt, she held her arms out for her son.

The stones near the top of the rearing black spur were slick with blood. It caked on Aurian's boots and coated her hands where she had used them to help her scramble up the last steep stretch to the summit. With a shudder, she wiped her sticky hands on the hem of her much-abused cloak, and longed for a mug of good strong ale to clear the metallic stench that caught the back of her throat.

Aurian looked back and saw Chiamh down below, waiting at the foot of the ridge with Wolf, while Anvar followed close behind the Mage. He too was tight-lipped and pale. Thankfully, there had been fewer deaths among the cats than Aurian had expected from Anvar's terse account of the battle, but some of the injuries they had witnessed on their way across the canyon had been dreadful. Having been apprised by Shia that Hreeza's life was not in danger, Aurian had lingered to give assistance where she could, though even with Anvar's overtaxed strength to draw upon, and the power of the Staff, her contribution seemed woefully inadequate.

Khanu, his heavy fur torn out in patches and one ear ripped and bleeding, had come across the canyon to meet the Mages and escort them to Shia in safety. When they reached the summit he led them proudly through the crowded ranks of felines that waited there. The assembly was a breathtaking sight. One great cat alone was awesome in size and power, but to see so many ... Wonderingly, Aurian swept her eyes across them all, taking in lithe, muscled females and heavy-boned males resplendent in their shaggy ruffs; grizzled veterans, leggy youngsters and fuzzy, gold-dappled black cubs, with paws and ears too big for them yet, that made her smile. A hundred gold eyes flashed and flared like a dragon-hoard in the early sunlight as the great cats watched her pass, each one of them tense with silent curiosity. Aurian, looking at their big curved claws and gleaming fangs, was suddenly very glad that she had Shia to sponsor her here. She was an interloper and a hated human, and had she been alone she would not have lasted long enough to draw another breath. With a shiver of surprise, she suddenly remembered her first meeting with Shia in the Khazalim arena. The bond between them was so strong now, it seemed impossible to believe that her beloved companion had very nearly killed her.

Shia was near the tip of the spur, watching over Hreeza. The old cat, though battered and bloody, raised her head with stubborn pride to look on as the Mage rushed to embrace her friend. 'Thank the gods you're safe,' she told the cat. 'How did you come unscathed through all the fighting?'

'Most of them were very glad to see me,' Shia replied smugly. 'Though there is one who was not.' Aurian followed her glance towards an enormous cat that lay nearby, its heavily muscled body limp in death. Shia looked back towards her people. 'Gristheena has been vanquished!' The thunder of her mental tones rose to match the challenge of her roar, which shook the very stones beneath them. 'Who is leader now?'

'Shia! Shia!' The sheer volume of the response was almost enough to batter Aurian to the ground. It took all her self-control not to clap her hands over her ringing ears.

'No.' Shia's answer stopped them in mid-roar.

For a moment there was utter silence, then an ancient, hollow-eyed Chuevah called out from the rear of the ranked cats. 'If you will not lead us, who will?' There was a brief scuffle as her friends tried to silence her, then the harsh old voice rang out again: 'Well, somebody has to say it! Don't be a fool, young Shia. You must lead us. Do you want us to go through this again?' Her bony paw swept out to indicate the many wounded who lay in the bottom of the crater. 'Our people have suffered cruelly in this last evil winter, and

129

through the injustice of Gristheena's rule. Our numbers are sadly diminished. A strong First Female is essential now, or the tribe will die. Would you weaken us further by wasting our best in challenge after challenge, until a new leader should emerge?'

Though the cantankerous old feline had spoken out of turn, murmurs of assent greeted her words.

'Be still!' Shia interrupted them. 'Taheera speaks wisely, does she not? Yet she is old. Too old, Gristheena thought, to be of any further use to the tribe. Too old to challenge. Only the strongest have been permitted to remain with our people. Only the strongest could rule. Yet see to what end our reverence for strength has brought us.' Now it was her turn to remind them of the cats that lay in agony below.

'My people, it is time for change. We must maintain our prowess, certainly; encourage, instruct and nurture our hunters and warriors for the good of the tribe. But let wisdom lead us.' Shia paused, and her golden gaze swept across the assembled cats. 'By right of challenge, the leadership is mine, but I cannot stay to lead you. The bonds of friendship hold me, and my path leads elsewhere, for not only here on Steelclaw is the safety of our people threatened. With your agreement, I will appoint another to rule in my absence. I will entrust the safekeeping of our tribe to the brave cat who dared, against all hope, to challenge Gristheena; the wise cat who brought home your exiled elders and den mates, and saved them from starvation in the mountains. O cats, have you learned from the slaughter and suffering? Will you abandon the law of claw and tooth and terror, and put your trust in wisdom? Will you have Hreeza as your leader?'

'What?' Hreeza demanded. 'Me?'

Aurian felt the warm edge to Shia's thoughts that denoted humour. 'Of course, old friend,' the great cat said. 'Who better?'

The cats stared at one another, thunderstruck. Shia's return had set them in a turmoil. At first they had been wild with elation over the reappearance of their long-lost leader, then horrified by her friendship with, of all things, certain humans. Aurian's help with their wounded had gone a long way to reassure them that not all two-legged folk were evil, and by the time Shia had warned them of her imminent departure they had been dismayed by her decision to leave them once again. But though the bitter lessons of the previous night had left their impact, and made them ready to listen to her stirring words, acceptance was another matter. Dispensing with the rite of challenge went against every belief that the tribe possessed.

There was a long moment of silence. Then a lone voice spoke up from the rear of the gathering. 'Well, I say we should have Hreeza as our leader.' It was the indomitable Taheera again. 'What do we have to lose?' the old cat went on. 'We followed the other way for so long, and see where it has led us. We old cats have lived for many seasons. We have hunted in our time, and borne cubs; we have survived through famine and sickness, battle and conflict within and beyond the tribe. We remember; we are wise. Should we be discarded because we are too old to fight and hunt and bear young? Why does the tribe not use our knowledge? Let Hreeza try, I say – and we old Chuevah will help her. Give her a chance. If she fails, we can always go back to the old way.'

A roar of assent broke out as the old Chuevah raised their voices to support her. The younger cats murmured amongst themselves, indecisive, and reluctant, perhaps, to let go of their authority. 'Fine words,' one of them said, 'but what if we need to defend ourselves? How can an old cat lead us in battle?'

Shia added the weight of her words to the debate. 'Hreeza must choose a battle leader from the cats in their prime. She may also appoint a hunt leader from those who are most skilled. Give her a year, and see what happens. Under Hreeza's rule, I am certain that the tribe will prosper.'

'It had better prosper,' muttered one lone voice from somewhere in the crowd, but apart from that, there were no further objections. 'Hreeza for leader!' Taheera roared, and as the other cats joined in the very mountains trembled. 'Hreeza! Hreeza!'

Hreeza turned to Shia with blazing eyes. 'Now look what

you've done, you young fool,' she snapped, but Aurian could see that she was secretly delighted.

'Here, let me look at those injuries,' she told the old cat. 'Goodness knows, you'll have a busy time ahead, so you'd better start off your reign in perfect health.'

Anvar pulled from his pocket the carved bone whistle that had been given to the Mages to summon the Skyfolk from the air. 'And once you've healed Hreeza, we must go home,' he said firmly.

Aurian looked around at the soaring mountains of a foreign land, and sighed. 'I would like nothing better – if only we had a home.'

9

On the Wings of the Wind

The sun was reaching its zenith when Chiamh emerged from the shadowy entrance to the Xandim fastness. He noted the hour with some surprise. Had he really slept so long? At about the same time the previous day, he had been flown back by reluctant Winged Folk from Steelclaw, along with Shia, Khanu and the Mages. All of them had been chilled to the bone and lightheaded from exhaustion, and no one really had the energy to answer the anxious entreaties of Parric, Schiannath, and the others who had waited behind. Much to the evident frustration of the temporary Herdlord, they had spent some time answering only the most urgent of his questions while they shared the bowls of stew and the hot spiced wine that Iscalda had prepared. Then Anvar, concerned at Aurian's evident weariness, had cut the meeting short with a brusqueness that had brought a scowl to the face of Parric, who had already been annoyed at having to stay behind to find accommodation for the new influx of outlanders, and calm his people after the shock of Meiriel's attack.

The Windeye, glad to make his escape at last, had sought his chambers as quickly as possible. After the harrowing events of the previous night, he had flopped down on his hay-stuffed pallet and fallen asleep fully clothed, before he even had time to pull the fur covers over himself.

When he finally awakened, Chiamh had still felt heavy-eyed with lack of rest. In an attempt to revive himself, he had decided to go and bathe in the icy pool at the bottom of the nearby waterfall. Wrapping a change of clean clothing in a thick warm blanket in which he would wrap himself until he dried, he set out through the labyrinth of passages towards the entrance of the fastness.

133

Now he stood to one side of the great arched doorway, yawning and stretching, and looked across the steeply sloping green expanse that lay below the massive stone edifice to the vast open vistas beyond, where the land dropped down towards the sea. The day was cool, with a brisk wind that harried the ragged knots of grey cloud across the sky, and sent beams of sunlight stalking across the land between the drifting showers, to patch the dull greens and duns of the woods and grasslands with pockets of emerald and gold. Brighter still, however, were the hues of the colourful tents that dotted the meadowland before the fastness.

The Windeye exclaimed aloud in astonishment to see the vast encampment of Horsefolk that had sprung up in his absence, in response to the messages that he and Parric had sent out before they left for the Tower of Incondor. So much had happened since then that he'd forgotten about sending out the summons, and last night he had failed to see the dark outlines of the tents in the rainy darkness. Besides, he'd had far more pressing matters to concern him. The Xandim, however, had answered the Herdlord's call. From the different and distinctive designs on the hide tents, Chiamh could see that they had flocked in from every region.

At the sight of so many folk thronging the meadow, the Windeye took an involuntary step backwards into the shelter of the entrance tunnel. He had never seen such a crowd of people all together, and their presence unnerved him a little. He had lived most of his days in enforced solitude before the coming of the outlanders had changed his existence, and though he revelled in the warmth of his newfound companionship and acceptance he still found himself longing, on occasion, for the peace and solitude of his own little vale, and the airy freedom of his Chamber of Winds, where he could reflect and meditate for a time on the incredible and portentous events that had overtaken him lately.

On impulse, Chiamh decided to change his plans and go home for a little while. He could just as easily bathe in the stream-fed pool in his valley, and he really ought to check his living-cavern to see that everything was still in order. That, at least, was what he told himself. In reality, the Windeye was running away – but that was something he would rather not think about.

First of all, however, he had to get through the busy encampment without being seen, but to one of his calling that presented no difficulty. Entering a pool of shade within the depths of the passageway, Chiamh took up the insubstantial shreds of shadow and wove a mantle of twilight about himself. Securely concealed in his shadow cloak from curious eyes, he slipped towards the archway with a secretive smile.

'Ho, Chiamh!'

On hearing his name, the Windeye froze in his tracks with a cry of dismay. Turning he saw Aurian, silhouetted against the torchlit doorway of the inner hall. 'That's a very clever trick,' she said as she approached, 'but I should warn you – it doesn't work on a Mage. Why the disguise, my friend?' She smiled at him, and Chiamh's chagrin melted away.

'You should look outside,' he told her. 'It appears that the entire Xandim nation has camped in the meadow. I felt the need for solitude, and . . .'

'And I interrupted your escape,' Aurian apologized.

'I don't feel any need to escape you. I just wanted to go home for a time . . .'

'Isn't this your home?'

Chiamh shook his head. 'I live further up the mountain – usually. It is very beautiful there.' Suddenly, he decided that maybe solitude was not so attractive after all. 'Would you like to see it?'

'Is it very much further?' Aurian, profoundly glad to be off the broad cliff path at last, stood at the top of the incline that snaked up the crag behind the fastness, and looked out across the windswept expanse of the mountain plateau. She could see no sign of another valley anywhere, and she did not want to stay away from Wolf too long. He had been sleeping contentedly when she left him, guarded by the hovering presence of Bohan and the two wolves, who had finally limped back to the fastness, footsore and defeated, while she and Anvar had been on Steelclaw. They had greeted the cub ecstatically, and one or both of them had been at his side

135

ever since. Although her son appeared to be suffering few ill effects from his abduction, he had been badly frightened, and the Mage wanted to be nearby should he need reassurance – although, in truth, the cub seemed quite happy with Bohan and his lupine guardians. None the less, Aurian had been hovering over him all morning, since she had awakened, until both Anvar and Shia had chased her out to get some air – and some peace and quiet for themselves.

Anvar had needed to spend some time with old Elewin, who had been longing to see the young servant from the Academy whom he had once protected. Now, it seemed, their positions were reversed. The steward, already enfeebled by his illness, had taken Meiriel's death very badly. He seemed shrunken, somehow: listless and morose and suddenly very, very old; and Anvar, his brow furrowed with concern, had gone to see if he could cheer his former mentor. Shia and Khanu also had plans: to make a brief trip back to Steelclaw – on foot this time – to see how Hreeza was faring in her new role as First Female.

Suddenly Aurian realized that the Windeye was speaking, and wrenched her thoughts back to the present in time to hear his reply to her half-forgotten question. Chiamh pushed a windblown lock of hair out of his eyes. 'My valley is a good league away, maybe, and part of it uphill again.' He noted Aurian's hesitation with a pang of disappointment. He had been looking forward to showing her his home – he had not realized how much, until now. Then an idea struck him. But could he do it? Suddenly, his mind was made up. He turned to Aurian and grinned. 'On horseback, it would take no time at all.'

'But we don't have a horse,' Aurian objected. The Windeye grinned broadly. 'Do we not? Stand well clear, my friend, and I will show you a wonder.'

Aurian knew, in an abstract sense, that the Xandim were shape-shifters, but because of her absence in Aerillia she had never actually seen the change take place. She looked on, wide-eyed with amazement, as Chiamh's outline blurred and expanded; his bones thickened and his head and neck grew heavy and long as his position altered to a four-legged stance. All at once, the transformation was complete. In the place of the Windeye stood a stocky, shaggy-maned bay horse.

'Oh, Chiamh,' Aurian breathed. She could hardly believe her eyes. Hesitantly she approached the horse, not sure whether she dared to touch him. This was not truly an animal after all, but a man. He's also an ally and a friend, Aurian told herself firmly. Screwing up her courage, she laid a gentle hand on his warm, thickly muscled neck.

Startled, Chiamh sprang back with a snort, unable to help himself. His mind worked somewhat differently while he was wearing his equine form, and it was unnerving to suffer the touch of an unfamiliar human hand. For a moment, he was tempted to change back again. He doubted whether he could hold to his offer to let her ride. Normally, for one Xandim to ride another in horse-form, there would have to be great need, or great intimacy between them. He and Aurian had become friends in a very short time, but . . .

The Windeye noticed that Aurian was standing back now, not sure whether to approach him again. She was frowning, and subtle changes in her posture and her scent betrayed her anxiety. He hated to see her frown – and all because he had wanted to show off, he realized guiltily. Did she not have enough to worry about, besides the fey humours of a half-wild horse? All at once, his mind was made up. Had they not journeyed together on the wind? And was this really so very different?

Taking firm control of his equine instincts, Chiamh stepped forward. Aurian reached out a hand, then hesitated, plainly uncertain, and the Windeye cursed himself for not explaining matters more fully to her before he had transformed himself, for neither his Othersight nor mental communication would work while he wore his equine form. For an instant, he considered changing back, just to speak to her – but no. He would probably never summon up the courage to do this again. Instead, he took another step forward, and rubbed his long nose against her outstretched hand.

At the Windeye's gesture, the Mage found herself relaxing. She stroked the soft, bristly nose, and smiled.

'Chiamh, this is amazing! I wonder how you do it,' she said softly. Chiamh snorted, flicked his ears and shook his long black mane, and Aurian laughed with pure delight. But at the back of her mind, she was still aware that time was pressing. 'Are you sure you still want me to ride? Is it really all right?'

The Windeye looked at her, and nodded his head up and down vigorously.

'Thank you,' Aurian said, 'but I'll need something to stand on, since you have no saddle. You're taller than I thought you'd be.' She looked around until she spotted a place where a small outcrop of rock poked above the turf at the top of the cliff. 'That should do.'

Chiamh, following her pointing finger, walked over to the place and stood patiently while Aurian scrambled to the top of a large, lichen-covered stone. As she threw a leg across his back he gritted his teeth and closed his eyes, mastering the urge to flinch away, but once she had settled on his back he felt better. She had done this before, he noted with surprise. Her legs clasped firmly but not too tightly, and she knew just the right way to distribute her weight to make things comfortable and easy for him. Suddenly Chiamh began to relax and enjoy himself. Once he felt her twine her fingers in the long, coarse hair of his mane he knew she was ready, and with a bound he was away, racing across the short, crisp turf of the plateau.

Aurian sat easily on the back of the galloping bay horse, her hair blowing behind her in the wind and her eyes watering with the exhilarating speed of Chiamh's running. The world went flashing past them, the bright spring flowers that dotted the grass blurring in a rainbow of colours beneath his pounding hooves. This was wonderful! Unable to help herself, she let out a wild whoop of delight that echoed back from the surrounding peaks.

The ride was over far too soon. Ahead of them, Aurian saw a pair of tall standing stones, the gateway to a narrow, pine-clad valley with steep, rocky sides. The Windeye slowed his wild pace, and came gently to a halt in the shadow of the towering stones. The Mage slid down reluctantly, and he backed away from her until he had sufficient space to change. Once again, Aurian saw his outline blur, and shrink, and resume an upright form – and Chiamh the man stood before her, slightly out of breath and grinning all over his face.

For a moment they looked at one another, beyond words, and then, as if at some unspoken signal, they rushed to hug each other. 'Chiamh, that was wonderful,' Aurian told him as they parted. 'I'll never forget it as long as I live.'

'Nor will I,' the Windeye assured her. Holding out a hand to her, he added: 'Come – let me show you my valley.' Hand in hand, they stepped out of the plateau's sunlight, and into the cool shadow of the pines.

'Has Wolf recovered from his ordeal?' Chiamh asked. They had bathed – very briefly – in the icy mountain pool, and now were sitting by a hastily kindled fire in the mouth of his cave, sipping hot herb tea and looking down the valley past the shadow of the great rock spire that towered above the Windeye's dwelling. Aurian, who was absently threading white starflowers into a chain, looked up at the sound of his voice and nodded. 'Seemingly – though he's still somewhat nervous. I think he had bad dreams last night, if a wolf can dream – but he seemed much calmer and happier today, or I wouldn't have left him.'

Chiamh nodded. 'You were right to come out, though. Apart from the fact that I am enjoying your company' – he smiled at her – 'you needed to put aside your worries for a while.' His face grew thoughtful. 'How long is it, Aurian, since you had a chance to think of only yourself?'

Aurian was touched by his concern. 'Gods, I don't remember,' she sighed. 'Probably not since Forral died.' The memory, still painful after all this time, cast a shadow across the bright afternoon.

'Ah, Forral,' Chiamh said. 'Parric's friend, and Wolf's father.'

'Parric told you?'

'Briefly, when we first met.' The Windeye took her hand. 'I grieve for your loss,' he said softly, and Aurian knew they were not mere empty words. 'What happened after you and

139

Anvar came south? How came you by the Staff and the Harp?'

The Mage found herself telling him of their adventures. Though she tried to keep her tale brief, by the time she was bringing herself up to the present the sun was dipping towards the cliffs on her left and the air in the shadowed mountain valley was growing chill. 'And now,' she finished quickly, 'we have the Staff and the Harp, and we still must find the Sword – but it is hidden, and I haven't the vaguest idea where to begin to look.'

'I may be able to help, you know,' Chiamh told her. 'Perhaps if I make a seeing, I will be able to find where it is hidden.'

'A seeing?' Aurian leaned forward, her eyes lighting with a spark of hope. 'What is that?'

'It . . . I . . .' Chiamh flung his hands up helplessly, lost for word to explain. 'If you and Anvar come back here with me tonight, I will show you.'

'Of course we will.' Aurian squinted up at the sinking sun. 'But I think we should be heading back now, Chiamh. It's getting late, and Wolf may be missing me.' She sprang to her feet, and suddenly turned back to him as a thought occurred to her. She had been meaning to ask the Windeye . . .

'Chiamh, who is Basileus? Do you know? When I almost died he helped me – but *what* is he?'

The Windeye smiled enigmatically. 'I think he could explain that better himself. Now that you are back from Steelclaw, I'm sure you will be meeting Basileus again very soon – and so you should. But if you want to return to your son before nightfall, we have no time at present. Can you be patient a little longer?'

'I suppose so,' Aurian muttered ungraciously. Patience had never been her strong point.

Chiamh grinned. 'In that case – do you want to ride back again?'

Aurian's face lit up. 'Oh, yes!'

As Aurian and the Windeye, once again in his human form,

were clambering back down the shallow, zigzag cliff path that led to the fastness, Chiamh was first to spot the trouble. The Mage's fear of heights extended even to this broad trail, and the descent was proving much more nerve-racking than the climb had been. Cursing the overwhelming Magefolk curiosity that had led her up here in the first place, she had been hugging the cliff face all the way, and the one direction in which she had not been looking was down.

'Look down there!'

Aurian shot the Windeye a sour look. 'Do I have to?'

Chiamh, unexpectedly, did not smile at her discomfiture. 'I really think you should,' he said gravely.

'Very well – but we'll have to stop for a minute, or I'll get dizzy.' Steadying herself against the comforting wall of stone on her right, she looked down past the many-levelled crenellated roofs of the fastness. The snaking track was situated in a curve of the cliff that barely gave her a view of the great arched entrance, and the crowd that stood before it. Though dusk was falling fast, she could make out the dark shapes of many people, several of whom were carrying torches. Now that she was paying attention, the faint murmur of protesting voices drifted upwards on the wind. Aurian cursed. At the top of the entrance steps, Parric stood at bay with Iscalda and Schiannath; evidently the focus of the angry, spear-waving mob.

'Great goddess! We must get down there – fast,' Chiamh cried. Even Aurian could see the necessity.

'You go ahead,' she told him. 'I'll follow you as quickly as I can.'

The Windeye had clambered down to the bottom of the cliff before he could make out individual voices in the crowd. As usual the hectoring Galdrus was one of the most vociferous.

'Thick in the body and thick in the head,' muttered Chiamh to himself as he ran towards the mob; but it didn't make the warrior any less dangerous. Galdrus had long been the ringleader of those who had mocked and victimized the young Windeye. For an instant Chiamh's quick strides faltered, then he plunged forward again. The days of fearing

Galdrus and the others were past, now. It was time to consolidate the grudging respect that he had recently begun to wrest from his fellow-Xandim.

'We were promised a new leader, outlander,' Galdrus was bawling at the beleaguered Parric, 'yet the dark of the moon is three days away and we have heard no word from you. We want no more of you!'

Many voices took up his cry.

'You bring our foes, the Black Ghosts and the Skyfolk, upon us!'

'You defile our fastness with filthy wolves and outland magicians!'

'You consort with outlaws and exiles!'

'You have cursed our true Herdlord!'

'We want Phalihas!'

Other Xandim took up the chant. 'We want our Herdlord!'

'Free Phalihas!'

Parric was attempting to answer them, but his shouted words were lost in the roar of so many voices. The mood of the mob was turning uglier by the minute. Chiamh ran faster, and then one of them turned and spotted him, and he realized his mistake.

'There he is – the Windeye!'

'He's the one who sided with the outlanders!'

'It's all his fault!'

Some of the crowd stayed to hurl abuse at Parric, but a large group, headed by Galdrus, broke away and ran towards the Windeye, their faces contorted with hatred and menace. An icy knot of terror congealed in Chiamh's stomach. He stopped and half-turned, every instinct screaming at him to run; and then he changed his mind. His communion with Basileus and the coming of the outlanders had transformed his life; his days of running away were over. Snatching at the brisk wind that swirled around the front of the fastness, he gathered a handful and twisted it into the shape of a luminous, hideous demon. It was the worst mistake he could have made. Galdrus, and several of the others, had seen his demon before. It had terrified and humiliated them then, and the memory served to fuel their anger. What was worse, they knew now that, though it looked fearsome, it was only an apparition, and could not harm them.

'It's all right.' A bellow from Galdrus cut through the beginning cries of dismay and panic. 'It's just harmless Windeye trickery. Get him!'

The mob surged forward, but despite their leader's brave words few of them were willing to go near the demonic shape that hovered in front of the Windeye. Even Galdrus, for all his bluster and brag, was reluctant. For an instant, Chiamh gasped with relief – then someone stooped, picked up a stone and threw it. Before he knew what was happening, the Windeye found himself amid a hail of hard-flung missiles. His pursuers were finding their range now, and even in the deepening twilight were gaining accuracy. A small rock hit him on the shoulder with bruising force, and he cried out in pain. His demon flickered and began to fade – it was all that was keeping them from tearing him limb from limb, and he was losing it ... Even as he struggled to reform the apparition, another stone went whistling past his face, cutting open his cheekbone close to his eye. With a curse, Chiamh let his demon scatter to the winds, and took to his heels.

As he ran back towards the cliff path, the Windeye heard the howling of the mob close – too close – behind him. Many missiles struck his back, bruising and winding him, but even in agony, with every breath a hard-won fire in his lungs, pure terror gave him the impetus to keep scrambling forward, praying to the goddess that he would not miss his footing in the gathering dark. Then a stone struck his head, and for an instant the world flashed black as he fell. Half-stunned and bleeding, he struggled to make himself rise, but he felt sick and dizzy, and his limbs would not obey him. They were almost upon him ... He saw their faces contorted like the bestial face of his demon; their hands reaching greedily towards him ...

... And suddenly stop, as though they had run into a solid but invisible wall that shimmered as they touched it with an unearthly silver light.

Then Aurian was kneeling beside him, her eyes flaring icy silver with anger; the Staff of Earth burning in her hand with its uncanny green light as she used its powers as a barrier to shield the Windeye from his assailants. She turned him gently, her face dimly lit by the glimmer of her shield, and Chiamh felt an uncanny tingle sweep through him as she quickly scanned his body with her healer's senses, seeking, he knew, any evidence of broken bones or internal hurts. As she laid a gentle hand on his forehead, all his pain vanished, and he could breathe easily again, though somehow he felt so sleepy ... Chiamh struggled hard to hold on to consciousness, reminding himself that they were not out of danger yet.

'You were lucky,' murmured the Mage wryly. 'If you can call it lucky to be almost stoned to death by these stupid, bloodthirsty animals. The fact that they couldn't see you clearly was probably all that saved your life.' She glanced up at the rabid crowd that surrounded them, still trying fruitlessly to break through the silvery, shimmering barrier she had created. Many now had drawn their swords, but most of them recoiled, Chiamh noted with satisfaction, from the savagery of her look, and suddenly began to seem far less enthusiastic about the attack.

'Bastards!' Aurian muttered, scowling. She lifted a hand, and suddenly, briefly, the barrier flared crimson with heat – and the swords followed suit. Galdrus and his supporters fell back, screaming, dropping their glowing weapons and clutching at burned hands.

'That'll teach them,' Chiamh heard Aurian chuckle. Through the gap that their attackers' retreat had created, he saw another uncannily glimmering light approaching, and wondered for an instant if the blow to his head was playing tricks with his eyes. Then he heard a wild, unearthly music that was so beautiful that it brought tears to his eyes, and with a shock he saw that even to his own poor eyesight the notes were clearly visible, swirling on the air like a mist of stars. And as the starsong fell on Galdrus and his followers, one by one they crumpled and fell to the ground as if asleep.

The eerie effulgence grew brighter, and Parric, Sangra, Iscalda and Schiannath came striding up to Aurian's barrier. Anvar was with them, and cradled in his arm he carried the Harp of Winds, still playing it as he walked.

'Anvar! Oh, but you're a welcome sight!' Aurian dropped her shield and rushed to embrace him, and as Harp and Staff met the night around them exploded into beams of coruscating light that shot skyward in a crackling aurora of silver-blue and green.

Parric and the others leapt back hastily. 'Be careful with those bloody things!' the cavalry master yelled. 'You'll blow us all to smithereens!'

The two Mages looked at each other and burst into peals of laughter, and it was the sound of their mirth that followed the Windeye down into the darkness at last.

'What did you do to them?' Aurian indicated the unconscious Xandim on the ground.

'Took them out of time, using the Harp.' Anvar grinned. 'I didn't realize how effective it would be. It seems to have a facility for that kind of magic – probably an effect of all those ages spent by the Cailleach's Timeless Lake. I did the same with the remainder of the mob, the ones who didn't go after Chiamh, but it's only a temporary solution. The Xandim who didn't join the riot are far from happy with their companions' fate. We need to solve the underlying problem, and quickly.'

Parric glared at him. 'The underlying problem is my business,' he said coldly. 'I am the Herdlord, after all.'

The cavalry master's response was so uncharacteristic that Aurian stared at him in surprise. 'What's got into you?' she asked him. 'It's the business of all of us, if we want to retain the help and support of the Xandim. It'll take all our brains to come up with the best solution, and we'll especially need Chiamh.' She stooped to check on the unconscious Windeye. 'Poor man. I'd no idea they hated him so much.'

'The Xandim are like a lot of people: scared out of their senses – or their sense – by the unknown.' Anvar put in, and Aurian noticed that his eyes were on Parric as he said it. She sighed. What had been going on between the two men in her absence? Drat them, she thought resentfully. It seems I can't let them out of my sight for a single afternoon without something going wrong. With a shrug, she shelved the problem until later.

'Are you going to leave poor Chiamh on the damp ground

all night?' she said sharply. 'Help me get him back to the fastness. Once he's feeling better, we can deal with this crisis and decide what to do next.'

Anvar grimaced. 'That,' he muttered, 'will be easier said than done – and it's not our only worry.' His face grew grave. 'Aurian, I was coming to fetch you when all this happened.' With a wide swing of his arm he indicated the unconscious Xandim. 'Chiamh is not the only one who needs your healing tonight. It's Elewin . . . I don't know what's wrong with him, but – oh, never mind.' Abandoning the struggle to explain, he hauled on her arm. 'You'd best come quickly, and see for yourself.'

The old steward was dying. Aurian knew it the minute she walked into his chamber. He lay limply on his pallet, his sunken skin aglow with a pale translucence that sent a familiar shiver down the Mage's spine. The irregular rasp of his shallow breathing scratched at the room's unnatural, waiting silence. Because of her previous encounters in Death's realm, Aurian was preternaturally aware of the Spectre that lurked in the shadows, biding his time. With an effort, she shook herself free of the eerie, clinging atmosphere. 'Build up the fire,' she told Anvar sharply. 'Send for some fresh torches.'

'That's right, boy, and be quick about it. I can't see my hand in front of my face.' Both Mages swung round at the sound of the cracked old voice, and Aurian heard Anvar gasp. That had always been one of Elewin's favourite phrases. Unbidden, a memory rose of sharp autumn evenings in the Academy, and the old steward using those very words as he scolded the tardy servants into lighting the lamps. Aurian compressed her lips and shook her head. It boded ill that Elewin's mind was wandering back into the past.

Parric and Sangra had followed the Mages into the room. 'What happened to him?' the cavalry master demanded. 'He was fine yesterday – at least, no worse than he usually is.'

'Since Chiamh healed him last time, he's been much better,' Sangra put in.

Anvar was flinging fresh wood on the fire, and the two

warriors went to the foot of the pallet, murmuring to one another in worried voices while the Mage knelt down by Elewin's bedside, looking at his face in the light of the renewed flames. The steward turned his head to look at her. 'Lady, tell them to stop whispering,' he said fretfully. 'I don't like it when they whisper.'

'All right, Elewin. They won't do it again,' Aurian soothed him. As she spoke, she was scanning him with her healer's senses, but they only told her what her instincts already knew. Sickness and injury she could counter, but age and despair she could not fight. The steward's body was failing. She already knew that her patient had fought valiantly, again and again, these last months, against illness and hardship, but something else had laid him low at last. There was a shadow over his spirit that she could not pierce, and she wondered what it was that had caused him to loose his grip upon the reins of life.

'Elewin, why?' she asked him directly. 'After you've come so far, what has made you give up now?'

'Lady, please don't plague me.' The voice was little more than a petulant whisper. 'I am tired now. I've had enough of struggle. I want to rest.' He turned his face away from her to stare into the shadows, and Aurian felt a chill creep up her spine as she saw his eyes focus on the Spectre that only she, of all the others in the room, could see. She shook her head. It would not be long now.

'Meiriel's death hit him very hard,' a soft voice murmured in the Mage's ear. She turned to see Anvar kneeling at her side, his face drawn and haggard with grief. 'Aurian, please – is there nothing you can do to help him?' he begged, and she remembered the fondness that had always existed between the young man and the old when Anvar had been a servant at the Academy. Now, his voice was taut with strain – the effort, Aurian knew, of denying the inevitable.

'You were with Elewin this afternoon. Was he like this then? Did anything happen, to explain why he should sink so fast?' she asked her soulmate. No matter that it was hopeless – for his sake, she couldn't just give up. She saw him take the old man's hand, and hold it tightly.

147

'He talked a lot about Meiriel ... and then he grew more and more quiet, and when he did speak, his mind seemed to wander more and more.' Anvar was frowning with the effort of remembering. 'Then he started to complain of being tired, and when he lay down I couldn't make him get up again ... Aurian, I've seen this before.' His voice was muffled with grief. 'It happened to my grandpa, the winter you came to the Academy. It was as though he just gave up. But it took weeks then, not hours ...'

Aurian felt a draught at her back as the door swung open and Chiamh came limping in, still covered in dust and sporting bruises. She had left him asleep in his own chambers, his healing sketchy and incomplete, to race to Elewin's side.

'Why didn't you send a message?' the Windeye demanded, glaring at her as he joined the Mages by the bed. 'I care about the old one too, you know.' His eyes followed Aurian's gaze into the shadowy corner, and she knew that he also saw what lurked there. He shuddered, and fell silent.

'Take good care of your mistress, Anvar.' The Watchers swung round, startled by the sound of Elewin's voice. 'You've turned out better than anyone expected, except me,' he went on. 'You've well repaid my trust in you, lad – I'm proud of you.' He turned away from them again, his grey eyes dark with pain. 'Prouder than I am of myself,' he murmured. 'Meiriel was ill – she couldn't help herself. Finbarr's death had turned her mind. I was supposed to be watching over her; taking care of her. It was the least I could do after betraying Miathan...' Tears were running down the steward's face. 'But I failed her,' he whispered. 'I failed them all. Too old, too feeble. I'm sorry ...' With a sigh, his last breath left him.

'You old fool!' Anvar cried savagely, his voice cracking with grief. He pounded the bedclothes with his fist. 'They weren't worth it!'

Aurian captured his flailing hand. 'Duty was Elewin's life,' she said softly. 'He had no family save the folk at the Academy. Duty and loyalty were everything to him – and I suspect that's what kept him going through these last hard months. Once he became convinced that he had failed on both counts ...' She shook her head sadly. 'Poor man.'

148

Chiamh buried his face in his hands. At the foot of the bed, Sangra was sobbing in Parric's arms. Holding one another, the Mages grieved together. Aurian looked over Anvar's shoulder into the shadows where Death had stood, but the corner was empty of the Spectre's presence now. This time, he had not been cheated – but then his coming had been welcomed by the one he sought. After long years of loyal service, Elewin had found his well earned rest at last.

10

Within the Crystal

In a prominent place on the wall of the Academy kitchen was a carved wooden rack bearing eight globes of shimmering crystal, each of which had once glowed softly with a different coloured radiance. Identical racks were housed in the old servants' quarters and in the gatehouses at the top and bottom of the steep path that went down from the top of the promontory to the river. Now, however, five of the crystals in each set were dark and lifeless – their Mageborn owners would issue orders and impose their will through them no more. Only three, the red, the silver-white, and the green, still shed their light.

The crystals caught the eye of Janok, head cook of the Academy, as he swept his gaze around the kitchen to make sure that the menials were all hard at work. He stood rubbing his fingers over his bristly chin, and looking at the globes and wondering. Only two days ago, the fifth, the blue-violet crystal, had been snuffed. The Lady Meiriel had perished, too. Not many of them left now, Janok thought. His masters were dying out at last.

Janok, unlike many Nexians, bore no particular hatred of the Magefolk. Why should he, when they had furnished him with such a comfortable existence? So long as their meals were plentiful, appetizing and available on demand, they let the head cook run his little domain in any way he chose – and since he enjoyed the favour of his powerful masters, none of the other menials dared oppose him. But how much longer would this satisfactory situation last? As the Magefolk numbers gradually decreased, Janok had begun to feel the first proddings of alarm.

Two matters gave him cause for concern: if a similar fate should befall Miathan and Eliseth, would he be able to hold on to his position of authority and prevent the other servants turning on him – and would the time spells they had placed on their supplies last beyond their deaths? If Janok could only get his hands on those provisions, so much badly needed food could obtain him anything he wanted, down in Nexis.

Of course these preoccupations were greatly dependent on his third chief concern. The head cook looked at the green crystal and scowled. The spark of light in its core was small and dim, indicating that its owner was still very far away – which was fine, as far as Janok was concerned. The further away she stayed, the better he liked it. The Lady Aurian – in his mind he turned her title into an epithet – had been responsible for robbing him of the drudge Anvar, and elevating the lad to a position of merit and trust. Even after all this time, he still flinched from the memory of the punishment that interfering red-headed bitch had earned him for allowing the escape of the young servant whom Miathan hated.

Recently, however, it had come to Janok's notice that, little by little, the green glow of Aurian's crystal was growing brighter. Wherever she had been all this time, she was apparently on her way back – and what would happen then? Janok knew to his cost that whenever she entered the game of power the rules had a way of suddenly changing – and that made him very uneasy indeed.

Even as Janok pondered, one of the other globes flared to a bright silver-white, and began to pulse in a regular pattern. The head cook muttered a curse, and reached out hesitantly to pick up the crystal. The Lady Eliseth had never had the best of tempers, but lately she had been growing positively baleful, to the point where the big man had found himself dreading her summons. What did she want now? One thing was for sure: it would only make matters worse if he kept her waiting. Janok shrugged and tightened his fingers around the crystal to activate its power, and then replaced it in the rack. A patch of silvery luminescence, half as wide as Janok's outstretched arms, shimmered into place above the fist-sized globe, and an image of Eliseth's face materialized in the centre of the light.

Janok assumed an ingratiating pose. 'How may I serve you, Lady?' he asked.

'With more alacrity,' the Weather-Mage snarled. 'How dare you keep me waiting, Mortal?'

'I beg your pardon, Lady,' Janok replied with a bow. He had already learned to his cost that in this waspish mood she would only be further angered by excuses. 'How may I make amends for my neglect?'

Eliseth's eyes narrowed, as though she was searching for something in the content or the tone of his question at which to take further offence, then, to his relief, she dismissed the matter with a shrug. 'I need Inella,' she snapped. 'Is the little wretch down there with you?'

'Alas, Lady, I have not seen her all morning. I thought she was in your chambers.' Janok fought to hide his triumph at the Magewoman's scowl of annoyance. I knew the brat would slip up sooner or later, he thought smugly.

'Well, don't just stand there smirking, you idiot! Find her, and send her up to me – and don't be all day about it.'

Before Janok had time to reply, Eliseth's image vanished, and shadows swarmed back into the corner of the kitchen. Sensing his temper, the scurrying kitchen menials, who had all paused to eavesdrop on his conversation with the Mage, suddenly became very noisily busy, and his thoughts were drowned by the sounds of scrubbing, slicing, scraping, and stirring.

'Quiet!' the head cook bellowed, and muttered a curse. As if he hadn't enough to do, without wasting half the day looking for Lady Eliseth's scheming little maid. Then his mood lightened. If the Weather-Mage was displeased, then not only would she punish Inella – and not before time, Janok thought – but he could probably get a blow or two in himself, as he had been itching to do for so long, without suffering any retribution from the girl's mistress. Janok grinned. Enjoying the security of Lady Eliseth's protection, Inella had been defiant and pert, and had undermined his authority with the others. He had waited ages for the brat to fall from grace – and now, it seemed, he would get his revenge at last. Janok grinned. There weren't many places to hide in the hilltop Academy compound. He would find her. In no time at all.

Many of the cool stone storerooms behind and beneath the Academy kitchen were forbidden to the menials who worked there, for most of the extensive stock of provisions hoarded within had been taken out of time by the Magefolk. Thus, while the city below them starved and struggled and suffered through the shortages that followed Eliseth's grim winter, the Academy and its occupants were independent, well supplied, and therefore in control. Their accumulated foodstuffs could not even be taken by force or stealth, should any Mortal be brave or foolhardy enough to try. The time spell not only preserved the supplies, but prevented any of the Mortal servants from purloining any desperately needed food to smuggle down to their hungry friends and families in the city below.

The hiding-place was small and awkward to reach, especially in the darkness, but at least it provided a temporary respite from Janok's brutality and the cruelty of the Mages. Zanna still hurt from the beating the head cook had given her when he had discovered her in the great library, but it had been nothing compared to the discovery that, when the Lady Eliseth was displeased, she could inflict pain worse than any beating without even lifting a finger.

The girl wiped a tear from one smudged cheek with trembling fingers and twisted her body in the cramped space, wishing she could find a comfortable position for her aching bones. She had come down to one of the few accessible storerooms, after her mistress had dismissed her for the night, to keep out of Janok's way – for now that the Lady was displeased with her, she knew he would feel free to abuse her as he wished. If only she had been more circumspect in her dealings with him in the past! She'd suffer for it now – but here, at least, she would be safe for a time. But she would have to emerge in the morning, and what would Janok do to her then? Suddenly, she had run out of time, and it was running out for her father, too. Zanna only wished that the cramped little nook behind the great stoneware crocks of flour, honey and beans could provide a sanctuary from her worries and fears – and the reminders of her own failure.

Lately, she had dared to hope for a time that there would be a way to free her father. Vannor had managed to smuggle her a message, hidden beneath the dirty dishes on a tray, that told her of the hidden escape route through the catacombs that ran beneath the library, and thence into the sewers. But only today, Zanna had slipped away to investigate, and discovered that the wrought-iron gate that had guarded the ancient archives was securely locked. To make matters worse, she had been caught in her investigations by Janok – and though her punishment had been bad enough, the worst of it was that he would be watching her like a hawk from now on. She dared not go near the library again – not without a damn good reason.

I convinced myself I was so clever, Zanna thought bitterly. *What a wonderful notion: become a servant at the Academy, and spy on the Magefolk. And then dad was captured ...* She choked on a sob. *I was going to release him, and we would both escape.* Another sob forced its way out. *But I can't rescue him – I've thought and thought, and there's just no way to get him out of the Academy past the guards. And he's in such pain ... The Archmage is killing him, bit by bit, and I can do nothing to prevent it. I can only watch him suffer ...*

The problem was, she was afraid that she could not watch Vannor suffer – not for much longer – and keep her feelings hidden from her mistress. Zanna was terrified that she would give herself away to Eliseth, and what would become of her then? Already she was taking too many risks, and spending too much time away from the tower in search of some way out for herself and her father. The terrible events of today had shown her that. But she had been so desperate to get away ... *If only she could* think ...

You came here to think! Zanna berated herself disgustedly. *But you aren't thinking. You're hiding in the storeroom, snivelling ...* Impatiently, the young girl dashed the tears from her eyes. *This skulking around and bawling like a lost calf is getting you nowhere,* she told herself. *This* was your idea – you wanted to do it. What happened to your nerve? You always looked up to Maya and the Lady Aurian. You wished you had their courage. Well, girl, now's your chance. You always prided yourself on your brains, so use them now.

Vannor's daughter was heartened by the thought of the two women she admired so much. Just knowing they were still opposing Miathan and Eliseth (for she had overhead from the Weather-Mage that Aurian was still alive, and clung stubbornly to the conviction that, although Maya had been missing for so long, she could not be dead) gave Zanna fresh courage. If Lady Aurian were in my position, she pondered, what would she do? Oh, if only she could be here. If only I could ask her advice . . .

Wait a minute – perhaps I can! Zanna sat bolt upright, her heart pounding with excitement. But would it be possible? Could it reach that far? You'll never know until you try, she told herself firmly, remembering the rack of crystals that hung on the kitchen wall. Only that day, when Janok had caught her, he had picked up Lady Eliseth's silver-white globe, waited until it had begun to shimmer, and spoken into it. 'I've got her,' he had said, and the Magewoman had answered. Lady Aurian's crystal was the green one, Zanna knew, and it still contained that telltale spark of light to show that it was active. If only she could use it to communicate – but not the globe from the kitchen. It would be missed. In the deserted quarters that had belonged to the household servants, however, there was another rack, forgotten and gathering dust . . . It was a small, faint hope, but it warmed the heart of Vannor's indomitable daughter. Forgetting her hurts and despair, she began to make plans.

'Tomorrow I plan to release some of our stored food to the Mortals of Nexis.'

'You plan to do what?' Eliseth cried. 'Miathan, have you lost your mind?'

To her irritation, the Archmage remained unperturbed. 'Here,' he said, producing a flagon of pale wine with a flourish from underneath his cloak. 'While I was down checking the supplies, I found a flask of your favourite.' With a negligent flip of his hand he tossed it to her, and Eliseth cried out in alarm as her fingers slipped on the smooth glass and she almost fumbled the catch.

'Damn you, Miathan – stop acting the fool,' she snapped. 'I know full well that the wine is only a ruse to distract me.' She placed the flask on her table without offering him any of its contents. 'Now – what's all this nonsense about giving our valuable food to those worthless, whining Mortals?'

Miathan sat down, uninvited, on one of Eliseth's chairs by the fire, absently stroking the white fur that draped it as he spoke: 'It isn't nonsense, Meiriel's death set me thinking . . .' His face darkened at the memory, and Eliseth too suppressed a shudder as she remembered being awakened, the night before last, by the wrenching agony of the healer's death throes. Though the pangs had been muted by distance, it had still been plain how Meiriel had died – and by whose hand.

'Pay attention!' Miathan barked, making the Weather-Mage jump. 'It's important that you understand what I'm doing, and why. Though your attempts at scrying have found no trace of Aurian so far, Meiriel's death should serve as sufficient warning of her capabilities. When she returns to the north – and return she will – we must be ready. We need the Nexian Mortals on our side; fortunately, most of them have scant intelligence and very short memories. If we claim it was Aurian who caused the winter and you who ended it, and then proceed to feed the starving rabble, we stand a chance of winning their support.'

'I don't like it,' Eliseth said automatically. 'Why, the very idea of grovelling for the favour of those lowly vermin! And we may need that food . . .'

'Spring is here, you idiot!' the Archmage roared. 'The Mortals are starving *now*, because nothing has had time to grow. In a few months there'll be plenty of food for everyone, thanks to the botch you made of keeping control of your winter, and the power of our provisions as a bargaining tool will be lost.'

Eliseth bit her lip to keep from betraying her anger. 'Very

156

well,' she shot back at him. 'Do as you will. Squander our supplies if you feel you must, but in return I want a favour.'

'What favour?' Miathan's eyes bored into her. She could actually see him bristling with suspicion. The Weather-Mage shrugged.

'No great thing,' she replied silkily. 'While you are dealing with matters here in the city, it would still be to our benefit if I could extend my scrying to get a glimpse of Aurian . . .'

'Face it, Eliseth – your powers don't allow that,' the Archmage snapped impatiently. 'How many times now have you tried and failed? Since Aurian reached the mountains, something has been shielding her.'

'And we must find out what it is,' Eliseth insisted. 'Miathan, listen. You prevented me from torturing Vannor to boost my powers – you said you wanted to experiment on him yourself. Let me try now, as the favour I asked of you. The merchant will still be alive when I've finished, you have my word on it.'

'Though, knowing you, he may well wish that he was dead,' Miathan said drily. 'Very well, Eliseth. You may try, if it will amuse you. Do what you must, within reason, to get results, but remember . . .' He leaned close, glaring fiercely into her eyes. 'I want Vannor alive, for a number of reasons. If you kill him, on your head be it – or on your face, at least.' His smile was cold and cruel. 'It would be interesting to see what effect another twenty years would have on those flawless features . . .'

Eliseth shuddered. 'I'll be careful, Archmage – I swear it.'

'It's up to you – you know the consequences if you are not.' With that parting shot, the Archmage got to his feet and left without another word. The Weather-Mage stared at the door as it closed behind him, and clenched her fists so tightly that her fingernails cut into her palms. One day, Miathan, she thought, I'm going to kill you.

Eliseth wrapped a white linen kerchief around her long, pale fingers, and used it to pick up the flagon of wine. Lifting it up to the firelight, she studied the amber flicker of the dancing flames through the pale, clear liquid, and sighed.

Though Miathan's cellars had been extensive, this was almost the last of the white. The Archmage preferred the richer, robust vintages with sparks of fire and ruby smouldering in their dark depths. Well, there was no help for it – not yet. 'When I am Archmage,' Eliseth murmured, 'things will be different.' A smiled curled the corners of her lips. But there was much to do before that day could arrive . . .

The Weather-Mage focused her powers on the angled glass facets of the flagon, and tightened her hand around the slender neck. The creation of her winter, and her subsequent researches in Finbarr's neglected archives, had taught her much about the forgotten and forbidden spells of the Cold Magic. At her word, the flames in the fireplace cringed back like beaten curs and flickered blue, and the light of the candles shrank and dimmed. A wisp of icy vapour came curling through the air to settle on the flask, to hide the wine within beneath a glittering white film of frost.

'Enough!' Eliseth banished the spell before the liquid could freeze and spoil, and, still holding the flagon carefully in its cloth, went to pour the chilled wine into a crystal goblet. She went to her favourite chair by the fireside and sat sipping appreciatively, reflecting on the irony of such ancient, powerful and lethal magic being harnessed for so mundane a task. Then again, why not? She felt the need to pamper herself a little tonight. Her spirits needed lifting, for lately things had not been going well.

It had been a mistake, she reflected, to take her frustrations out on her maid, although the lazy little slattern had deserved to be punished. Eliseth took another delicate sip of wine, reliving the memory of the girl's distress as she had stood, frozen and immobile, in the middle of the room, only her eyes reflecting her terror as the Weather-Mage stood over her, flexing her fingers to tighten the ache of burning, icy cold around Inella's body. Only afterwards, when she had caught the expression of veiled resentment in her servant's eyes, had Eliseth realized her error. Though tormenting the maid had given her a satisfying and much-needed outlet for her recent frustrations, it had possibly caused irreparable damage to the child's loyalties – and these days, the Mage-woman reminded herself, she needed to foster what support she could get.

With gentle fingers, Eliseth smoothed away the wrinkle of a frown. Since Miathan's spiteful spell that had burdened her face with ten additional years of age, she had been forced to take great care of her beauty. All was not lost, she reassured herself. She had been quick to note the darkening bruises that disfigured Inella's arms and face, and the hunched posture and stiff, awkward movements that betrayed other damage, out of sight: a gift from Janok, no doubt. Perfect! Eliseth found her smile again. The head cook had played right into her hands. She would turn a blind eye for a while, and let him brutalize the child – and then she would punish him and rescue Inella, earning the maid's gratitude once more.

Mortals were so easily manipulated – with one single, in-furiating exception. As she thought of Vannor, Eliseth found herself beginning to scowl again. Leaping to her feet, she re-filled her goblet from the frosty flask, and gulped down the fragrant wine to cool her anger. For many days now, while the moon passed through half its cycle, she had been trying to persuade Miathan to let her use the dark energy of the Mortal's fear and pain to fuel her power. That first night, when she had gone to the merchant's chamber to try her luck, the Archmage had forbidden her, and had been spite-fully keeping Vannor to himself ever since. He could not seem to see how essential it was that Eliseth extend her scry-ing to pierce the miles of distance that separated her from Aurian. The former leader of the rebels was the key, of that she was certain.

The Weather-Mage snarled a curse. Miathan! He had in-sisted that Vannor's strength must be husbanded, and that he must be spared from any severe or crippling injury, the shock of which might kill him. What nonsense! That mer-chant was strong as an ox – strong enough to have learned to resist what suffering Miathan had chosen to inflict. That doddering fool of an Archmage was growing soft. Or was he? It was always a mistake to underestimate Miathan's cunning, as she had learned to her cost. Did the old fox have plans of his own for Vannor? Or was he simply trying to limit Eliseth's power? Well, whatever he was up to, it wouldn't work. She'd had enough of waiting; enough of holding back. Fuelled by the wine she had drunk, her resolve leapt up like a white-hot flame within her. Smiling, she went to seek her crystal, so that she could call the gatehouse and summon two of the mercenary guards who were stationed there to assist her with the merchant. A plague on Miathan, and his damned experiments. But she had worn him down at last. So long as she didn't actually kill Vannor, the Archmage could scarcely complain of what she did to the Mortal – not if she achieved results. And tonight she would succeed at last. She would find Aurian, whatever it took to accomplish the task.

Vannor was lying huddled on Aurian's bed as Eliseth stalked into the chamber, flanked by the two stone-faced mercenaries. At the sound of her entrance he hauled himself to his feet and straightened in a posture of insolent defiance, as though he had nothing to fear from her. But the Weather-Mage had seen, for a fleeting instant, the way his face had blanched at her approach, and had glimpsed the shadow of dread, now veiled, that lurked behind his eyes.

'Still on your feet, Vannor?' she mocked him. 'Evidently the Archmage has been too lenient with you. But now comes my turn.' Her voice dropped to a snarl. 'Tonight you will assist *me*.'

'I'll assist you in nothing,' Vannor blazed, 'as I told your master before you.'

'Indeed.' Eliseth's voice was icy with anger. 'That remains to be seen.' At her signal, the two guards rushed forward and seized the merchant. Turning her back on Vannor and beckoning the mercenaries to follow with their captive, she walked back into the living chamber and laid her crystal on the polished wooden sill of the narrow window, placing two candles so their light reflected in the diamond panes and angled into the glittering facets of the gem. 'Now, Mortal.' She looked back at Vannor, held tightly in the grip of his captors, in much the same way as she might have regarded an insect. 'Let us test the measure of your defiance.'

Her dispassionate gaze turned to the guards. 'Something small at first,' she mused, calm as though she were selecting silks in the marketplace. 'Yet something that will serve as a permanent reminder never to defy the Magefolk. A hand, perhaps. The right hand, so he will never take up a sword in rebellion again.'

'No,' Vannor howled, thrashing and writhing in frantic desperation to escape as the mercenaries manhandled him into position with his hand held flat against the smooth surface of the table. Still he continued to struggle, until the Weather-Mage, with a small exclamation of annoyance, lifted her hand in an abrupt, sharp gesture. All at once, the merchant found himself unable to move, unable to speak; his limbs and tongue wrapped in a gelid shroud of icy cold that struck agonizingly through to his very bones. His eyes were frozen open, looking down at the hand that lay limp and helpless, white against the darkly glowing wood of the table. There was no way he could avoid seeing what they did to him. Only Vannor's mind was still marginally under his control, and it could do nothing but curse impotently to articulate the terror and fury that he was unable to voice.

Eliseth, however, seemed able to hear his very thoughts, now that his tongue was stilled and he was a prisoner of her magic. 'Much better,' she murmured, with a complacent little smile. 'The power of your trapped emotions is increased if they have no means of expression.'

The merchant, helpless and in anguish, attempted to distract his roiling thoughts by imagining, in cold, precise detail, just what he would do to her if only he were free, but the Magewoman merely laughed. 'Hatred will serve my purpose just as well,' she told him, 'as will your despair. There is no escaping me now. You have no choice but to betray your friends.'

From the corner of his eye, Vannor glimpsed a flash of silver and heard the rasp of steel as one of the mercenaries drew his blade. The merchant's blood turned to ice. Cut off his hand? No they couldn't! They –

The guard reversed his sword, holding it point up, high above the table. With the hilt in both hand, he brought it smashing down, the blade's keen edges a silvery blur passing perilously close to the merchant's face. Vannor's world exploded in a flare of white-hot pain. His mind erupted in a soundless shriek as the heavy steel pommel of the hilt hammered once, twice, three times into the back of his hand, mangling and crushing the flesh and delicate bones into a bloody pulp.

'Enough.' As though it came from a great distance, Vannor heard Eliseth's cool voice faintly through the buzzing in his ears. He wanted to let go, to lose this agony and shock and outrage in the dark haven of blessed unconsciousness, but the Mage's spell held him like bands of iron, preventing such an easy escape. That bloody evil, foul-minded bitch, Vannor raged inwardly – but no; she had said she could use his anger just as well. *I won't permit this*, he thought. *I'm damned if I'll let her use me.*

With a wrenching effort, he turned his mind away from the pain and mutilation to concentrate on good things: the wealth and luxury of former days, when he was head of the Merchants' Guild; the warmth of comradeship, with Forral and Aurian, Parric and Maya. He thought of loved ones: Zanna (no – not Zanna! Vannor remembered the risk just in time). Instead he thought of his lovely first wife, and Sara ... But, to his astonishment, it was the memory of Dulsina, his clever, sensible housekeeper with the compassionate heart and acerbic tongue, that gave Vannor the strength to defy his tormentor.

Without sparing her prisoner a further glance, the Weather-Mage turned back to her crystal and let her mental energies flow into the fist-sized gem that sparkled in the candlelight by the window, against a backdrop of velvet night. Then, bracing her mind, she opened herself to Vannor's pain and terror, stoking her powers with the pounding waves of negative dark energy that emanated from her suffering victim. It had taken many hours of exhausting and painstaking practice to allow her to reach this point, where her inner vision would expand to see Beyond, but now ...

Eliseth half-closed her eyes as the crystal's brittle rainbow glitter blurred and merged into a misty, opalescent haze – and within ... 'Ah.' The Weather-Mage breathed out in a long sigh of satisfaction. 'Now I have her!'

Eliseth's first impression was the warm gold flicker of fire-light, then, as they came more clearly into focus, she could see Aurian and Anvar sitting very close together. The Mages and two Mortals, a male and a female, were talking to some-one else, who seemed, frustratingly, to be constantly beyond the range of her vision. She frowned and narrowed her eyes, pouring all her concentration into the crystal in a desperate attempt to discover the identity of the fifth person, but all she could perceive was a shape cloaked in shadow, human yet not human, that flowed and shifted in her vision, defying all her attempts at definition. With an effort, Eliseth focused into the vision until she could hear what was being said – and to add to her vexation it seemed that there was a sixth person within the chamber. Someone else was clearly being addressed by Aurian and Anvar and the odd, hidden being. Someone whose replies could not be heard, and whom the Weather-Mage, try as she might, could not see at all.

Aurian took a sip of syrupy mead from her cup of carven horn, and Chiamh saw her trying to suppress a grimace at the cloying sweetness of the drink. Though the Xandim brewed a more than passable ale, this stronger liquor was traditionally served on occasions of great formality, such as serious (if unofficial) councils. Today, they had gained a res-pite from the demands of the Horsefolk so that they could bury Elewin. Tomorrow, however, there would be hard de-cisions to make concerning the future leadership of the Xandim and the part they would play in Aurian's fight against the Archmage. Tonight, Parric, Chiamh, the Mages and Sangra had met privately, not only to share their grief over the passing of the steward, but also to confer together in the hope of coming up with some plan, or strategy, which they could present to the gathered Horselords in the morn-ing.

Parric took a swig from his horn cup and cast his gaze

around the solemn assembly. 'I know that no one feels like making hard decisions tonight,' he said heavily, 'but after what happened yesterday we had better come up with something, fast. It's the dark of the moon again, so that I can be challenged, and I don't want or need to be Herdlord any longer. Besides,' he added wryly, 'I'm not going through a fight like that again for anyone. Surely there must be someone from the Xandim who can take over – someone sympathetic to our cause. What happens, under Xandim law, if the Herdlord doesn't want to defend the leadership? Can we nominate someone?'

'Well?' Aurian prompted Chiamh, who had been sitting lost in silent thought. The Windeye turned his attention back to Parric's question. 'Yes,' he said. 'With your approval, another challenger can step forward in your place – but he must fight for the leadership none the less, if he is opposed. But who would you choose to lead in your stead?'

'Schiannath,' Aurian said firmly. 'Apart from you, Chiamh – and obviously you can't become Herdlord – he's the only one of the Xandim on whose support I can count.'

'But wait,' Anvar interrupted. 'I thought Schiannath had tried to become Herdlord before, and been beaten. So how can he challenge again?'

'Because Parric has nominated him,' Chiamh replied. 'In essence, he is acting for another, not himself. There is no doubt that Schiannath will order the Xandim to aid you if he becomes Herdlord. At present, Lady, he connects you with all his recent great good fortune. Anything that he can do to assist you, he will.'

'But I didn't do anything for him, really,' Aurian protested.

The Windeye shrugged. 'No? Had it not been for you, Parric would never have come to our lands. I would not have been forced to take action against the Herdlord, and Phalihas would, in all likelihood, have maintained his rule. Schiannath would still be an exile, and his sister imprisoned in her equine form. Do not protest his devotion, Aurian. It is not unearned, and at the moment it is all to your advantage.' Though Chiamh had been striving to keep any part of his inner feelings from showing in his voice, there must have been something – the slightest trace of hesitation or a hint of bitterness – that betrayed him.

Frowning, Anvar looked at the Windeye. 'You said Aurian's advantage. Are you implying that it may not be to the advantage of Schiannath or the Xandim?'

Chiamh hesitated. Within the last few days, strong memories of his seeing of long ago had begun to haunt him. So far, everything had come to pass as he had foreseen. He had assisted Aurian and Anvar in their struggle against the Evil Ones, and Schiannath, too, had played his part. There was only one part of the vision that had not yet become manifest: the chilling prophecy that the arrival of Aurian spelled the end for the Xandim race. For days now he had been struggling with his conscience, wondering whether he ought to let the Mages know what he had foreseen. Did Aurian not have enough difficulties to deal with already? Was it fair to increase her burden with the fate of a race that was not even her own? On the other hand, should he not warn her that there might be grave consequences to her actions? If he did not, and the worst came to happen, would he not share the blame? Yet if it was a true seeing, could disaster be averted whether he spoke out or not? Chiamh could feel Aurian's eyes on him. Anvar too was frowning, now. The Magefolk would clearly not be satisfied without some kind of explanation.

'Very well,' the Windeye said at last. 'I probably ought to tell you – not that it will make any difference ...'

'*No! Do not!*'

Chiamh started as the voice of Basileus resounded sharply within his mind. Judging by Aurian's astonished gasp and the widening of Anvar's eyes, he guessed that the Mages had heard the Moldan too. The Windeye saw the sharp glance that passed between them.

'Who the blazes was that?' Aurian demanded. 'Surely it was the same being that defended me against Death. And why shouldn't you tell us – whatever it is? If it's something we need to know ...'

'*It is something they do not need to know.*' The Moldan's

165

mental tones were stern and implacable. *'Little Windeye, you must not do this,'* he went on, and from Anvar's scowl, and the angry tightening around Aurian's eyes, Chiamh realized that Basileus was now addressing only himself, and the Mages could not hear.

'You and I both know what you foresaw,' Basileus continued in gentler tones. *'When Aurian takes up the Sword of Flame, her actions may indeed put an end to the Xandim – but there is more at stake here than the fate of a single race.'*

'That's very well for you to say,' Chiamh retorted, so angry he barely remembered to keep from speaking the words aloud. 'It won't be your race that is wiped out.'

The Moldan sighed. *'Young Windeye,'* he said gently, *'my race was incalculably and irretrievably injured long ago by the Wizards. The Moldai, of all the peoples of the world, know what damage they can wreak. To save the world from this new evil power that has arisen among them, I would gladly sacrifice myself, and what remains of my race. It may yet come to that – or it may not, for Moldai and Xandim both. Your vision may have been obscure or misleading, and let us hope that it is so. But whether you were correct in your interpretation or not, you have no right to burden these Magefolk with your fears and doubts. If you reveal what you know, you may hinder them in their fight; and if the Evil Ones should prevail, then that will almost certainly spell the end for the Xandim race.'*

Chiamh knew, to his sorrow, that Basileus was right. The Windeye had reached this same hard decision on that night, several moons ago, when he had discovered dread tidings of evil on the wind, and then seen those clear and shining beacons of hope in the south: Aurian and Anvar, with whose fate he had become so entwined. He bowed his head in acknowledgement of the Moldan's wisdom. 'I understand,' he replied softly, still taking great care to shield his thoughts from the Mages. 'The burden must be mine alone.'

The Weather-Mage cursed, and threw down the crystal. This was getting her nowhere! A plague on Aurian – how had the bitch managed to foil the penetration of Eliseth's vision? Scowling, she turned to see the two mercenaries looking at her, obviously awaiting further orders. Between them, Vannor still stood frozen in her spell, though his face was grey and his expression blank. Yet though he clung to consciousness only because of her magic, the merchant's eyes still smouldered with an unquenchable spark of defiance. Had his dogged resistance been the barrier that had foiled her attempt to spy upon her enemy? Well, she'd get no further use out of him tonight – that much was clear – but she would see his stubborn spirit well and truly broken before she attempted to use his energies again! With a wave of her hand she banished her spell, and the merchant's knees buckled as blood began to ooze from the lump of mangled flesh and shattered bone that had been his hand. The mercenaries quickly grabbed an arm each, and hauled him back upright.

'Release him,' Eliseth snarled at the guards. 'Bind his hand – I don't want him bleeding to death.' Scooping up her crystal, she stalked from the room as Vannor crumpled to the floor.

As the Weather-Mage descended the curving stairway to her rooms, her temper began to cool a little. After all, her efforts had not been entirely fruitless. She had at least discovered that Aurian was planning to return to the north, and that the Mage had enlisted the Xandim to help her. Eliseth nodded grimly to herself as she swiftly consumed fruit and wine to help restore the energies depleted by her magic. Very well. It was time to put some of her own plans into action. There was little she could do about Aurian's mysterious southern allies, but the Mage would find little aid within her own lands, should she dare to return. And if Eliseth wanted to set a trap, then Vannor would be the perfect bait. She simply needed a Mortal agent to infiltrate the rebels, and tell them the sad news of their former leader's capture, and she suspected that she knew the very man to do it. Without further delay, she wrapped herself in her darkest, warmest cloak, picked up her staff and left the tower.

The Weather-Mage slipped across the courtyard, avoiding the shimmering pools of moonlight, invisible save as a deeper sliver of shade within the shadows of the walls. The solitary guard in the upper gatehouse never saw her pass him. The cluster of armed mercenaries that now guarded the lower gate had been told to watch for intruders, not people going out. Besides, they were deeply engrossed in a game of dice. Eliseth made a mental note of that. Come tomorrow, those buffoons would be regretting such inattention whilst in Magefolk employ. Shrugging the matter aside, she drifted silent as a wraith across the bridge, and vanished into the shadows of the city.

11

Killers of the Night

Pickings that night were even more scant than usual. Grince was driven by his own hunger – and the more pressing needs of his small white companion – from his usual safe haunts within the Grand Arcade. Though the streets were cold and dangerous, there was always the chance that a sharp lad like himself could come by something or other to keep body and soul together for another day – especially when that lad was getting better all the time at his newfound trade of thief.

It was hard to leave his home, though – even for a few short hours. Grince's cosy lair in the labyrinth of the arcade's deserted storerooms showed ample evidence of his burgeoning skills. He had found a small chamber at the end of a dusty passage, and had concealed the door from prying eyes behind a pile of boxes, planks, broken crates and casks and any other rubbish he could find. Having wedged the door ajar just enough for a skinny boy to worm his way through, he had constructed his own entrance at the bottom of the tottering stack of camouflage using two casks, with the ends knocked out, laid in line to make a narrow tunnel through the pile of junk. Apart from this access into the arcade, the room also had a high, barred window, now screened and draughtproofed with old sacks tacked to the wooden frame, through which the young thief could reach the alley outside.

Within his hideout was a magpie-nest of odds and ends that Grince had scavenged, found or liberated from their previous owners. In a box were his utensils – a dented tankard, a patched and battered cooking-pot, and two chipped bowls (now used by the puppy) that had all been gleaned from a rubbish-heap behind a tavern; a carefully straightened spoon with a consequently wavy silhouette; an eating-knife with a broken haft and four wooden trenchers, of which Grince was especially proud, which had once been the ends of the casks that formed his entrance tunnel. The porridge pot, the original theft that had started his career, held a supply of water now, painstakingly transported from the pump in the arcade, as did a large, tightly lidded crock that had originally, and all too briefly, been filled with sticky sweet honey.

The young thief's bed took up an entire corner. He had laid down an old door to shield his body from the cold that seeped up from the stone floor, and had strewn a thick layer of straw over the wooden panels. On top of these he had piled a rainbow of tattered snippets: every rag he came across and any scrap of cloth he could steal from the unsuspecting tailors and dressmakers of the arcade. Each day, when the night's business of survival was done, the weary boy and his dog would burrow into the snug warmth of the mounded scraps like rabbits vanishing underground.

Grince had snatched two thick blankets of creamy, undyed wool from a washing line in the north of the city, much to the puzzled dismay of the goodwife who had hung them there in the confidence that the walls of her backyard were unscalably high. These were spread over his nest, adding weight and warmth and keeping the tottering structure together, and crowning it all was his prize – a heavily fleeced sheepskin that had vanished one night from a tanner's shop near Greenmarket square.

Since he had come by the sheepskin and blankets, Grince had taken the swathes of thinner cloth – filched from the great stored bolts used by the arcade's seamstresses – that had originally served him as bedcovers, and hung them from the walls of his lair, where they brightened up the room with their colour, and kept out draughts a treat. He had nowhere to make a fire, nor would it be safe to do so, but a motley collection of lamps, both brightly polished household treasures and dented old relics with cracked and soot-stained chimneys, stood safely on another box in the centre of the chamber, along with candles of both beeswax and tallow.

Grince kept a battered bucket in one corner for his own

waste, with a piece of wood, weighed down by a stone, on top for a makeshift lid. A straw and sawdust-filled box stood nearby for his dog to use. Each night the boy was forced to make two awkward peril-fraught journeys outside to empty these down a nearby drain.

His treasures were strewn about or propped on makeshift shelves of plank and brick. An old sword, its blade broken off a foot below the hilt, that came in useful for prying open windows. Mismatched items of clothing that had come from washing lines all over the city. A pile of odd gauntlets, woollen mittens, scarves and kerchiefs, that Grince was sure would come in useful for something – sometime. Assorted needles, spools of cotton, hanks of wool and twine, odd-shaped bits of wood and a collection of rusty nails that came in useful all the time. A precious tinderbox and a bottle of lamp-oil, that he refilled when he had the chance. A twinkling assortment of combs, clips, rings, and trinkets, whose value he had no means of assessing – nor was there any way of selling them. Grince kept them because their sparkle cheered him, and because they made him feel like a proper, bold and daring thief. He kept them on a shelf by his bed, along with his chiefest treasure – a long, keen dagger with a jewelled hilt, a lucky find that he had taken (even now his gorge rose just to think of it) from a drowned corpse washed up on the riverside mud.

In a sack suspended from a hook in the arching stone ceiling Grince kept his food supplies, when there were any to be had. It was the only way, he had discovered, to keep them safe from the marauding rats that could not be kept out, no matter how hard he tried. Tonight, however, for all his scavenging around the arcade, the sack hung flat and empty, and his puppy Warrior was beginning to whimper with hunger.

Grince sighed, and took a last, wistful look around his hideout. He was constantly amazed by his own ingenuity. It was a far better home than the squalid hovel he had shared with Tilda – and it was all his own. There was no one here to curse or cuff or beat him; none of the drunken scum who were his mother's customers trooping in and out. When he got lonely, there was always Warrior – the best friend a boy could ever want – to keep him company. Though he was building up a wary confidence in his own abilities, the city held a multitude of dangers, and he was always reluctant to leave this place of safety. What if something dreadful happened to Warrior in his absence? What if someone else should find the place, and turn him out? What if . . .

'Oh, don't be so bloody stupid,' Grince growled to himself. After all, it wasn't as if he had any choice. It was either steal or starve. He didn't mind going hungry himself, but for Warrior it was unthinkable. The dog was growing rapidly, and needed all the food he could get. Grince picked up the squirming white puppy and petted and hugged him before putting him in his special basket, also filched from an unsuspecting merchant in the arcade, which had a lid that tied shut with a piece of twine, and a handle so that it could be hung from the same ceiling hook as the food sack. By the time Warrior outgrew it, he would also be big enough to defend himself from the huge, marauding rats – but in the meantime his anxious master was taking no chances.

Thrusting his dagger and broken sword into his belt, Grince put on his outdoor 'cloak' – a garment of which he was very proud, for he had made it himself, and a great deal of thought had gone into its invention. One of his mother's regular clients, a one-legged seaman forced on to shore by his disability, had taken to the youngster and had taught him to use a needle – with the wholehearted approval of the lackadaisical Tilda. Though Grince had spurned such nonsense as only fit for girls, old Tam, the sailor, had quickly – and forcibly – corrected this notion, and the boy was glad of his teaching now, in the chilly nights of the northern spring.

Grince had cobbled together his peculiar piece of apparel from bits of leather and fur, fustian, velvet, brocade, and any other scraps of warm fabric that he had been able to find among the stalls and storerooms of the arcade. Its patchwork of varied textures and hues broke up his outline and helped him blend into the shadows. It was short enough to leave his feet unencumbered for running, and loose enough to be slipped off at an instant's notice – or in the clutch of a grabbing hand. Unlike a normal cloak there were slits in the

172

sides that he could put his arms through to snatch a cooling pasty or cut the strings of a purse, and the inside was lined with a multitude of pockets to carry home his spoils.

Old Tam, in addition to his sailor's skills with a needle, had possessed a fund of outrageously tall stories with which he had bribed the boy as they worked. Grince particularly remembered the tale of a magic cloak that made its owner invisible, and he liked to think of his cloak having similar powers, though he had far too much sense to put it to the test. None the less, it was his special thief's cloak, and it gave him confidence. Though it would have been too conspicuous during the day, he never went out at night without it.

Thus equipped for the night ahead, the boy stacked some wooden boxes to act as steps up to the high window of his lair, and blew out the candles and all of the lamps save one. Squirming between the bars, he dropped down into the alley below and vanished into the maze of darkened streets.

Grince slid through the shadows like dark water running downhill towards the river and the docks, heading in the direction of the merchants' warehouses, and the possibility of stored food. It was cold outside, but in his cloak he was safe. The other denizens of the night were far too intent upon their own business to take any notice of him; a small boy was clearly no threat to them and he had nothing that they could possibly want.

As it happened, the boy did not have to go as far as the river. His chiefest skill was burglary, and the looming, tottering houses in the old quarter, with their overhanging storeys, crumbling masonry and loose-fitting windows, had always provided him with the easiest pickings – when there was any food within. Tonight he was lucky. His third such foray (the first having produced one ancient, wizened apple plus a few small shellfish from the river that he ate on the spot, and the second nothing whatsoever) provided him with a stub of candle, half a dozen oatcakes and a small, stale meat pie of indeterminate ancestry. Slipping his spoils into a deep pocket within his cloak, Grince blessed his luck as he wormed his way out of the forced window back into the street, and headed for home.

173

It was later now, and the streetfolk were becoming desperate. Grince hugged every scrap of cover he could find on the way back and gave a wide berth to the starving derelicts that remained. A few narrow escapes in the past had taught him to be circumspect. While he had lived with Tilda, he had never known anyone desperate enough to eat human flesh, but these days he was not so sure. He had overheard rumours of gangs who roamed the streets in the guise of beggars to let them get close enough to their victims – and then it was too late.

There were, however, certain advantages to this perilous hour, for the doors of the taverns were beginning to open now, and their occupants were spilling out into the streets. With luck, Grince might encounter a number of drunks on his homeward journey – and a drunken man, off his guard and bent on weaving home, was a far easier mark than a guarded, sober man for a young pickpocket who was just learning his trade. Unfortunately, however, Grince's luck seemed to have run out for the evening. The impoverished folk of the city were growing more and more desperate in this hungry spring, and more and more were taking to the streets in the hope of robbing their more fortunate brethren who had anything at all worth stealing. People were more on their guard now, and tended to go about in groups for their own protection. When a likely prospect did present himself, the competition from bigger, well armed ruffians was more than one small boy could handle. Time and again, the boy would be sidling up to a potential victim, only to be beaten to the mark – usually by armed thugs who did not stop at the mere picking of pockets, but had murder in mind.

With some mixed feelings, Grince decided to give it up for the night. In the end, his safety was more important than a couple of coppers in a leather purse. After all, he had responsibilities. He shuddered at the thought of what would happen to his dog if he should be killed out on the streets. The mere idea of poor Warrior, shut in his basket and slowly starving to death, was enough to make the young boy cautious. Because of this, though he did not realize it, the white puppy had probably saved his life on several occasions.

Grince was looking forward to seeing his small companion again. Warrior, like his master, had become used to eating all manner of things in his short life. He would enjoy the meat pie; and afterwards they could snuggle up together in the warm and cosy bed, safe from the violence of these cold, damp streets. These happy thoughts gave impetus to Grince's feet as he turned homeward. Familiar as he was with all the short cuts, it took him very little time to get back into the tangle of alleys that ran behind the Grand Arcade. Grince slowed his pace then, and began to creep forward cautiously, reminding himself that this was one of the more dangerous parts of his journey. He must be sure that no one saw him approach the arcade or climb in through the window, or the secret of his hiding-place would be out.

There was one last, broader lane to cross before he could duck into the narrow passage that backed on to his home. He would have to be careful here – the thoroughfare was usually the haunt of beggars. As he crept stealthily forward, Grince heard the sound of footfalls, soft but brisk, coming from the street ahead. He froze like a rabbit that scents the hunter, flattening himself against the cold, damp wall and peeping warily round the corner of the building to look into the lane. In the distance a tall figure came into view, all details of its identity concealed beneath a billowing hooded mantle of midnight black – yet there was something about it that made the young boy shiver and shrink further back into the shadows, lest the dark void that concealed the shrouded face should turn his way and transfix him with its blank, arcane regard.

Oh, grow up, Grince, he told himself in withering disgust, as the figure came nearer. It's only some damned mark who's stupid enough to be wandering home alone at this time of night. Do you want to miss a chance like this? You'd never get at a pocket through that big loose cloak, but maybe begging would work ... Maybe it would, but Grince would never find out, because there was no way, no way at all, that he could force himself into the open to accost the eerie stranger. His heart laboured and sweat sprang out on his forehead, icy in the chill of the night. It felt as though his feet had been nailed to the ground. Though he had been too intent on the approaching nightmare to see them go, he suddenly noticed that the lane had suddenly emptied of beggars, apart from himself.

Huddled into the folds of his patchwork cloak with his guts knotted in terror, Grince shrank back into the shelter of his alley and watched the looming figure pass. Once it had gone on beyond his hiding-place, he felt limp and shaky with relief. None the less, he would not, dared not move until the shrouded shape was completely out of sight. Grince closed his eyes and listened to the receding tap of footsteps, praying that they would soon be gone.

The sound of footfalls stopped abruptly, and the boy felt a chill go through him. Was the figure turning? *Did it know he was there?* Though Grince was afraid to look, the fear of not knowing if he was being stalked was far worse. After a brief struggle with the shreds of his courage, he opened his eyes and sneaked a quick look round the corner.

'Alms, great Lady? Spare a copper for a poor old blind woman?'

Grince started at the sound of the quavering voice. To his dismay, he saw a beggar grope her stooped and halting way towards the brooding figure. The unsuspecting crone had claimed that she was blind – he supposed that accounted for the fact that she had not run off in terror, as the other beggars had. But how had she known that the mantled stranger was female? The old woman shuffled forward, into the dim pool of light from the lamp that hung on the corner building at the end of the street. The figure in the black cloak stepped forward, arm extended, and Grince, astounded that the blind crone should have met with such easy success, thought: damn – what was I afraid of? I've missed my chance. Then that thought, and all others, fled from the young thief's mind. The outstretched hand flashed white in the light of the lamp as it touched the crone, and the blind old beggar crumpled into a limp, dark heap of rags on the cobbles. Grince heard a soft laugh, as chill and cheerless as a winter's dawn, as the figure went on its way, rounding the corner and passing out of sight.

176

Minutes crawled by, and the slumped shape of the beg-gar-woman in the roadway did not move. It was much longer than that before the terrified boy dared venture from his hiding-place. Cold and hunger drove him out in the end, as did the threat of the impending dawn and the thought of his poor puppy, still shut in its basket and cold and hungry too. In order to reach his own alley, Grince had to cross the street and go almost as far as the lower corner – much too near, in his estimation, to the body of the crone. But if he wanted to reach the longed-for safety of his lair, it would have to be done. I'll just run, he thought. I'll run right past her, and I won't look, because if I do . . .

When it came to it, of course, he couldn't help but look. Though he ran as fast as he could, especially when he neared the shapeless heap, it was as though Grince's eyes had been hooked by a fishing line that the body was reeling in. For many nights afterwards he had reason to curse his curiosity. His footsteps faltered, and his breath congealed in his throat at the sight before him. Though the body was gro-tesquely twisted, the face was half-turned towards, the milky, sightless eyes turned up in death. In the lamplight, he could see the bloodless pallor of its sagging, wrinkled skin, and the expression of stark terror sealed into the features in that last moment of fading life. On the old woman's forehead, like a brand, was the mark of a hand that burned in flaming silver.

Suddenly, Grince found his wit again. With a yelp of ter-ror he fled back to his den in the arcade, tumbling in through the window without a thought for the drop on the other side. Without pause, he snatched down Warrior's bas-ket and dived into the spurious safety of his bed, where he huddled, wild-eyed and trembling, clutching the puppy to him for comfort, biting his lip to keep back tears. It was a good thing he had Warrior, he thought. Without the dog to care for, he doubted that he would ever find the courage to venture out into the streets again.

Though the night-time thoroughfares of Nexis were aswarm with the usual human detritus of beggars, whores and foot-pads, Eliseth made her way through the dark back streets

177

without concern. Even though she was disguised by the billowing drapes of her hooded cloak, there was an aura about her: a sense of presence that bespoke both power and peril. Only one had dared approach her, and that one had been blind. Almost contemptuously, Eliseth had extinguished the faltering flame of the old beggar's life with a single touch, taking in its energy to add to her growing powers. To her surprise, even such a used and faded existence had provided a tingling jolt of energy that coursed through her veins like wine and felt so good – so very good – that she understood at last why Miathan had become addicted to his human sacrifices. Well, well, she thought. We live and learn. I must look into this matter further – but not tonight. Tonight the Weather-Mage had other business, and her hurrying steps had almost brought her to her goal: the place she had located by scrying crystal; the home of the one she sought.

The bakery had been repainted on the inside and limewashed without, and the floors and windows sparkled. The crumbling brickwork and the sagging roof had all been well repaired. Bern had worked hard to undo all the depredations left by his father's neglect – with one exception. The business was still a failure for one single, simple reason: there wasn't a scrap of flour to be had in Nexis for love or money.

Bern was sitting, as was his habit these long, sleepless nights, in the downstairs room that was the bakery itself, a bottle at his elbow and his feet up on a convenient ledge in the warm brickwork of the older, smaller oven. Almost as a ritual, Bern still kept the great fires of the ovens alight; both the original one and the larger one he had built to augment it in more hopeful days, when Torl was newly dead and the business was his own at last. They warmed the house, but did little to assuage the cold, creeping sense of failure within the baker's heart. He had betrayed the rebels and murdered his father to get this business for himself – and what had been the point? Supplies of flour and yeast had run out during the dark and endless winter, and the girl he had planned to marry, a dark-haired lass with flashing eyes, the daughter of a widowed dressmaker who lived nearby, had left him when his black moods and evil tempers had become too much for her to bear. Bern cursed aloud. It was so bloody unfair! As soon as he had achieved his lifelong ambition, the glowing dream had turned to ashes in his hands.

In the midst of his brooding Bern must have dozed, for he was jolted rudely awake by the slam of a wind-caught door. The curse that instantly sprung to his lips died there, un-uttered, as he opened his eyes to see a tall, black-cloaked shape that towered over him, its face concealed within the shadows of a hood. His hand, flung out instinctively to reach the long iron poker, the nearest available weapon, froze in midair. Then, without a word, the figure extended white and shapely hands, and pushed the hood back from her face. 'You!' Bern gasped, and then, stuttering apologies, he fell to his knees before the figure of the Weather-Mage.

Eliseth laughed. 'Indeed, Mortal, it is I. Did you never think, after the night you came running to the Academy to betray your father, that you would see me again?'

Bern, who in fact had thought no such thing, remained grovelling in terrified silence. The Magewoman laughed again, and stepped over his prostrate form to take the best chair by the fire. 'Have you fallen on such hard times, baker, that you offer no refreshment to your guests?' she asked him sharply.

'My Lady – I beg your pardon.' Bern leapt up on shaky legs and ran to fetch a crystal goblet that had been part of his mother's dowry, and a flask of good wine, all too scarce these days, which he had been saving for a celebration – or an emergency such as this. Setting them on the low table before his terrifying guest, he poured for her with shaking hands, while Eliseth pushed back her heavy mantle and held out her slender white hands to the dancing flames. Taking his own cup, still filled with the rough, inferior stuff with which he had been drowning his sorrows, he took the other chair, restraining himself with an effort from pushing it further away from the cold-eyed Mage. All the while, his mind was racing. What could she want from him? How could he possibly placate her?

Eliseth, watching him sidelong from under her lashes, let

the baker writhe in silence for a while before putting him out of his suspense. At last, when she judged that his curiosity and fear had reached exploding point, she began to speak.

'Mortal, you once did the Magefolk a great favour by disclosing to us the location of the rebels that infested our city. Such loyalty is to be greatly commended; and now I find I must count upon it once again.' Swiftly she outlined her plan for his betrayal of the rebels, watching his eyes first widen in amazement and then narrowing in calculating greed. Eliseth smiled to herself. She had gauged his nature to a nicety. When she had finished speaking, she sat back in her chair and took a sip of the disgusting wine, wondering what this base and lowly Mortal would dare ask of her in return.

Bern's request took her completely by surprise. 'What?' she gasped. 'Grain? Are you certain?'

The baker nodded, his expression avid. 'Lady, there is no flour in Nexis. I'm a ruined man – I can't run my business. Think what it would mean to me to be the only working baker in the city. And I did hear rumours,' he added slyly, 'that the Magefolk have all sorts of supplies up there in the Academy.'

Eliseth made a mental note to investigate the source of such rumours, and turned her attention back to Bern. It was difficult to suppress her smile as she answered. 'Of course you may have the supplies you require,' she told him graciously. 'But on one condition – you must set out this very night.'

Bern looked thunderstruck. 'Why yes, my Lady, of course, but . . .' He swallowed hard. 'How shall I make arrangements to collect my grain?' he stammered.

Eliseth marvelled at the man's temerity, even though he had shrunk from actually suggesting that she might not keep her word. 'That can be dealt with at once,' she told him crisply. 'Have you a secure place to store it in your absence?'

Bern nodded, and led the way to his storeroom in the cellar. The Mage nodded her satisfaction. 'Now – be silent,' she commanded. Reaching with her mind to the location of the Academy supplies, she poured her powers into an apport spell. There was a flash, a roar of displaced air – and the cellar was filled from floor to ceiling with bags of spilling golden grain.

'Oh – Lady!' The baker's expression told Eliseth everything she needed to know. 'After this I'll do anything for you,' he blurted. 'Anything at all.'

'You already know what I require of you.' The Mage had had enough of the Mortal. She wanted him on his way, and out of Nexis before the morning. Leading him from the cellar, she shut the door firmly behind them and passed a hand across the wood, watching the wardspell shimmer into place like light on water. 'Now,' she told the baker. 'Pay attention. To protect your precious supplies, I have spelled the door and the grating to kill anyone who touches them.'

The baker's avaricious eyes grew round with dismay. 'But, Lady . . .' he stammered.

'As soon as you return, having successfully completed your mission,' Eliseth went on crushingly as though he had not spoken, 'you will report to me at the Academy, and the spell will be removed. That is all. Make your preparations, Mortal, and leave immediately – lest I should be tempted to regret my generosity.'

There was no need to say more. Eliseth knew that he was hers. As she left the bakery, she could no longer hide her smile, thinking of Bern's dismay when he returned from his dangerous assignment to discover that free supplies had been given out by Miathan the very day he had left – and gloating over the thought of the Archmage's baffled fury in the morning, when he discovered that most of his grain supplies had mysteriously vanished.

The slow hours of darkness crawled by as Zanna waited. Now that she had a plan, her spirits fluctuated wildly with an unsettling mix of excitement and trepidation, and she could scarcely wait to leave her hiding-place in the storeroom and get moving. Unfortunately, the last thing she needed at this point was to run into Janok. Zanna knew she would have to curb her impatience as best she could, and wait until everyone – especially the brutal head cook – was sure to be asleep.

181

Getting out of the storeroom in the darkness was a night-mare, but even if Zanna had remembered to bring a candle she dared not risk a light. She was forced to worm her way out of her cramped lair on hands and knees, feeling blindly ahead for the stacked barrels, bags and crocks that turned the room into a maze of hazards. It seemed to take for ever. She was stiff and aching from Janok's beating, and after so long a wait every movement made her muscles scream in protest, but that was the least of her worries right now. Zanna felt lost and disorientated, her head spinning dizzily. Surely it was such a small chamber that she must have reached the wall by now?

Her heart leapt into her mouth as she felt a pile of sacks begin to totter and fall. Reaching up quickly, she tried to steady it, but to no avail. The breath was knocked out of her as several lumpy, laden sacks landed on top of her. Potatoes, from the clean, sharp, earthy smell. For an instant of frozen terror she simply lay there, waiting for the crash that never came, then carefully began to lever herself out from beneath the heavy bags. Thank the gods, she thought as she rubbed her bruises, that one of the crocks didn't go over. After an-other long moment of groping, she scraped her knuckles on a cool rough surface. She had reached the wall at last. She took the best guess she could at the direction in which the door lay, and was lucky. The spaciousness and empty air felt so good beyond her seeking hands. Oh, what a blessing it was to be able to stand up again, and move unhindered. She went slowly down the dark passage, feeling her way with one hand on the wall.

The kitchen, though shrouded in shadow, seemed dange-rously bright after the pitch-black corridor. Dark humped silhouettes against the dim, smoky light of the banked fires showed the positions of sleeping menials, and Zanna found herself thinking it was a measure of Janok's cruelty that he would not permit his few helpers to take over the almost deserted dormitory of the household staff. He goes grovell-ing and creeping around the Magefolk, she thought resentfully, but he treats us worse than animals, because it keeps us cowed so that we do his bidding. And because he enjoys the sense of power . . . Zanna shuddered, and tried to put him out of her mind. The thought of him made her sick and afraid to her very soul.

The door that led from the kitchen into the Great Hall was on the far side of the room. It took more courage than Zanna had known she possessed to cross that broad expanse of kitchen floor. Only the thought of her dad, imprisoned and suffering, could make her take that worst, first step, and keep going thereafter. Guiding herself by the faint glow of the fire, she slid from shadow to shadow towards the door, giving the slumbering menials a wide berth. Though her feet were silent, surely someone must hear the beating of her heart.

As she passed the sinks, a dull gleam of red caught Zanna's eye, as though an ember from the fire had somehow rolled into the shadows underneath the deep stone basins and was slowly dying on the cold damp floor. What in the world . . ? Zanna's heart leapt. It couldn't be, could it? Stooping quickly, she nicked her scrabbling fingers on the razor-keen edge of a long, broad-bladed knife. She snatched it up quickly, her bloody fingers slippery on the smooth bone handle, and felt instantly amazed at the difference a weapon made to her faltering courage. With considerably lifted spirits, the young girl finally gained the door, and slipped gratefully out into the cool, musty darkness of the deserted Great Hall.

Zanna darted over to crouch down beside the panelled wall beneath the overhanging minstrels' gallery. There she stayed for several minutes, until her heart slowed and her breathing steadied and her trembling stilled. Though a little light filtered from outside through the row of tall windows to illuminate the stark black columns of the double row of pillars, the vast, echoing chamber seemed very dark after the half-light of the kitchen. As she waited for her eyes to adjust to the difference, Zanna turned her weapon over and over in her hand. She supposed it must have been knocked from the table or the bench and accidentally kicked beneath the sink, where it had been lost in the shadows until that stray gleam of firelight had picked it out for her eyes. Janok must truly have been preoccupied today, if he had not noticed it was missing. Usually, he kept a careful tally of the knives.

The thought of the brutal head cook was enough to spur Zanna into action once more. Levering herself away from the wall, she turned to her right and made for the corner where an elegant spiral of open wooden steps curled round a carven pillar and led up to the minstrel's gallery. There was no way to get up those steps silently – the Great Hall had been designed to carry sound. Zanna froze, horrified and startled, as the hollow shuffle of her footsteps was magnified into sibilant echoes that whispered around the massive chamber. She had to take herself sternly in hand and remind herself that she was the only one there before she could find the courage to continue.

Luckily, the gallery itself was carpeted for the comfort of visiting musicians. Zanna finally gave in to her wild urge to run. Holding the knife carefully at arm's length, she pelted down the long side of the hall, through the flickering patches of dark and light made by the line of windows. Turning left at the bottom, she found the curtained upper door that led to a short corridor and thence through another, plainer door into the quarters of the household servants.

Had Zanna but known it, she was lucky. In Elewin's day, both doors had been securely locked, except when the hall was in use, to prevent the servants' taking a shortcut through the hallowed chamber from their quarters to the kitchen. Now, however, the dormitory had so few occupants that such traditions had been permitted to slide. The second door opened for Zanna, as she had been confident it would, and she permitted herself a sigh of relief at last. Nothing could stop her now. Because of the two closed doors and the stretch of corridor between, she didn't hear the sound of the kitchen door opening into the Great Hall, and softly closing again.

On a shelf at a convenient height beside the door, Zanna found a tinderbox and candlestick. Laying her knife down on the shelf, she lit the candle after several shaky attempts, and then cursed her own stupidity. What if someone – even the Archmage, she thought with a terrified shudder – should be crossing the courtyard, and see the gleam? Shielding the flame with her cupped hand she ran to close the curtains across the three windows spaced at regular intervals down the length of the dormitory. Once that was done, Zanna felt much more secure. Lifting her candle high, she passed the lonely row of neat and unused beds and crossed back to the corner near the door, where the rack of twinkling crystals glittered with cold fire as they caught her tiny flame. Holding her light close to the gems, she moved her hand along the rack until she found a glimmer of green.

At last! Vannor's daughter replaced the candle on the shelf and was reaching out to take the crystal when the door burst open with a crash.

'Got you, you little bitch!' Rough hands spun her and grabbed her arms with bruising force, making Zanna cry out with pain. Struggling was useless, against that enormous strength. The candlelight made red reflected gleams in Janok's eyes, giving him the look of some brutish wild beast. Zanna's mind went blank with terror. It was all over now. He had caught her here in this deserted place where there were no witnesses and no one would hear her screams.

Janok chuckled, enjoying her fears. His hands tightened around the tender flesh of her arms, making her whimper. 'Well?' he said. 'And why are we creeping around the servants' dormitory in the darkness, I wonder? Were you trying to find a lover, by any chance? I'll wager you've never had one, such a plain little thing as you are; but you're a year too late, my girl. All those fine, handsome young men have left or been slain and there's no one in this place to bed you. No one but me, that is.'

What would anger him more? To reply or not? Zanna had little time to reflect on the decision. His hand lashed out, hitting her, hurting her. She felt a warm trickle of blood crawl down her chin. Janok was pressing his weight against her, pinning her body against the wall. His hairy arms encompassed her; his sweaty body was pressed against her flesh. She could feel the moisture, warm and clammy, seeping through the thin fabric of her blouse, and swallowed down on the acid nausea that came boiling into her throat.

His foul breath, and the greasy stench of his unwashed body, made her retch.

Janok pushed at her lower body, hard and excited. Zanna tugged one hand free and jabbed at his eyes with rigid fingers, but he caught her wrist in a merciless grip and held her hand, helpless, above her head. Holding her in place with one arm and his knee, he ripped at her clothing, pulling her blouse away in tatters. Zanna felt cold air wash over her breasts and turned her head away, aghast as his rough fingers squeezed her flesh. Then the hand was fumbling lower, lifting up her skirts and feeling underneath. She knew what would come to her now: had she not seen it happen, many times, to helpless, shrieking, weeping kitchen maids?

Zanna wriggled helplessly, desperate to escape. Against his size and strength her efforts were hopeless, but they angered him none the less. Enraged and excited, he slammed the back of her head against the wall, and from the corner of her eye she saw the crystals tumble from the rack. Their fiery glitter in the shivering candlelight matched the dazzling dark-bright pain that shot through her skull. Aurian, she thought desperately, but the Mage was far too far away to help. It was all up to Zanna now – and what could she do against a man so much bigger and stronger than herself?

Again Janok hit her, first with his open hand across her face, then, when that failed to cow her, two or three lower blows with his fist. That stopped the fight in her. Zanna sagged against the wall, gasping for breath, his strong grasp all that kept her from doubling up in agony. Briefly, she was beyond all conscious thought.

'Now!' With an iron grip on one arm, Janok dragged her towards the nearest row of beds. An odd, dizzy, disconnected thought shot through Zanna's innocent mind: after all his brutality, why was he being so particular now? He might as well have knocked her to the floor, and taken her, and had done with it. Then Janok threw her face-down on the bed, keeping her pinned down with one hand while his other groped to free himself from his fetters of clothing.

This momentary distraction was all that Zanna had been

waiting for. She had gone beyond reason and was working on pure instinct – and it was all the more unexpected to Janok, for he thought he had her cowed beyond resistance. Writhing away from the palm that pressed her down, she managed to turn herself half around, and bit into the arm that held her with all her might. Janok howled, cursing, flailing at her with his free hand, making her vision explode into stars. Zanna held on grimly. Coarse black hairs tickled her throat, and the salt metallic taste of his blood made her retch, but she still hung on, biting deeper and deeper. It was her only chance to escape him. What had she to lose? In a surprisingly short time Janok relaxed his grip and she slid out from underneath.

Tripping over the tatters of her skirt, Zanna scrambled, half-stumbling, across the room, the head cook's grasping hands and bruising fists snatching at the air an instant behind her. She had only one thought in her mind as she shot towards the door – and the shelf nearby. In the moment that it took to haul herself up by the smooth, slippery edge, Janok had laid hands on her again; but Zanna's groping fingers had knocked down the tinderbox, and found the knife that she had laid down only minutes before.

The girl could sense Janok's surprise – almost disappointment – as she ceased to fight him. 'Ah,' he muttered, pressing her body against the wall. 'I knew you wanted it. Of course. They always do.'

'Yes,' she murmured, 'but I would like to see your face.'

'Naturally.'

Zanna felt his hard hands upon her as he turned her round. She felt him press against her, even as her fingers clenched about the knife that was half-hidden in the torn remnants of her skirt. Then the blade was embedded hilt-deep in his belly, and Janok doubled up, screaming, his blood gushing out all over her hands. At that moment, Zanna felt nothing but a burning, all-consuming hatred. Remembering something that Parric had told her long ago, she took a firm grip on the slippery haft and thrust the knife downwards with all her strength, to slice the blade into Janok's guts. He fell to the floor, shrieking and clutching

187

himself, rolling and writhing in the spreading pool of his own blood.

It was taking him a long time to die. Zanna, frozen with shock, felt a stab of panic. What if someone heard him? She had to get out, and fast. There was no time to look for the correct crystal – she simply gathered them all as she found them, crawling on her hands and knees to scoop up the scattered gems and dropping them into a twist of cloth torn from her ruined skirt. As soon as she had them all, she fled out of the door opposite the one she'd entered.

Without any thought now for stealth, Zanna clattered down the wooden staircase and into the refectory below. There she paused, shudders running through her, with her back pressed against the outer door like a hunted beast at bay. Her head was whirling and her knees had turned to water. She looked down at the stinking, sticky blood that coated her hands and the front of her body, and doubled over sharply, vomiting. When she had emptied herself, she straightened shakily, automatically wiping her mouth on her bloody arm – an act that set her retching again. Zanna took great, gulping gasps of air and forced herself to be steady. So she had killed a man; well, there was no leisure to think about that now. Her dad needed her, and time was running out.

All sounds from the floor above had ceased. Slowly, Zanna began to realize that if Janok's screams had been heard, then someone would have come long before now. The remoteness of the servants' quarters from both the kitchen and the guardpost at the far side of the courtyard had saved her. Relief washed over her. She dropped to her knees in a patch of moonlight from the window, wishing that she'd had the sense to remember the candle. Well, she'd just have to wish. She wasn't going back up there, past Janok's body, to get it – not for anything.

The crystals rattled on the wooden floorboards as she spilled them from their makeshift bag. They all twinkled enigmatically in the dim, cold light, but only two held sparks of bright fire in their hearts: the crimson and blue-silver gems. But somewhere among them was another, which held a slumbering spark of green. One by one Zanna held them up to the moonlight, peering into their jewelled depths, until she found the one she sought. Kneeling like a statue in the beam of light, she cupped the crystal in her hands, and, with a prayer to all the gods she knew, she concentrated on the image of the Lady Aurian.

12
A Cry for Help

What Aurian liked best about the Xandim fastness was the
way in which the interior was completely at odds with the
outside. Though the exterior of the massive structure stood
foursquare and blocky, consisting of straight lines and sharp
angles, it was revealed, to any with the eyes to see, that within
those walls the building was not an inanimate human artefact
after all, but a living being. The passages and chambers had
floors and walls that grew into one another with no visible
join, ceilings that were vaulted and ribbed with what looked
like arching bone; everything from windows to fireplaces,
from lintels to torch-brackets, from the benches that grew
out of the walls at comfortable human sitting-height to the
broad stone shelves that the Xandim covered with fleeces
and heather to make comfortable beds, possessed a seamless
fluidity of line that could only be organic in nature.

Chiamh had housed the Magefolk and their companions
in a complex of rooms towards the rear of the fastness, in a
square turret that rose above the main bulk of the building
and abutted the cliffs that towered behind. There were two
floors in the squat tower, each consisting of an interlinking
cluster of small chambers reached by a twisting staircase with
a heavy door at the bottom that blocked off access to the turret. The quarters were cramped but cosy and easier to heat
than the vast, echoing rooms in the main part of the building,
and everyone felt a measure of security in staying together.
Even Parric, much to the evident annoyance of the Xandim
Elders, had rejected the Herdlord's official quarters in
favour of lodging with his friends.

Aurian and Anvar shared two chambers on the upper
storey with Shia, Khanu and the wolves; Bohan and Yazour
occupied the room adjoining and Chiamh slept in an annexe

beyond. Schiannath and Iscalda, still somewhat unsure of
their position among the Xandim after their exile, had
elected to remain with the Magefolk, and shared the lower
floor with Parric, Sangra and Elewin, before the old steward
had passed away. Following Elewin's death, Yazour had
decided to move downstairs to be near Schiannath and
Iscalda, with whom he had become fast friends. This alle-
viated some of the overcrowding on the upper storey, for the
great cats took up an astonishing amount of space, and the
wolves preferred to claim a small territory of their own, away
from too much human disturbance. They had a den beneath
the table, where they had scratched up and shredded an area
of the woven rush matting to create a bed that Aurian had
augmented with the remains of her tattered threadbare old
cloak.

Chiamh, considering the needs of the non-humans of the
party, had chosen these quarters with great care. The gap
between the window in Bohan's room and the cliff face was
little longer than two spans, and he had constructed a rough
but functional bridge across the intervening space from a
sturdy plank lashed securely into position. Shia, Khanu and
the wolves could cross this and gain access to a series of narrow ledges and trails that led on to the broader reaches of the
Wyndveil, where they could hunt and roam as they pleased
without having to run the gauntlet of the Xandim camped
both within and without the fastness.

Though Aurian and Anvar had not been in these quarters
long, their small chamber was already cluttered with signs of
their occupancy. Leaning heavily on Parric's authority as
Herdlord, they were putting together a new set of gear for
their northward journey. Piles of clothing lay across the bed
and benches, including britches and tunics of soft leather;
shirts, of linen and of wool; boots of sturdy but supple hide;
and long, thick mantles of woven wool, dyed in the mingled
greens and golds of the grasslands, with additional cloaks of
thin oiled hide that would pack small in a saddlebag, to wear
when it rained.

To Aurian, the room looked warm and homely. A soot-
smeared copper pot of water steamed gently at the edge of

the blaze in the great fireplace. The table was scattered with plates and cups made of horn or bone; a jug of water, a flagon of ale and a flask of mead; small leather pouches of dried berries, blossoms and leaves for making a variety of teas; and emergency supplies of bread, cheese and fruit, because it was such a long trek to the stillrooms and the pantries.

The Staff of Earth and the Harp of Winds had been propped against the wall in the furthest corner of the Mages' bed, safely away from curious hands and careless feet. Their mingled radiance, a changeful amalgam of green and shimmering silver, conflicted with the warmer, saffron glow of lamps and fire, to cast a rippling light like the sun through beech leaves across the faces of those assembled in the chamber.

Aurian and Anvar, seated on the bed with Wolf in Aurian's lap, were listening in wide-eyed amazement to Basileus recounting the history of the Moldai. Shia and Khanu had not yet returned from visiting Hreeza on Steelclaw and Bohan was asleep next door. Parric and Sangra, unable to participate in the weird, four-way mental conversation of Mages, Moldan and Windeye, had gone off together to drink to the memory of Elewin. Chiamh, who had heard Basileus tell his tale before, was barely paying attention to the Elemental's words. Instead he was peering with rapt fascination at the game the Magefolk were idly playing between themselves as they listened to the Moldan speak.

Aurian would lift her hand to let a small green fireball materialize like an unfolding blossom above her palm, and with a quick, flicking gesture would launch it into the air. Obeying the dictates of her will, it would dive and dodge in a swift, twisting path between hangings, sconces, and furnishings. Anvar would follow suit with an incandescent globe of his own in blue fire, and would send it after Aurian's fireball, trying to catch the glowing sphere as it darted to and fro across the chamber; the difficulties of fine control being compounded, of course, by the fact that both Mages were also paying attention to the Moldan's words. Aurian was using this game to help her soulmate improve his facility with Fire-magic – never his strong point, and a form of power that could not be boosted by the Hard of Winds, whose element was Air. Chiamh, squinting critically up at Anvar's wavering, sloppy efforts, which had a tendency to weave and plunge erratically around the room emitting a trail of cobalt sparks, decided that the Mage was badly in need of the practice.

As the Moldan's tale unfolded, however, the participants gradually forgot about their game, and left their fireballs to bob aimless and neglected, clustering like a swarm of fireflies against the ribbed stone of the ceiling. There was no doubt that Aurian and Anvar were both enthralled, and Chiamh admired both the power and the cunning of the Earth-Elemental in being able to distract Aurian, in particular, from asking some very awkward questions.

Aurian, however, had a whole series of questions that she did want to ask Basileus. Though she was still annoyed by the Moldan's refusal to disclose the substance of his private conversation with Chiamh, she trusted the Windeye and was beginning to trust Basileus; moreover, she recognized immovable stubbornness when she saw it. As Anvar had slyly reminded her, such obduracy was part of her own character. Though the Moldan had assured her that what he had discussed with Chiamh was a matter for the Xandim, and nothing to concern her, it was her nature as a Mage to be curious, and to want to meddle, none the less. That same curiosity, however, had led her to shelve the matter for the time being (she would probably stand a better chance of prying the information out of Chiamh anyway) in favour of the incredible experience of conversing with a being who was as old as the hills themselves.

'And you say this mad Moldan is imprisoned under the Academy?' she asked Basileus in shocked tones.

'Indeed he is, and has been for many a long age. If Ghabal was mad before, I can scarcely imagine his state of mind by now.'

Anvar, who had been lucky to survive a confrontation with one of the powerful Earth-Elementals, and had also spent hundreds of hours down those very tunnels with Finbarr, was similarly horrified. 'Gods, I hope Miathan doesn't find it down there.' He shuddered. 'Such a discovery might solve our difficulties where the Archmage is concerned, but it'll leave us with worse problems than ever – if there's even a city left to return to, that is.' With a chill, he wondered if Basileus knew about his battle with the Moldan of Aerillia Peak – and how the Moldan might react if he found out.

'Don't go borrowing trouble,' Aurian warned him, referring not to the words that he had spoken aloud, but to the small, scared thought that she had picked out of her soulmate's mind. Before Anvar could reply, however, Aurian was sure she heard another mental voice – a thin, weak call that seemed to come from very far away.

'Did anyone else pick that up?' the Mage asked sharply.

'Pick up what?' Anvar sounded puzzled.

'I could have sworn I heard, very faintly in my mind, a strange voice calling my name.'

I heard nothing,' said the Moldan.

'Nor I.' Chiamh shook his head.

'I must have been imagining things.' Aurian rubbed her eyes. 'Maybe it's time we all got some sleep. We've another difficult day tomorrow ... There it is again!'

Signalling the others to be silent, she closed her eyes, straining her mind to catch the elusive wisp of thought: that faint and faraway calling of her name. For a moment there was nothing. Had she imagined it? But no. Suddenly it came again:

'Lady ... Lady Aurian? Oh, please be there. Please answer me – *please.*'

'There *is* someone there – and she's calling for help,' Aurian told her companions. 'It's very faint, but with the Staff to boost my power I can probably reach her.' Quickly, the Mage leaned back across the bed to reach the Artefact.

'Be careful,' Anvar warned. 'What if it's Eliseth? She might be trying to trap you again, as she did in the desert.'

Aurian scowled, not liking to recall the time the Weather-Mage had almost duped her into killing both herself and Anvar. 'I almost hope it is Eliseth,' she said grimly. 'Now that I have my powers back, she'll find me a very different proposition from last time.'

As her fingers closed round the Staff, the Mage felt its power run glowing through her veins like molten fire. Her own magic blazed up fiercely within her, augmented by the strength of the Artefact. 'Anvar, Chiamh,' she said quickly, 'take hold of the Staff so you can link your minds to mine. Whatever this is, I want you to hear it too.' As she felt their thoughts join her own, she closed her eyes and concentrated all her power on the faint and faraway whisper.

When Aurian stretched forth her consciousness towards the distant cry, the mental voice seemed to leap towards her, as though the caller had been shut away in another room, and a door had suddenly opened between the two. The summoner sounded desperate now, and close to tears.

'Here I am,' Aurian cut through the anguished pleading. 'Who are you?'

'Lady Aurian? Is it really you? Oh, thank the gods! I didn't think I'd ever find you. Lady – it's me, Zanna. Vannor's daughter.'

'*What?* How in the world have you managed to reach me like this?'

'Through a crystal, Lady. The ones you used to summon the servants in the Academy. I disguised myself as a servant and came here to spy on the Magefolk, but now the Archmage has captured dad . . .'

With mounting horror, Aurian listened to Zanna's story. How long had it been, she wondered guiltily, since she had spared even a thought for Vannor? She had always been fond of the merchant, and the thought of him, helpless and suffering in the cruel hands of Miathan and Eliseth, made her blood run cold. And as for Zanna . . . The Mage was staggered by the courage and daring the young girl had shown – and appalled to discover that she herself had set the example that Vannor's daughter had been trying to follow. Why, she's little more than a child, thought the Mage – and was rapidly forced to revise her opinion as Zanna told her how Janok had met his end.

'But someone may discover that he's missing at any time,' Zanna finished, 'and I've got to get dad out tonight – there'll never be another chance. But how can I get him out of the Mages' Tower, and even if I do, what then? Dad told me there's a way out through the tunnels underneath the library,

195

but the door to the archives is always locked, and I can't get in.'

'Yes you can,' Aurian told her quickly, 'and I'll tell you how to do it. But keep the crystal with you, just in case you need to speak with me again. Besides,' she added with a smile, 'I'll want to know how everything works out. Now listen carefully, Zanna. This is what you must do . . .'

When she had completed her instructions to the girl, Aurian took leave of Zanna with some misgivings. She had tried to remain encouraging and positive, but in her heart she knew there was a great deal that could go wrong with Vannor's escape.

'Try not to worry too much,' Anvar told her. 'You've done all you can, and Zanna lacks neither common sense nor courage. Imagine, a young lass like that killing Janok!' His eyes lit up with savage joy, and Aurian remembered how he had suffered at the brutal head cook's hands – and indeed how his ordeal had led to their own meeting.

Before she had time to reply, however, her thoughts were knocked out of her head by a stentorian mental bellow loud enough to rattle her brains within her skull.

'Aurian – quick! Your misbegotten Horsefolk are shooting at us!' The voice that roared through the Mage's mind had come from Shia.

'Damn and blast them!' Almost before the words had passed her lips, Aurian had returned Wolf to his foster-parents and was out of the chamber with Anvar a split-second behind her. Chiamh came groping after them as quickly as he could manage, but he had more sense than to call on them to wait. Instead, he hammered on the door of Parric's chambers to warn the Herdlord of impending trouble. Parric and Sangra, fortunately not yet the worse for ale, came out at once, followed by a tousled Iscalda, rubbing sleepy eyes. Schiannath and Yazour, however, were nowhere to be found.

The Mages had scarcely reached the bottom of the stairway when they were halted by an urgent warning from the Moldan: *Wizards – beware. The Xandim have taken up arms against you and the Herdlord. They already hold the outer doors, and are heading this way even as we speak.*

196

Anvar muttered a livid curse. As one, the two Mages dodged back upstairs, barring the door behind them. Already, Aurian was in contact with Shia; the cats, relying on their night-vision, had managed, so far, to dodge the arrows and had retreated partway up the cliff path. Apparently the Xandim bowmen were trying to pluck up enough courage to pursue them – a foolhardy business in the daylight, let alone in darkness. The Mage quickly told Shia what was happening within the fastness and warned her friend not to come any closer. 'If they keep after you, head for Chiamh's valley – once you've passed the standing stones they won't dare follow you further.'

'Only if there's no alternative,' Shia insisted. 'I want to be near enough to help if you need me.'

On the first landing, they met Chiamh and the others, looking grim. 'Schiannath and Yazour are somewhere within the fastness,' the Windeye told the Mages. 'They must be found and warned, if it's not already too late.'

It is not,' the Moldan told those who could hear him. '*They went to the stillrooms by the back route. As yet they are undiscovered.*'

When Chiamh passed on the message, Iscalda shouldered her way forward. 'I will go. Schiannath is my brother.'

'Wait.' Anvar stopped her with a hand on her arm. 'I'll go. Basileus can guide me to them.' Seeing Aurian opening her mouth to volunteer, he was quick to forestall her. 'No, love. I'm the obvious choice – you're still recouping your energy after being wounded and then fighting on Steelclaw. I'll be much quicker on my own.'

Aurian scowled. 'Blast you,' she muttered. 'I hate it when you're right. Take care, then – and hurry back.' She went with him to the bottom of the stairs and hugged him hard before letting him out. Anvar heard the thud of the bar dropping back into place behind him, and shivered. Suddenly he felt very exposed, and very much alone. 'You and your bloody heroics,' he muttered to himself. Turning to his left, he sped off down the passage on flying feet. The sooner he got back behind the dubious security of that thick oak door, the better he'd feel.

Schiannath had been showing Yazour around the vaults beneath the stillrooms; in particular, that part of the network of cellars where the Xandim stored their supplies of ale and mead. Though the actual kitchens of the massive building were very basic, because the Horsefolk preferred to do most of their cooking – and eating, for that matter – in the open air, each wandering band was expected to supply a tithe of the fruits of their hunting and gathering to be stored in the fastness, to feed those, such as the old and the sick, who dwelt within. These inhabitants, who usually could not hunt for themselves, worked to preserve the food, so that a store of provisions was always on hand for emergencies such as drought or siege.

The old folk were also the brewers of the tribe, trading the results of their labours for other necessities from the hunters and craftsmen. Their stocks of liquor, though generally un-guarded, were carefully tallied and fairly distributed in a system of barter which most of the Xandim were content to honour. Nevertheless, when Schiannath and Yazour, sitting swapping battle yarns late into the night, had run out of ale, the former outlaw had not thought twice about an expedition to the vaults to 'liberate' some more. Had Yazour but known it, this was just the sort of misdemeanour that had always been getting his friend into trouble with the Elders and the Herdlord in Schiannath's younger days.

Despite the Xandim's airy assurances that there was nothing to worry about, Yazour felt a creeping sense of un-ease as they hauled open the great trapdoor in the back of the furthest stillroom, and ventured down the flight of smooth stone steps that led into the vaults. At first, he simply decided that the ale he had already consumed was inflaming his imagination. It was cold underground, and the air had a dry, dead, heavy feel. As they walked along the low, arched passage at the bottom, the stealthy patter of their footfalls was echoed over and over by the rounded walls, until they were surrounded by a sound like the beating of hundreds of soft wings. The amber flame of the torch that flickered in Schiannath's upraised hand chased the silver veining in the stone with threads of gold, and sent their shadows leaping up

the curving walls like beings with a life of their own, reminding Yazour, most unpleasantly, of Aurian's harrowing,
blood-chilling tales of the Death-Wraiths.

With every step he took, the young captain's sense of unease was growing. He put it down to the uncomfortable,
closed-in feeling of being underground, with the awareness
of the gigantic mass of stone above his head; but when he
and his companion reached the place where the vaults
opened out around them into a maze of interconnecting cellars divided by great arches of pillared stone, his warrior's
sense of unseen danger increased. Anyone – or any*thing*, he
thought uncomfortably – could hide in this labyrinth of
chambers, and sneak up on its prey unseen.

'The food comes first,' Schiannath's whisper made Yazour
jump like a startled rabbit. 'They store the ale further in,' the
Xandim continued, oblivious of the effect he was having on
his friend's overstretched nerves. 'They hope that we out-
siders will get lost before we find it.'

As he walked on through the cobwebbed, cavernlike
chambers stacked haphazardly with barrels, chests and sacks,
Yazour inwardly mocked himself for being such an old
granny. Look at Schiannath, he told himself. He isn't scared
of the dark! As an attempt to buoy his courage, it was singu-
larly unsuccessful. Try as he would, he could not shake the
crawling between his shoulderblades that told him he was the
target of unseen eyes. But having followed his companion so
far now, there was no way he could retreat without looking
like a cowardly fool. He would rather die than lose face
before Schiannath – and, more important, Schiannath's
sister, when she should come to hear the tale. The sooner
they found the wretched ale, the sooner they could be gone –
and so Yazour clenched his jaw, loosened his sword in its
sheath, and continued to follow the Xandim.

Then out of nowhere came a puff of wind, and the torch
went out. Darkness fell around them, so thick and heavy that
it seemed as though some god had dropped a velvet cloak
across the world.

'Plague take it!' Schiannath cursed, his words drowning
his companion's gasp of shock. Yazour, fighting panic, could

199

hear the Xandim swearing softly as he groped for flint and striker, and then a tiny, metallic clatter as one or both implements fell to the floor.

'You clumsy fool,' Yazour hissed in a ferocious whisper, groping in his tunic for his own firemaking tools with hands that trembled. In the Reaper's name, where had he stowed that blasted flint? He couldn't stand the way this darkness pressed in on him – and without some form of light they stood little chance of finding their way out of the cellars at all.

Schiannath, it seemed, had been thinking along similar lines. 'Well, at least we won't starve down here,' he muttered.

The grim humour did much to restore Yazour's courage. 'If we could only find that accursed ale, it wouldn't matter how long we had to stay. And that's just as well,' he added sheepishly, 'since the idiot who called you a fool seems to have left his firemaking gear in his other tunic.'

Schiannath burst out laughing. Yazour felt a hand brush his sleeve in the darkness, and then his companion's strong, warm fingers tightly clasped his own.

'It won't do to get separated,' the Xandim said softly. 'Now – I'm going to move to my left, until we find a wall to guide us.' Using the wall to navigate, they turned themselves round and began the hopeless business of trying to backtrack their way through the cellars.

It was hard to keep track of time in the darkness. It seemed to Yazour that they had been groping their way blindly forward for hours, though he knew, from his lack of hunger and thirst and the reserves of strength he still possessed, that it could not be possible. None the less, when he caught the first faint faraway glimpses of torchlight bobbing enticingly ahead of him in the depths of the vaults, he could have fallen on his knees and wept with gratitude. A hoarse, glad cry from Schiannath proved that the Xandim had seen them too. As one, still clasping each other's hands, the two rushed forward together, yelling to attract attention. Yazour and Schiannath only discovered that they had drawn the wrong kind of attention to themselves when they ran headlong into a ring of bristling steel.

With the help of Basileus, Anvar found his way through the snarl of torchlit corridors that branched like arteries within the heart of the fastness. The further he went, the narrower, dustier and less well lit the passages became, until he needed his Mage's night-vision and was forced to slow his pace because of the worn and cracked stone floor. In the same way that he had once guided Chiamh through his ventilation ducts, the Moldan sent a slip of glowing vapour ahead to mark the route at every intersection; but Anvar still found himself thinking ungratefully that the Earth-Elemental could have made his innards a great deal less complex. The Mage's own innards churned with tension even as he ran. Though Basileus had promised to warn him of the proximity of any armed foes, he was half-expecting to run into trouble around every blind corner. After what seemed an age, he had still not reached a turning he recognized. 'Are you sure this is the right way?' he demanded of Basileus.

'I am taking you through the old back corridors,' the Moldan replied testily. 'Unless you would prefer the quicker route, which is swarming with Xandim warriors.'

'In that case, this route is fine – so long as we get there in time.'

'We are too late to prevent your companions from being captured, but as yet they are unharmed. They were followed to the vaults and ambushed there, for I had no way to warn them. I tried to conceal them by blowing out their torch, but alas, it only made them walk into the hands of their captors, believing they were being rescued.' The Moldan sighed. 'The mistake was mine,' he confessed. 'The ways of Mortals are still strange to me, though I believe that ultimately my interference has made little difference. Yazour and Schiannath are being held under guard in the stillrooms until the rest of you have been taken.'

'What? Why the blazes didn't you warn me they had been captured?' Anvar protested.

'I am warning you.' Basileus sounded completely unruffled. 'To worry you sooner would have served no purpose. Now, Wizard, stop and pay attention. The next two turnings will bring you to the stillrooms. You must prepare yourself to fight.'

In the stairwell of the turret, Aurian and her companions

201

were also preparing themselves. She and Parric were guarding the door, listening with mounting dismay to the growing clamour of hostile voices on the other side. Already, their surrender had been demanded, and denied. Sangra and Iscalda waited with drawn swords further up the staircase, while Bohan remained in the Mages' chamber guarding Wolf. The Windeye was sitting slumped like a rag doll on the bottom step, his spirit gone from his body to ride on the slip of draught that blew around the edges of the oaken door, to watch the enemy assemble on the other side.

'Lady, they are armed with swords, bows and axes.' His voice echoed hollowly in Aurian's mind. 'They carry torches, too. We cannot hold them off for long, especially if they use fire. We must prepare to flee.'

Aurian gritted her teeth. 'Curse you, Chiamh, I'm not fleeing anywhere. Not without Anvar.' Beside her she felt the cavalry master stiffen, and before he had a chance to open his mouth she snarled: 'Whatever it is, Parric, I don't want to hear it.'

Chiamh's eyes snapped open as he returned to his body. 'I do not propose that we abandon Anvar. Nonetheless, we must prepare,' he told her firmly. 'Our only possible exit from this trap is the way the animals take – across the plank.'

Aurian's blood ran cold at the thought of that fragile makeshift bridge, and the narrowness of the fingerhold ledges and crumbling goat trails beyond. Her curses drowned out the rest of Chiamh's words, and were drowned in their turn by the crunch of an axe blade biting deep into the door. Before anyone had time to react, the panels juddered beneath another heavy blow.

'Come out, you traitorous freak, before I come in to get you and those skulking outland scum that you've befriended.'

A third splintering crash sent a thin crack snaking down the wooden panel.

Chiamh's mild brown eyes sparked bright with anger. 'Galdrus! I might have guessed,' the Windeye muttered. 'Come out, indeed! We'll see about that.' His eyes flared silver as he twisted the whistling draught to form an illusion and strained to project it simultaneously to the other side of the door.

202

The Mage, in the meantime, was projecting her own thoughts to seek the minds of the wolves upstairs. Quickly she transmitted an image of their danger, followed by a series of mental pictures that showed them picking up Wolf and taking him across the bridge, up the cliffs and across the plateau to the safety of Chiamh's vale. So long as they were quick enough to dodge the eunuch they would be all right, and she knew that Bohan, who had always vied with them jealously for the care of her son, would follow the wolves to safety; though (she prayed to all the gods) he would not be quick enough to catch them.

As an afterthought, she made brief contact with Shia, who, as Aurian had suspected, was still waiting with Khanu at the top of the cliff path.

'Are you mad?' the great cat muttered when the Mage had explained her plan. 'Oh, never mind – I'll come down to help them, before that clumsy great ox falls off the cliff or chops someone's head off by mistake. Khanu will guard the cliff path, though your chicken-hearted grass-eaters have shown no signs of approaching us so far.'

Shia and the eunuch had always shared a special bond, and Aurian felt easier in her mind knowing that the cat was on hand to guide and help him. Having done the best she could for Wolf and Bohan, she stifled a pang of fear for the eunuch, who would be forced to scale those perilous cliffs in darkness, and turned back to assist Chiamh, who was clearly struggling with difficulties of his own.

Bohan was standing, rigid with tension, near the door of the Mages' chamber, straining his ears to catch a hint of sound from the stairwell to let him know what was happening two floors below. His sword, clutched in one enormous hand, looked like a toy against his massive bulk as he guarded the wolves who protected Aurian's son.

From their den beneath the table, two pairs of eyes, flashing green with reflected firelight, observed the eunuch even as he was watching them. The she-wolf crouched slightly behind her mate, shielding the cub that was their charge. It was not such an easy task as it seemed. In the past few days

Wolf's eyes had opened properly, and he had turned into a small grey bundle of curiosity, exploring his surroundings on stubby, unsteady legs with the relentless fervour of all new creatures. And like all new creatures who have been cosseted and protected from birth, he had no idea now of the danger that faced him. He could recognize the shape and scent of Bohan, familiar and loved, who stood nearby, and he wanted to play. Time and again he tried to escape his guardian and reach the eunuch, and repeatedly the she-wolf stopped him with a firm paw and a soft but warning growl, making the cub whimper in frustration.

Bohan stiffened at the sound of Wolf's distress. He'd always hated to relinquish responsibility for the cub to its lupine foster-parents. Lacking Aurian's Mageborn facility for communicating with the wolves, he saw them only as dangerous wild animals, and did not trust them. The main flaw in his thinking – that Wolf himself was such a beast – he discounted. The cub was Aurian's son, enchanted, and one day he would be returned to human shape. If Bohan's beloved Lady had said so, that was good enough for him.

Wolf whimpered again, and the eunuch scowled, fighting the urge to scoop up the cub and put him safely in his deep tunic pocket, as he had so often done. He half-stooped to peer beneath the table, and the male wolf met his approach with a warning snarl that made Bohan take a hasty step backwards from sheer surprise. As a rule, the wolves seemed well aware of those with whom they shared their guardianship, and treated Aurian's companions as part of their new pack.

With a sudden flash of bone-white fangs, the wolf leapt for the eunuch's throat. Bohan, already off balance, threw himself backwards, his sword flailing fruitlessly at empty air as he fell. In an instant of blinding terror, he waited for the ripping teeth to sink into his flesh, but his attacker was no longer there. The she-wolf, with the cub dangling from her jaws by the loose fur on his neck, was dashing towards the open window, her mate a flashing silver shadow at her heels. In a bound, they reached the sill and were gone.

Bohan's mind roared out the bellow of rage and anguish that his mute throat could not voice. Aurian had trusted him to protect her son and he had failed her. Without pausing to think of the consequences, he ran to the window and climbed out on to the slender makeshift bridge.

A dew of sweat glittered on Chiamh's brow, reflecting the eldritch silver blaze of his eyes as he fought to maintain his phantasm on the other side of the door. He had given up his demon – they were far too familiar now with that apparition – in favour of an image of Shia, who stood snarling before the door with her long black tail lashing and her eyes flashing crimson fire above her bared and fearsome teeth. At first it had duped the hostile mob – he had heard their cries of fear and alarm through the thick wooden panels, and for some minutes now the axe-blows on the door had ceased. But the deception couldn't last much longer. In order to maintain the illusion, he had to keep his mind within his body, but without being able to see what was on the other side of the panels he had no idea of the accuracy of the image he projected, nor how he should make it act in response to what was taking place. It was extremely difficult, in any case, to work at all, let alone on such an ambitious scale, with the slender tendrils of draught that were the only air currents small enough to pass through the sides of the door frame.

All too soon, they saw through the deception. There was a chorus of jeering yells and angry curses from the other side of the door, and suddenly the axe came smashing down again to bite into the weakening wood. Muttering a vile oath that he had learned from Parric, Chiamh braced himself and tried once more. The phantasm was Aurian herself this time, her green eyes blazing, the Staff of Earth in her hand emitting bolts of emerald fire. Again, the Windeye heard the stifled sounds of a scrambled retreat, but his relief was short-lived. He leapt back with a curse, his illusion crumbling away to nothing, as blows rained down on the door, which was beginning to splinter under the repeated assaults. Now what?

The Windeye felt a cool hand on his arm and turned to find himself face to face with Aurian. Her presence startled him – he had been concentrating so hard that he had forgotten she was there. 'Here – let me help.' The Mage raised her hand, her eyes narrowed in concentration, and the thunder of axe-blows ceased. There was a sudden, ominous silence on the other side of the door.

'What did you do?' Chiamh gasped.

'I took your would-be woodman out of time.' Her eyes glittered in the gloom with a dangerous light. 'That should give them something to think about for a while.'

Chiamh sagged against the wall, only realizing now how much his previous efforts had exhausted him. 'Couldn't you take them all out of time?' he ventured hopefully. 'Just until we escape?'

'Would that I could.' Aurian shook her head regretfully. 'I can only work the spell on one thing at a time, and within a very short distance. Once I had taken out a few of them, the rest would simply retreat out of range and wait to ambush us when we came out. We need Anvar to do more – with the Harp he has the power to freeze a number of enemies, as he did the other night. He left it behind, but it's attuned to him, as the Staff is to me. There are rules governing the use of the Artefacts. I can't wield it alone without wresting it from his control, and that's not only dangerous in itself, but for other reasons it's the last thing we would want to –'

Their assailants had found their courage again. Both Mage and Windeye leapt back, retreating in a frantic scramble up the stairs, as a hail of arrows thudded into the door. 'Blast them!' Aurian cried, as she heard the telltale crackle of flame. Already the smell of burning wood was drifting up the stairwell. Dark scorch marks were beginning to form around several spots where the heads of the flaming arrows had lodged in the wood, and thin skeins of smoke were drifting through the cracks in the door. The Mage's blood ran cold, thinking of Anvar trapped elsewhere within the fastness, and herself unable to defend this one sanctuary against his return, or get out past the attackers to go to his aid.

Parric grabbed her roughly by the arm. 'Come on,' he yelled. 'We can't stay here now that the bastards are using fire. We've got to get out!'

13

Through Earth

'This isn't going to be easy,' Zanna warned herself as she crept out of the lower entrance to the servants' quarters and darted back across the broken flagstones towards the kitchen. Though her talk with the Lady Aurian had stiffened her courage and given her hope, the Mage had not been able to provide the food and sleep that she desperately needed. Zanna's mind was dulled; her limbs felt heavy with fatigue – but there could be no rest for her in the foreseeable future. The Lady could not be there to help her should she make a mistake or run into danger. She had only her own wits to rely on now. The hours before dawn would be brief indeed for all she had to do, and there was no guarantee that she would succeed at all.

It took more courage than she had known she possessed for Zanna to go back into that kitchen with its uneasy sleepers – and worse still, its lingering memories of Janok. Though she had taken the Mage's advice and replaced her torn, bloodstained rags with warmer clothes from the abandoned closets in the female servants' dormitory, she shivered with more than the cold as she carefully lifted the latch and opened the heavy door just enough to edge her slight body through the gap.

The cavernous chamber was darker now, for the fires had burned down, but as Zanna slipped inside and closed the door behind her she heard a sleepy, querulous mumble from the shadows near the hearth as one of the menials stirred and rolled over, disturbed by the sudden draught. Without thinking, she dived into the dank, dark space beneath the sinks and froze, her heart hammering, her knuckles pressed tightly to her lips to still the sound of her breathing. Eventually the stretching silence reassured her that the sleeper had gone back to his dreams, but she waited a little longer, afraid of disturbing him again if she tried to move out of her bolthole.

Remembering her previous lucky find of the knife beneath the sinks, Zanna groped cautiously around her in the darkness, but such good fortune could not be expected twice in one night. All she found beneath her fingers was greasy dirt, and the stiff remains of an ancient floorcloth. When she finally encountered a cluster of clinging cobwebs whose owner scuttled across the back of her hand before dropping to the floor, that finished it. She snatched her hand back with a shudder, biting her lip to stifle a scream, and decided it was about time she got moving; even though the small, detached voice of common sense that always lurked in the back of her mind was pointing out the irony of someone who'd had the courage to stick a knife into a man twice her size being afraid of a little spider.

As she crept out of her hiding-place and ghosted through the silent kitchen, Zanna went over the Lady Aurian's instructions in her mind. It was fortunate that she was sufficiently familiar with the contents and organization of the room to find what she wanted without a noisy search, or the need to risk a light. None the less, she picked up a handful of candles and a tinderbox, knowing she would need them later. Moving as quickly as she dared, she took one of the shallow baskets that were often used to carry food and crockery to and from the Mages' Tower, dumped her candles inside, and added three goblets, wedging them carefully so that they would not rattle and clink.

Crossing the kitchen to reach the pantry where Janok kept (*had* kept, Zanna reminded herself with a shudder) his immediate supplies was the worst part of the business. She had been dreading the moment when she'd be forced to pass close to the huddled sleepers near the hearth. Holding her breath, she crept carefully past them on tiptoe, gripping the handle of her basket so tightly that the twined wicker dug into her palms. Each time one of the humped figures near the fire turned in its blankets or sniffled or sighed in its sleep, she froze like a hunted animal, so that her progress was slow and achieved in a series of halts and scurries, like one of the mice that darted by night across the kitchen floor – the same mice whose frantic scamperings for cover she could hear when she finally gained the relative safety of her goal.

It was pitch black in the pantry, so she closed the door behind her and risked a candle, though it was difficult to strike a spark when her fingers shook so badly. Securing it to a shelf with a glob of dripped wax so that she could have both hands free, Zanna rummaged quickly among the stores for bread, cold meat and cheese, then checked the wooden racking beneath the shelves for wine. When the cool, smooth side of a flask met her questing fingers, she dumped it in her basket with the rest of her gleanings, blew out the candle, and left the mice to their feasting with greater sympathy for the little beasts than she had ever known before. Retracing the nerve-racking journey across the kitchen as quickly as she dared, she slipped back outside as silently as she had come, and ducked across the narrow alley to the infirmary that had once been Lady Meiriel's domain.

For a dreadful moment, Zanna thought the door was locked, but a sturdy shove proved that its handle had simply stiffened from disuse. It shot open with a protesting groan and a bang that brought her heart into her throat. Damn, oh damn! Not in the dead hour of the night when the noise would carry . . . Not when she was so near the gatehouse . . .

Zanna's inarticulate prayers were drowned by the clatter of running feet across the courtyard. Instinctively, she looked around for a place to hide, but there was nowhere to go except the infirmary – and that would only buy her worse trouble than she already had. An attempt to run at this point would get her an arrow in the back and no questions asked.

And then it was too late for thinking. A massive shadow loomed in front of her, and she shrank back against the door frame with a cry of terror as the point of a sword was pressed against her throat.

'Why, bugger me – it's a girl! Marek, stop standing there picking your nose, and bring that lantern over here.'

Zanna blinked as a dazzling light shone into her face. Beyond it, the two guards were still nothing but anonymous, hulking shadows.

'Aren't you the Lady Elisèth's little maid?' the same voice demanded. 'Thara's titties, girl – I bloody nearly gutted you for a prowler! What in all the festering hells are you doing out here in the middle of the night?'

Almost absent-mindedly, the guard lowered his sword, and its removal came as such a relief to Zanna that she found her voice, and her wits, at last. 'It wasn't my idea,' she muttered, with just the right note of sullen resentment. 'Lady Elisèth can't sleep, can she? So she hauls me out of bed – after I've been up half the night in any case ruining my eyes with her wretched sewing – and sends me down to fetch her something to eat.' For proof, she held up her basket.

'Listen, girl – I don't know what your game is, but the watch before we came on duty told us that the Lady had gone out just after midnight. She slipped past the gatehouse and never said nowt, but young Feddin saw her all right. And she hasn't come back while we've been on duty, so what do you have to say to that?'

'You must have been asleep on watch, then,' Zanna retorted brazenly. 'Why, the Lady came back hours ago. Would you like to come up with me to the Tower, and explain that you didn't see her?' She stood rigid to keep her knees from trembling, and prayed to all the gods that they wouldn't be brave enough to catch her out in the lie. 'I wouldn't if I were you,' she added, seeing them hesitate. 'She gets madder than a scalded weasel when she can't sleep.' For good measure, she pushed back her hair from her face to let them see the bruises that Janok's fists had left.

Fortunately, as she had guessed, these musclebound mercenaries were all very much in awe of the Weather-Mage's temper.

'That's all very well, but what were you doing in the infirmary?' the other guard demanded, changing the subject hastily.

Zanna sighed with relief. Here, at least, the truth – or almost the truth – would serve. 'She wanted some herbs, to make a sleeping draught. And I'm late already, because I dropped my lantern in the courtyard, and I didn't dare go back for another. Please – won't you help me find what she wants, so I can get back as quick as I can? The way she is tonight, I'm scared to keep her waiting.'

'Of course we will, lass,' the first guard told her kindly. 'I'm sorry we stopped you, like, but it's our job. Hey, Marek – give me that bloody lantern. The poor girl needs to see what she's doing, you know.'

Because the Lady Aurian's instructions had been very explicit, Zanna found the herbs she needed with little difficulty. Bidding a grateful farewell to the guards, she hurried back across the courtyard to the Mages' Tower on shaky legs. Gods, that had been a narrow escape, and the danger wasn't over yet. Why the blazes had the Lady Eliseth gone out tonight, of all nights? Now, Zanna could only pray that she'd have time to free her father before the Magewoman really did come back, and give the game away.

'Could you two handsome, hard-working gentlemen use some wine to cheer your night? I brought it for Lady Eliseth, but she's asleep, and we wouldn't want to waste it, would we?' Zanna held out her basket hopefully. Since she had never in her life tried to be coquettish, and could only rely on memories of the way her elder sister used to behave with the boys, and the antics of the kitchenmaids, she could only hope it came out right.

Zanna's knowledge of soldiers was as scant as her experience of flirting, or she would have been less surprised at the success of her ruse. When it came to an offer of wine, the purveyor would need to be a whole lot plainer than herself to be rejected. As it was, the faces of the soldiers who guarded Vannor's door lit up like beacons. They were an unprepossessing pair; the first a mangy bear of a man covered as far as the eye could see in a mat of curling red hair. The second, smaller and wiry, might have been handsome once, but his face was disfigured down one side by a ragged red scar that twisted his mouth awry. That in itself was not so bad, thought Zanna, but his eyes were cold and narrow, with the feral, pitiless gaze of a man who lived to kill.

At least the big ruddy-haired guard was smiling. 'Why, that's a kind thought, little lass,' he said, reaching greedily for the flask.

211

'Just a minute,' the other, more suspicious but less quick on the uptake, cut in. 'Why in the name of all the gods should some skirt be bringing us food and wine at this time of night?'

'Not because she fancies *you*, that's for sure,' his companion jeered. 'Why d'you think, you idiot?' He took a long swig from the flask. 'It gets lonely down in them servants' quarters, doesn't it, my pet?' He turned to Zanna with a lewd wink.

'Oho,' said the small man, catching on at last. 'Don't hog the lot, then.' He made a grab at the flask. 'I'm sure the little lass can't have meant it all for an ugly old bastard like you.'

'Help yourself. It tastes a bit off to me – but I suppose it's just the sort of horse's piss these Magefolk bastards would like.' The big guard handed over the flask and wiped his mouth. 'I'm more of a beer man, myself,' he added. Just as Zanna was reflecting that she needn't have bothered looking for the goblets, she found herself swept up in a pair of hairy, brawny arms. 'And a woman's man,' the guard went on, leering into her face.

Zanna gritted her teeth, forced herself not to struggle, and from somewhere or other managed to dredge up a smile. 'We'll have to see about that, won't we?' she replied, and wondered how she could keep her voice steady as she felt his hand creep up beneath her skirts.

'Here, hold on!' A rough hand grabbed her arm and spun her away from her admirer. 'What about my turn, you stinking sack of dung!' The second guard, scowling darkly, thrust the flask of wine into his companion's hand. 'Here – you didn't have much,' he said with mock-generosity. 'You finish it, while I get acquainted with the little lady.' Forcing Zanna against the wall, he covered her face with slobbering kisses while she fought against nausea and willed herself to keep still and endure it.

'Rot you!' The first guard drained the flask and flung it away to crash against the wall. 'Give her back, you pox-ridden little bastard. I had her first!' With a meaty hand that covered most of the smaller man's shoulder, he pulled his rival away.

212

The little killer grunted a curse and went for his knife, and Zanna seized the moment to wriggle free. 'Quiet!' she hissed. 'Do you want to bring the Magefolk down on us?'

As the thought penetrated what passed for their brains, the guards stopped grappling and turned to gape at her sheepishly. Zanna forced another smile. 'There's no need for all this fighting,' she said winningly. 'Why, we have the rest of the night in front of us.'

'What a clever little lass you are,' the big guard beamed. 'Come on, lovey, what about a kiss for me?' He reached out to embrace her – and toppled, choking, with his rival's knife between his shoulderblades.

The man with the killer eyes planted a booted foot in the other's back and wrenched his knife out of the body. 'And now *we* have all night – just the two of us.' Clutching the bloody blade, he advanced on Zanna, grinning nastily as she backed away. 'Don't be shy, little lass. To start with, let's see what you're like under all those clothes.'

Suddenly, his eyes glazed over. 'Gods, what's happening? You bitch, you've poisoned me . . .' He staggered, and went down like a felled tree as the handful of powdered herbs that Zanna had dumped into the wine took effect at last.

Zanna slumped against the wall, breathing deeply, until the dizziness cleared from her brain and the urge to throw up was under control. Then, stooping swiftly, she scrabbled at the belt of the big, ruddy-haired guard, searching for his keys; the task made all the more difficult because she couldn't bring herself to look at him. A lecherous fool he might have been, but he'd seemed harmless enough – after all, her behaviour had looked like an open invitation – and he had spoken to her kindly. Now he was dead, and it was all her fault. 'I didn't want this. I only meant to drug them,' she muttered helplessly, but it did nothing to erase the sick sense of guilt that rose up to choke her.

To confound her expectations, there was no ring of keys on the guard's belt, but after a fair amount of cursing and a further rummage through the dead man's pockets Zanna finally found what she sought. Praying that it really was the right key, she fitted it into the lock, and sagged with relief as it turned over with a click. She took the key with her as she glided silently into the room beyond, and closed the door behind her.

There was no light in the living chamber save a cluster of dull rubies that must be the dying embers in the hearth. Zanna, familiar with the placement of the furnishings, crossed over to the table and lit a candle, but what she saw there in the growing light sent her reeling backward with a stifled cry of horror. The once-smooth wood of the tabletop had been gouged and splintered, and its surface, like the floor below, was stained and spattered with rusty smears of blood. 'No,' she whispered, stricken. 'Oh, dear gods, no!' Surely, after everything that had happened, after all she'd been through, she couldn't be too late?

Zanna fought the most difficult battle of her life not to run right then. She didn't want to know, couldn't bear to see what might await her in the next room. Yet she had to know; she couldn't risk not knowing. 'Don't be a bloody fool,' she snarled angrily at herself. 'Would the Lady Aurian turn tail like a coward and run?' Holding on to the thought of the Mage for courage, she picked up the candle – ignoring the stinging drops of hot wax that spilled across her shaking hand – and walked resolutely into the bedchamber.

He lay across the bed like a broken toy with limbs askew, his body limp and unmoving and his sunken face a ghastly, ashen grey. Blood streaked the green silk coverlet where it had seeped from a bundle of inexpertly wrapped rags that were bound around his right hand. Zanna could see no movement of breath beneath the gory ruin of his shirt. Try as she would, she could not make herself approach him. 'Dad,' she tried to whisper, but the word could not struggle past the choking constriction in her throat. She took a hesitant step towards him, and another, but it seemed the very air had turned solid to resist her.

'Dad – oh, dad!' With no memory of how she had come to be there, she found herself kneeling by the bed and sobbing heartbrokenly into the cool silk of the quilt. Once released, her tears could not be stemmed. Without a thought for her own danger, Zanna abandoned herself to her grief, her body

214

shuddering with great, racking sobs as she mourned the father she had come too late to save.

'What . . . Who . . . *Zanna?*'

But it wasn't the voice that first penetrated her grief – it was the cold, weak hand that stroked and rumpled her tousled hair. Zanna sprang backwards with a yelp of shock, stumbled, and sat down hard on the floor. She looked up to see her father, propped weakly on one elbow, squinting blearily down at her.

'It *is* Zanna. What are you doing here?' he croaked. 'I thought I was dreaming . . .'

'I thought you were dead!' Zanna cried, still half-afraid to approach him; not daring to believe that her dad was really there, and living, and talking to her.

The ghost of a smile softened the merchant's haggard face. 'No, love, I'm not – though the way I feel, I'd probably be better off.'

'Don't say that!' Zanna felt a surge of anger. 'Damn it, if only you knew . . .'

'I'm sorry.' He reached out to hug her, and fell back limply, his face blanching bone-white with agony as he moved the injured hand.

Zanna flew to his side, exerting all her strength to haul him up and prop him against the pillows. Sweat sprang on his brow and she saw him clench his teeth against crying out – so that, as he imagined, she wouldn't realize how much the movement hurt him. She hugged him as hard as she dared, so glad to see him that she wanted to weep again; but now she knew he was still alive there were priorities more urgent than rejoicing, more important even than finding out just what the Mages had done to him. There was so little time to spare and, hurt as her father was, how the blazes could she manage to get them both out of the Academy?

'Is there any water?' Vannor whispered. Zanna ran to fetch a goblet, and as an afterthought added a dash of strong spirits that she found in a flask on the nightstand nearby. She held it for Vannor as he drank, noting with some relief that a little of the colour was returning to his face. 'Dad,' she told him urgently, 'listen carefully. I've come to get you out of

215

here. This is our one chance to escape, but we'll have to hurry. I've . . .' But the words stuck in her throat. How could she tell her dad, who still thought of her as his little girl, that she had killed two men tonight, and they must escape before the bodies were found? 'Look,' she temporized, 'the Lady Eliseth has gone out into the city, but she could come back any minute, and we have no time to waste. If I helped you, do you think you could manage to walk?'

The old well remembered gleam lit her father's eyes. 'To get out of this accursed pit of vipers? I'd crawl on my hands . . .' He swallowed the word as if it pained him. 'Well, I'd crawl, anyway,' he finished lamely. 'Come on, lass – help me up. And bring that brandy with you, if you can carry it. We might need it before we're done, if only to keep me going.' He grinned at her as though she were another man, a comrade in arms, and Zanna's heart swelled with pride. 'I do take it,' he added, 'that having achieved this much, you have a plan to get us out of here?'

'Blast it!' Zanna struck her forehead with her open palm. 'I almost forgot about the bloody key.'

'Zanna!' Vannor's reproof was a father's instinctive re-action. 'You never learned that kind of language from me.'

'Yes I did, though,' Zanna chuckled; but as her head was buried, at the time, in the depths of the Lady Aurian's closet, she doubted that he'd hear her. She rummaged quickly through the folded clothing within until she found a faded old grey robe, such as the Magefolk wore. Pulling it out of the stack, she dipped her hand into the pocket as the Lady Aurian had instructed her, and sighed with relief as her fingers closed around a twisted shape wrought of ice-cold metal. She pulled it out, and there it was, glittering in the candlelight – an intricate key that looked like a tangled fili-gree of polished silver. Aurian's key to the archives – and Zanna's key to freedom.

She thought she would never get her father down the winding staircase of the Tower. To Zanna's overstrained nerves, the descent seemed to take for ever. Even though he was clinging to the banister with his left hand, and his daughter supported him with her shoulder beneath his arm

216

on the other side, Vannor still stumbled occasionally, and staggered like a drunken man. Time after time, she thought that he would send them both tumbling – and, while the curve of the stairs would prevent them from falling right to the bottom, she knew his injury would not withstand such a battering, and didn't want him passing out from the pain. Added to that danger was the ever-present risk of meeting the Lady Eliseth, coming back from wherever she had been.

By the time they reached the bottom of the staircase, Zanna could have wept from a combination of relief and weariness. In addition to helping her father, she was hampered by the basket with its essential food, which she had picked up on the landing where she had left it beside the bodies – one sleeping, one dead – of the guards. It proved useful for carrying the flasks of spirits and water that she'd dipped from the ewer in her father's rooms, but even with the wicker handle hooked into the crook of her elbow it was clumsy and awkward to carry, and it effectively tied up the hand that she needed to hold on with, should Vannor fall. Already she was trembling from the strain of supporting her father's weight, and who knew how far they still had to go?

As they crossed the threshold, the cold night air seemed to revive her – that and the escape from the oppressive atmosphere of the Tower itself. Fortunately, the journey across the courtyard to the library was not a long one, though it took much longer than it should have done, at the slow and halting pace that was all Vannor was able to manage. The moon was almost dark, and in any case had set long ago, so there was no light to betray the fugitives. No guards appeared to stop them, and no Lady Eliseth, terrifying in her wrath, leapt out of the shadows to demand an accounting of the two escaping Mortals. It was almost too good to be true; but Zanna, shivering in the pre-dawn chill, had a sinking feeling in her bones that she had already stretched her luck about as far is it would go. She could not rely on it for ever – or for long.

The library, in darkness, was a maze of obstacles, and Zanna was forced to find the way to the inner door with only her memory as a guide. Time and again, she heard Vannor's muffled curse and felt him stagger as they collided with unseen hazards – tables, chairs, and protruding stacks of shelves. At least, she comforted herself, they would not have to worry about leaving a trail. The fastidious Lady Eliseth had been spending a good deal of time in the library lately, and had come up with a spell of Air to get rid of all the cobwebs and dust.

When they reached the rear wall, Zanna was forced to leave her father resting while she groped her way along with outstretched hands, feeling for the grille of wrought iron that was the archive gate. At last she found it, and fumbled for the lock plate by touch alone. And after a desperate struggle to fit the key into its hole, Zanna felt the door swing open on its well oiled hinges, making not the slightest sound to disturb the profound peace of knowledge's domain. Quickly, she groped her way back along the wall to fetch Vannor, and found him by touch, slumped at the table where she'd left him.

'Dad! Come on – you can't sleep now!' Though she shook him as hard as she could, it took him a long time to awaken. Mumbling a string of lurid curses that, had he been in full possession of his wits, he would have killed anyone else for speaking within her hearing, he staggered after her, dragging on her hand like a shipwreck victim clinging tightly to the one last floating spar. Zanna pushed him through into the archives ahead of her and, reaching through the metal grille, locked the door behind her and pocketed the key with an audible sigh of relief.

It was not over yet, however. Despite the fact that they had escaped the Magefolk, for the time being at least, the worst was still before them, as Zanna soon found out. Dragging Vannor behind her, she groped her way through two turns of the passage before risking a light, but when she finally dared set a spark to one of her candles she was glad she had waited no longer. The fragile flame revealed a narrow, low-ceilinged corridor with rough-hewn walls – and, not half a dozen paces in front of them, a steep stairway that plunged downwards, into who knew what depths of darkness.

That was too much. Trembling at the narrowness of their

escape, Zanna decided that she and her father could go no further without rest, not if all the fiends of the infernal pit were howling at their heels. Vannor needed no convincing. Even in the time it had taken her to light the candle, he had slid down the wall into a huddled heap by her feet. Zanna cursed aloud. It's not fair, she thought wildly. Through most of her life, her dad had taken care of her. How had the tables suddenly turned?

The thought reminded Zanna of the Lady Aurian. Had she, too, felt this hopeless rage, this sense of helplessness, when she had been forced to flee Nexis? Well, she managed, Zanna thought sturdily, and so can I.

None the less, it took her a little time to revive her father. Fishing the single goblet from her basket, she mixed another measure of water and brandy, and held it to his lips. The drink seemed to revive him. Vannor spluttered, opened his eyes, and looked around him dazedly. 'Where the blazes are we?'

'In the catacombs, below the library – at least, we will be when we get down those stairs.' Zanna fought the urge to clutch her father's sleeve. 'Dad, I know you told me that the archives lead eventually to the sewers where you used to hide out. But do you know the way from here?'

'No, lass.' Vannor shook his head. 'Not from up here. We should keep going down, that's all I know. Keep heading for the older parts and the colder parts – that's what Elewin said – until we reach a cave and a crack and a tunnel with a rotted iron ladder. It leads to the sewers, and then we're halfway out.'

Wonderful, Zanna thought ruefully. That's a lot of help. Still, if we get lost down here, it should be beyond even the ken of the Magefolk to find us – and I'd rather suffer any fate than fall back into Eliseth's hands.

Smothering a sigh, she hooked the basket back over her elbow and picked up the candle in the same hand. Putting her free shoulder under Vannor's arm, Zanna helped her father struggle to his feet and, half-leading, half-supporting him, she guided him down the steps and into the un-fathomable darkness that lay beyond.

14

Through Fire

'How many guards are there?' Anvar asked the Moldan.

'One round the corner, in the junction of the corridors,' Basileus replied. *'Two in the doorway, and the rest inside the stillroom guarding the prisoners – a dozen guards in all.'*

'A dozen?' Anvar gasped in dismay. How would he deal with so many? Aurian, who had been taught by the world's greatest swordsman, and had practised the arts of combat for most of her life, might have considered such odds, but he knew his own limitations. Still, perhaps he could simply take them out of time . . . Even as he reached behind him for the Harp that was usually slung on his back, he realized that in all the hurry and confusion he had left it behind in his chamber. He swore bitterly. How could he have been so stupid? And more to the point, what was he going to do now?

'Fear not, Wizard,' the Moldan told him. *'I will arrange a diversion. Be ready to act when I give the word.'*

Anvar flattened himself against the wall and waited, swallowing to ease a throat gone dry with nervousness. Even as he tightened his grip on a swordhilt that felt cold and slippery in his hand, he could feel, with his Mage's senses, the tingling pulse of life through the silver veining in the smooth, dark stone that pressed against his shoulders. How in the world, he wondered, was Basileus going to distract the guards? What could an inanimate being such as the Moldan do to affect the outcome of the impending fight? It took all of Anvar's self-control not to leave his body right there and then and send his consciousness ahead up the passageway to see what was happening. He knew better, however, than to make such a stupid error. What if more of the rebel Xandim should come this way while his body was unoccupied? No – he would have to trust Basileus, bide his time, and wait.

Schiannath could barely contain his anger at the base treachery of his compatriots. Even though he was helpless – lying, bound hand and foot, next to the stillroom wall – it did not stop his mind from struggling against his fate. Blood kept dripping down into his eyes from a cut in his forehead, and he was bruised and aching from blows of fists and feet, for he and Yazour had sold their freedom dearly. But Schiannath was less concerned with his hurts than with the gut-wrenching fear of being captured and imprisoned, once again, by his own people. His return from exile had been like waking from the terrors of an evil dream, and now, it seemed, the nightmare was starting all over again. What would they do to him this time?

In an effort to control the panic that rose up in him like choking bile, Schiannath distracted his frantic thoughts by trying to make sense of what was happening. Why had the Xandim rebelled against Parric now? Even if the Herdlord was an outlander, he had won his challenge fairly, by all accounts – and what was more, he had promised to relinquish his rule once his companions had been rescued. With the dark of the moon bringing the chance of a new leader tomorrow night, what was to be gained by this uprising? Was it really so important, this Xandim tradition that all aliens must die? As far as Schiannath was concerned, the oddly assorted band of northerners had been better friends to him than any of his own race – with the exception of Iscalda, of course.

Iscalda! What was happening to his sister now? It was a safe assumption that he and Yazour were not the only victims of this cowardly attack. What had become of Anvar, and Aurian, who had earned his undying gratitude for being the one to lead him, all too briefly it seemed, back to the acceptance of his people? Had they been ambushed, as he and Yazour had been? Had they been captured? Were they hurt – or even dead?

What did the Xandim have against these outlanders? Why did they hate anyone who did not belong to their own tribe? Then Schiannath thought of Chiamh, who was one of the Xandim; yet, before he had learned better, the former outlaw

221

had feared and mistrusted the Windeye as greatly as anyone else in his tribe. Schiannath looked up at the faces of his guards, who laughed and joked amongst themselves to fan the bright, false flames of their courage. He sensed fear in their studied indifference, their refusal even to acknowledge the presence of Yazour and himself, and knew it for an irrational, gut-level fear of any person or thing that was unknown or unpredictable – or simply different.

Curse them all! Schiannath could not believe that this could be happening to him – not again – not so soon after the last time. The unfairness of it all made him burn with anger. Half-blind with rage, he struggled against the rough thongs that held him, scoring and abrading the tender skin of his wrists. But they had bound him too tightly – they knew their job too well.

A movement caught the edge of his vision, and Schiannath turned his head to see Yazour also fighting to free himself. As their eyes met, the wild hope flashed through his mind that if they could stealthily move closer to one another, they might be able to untie each other's bonds. But one look at the guard – a stranger to Schiannath – withered that plan before it even had time to take root. Standing close to the prisoners with his sword out of its sheath, he did not take his eyes from them for an instant. Schiannath ground his teeth and swore softly to himself. By the goddess, there had to be something he could do!

Suddenly a cloud of greasy black smoke came billowing out of the empty fireplace, filling the room with an acrid haze. Schiannath stiffened as his guards cried out in alarm. Was there a way to take advantage of their distraction? But such considerations were quickly forgotten as more smoke – more and more – kept pouring out of the dark void of the stillroom hearth, and the chamber was obscured by a heavy, choking miasma that clung to everything it touched. Though he and Yazour were closer to the ground than their captors, and were therefore getting less of the noxious smoke, he could feel it attacking his own lungs now. His eyes began to sting and water as he fought, wheezing and gasping for a breath that he could not take.

'*Now!*' The voice of the Moldan resounded loudly in Anvar's mind. Taking a tighter grip on both his courage and his sword, Anvar rushed round the corner, to find the corridor beyond quite empty of guards. The reason for their absence became clear a moment later, when he saw the clouds of smoke that were billowing out of the stillroom door, and heard the curses and panic-stricken cries that came from within.

'You've set the place on fire?' he asked the Moldan, aghast.

'*No, Wizard – it is only smoke.*'

Anvar took as deep a breath as he could manage while the air was still clear, and braced himself to rush forward down the passage.

'*Wait.*'

Anvar ducked back round the corner with a curse. Just when he'd got his nerve up to go ... 'What now?' he demanded irritably.

'*Remember that you are a Wizard, and skilled in the magic of Air,*' Basileus pointed out with a trace of amusement. '*You, of all people, need not breathe the smoke.*'

'Plague take it! I should have thought of that,' Anvar muttered. With care, he constructed a shield of energy around himself that would permit clean air, but not the noxious smoke, to pass through. Thus equipped, he set off again down the corridor.

'*I should hurry if I were you,*' Basileus prompted. '*With regard to the smoke, I might have let my enthusiasm get the better of me.*'

The Mage didn't need telling twice. Already, great black billows were rolling out of the stillroom doorway and obscuring the passage. Erupting out of the dark cloud came several running figures, who almost knocked Anvar off his feet as they pounded past. Evidently the Xandim guards had given up trying to deal with the smoke, and were beating a hasty retreat. Though he was glad to have them out of the reckoning, their panic boded ill for Yazour and Schiannath. Anvar broke into a run.

It was impossible to see anything inside the stillroom. Not even the night-vision of a Mage could pierce the dark, obscuring clouds. Much as he wanted to call out to the two captives, Anvar forced himself to remain silent. He had no idea whether or not there were any guards left in the still-room, and the last thing he needed was to draw the wrong sort of attention to himself. Following the sounds of coughing, retching, and one weak voice (he could not tell whose) that cried for help, he groped his way across the room, tripping over benches and bumping into tables, until eventually he almost fell over the two bound bodies lying near the wall.

Schiannath and Yazour had not been idle. Once their guards' attention had been distracted, they had seized the opportunity to roll and shuffle along the wall until they were close together. With difficulty, they had manoeuvred themselves until they were back to back, and had been trying frantically to untie each other's bonds. But the knots in the thongs were tight and awkward to reach with bound hands, and increasing panic had made fingers fumble and shake. It soon became appallingly clear that they would never make their escape before they were overcome by the choking fumes.

Schiannath had looked into the face of death so many times over the last year that familiarity had blunted part of its terror. Instead of giving way to his fears, he struggled all the harder to free himself and his friend, but there was no way to combat the insidious smoke. It crept burning into his eyes and throat and lungs, until he was wheezing and gasping for breath, and blinded by his tears, so that he did not see the dark figure that appeared out of nowhere to stoop over him.

'Hold on, Schiannath – I'll soon have you out of here.'

'Anvar!' the Xandim spluttered. Had he not been so overjoyed, he could have wept with relief as he recognized the Mage's voice. Suddenly Schiannath felt a disconcerting tingle run through his body, and the smoke that surrounded him disappeared. For the first time in long, agonising minutes he could breathe easily, and the shock of the transition came very close to a thrill of ecstasy. Then the thongs around his wrists parted to the keen, cold edge of a blade, and his fingers were free again. Blotting his streaming eyes on his sleeve, the Xandim looked up to see the thinning black miasma held at bay beyond the walls of what appeared to be a bubble of clear air that encompassed Yazour, the Mage, and himself.

Yazour looked to be in a far worse state than the Xandim. He had barely been conscious at the time of Anvar's timely appearance. Now he was taking great, deep gulps of air as though they were draughts of the finest wine, and a little colour was beginning to soften the ghastly pallor of his face. Anvar knelt beside him, busily sawing at his bindings with his knife. 'Get your feet free, if you can,' he told Schiannath, without looking up. 'And hurry – we've very little time to spare.'

Schiannath wasted no time in asking questions. Once the two captives had been released, they scrambled to their feet, Anvar helping Yazour with a supporting arm around his shoulders while Schiannath took the Mage's sword and went in front. As quickly as they could manage, they groped their way through the thinning murk towards the door.

Without warning, a figure burst out of the smoke behind them and swung a sword at Anvar's head. Groggy as he was, Yazour's battle-trained reflexes held firm. He heard the whistle of the blade, yelled, and let his knees buckle, dragging the Mage down with him to one side. The sword flashed harmlessly past Anvar's right shoulder, to meet another blade in a spray of flying sparks and a resounding screech of steel on steel, as Schiannath, alerted by his companion's cry, pivoted and struck. Caught off balance by the sheer force of the blow, the attacker stumbled, leaving himself wide open to the other's thrust. For a fleeting instant, Anvar glimpsed the man's expression of terror and despair as he realized his mistake, and then he toppled, spitted on the point of Schiannath's sword.

The conflict had begun and ended almost before Anvar had time to realize what was happening. He clambered rather shakily to his feet as Schiannath pulled his sword from his opponent's body, gave the bloody blade a cursory wipe on the dying man's tunic, and returned it to Anvar, picking up the fallen man's sword for himself.

'Thanks.' The Mage took back his blade from Schiannath's strong, brown hand. 'It's a good thing for all of us that you're so fast – and you, too, Yazour.' He turned to the Khazalim captain, to help him up, but he was already on his feet.

'*You must waste no more time,*' Basileus warned Anvar. '*Your companions are besieged, and the fight goes badly.*'

'Come on,' Anvar told his companions. 'Let's get moving – Aurian needs us.'

Bohan had lost the wolves already. He was less concerned about the fact that he had also come within a hair's breadth of losing his life on the springy, slippery plank bridge that bent and bowed alarmingly beneath his weight as he crawled across it on his hands and knees. Though it was only a short crawl from the fastness window to the mountain ledge, much care had been needed to avoid a fall, and by the time he had reached the other side the wolves, still carrying Aurian's son, had vanished into the darkness.

The night was still black, with an hour or two of darkness yet to go before the dawn. The eunuch pressed himself against the steep and sloping face of the mountain. Forcing his thick fingers into a narrow, slanting fissure in the stone, he clung with all his strength to keep himself balanced on the ledge, which was scarcely wider than the span of one great hand. He had already discovered, to his dismay, that the slender crack to which he clung narrowed away to nothing in the direction he wanted to go, and without a handhold it seemed impossible, because of his massive bulk, that he could keep his body balanced on the ledge. Bohan closed his eyes in anguish. What could he do? Every moment he lingered here, afraid to go forward and refusing to go back, those accursed wolves would be getting further away with the child that he had promised to guard.

Though there was no rain now, the rocks were still slick from an earlier squall, and a thin, frigid wind whined and snarled as it snaked across the Wyndveil's bare flanks. Bohan, having spent his life in the broiling desert climes of the south, found himself shivering uncontrollably, and a knot of panic twisted in his breast. Though he told himself stoutly that he could stand any amount of discomfort from the cold, the growing numbness in his feet and fingers could only add

226

to the peril of what was already an appallingly difficult climb, and the longer he waited, the greater would be the risk of a lethal fall.

There was nothing for it. Bohan could not bear the shame of letting his beloved Aurian know he had lost her child. He knew that he must go on somehow and find Wolf, or perish in the attempt. Slowly, he began to inch his way along the ledge, his right hand feeling out ahead of him into the slim crack in the stone; all his concentration centred on the narrowing fissure that provided scant purchase for his abraded fingers.

And then, abruptly, the crevice ended. As the eunuch's groping fingers met with nothing but smooth stone he rocked for a horrifying instant, until his left hand, still securely anchored, brought his body back to lean, trembling, against the cold rock of the cliff face. But now he was putting too much weight on the fragile ledge beneath his feet. With a tearing crack, the lip of stone broke loose beneath him.

Parric, familiar with the sight of Magefolk at work, had been staying out from underfoot to give Aurian and Chiamh a clear field. While they were holding the attackers at bay, he had slipped upstairs to Sangra and Iscalda and told them to search the rooms and each pack up a bundle of necessities: cloaks, weapons, and any food that was lying around the chambers. He had known a retreat was inevitable, and wanted to be prepared. Now it seemed that the time had come.

When the flaming arrows thudded into the door, he ran downstairs and grabbed hold of Aurian's elbow. 'That's enough,' he cried. 'They're trying to smoke us out. We've got to go now, before it's too late.'

'No!' The Mage wrenched her arm from the cavalry master's grip. 'You take the others on ahead. I'm staying here until Anvar comes.'

'Have you lost your mind?' Parric roared. 'You don't know where he is, how soon he'll get here – or even if he's alive . . .'

'He is alive! Have you forgotten that one Mage can feel

227

another's death?' Aurian rounded on the little man, her eyes blazing. 'Don't argue, Parric. Get the others out of here, and I'll wait for Anvar.'

'Damn it, Aurian, you won't. Look at it!' The door was thick, and it would take some time for the fire to eat right through, but tiny yellow tongues of flame were already threading their way up the scorched panels. Chiamh was using up the supplies of water from the upstairs chambers to try to douse the flames, but the fire was burning hot and strong on the other side of the door, and soaking the wood on this side could only delay matters for a little while. It was growing uncomfortably hot in the stairwell. The air was thick and acrid with a haze of choking smoke.

'If you'll let me be, I'll try to quench these flames with magic,' Aurian snapped. 'Now get away from me, and let me concentrate.'

Parric, desperate now, racked his brains for a way to make the Mage see sense. It didn't help that he was consumed by a burgeoning resentment of Anvar, and all that Aurian's refusal to leave him implied. Reluctant as he was to hurt her, she was clearly beyond all reasoning, and there was no time to argue.

The Mage had turned her attention back to the burning door, and Parric seized his chance. He lifted his sword, to club her unconscious with the hilt.

A hand closed round his wrist.

'No.' Chiamh spoke very quietly, but there was a hard look in his amiable face that the cavalry master had never seen before. Then the amber eyes flared silver, and Parric felt the sword turn to burning ice in his hand. Swearing horribly, he dropped the blade, which clattered on the hard stone stairs.

'Will you be quiet,' Aurian snarled, without looking round.

Chiamh picked up the fallen sword and returned it to the cavalry master. 'For shame,' he said softly. 'You have no right to make such a decision for her. Go, if we cannot trust you. I will take care of her.'

Parric looked at the Windeye and shook his head. 'No.' He spoke through gritted teeth. 'I'll send Sangra and Iscalda, but I'm staying here. If you two idiots persist in this insanity, you'll need all the help you can get.'

228

'Very well – but no more treachery.' Chiamh's voice was still cold. Parric stifled his angry retort. Clasping his sword-hilt until his knuckles turned white, he looked over the Windeye's shoulder to see how Aurian was progressing.

The Mage had missed the tense exchange. She was struggling with problems of her own. It was a simple matter to control the flares and fireballs that she created herself with her magic, but this was wildfire – a natural force that was un-disciplined and untameable. Aurian bent as near to the smouldering surface as she dared to come, though the heat and the acrid smoke stung her eyes and caught in her throat and lungs to make her cough. She had been trying to use her powers to absorb the heat-energy of the flames, to cool and shrink them, but soon she realized, with a sinking in the pit of her stomach, that the fire was already too far out of hand for that. There had to be another way. If the door was eaten through, there would be nothing to keep the attacking Xandim at bay – and if Anvar should return now with Schiannath and Yazour, there would be a wall of fire between them and safety.

'Where are they now?' she asked Basileus, who had been keeping her informed as to the movements of her missing companions.

'Coming. Soon they will be here.' The Moldan hesitated. *'What will you do when they reach this place?'*

'I don't know.' The Mage's mental tones were edged with desperation. 'Is there nothing you can do to help?'

'Alas, it seems there is not. I have already tried to make a draught to quench the flames, but it only fanned them and made matters worse.'

'Yes, it would. But wait – hold on a minute.' The Moldan's words had given Aurian the glimmering of an idea. 'Chiamh,' she yelled. 'Quick – get over here!'

'I *am* here.' The Windeye's voice came from just behind her shoulder, making her jump. If his expression seemed a little strained, Aurian was too caught up with her plan to pay it much attention.

'Chiamh, you're our expert with air – do you think you could come up with some means of keeping the air away from those flames on the other side of the door?'

229

Chiamh's eyes widened with surprise, then his slow smile of understanding brightened his face. 'Ah,' he said. 'Very clever, Lady. Let me see what I can do.'

Aurian moved over to make room for him, and the Windeye knelt to join her near the door. Despite the heat, he shivered a little as his eyes glazed over with the uncanny, reflective quicksilver hue, his vision blurring and shifting to the translucent, sharp-edged, crystalline aspect of his Othersight. Dimly, he felt the Mage put out a hand to help steady his sagging body as he sent his mind forth beyond the burning door. The silver strands of air on the other side were blurry with heat and turbulent as a tumbling mountain stream as they rose and fell swirling around the fire, forming the draughts and currents that fed the greedy flames. The actual flames were barely visible to Chiamh's Othersight, appearing as faint and glimmering wraiths of their real selves. The impatient attackers who crowded the corridor at a safe distance from the fire could be seen as glowing phantoms, the auras of life-energy that surrounded them glowing with the angry crimson of blood-lust and greed. The Windeye shuddered, knowing that sooner or later they would have to be dealt with; but first, the fire must be put out.

Straining with concentration, Chiamh tried to take a grip on the twisting tendrils of air and push them away from the devouring flames. But because his spirit was out beyond his body, using energy to stay in this unnatural state, his powers lacked impetus, and he had nothing but the force of his mind to grasp and mould the silvery strands. The turbulence caused by the fire added to his difficulties, lending the air a force and strength of its own with which to defy him. Nevertheless, Chiamh persevered, though diverting the powerful currents of air was one of the most difficult things he had ever done. Though he could not extinguish the flames, he could at least slow the fire's advance, and gain Anvar the extra moments he needed.

Conditions were worsening in the stairwell. The moisture in the wood had been burned away now, and the flames were taking a stronger hold. The crackling of the fire grew louder, and the Mage was forced to help herself and Chiamh – and

Parric, who waited, hunched and glowering, some three or four steps further up – by creating, as Anvar had done, a shield around them to keep the smoke at bay.

Aurian, keeping her watch over the Windeye's body, knew that Chiamh was in trouble. She could see the ravages of the mental battle reflected in his face. Lines of strain had etched themselves deeply around his eyes and mouth, and his long brown hair, soaked through with sweat, hung down in tendrils that she had to keep brushing out of his uncanny silver eyes. Though she began to fear that he might harm himself, she was reluctant to break into his trance, lest she make matters even worse. She knew, however, from her own experiences of overextending herself, that Chiamh ran a grave risk of becoming lost in his own magic, with so much of his energy sucked away to fuel his powers that he would have no chance of returning to his body.

'Anvar, where are you?' She sent out a desperate mental cry, and prayed that he would be close enough to hear it. 'We can't hold on here much longer.'

'We're almost there.' Anvar's reply sounded faint and weary. 'We ran into trouble once or twice, but so far we've managed to fight our way through – probably because most of the Xandim are massed around your door.'

'Thank the gods you're all right.' It cheered Aurian just to hear him. 'Let me know as soon as you come within sight of our attackers.'

'Whenever you're ready,' Anvar responded wryly. 'We've reached the corridor junction now.'

'Good. I'll tell you when.' Aurian looked round at Chiamh, and was relieved to see that, though he was very pale, he looked awake and aware, and his eyes had returned to their normal shade.

'I heard you both,' he told the Mage. 'I'm ready.'

Aurian drew Coronach from its sheath. 'When I give the word, we're going out there to help Anvar,' she told Parric. Without giving him a chance to start arguing again, she turned back to the door, which without Chiamh's support was now collapsing in a mass of flames.

'Now!' As she cried the word with both her voice and her

231

mind, Aurian blasted the remains of the door with a bolt of energy that sent the flaming fragments exploding out into the corridor and into the crowding Xandim. They scattered, shrieking, beating at flying bits of burning wood and the sparks that lodged and clung to their clothing and hair. Aurian burst out into the corridor screaming a battle cry, with Parric and Chiamh close behind her. They tore into the disorganized cluster of Xandim like a pack of wolves.

Shia had sent Khanu ahead up the mountain to escort Wolf and his foster-parents to Chiamh's vale. Then, as Aurian had asked her, she had returned to the upper levels of the fastness, picking her way along the narrow ledges of the cliffs behind the massive building in search of Bohan. Though she hated to admit it to herself – almost in case, in some irrational way, the admission should make her grounds for concern a reality – she was becoming increasingly worried about the eunuch. 'Why can he not keep up?' Shia muttered to herself. 'Great clumsy ox – probably got his feet in a tangle.' That thought halted her with a shudder. On these ancient, crumbling cliffs, even one mistake would be fatal. She was nearing the fastness when the scream ripped through the night.

A scream? Shia's ears went back. It couldn't possibly be, but . . . With a snarl, she went leaping from ledge to ledge down the cliff as though pursued by a horde of demons. It was impossible to run on these narrow projections, but Shia, seething with frustration, scrambled down at a perilous speed, her claws extended to give her better purchase. When she reached the narrow chasm where the cliff came close to the fastness, her heart turned to ice within her. Bohan, his eyes bulging with strain in a face grey with terror, hung by his fingers from the last crumbling spur of the broken ledge that had nearly collapsed beneath the weight of his great body. Somehow, as he fell, he had managed to catch the edge of the broken stone, and was suspended there over the drop.

Even as she looked on in horror, his straining fingers

slipped a little further from the ledge. The cat darted forward and sunk her fangs into the back of Bohan's tunic, digging her claws hard into the stone to stop herself from slipping. The eunuch's weight dragged at her, wrenching the muscles of her jaws and neck, but she held on firmly, taking as much of the strain as she could from his arms and hands. It was all she could do to help him. Bohan himself would have to gain a better grip and pull himself back, but he seemed paralysed by terror, unable to risk what scant hold he had in order to inch himself to safety.

Shia's mind flew back to the tunnels beneath Dhiammara, when she had almost plunged into the chasm fighting the spider-creature, and he had performed the same service to save her life. Bohan had been her silent but staunch companion since the day she had escaped from the Khazalim arena, and had shared the days of her freedom ever since. He was her friend. She couldn't let him fall. Move, you great lummox, she thought desperately. Pull yourself up. I can't hold on like this for ever.

Clenching her jaws around the mouthful of cloth, she edged back a little, knowing the futility of trying to haul up the eunuch on her own, but with no other option but to try. The small, harsh sound of tearing fabric seemed to rip across the night, loud as a thunderbolt to Shia's ears.

Bohan!

The eunuch looked up into her eyes and said, quite plainly: 'Shia. My friend.' His fingers scrabbled fruitlessly at the ledge as the last of the fabric tore away, and then he was gone. Shia heard the thud of a body striking the rocks far below.

Then there was silence, save for the keening of the wind.

Shia sat back on her haunches and howled her grief at the uncaring mountains.

Anvar's world had become a nightmare of smoke, and blood, and flashing blades. Though Aurian had been training him in the use of a sword as they journeyed, this was his first real battle, and he discovered that as soon as he entered the mêlée all of her carefully ingrained lessons simply vanished from his mind. All he could do was respond to the challenges of each separate moment; the next foe that came at him, the next sword that was raised against him. Warm blood dripped from a shallow cut in his forearm, where he had caught the edge of a glancing blade, but in the heat of the fight he felt no pain. He blocked a blow; missed an opening and swore; turned his blade to meet the return stroke backhanded. He did not miss a second time. Aurian's training held true, guiding his instincts to slip his sword through his opponent's guard to rip the man's belly. The Xandim fell, to be instantly replace by another.

Anvar's sword had taken on a life of its own, hacking and piercing, parrying and blocking, and he was aware of nothing save the foes that surrounded him, and the shadowy shapes of Schiannath and Yazour on either side. Dimly, he knew that they were using their superior warrior's skills to help defend him, but there was no time now for thoughts of gratitude. His mind could only be fixed on his survival, yet somewhere, at the edge of his consciousness, he was always aware of the tall, flame-haired figure that he strove to reach on the other side of the frenzied, milling mob.

Aurian was coming closer now – or he was coming closer to her. With every minute that passed, there were fewer foes between them. The Mage dispatched an opponent and glanced up to meet his eyes. As the companions gathered together, Anvar felt the tingling force of the magical shield that she threw up around them, and saw the attacking Xandim drop back from the barrier of spitting sparks. With a surge of relief that the fighting might be over at last, he threw his power behind that of his soulmate, to extend and reinforce the shield.

'Back to the tower,' Aurian yelled, in a voice that would have done credit to Forral's battle-trained roar. But, even as the Mages met in the midst of the fighting, everything went horribly awry. Anvar glimpsed Sangra and Iscalda running down the tower steps, yelling something about a broken ledge, and wondered what the blazes they were playing at. Aurian, with her closer link to Shia, received the message an instant sooner. Anvar saw her falter, her eyes blank, her face stark-white. The enemy pressed in closer as the shield began to fail.

'*No!*' Even as the raw cry of grief was torn from Aurian's throat, his own mind was battered by the impact of Shia's emotion – and his own. Bohan? Dead?

'Look out, you fool!' a voice roared in Anvar's ear. A sword flashed up to block the blade that was whistling down towards him, and a shower of sparks scorched his face, narrowly missing his eyes. Anvar scrambled his wits together and plunged his own blade into the attacker's chest, whirling with the follow-through to see Yazour turn to face another foe who was coming in on his right. Beyond them Schiannath was protecting Aurian in a similar fashion, while Chiamh fought beside them and Parric, flanked by Sangra and Iscalda, defended the tower doorway.

'Aurian!' he yelled, and was relieved to see her eyes come back into focus, glittering a wrathful silver. Snarling an oath, she flung up the shield once more, with such force as to hurl several of the Xandim back along the passage. Anvar rushed towards her and seized her hand to drag her to safety, lest in her rage at Bohan's death she decide to take on the Xandim single-handed. Even in such a desperate moment there was comfort in that touch, and Aurian evidently had too much sense to prolong a fight against such odds. Taking advantage of their opponents' terror and dismay, the companions raced for the tower stairs. When all had reached the safety of the upper landing Aurian turned, eyes blazing, and flung a bolt of fiery energy at the sloping ceiling of the staircase below. Anvar's mind was battered anew by a cry of indignant pain from Basileus as the roof collapsed in a grinding avalanche of rubble and dust.

15

And Through Air

'I'm sorry, love – I can't go any further. I must rest for a while.' Vannor's voice was weak with fatigue and pain, and Zanna could feel his body trembling against her supporting shoulder as she helped him along the tunnel.

'All right, dad. If you can go on just a little longer, we'll find a room to rest in, as we did before,' Zanna told him, forcing a cheerful note into her voice. For his sake, she tried to keep from betraying her own exhaustion, and the fears and worries that crowded her mind. They were utterly lost in this maze of cold, damp tunnels, and rapidly running out of both food and strength; and injured as he was, her father had difficulties enough of his own to contend with. After every one of their halts so far, it had taken her longer to get him going again, and he was needing to rest more and more often. Zanna had had no chance to look at his injury – he would not speak of what the Magefolk had done to him, or let her unwrap the bindings on his hand – but she knew that it was bad. He ought to have rest, and proper care, and a physician – but it was only a matter of time before he would be in no condition to reach the help that he so badly needed.

Zanna lifted her candle higher, and looked along the passage for the darker shadow of the next doorway. The ancient archives beneath the library were honeycombed with alcoves, niches, and chambers of all sizes; some large enough to stretch far beyond the range of the fugitives' candlelight, and some so small that Vannor and his daughter could barely squeeze in together among ancient volumes and dusty stacks of crumbling parchment. In truth, Zanna much preferred the latter. They might be cramped and uncomfortable, and need extreme care with the candle to prevent a conflagration, but they were warmer, less draughty, and felt much more secure.

She didn't have to worry about what might be lurking in the darkness beyond the small, safe circle of flickering candle-glow. She had overheard Eliseth complaining that though Finbarr, the former archivist, had set spells to keep out rodents, cockroaches, and other small, destructive creatures, the magic had now started to decay through lack of upkeep; but it wasn't the idea of small beasties that bothered Zanna. What did worry her, however, was the unshakeable conviction that something else was down here with herself and her father. Something unseen, unknown, but unspeakably evil.

'Oh, for goodness sake,' Zanna muttered to herself. 'Don't be such an idiot. If you start letting your imagination run away with you down here, we'll be in trouble for certain.' Instead, she put her arm round her father and guided him towards the nearest dark mouth in the side of the tunnel.

To Zanna's irritation, the shadowed opening proved to be an alcove, not a doorway. Muttering one of Vannor's choicest oaths under her breath, she was turning to retrace her steps when the light of her candle caught a stray gleam low in her line of vision – the dull, cold shine of dark and pitted iron. She gave her basket to Vannor and left him to lean against the wall for a moment, while she peered close to investigate – and almost went sprawling down three deep steps. At the bottom, in the corner of the alcove – not in the centre of the wall, where she would have expected it to be – was a narrow wooden door.

It was locked, of course. Given the obvious secrecy of the entrance, Zanna had expected nothing less. All the same, it infuriated her. Because access was denied her, she felt that she *must* see what was inside – and it never occurred to her that a door, in these eerie depths, might be locked for a good reason: to keep things out, as well as hold them in. It was irrational, she knew, but suddenly that locked door came to represent all the other deprivations, abuses and insults she had suffered at the hands of the Magefolk ever since coming to the Academy. It was a symbol of their power over her, of what they had done to her father, and all they had denied her race. Bracing her feet and putting her shoulder to the door,

Zanna gave it a ferocious shove. No one could have been more surprised than herself when it shot open with a protesting creak and pitched her headlong into the blackness beyond.

The candle went out, of course. It fell from her hand, guttered, and rolled away into the darkness. Zanna lay there, shocked and bruised, all the breath knocked out of her. Her righteous anger was suddenly replaced by the chill of fear. *What had she done?*

But after the events of this night, she discovered a resilience she hadn't known she possessed. Don't be ridiculous, she told herself. How many locked and forgotten chambers must there be in this ancient labyrinth beneath the Academy? The lock was old – it had rusted and rotted, that was all, until even her own slight strength had been enough to force it. Anyway, Zanna – be practical. It was a place to rest.

'Zanna?' It was the querulous voice of an old man, and that frightened her far more than a fall into the darkness. Her dad had always been so vigorous. She'd never thought he would grow old . . .

'Don't worry – I'm here. I missed the step, that's all.' Zanna climbed painfully to her feet, but had no idea which way to go. The darkness was utterly profound. She was glad that she had Vannor to take care of, or she might be overcome by the sneaking fear that threatened to creep up on her and overwhelm her. It was on the tip of her tongue to ask him to strike a new light, but she remembered that, with his injured hand, he would not be able to manage it. Zanna took a deep breath. 'Dad, I'm all right, but I lost the candle. Can you keep talking to me, or calling out, to guide me back to you?'

'Of course I can, lass.' To her relief, he sounded much more like his old indomitable self. 'Don't be afraid now. Just follow the sound of my voice . . .' Even though his words were strained with the effort of fighting the agony in his wounded hand, Vannor rallied himself for the sake of his daughter. Zanna heard that newfound confidence, and rejoiced.

'Did I ever tell you about the time I met Leynard, and made my original deal with the Nightrunners? It was like this . . .'

At another time, Zanna might have been enthralled by the tale. Now, all her attention was on Vannor's voice itself. Following what she profoundly hoped was the direction of the sound, she stumbled forward, her hands groping blindly out in front of her. It wasn't easy. She made several mistakes at first, until the fading of the spoken words proved that she must be going the wrong way. After a time, though, her hearing seemed to have become preternaturally efficient in the absence of sight. Other senses also came into play – the cold caress of the draught that came through the open doorway on to her skin, and the metallic smell of blood from her father's hand.

'And so there we were, all dressed up in our solstice finery – except for Forral and the Lady Aurian, who'd been out sparring, would you believe – even on a festival day? The crazy fools. Well, your stepmother wasn't best suited, let me tell you – and when one of the soldiers came to the door and said they'd found a runaway . . .'

Zanna half-listened to the story. She had never heard this one before – and it concerned the Lady Aurian. But now, it simply served as a beacon to guide her to safety.

'Poor lad – a bondservant they called him, but a better word would have been slave. But the Lady protected him, and cared for him, and took him as her servant – and a good thing too, as it turned out, because in the end, Anvar saved . . .'

Zanna cursed as she tripped over a step, scraping her already abraded hands and banging her knee painfully. 'Dad?' she called.

'I'm here, love.' His voice was comfortingly close – as was the hand that groped for hers a minute later.

Zanna dared not betray her relief lest he discovered how afraid she had been in the first place. 'Can you hand me the basket?' she asked him. Once she had grasped it, she groped inside for the spare candles and the tinderbox. It seemed to take endless minutes before she got another candle lit, only to find it wasn't much help, because they had strayed into another large chamber. But that was no surprise to Zanna, who had been conscious of the echoes of Vannor's voice while she had tried to navigate herself out of the room. She simply took comfort in being able to see at all; and, especially, to see her father again.

'Come on, dad – we'll rest now.' Zanna guided her father down the steps and into the echoing chamber. Just inside the door, she took him a few paces to one side, to be out of the draught from the entrance, but near enough to it for a quick escape, and eased him down to rest with his back against the wall.

Vannor sighed. 'That's better,' he murmured. He accepted the flask from her and took a swig of water, while Zanna rummaged in the basket to find him some bread and cheese. When she turned back to him, he was fast asleep.

Zanna gently freed the flask from his limp hand. She took a drink for herself, nibbled hungrily at a little of the bread, and then settled down to watch over the slumbering merchant. It was surprisingly lonely being the only one awake in the darkness, but despite her own exhaustion Zanna felt that someone should be keeping watch. Besides, the unnerving atmosphere of the lonely catacombs made it impossible for her to fall asleep. If only she could rid herself of the feeling that she was not alone; that someone – or something – else lurked beside herself and her oblivious father in the darkness. 'Well, whatever it is, I hope it knows the way out of here,' she muttered stoutly, trying to stiffen her courage with common sense, 'because we need all the help we can get.'

It was no good. As time went on, the feeling grew and grew in her, until the idea of sitting around waiting for some nameless thing to pounce on her became unbearable. And to make matters worse, she was feeling increasing discomfort from the urgent need to relieve herself. Damn, Zanna thought, wishing she hadn't drunk that water. This would have to happen now. Where could she go? It seemed an un- forgiveable sacrilege to use a chamber full of ancient and probably priceless books as a privy. But there was no way in the world that she was going out into that draughty, open corridor, out of sight of her dad. She would simply have to find a corner, she thought, and do her best to clear a space.

Taking another candle from the fast-diminishing stock in her basket, she lit it at the first and stuck it on the bare rock near Vannor's feet. With only that frail slip of light to guide her back to safety, Zanna struck out, feeling her uncertain way along the wall of the chamber. She had not gone far before she started to regret her rashness. The vast, echoing darkness pressed in on her, and she was startled over and over again, until her nerves were frayed to tatters, by tiny rustlings and patterings beyond the range of her light. Once, she tripped over a scattered pile of books, and almost lost her candle.

That was quite enough, Zanna told herself. It had been a daft idea anyway, this wandering around in the dark when she ought to be resting and looking after her dad. And then a dreadful thought struck her. What if, in her absence, something horrible had crept up on Vannor while he slept? Looking back over her shoulder, she caught a glimpse of the tiny seed of light that was his candle, and felt somewhat reassured. None the less, she had left him alone long enough. Quickly, she found a spot, where the wall angled sharply round into another alcove that seemed to be clear of books, and squatted down to relieve herself. As she got to her feet she half-turned, holding her candle high – and light sprang into the shadowy depths of the recess to reveal the tall, thin figure of a man who loomed over her, his face a snarling mask of horror, with the glittering flame reflected in his glassy eyes.

The Mages and their companions retreated from the cloud of choking dust that billowed across the landing, and sought the sanctuary of the upper chambers. There they paused, some sitting, some leaning wearily against one another; all of them breathing hard from the terrors and exertions of the fight. Though no one had been seriously wounded, none of them had come out of the battle completely unscathed. After a moment, Iscalda found a water bottle in one of the packs, and began to rip an old shirt into bandages, for it was clear

241

that the Mage was too spent, for the moment, to attempt any healing magic. Aurian and Anvar, the only ones who yet knew of Bohan's death, clung to one another briefly, sharing their relief at finding one another safe, and their sorrow at the passing of their friend. All too soon, Aurian lifted her head from Anvar's shoulder.

'Forgive me, Basileus,' he heard her say to the Moldan. 'I hope I didn't hurt you too badly, but I had no other choice.'

'I understand.' The Elemental's voice was sombre. *'It was no great injury to a being of my vast dimensions – but it proved an unwelcome reminder of the powers your race can wield. Even now, the Xandim are hacking at my bones elsewhere, to break a path through to where you are, and I would put any blame for this business with them, rather than yourself. None the less, the time has clearly come for you Wizards to leave this place – for the good of us all.'*

'I'm sorry,' Aurian sighed. 'You're right.' Then Anvar sensed the mental shift as she turned her thoughts towards Shia.

It took all of Aurian's courage to ask the question, for she feared that she already knew the answer. 'Shia – what about Wolf? He didn't . . .'

'No. He is quite safe. Khanu is taking the cub and his guardian wolves to Chiamh's tower.'

Relief washed over Aurian in a dizzying wave. She felt almost guilty that she should feel so glad when the eunuch had perished. 'What happened to Bohan?' she asked softly.

'He fell.' The cat's mental tones were heavy with sorrow. 'I think the ledge cracked beneath his weight. I tried to save him, but . . .' It was clear that she was too overwhelmed to say more.

'And I sent him out there.' Though she spoke aloud this time, the Mage's voice was little more than a whisper. Abruptly she gasped, swore, and wrenched herself out of Anvar's arms, heading for the window. 'Shia – what about the ledge?'

'Gone for some distance – as is your bridge. You will find no escape this way.'

Aurian found her companions pressing round her as she leaned out of the window.

242

'We tried to tell you,' Iscalda was saying. 'The planks had gone . . .'

They were crowding her so closely that the Mage, with a stab of panic, felt in danger of falling herself. 'Get back,' she shouted, and pulled herself away from the terrifying drop, shaking at the thought of Bohan's fatal plunge to the rocks below. With an effort, she wrenched her thoughts away from the horror. She must concentrate now on surviving the present crisis.

'Everybody take what you need,' she ordered. Dashing across to her bed, and the assorted pile of baggage that lay beside it, she thrust the Staff of Earth into her belt and began to rummage in one of the packs for the whistle that would summon the Skyfolk.

'Here – use mine.' Anvar, the Harp now slung securely across his shoulders, was a step ahead of her.

'You signal them.' Aurian didn't want to lean out of that window again if she could help it. As she was stuffing the contents back into her disembowelled pack, she heard the first shrill blast go echoing out into the darkness. She only hoped that for once in their lives those wretched Winged Folk would hurry. 'How long do we have?' she asked Basileus

Long enough – if you are quick.

'That's a great comfort,' the Mage muttered irritably, but was careful not to project the thought.

'Is there no way I can help you?' Shia's voice came into her mind. 'It's a long leap in the dark, but I think I could reach the window . . .'

'No! Don't!' Aurian could not bear the thought of losing another friend to the fanged rocks at the bottom of the chasm. 'Don't worry – the Skyfolk are coming.'

'You'll be lucky.' Shia's mental tones were sour with disgust. 'I may have been running for my life at the time, but I distinctly saw those craven feathered traitors fly away when the Xandim began their attack.'

What? Aurian spat out a vile epithet that made even Parric raise his eyebrows in surprise.

'What now?' he asked.

'The bloody Skyfolk have deserted us,' Aurian snapped.

Parric gave her a knowing look that made her want to strangle him on the spot. 'Well, don't say I didn't warn you, after what you said to them the other day. You have to know how to handle folk, if you want to be a leader. You can't just – '

'That's sound advice, Parric, coming from the man who has skilfully handled the Xandim into attacking us,' the Mage retorted. Seething, she turned her back on him and went to join Anvar in the window embrasure. The trouble was, she knew that the cavalry master had a point. Without Raven there to control them, the winged escort that she had assigned to the Magefolk had been proving more and more restive and wilful; and the further they went from their mountain home, the more plainly reluctant they had been about their duty. Nevertheless, this cowardly desertion, just when they were needed most, came as a tremendous blow to Aurian's plans. Bitterly, now, she regretted the scathing words she had said to them the day after Wolf's kidnapping. At the time, she'd been so incensed by their lack of support that she had allowed her temper to get the better of her. But though they had seemed restless and unrepentant, she had thought she could heal the breach, in time. Unfortunately, what with Elewin's death and the attack of the Xandim, she'd never managed to make the time.

'What are we going to do?' Iscalda said. The Xandim woman's smoke-smudged face had the pale, set look of one who was reaching the end of her courage.

Luckily for Aurian, who had no reply to give, Schiannath answered for her. 'If worse comes to worst, we fight.' He drew his sword and went to stand beside the Mage. Aurian was buoyed by his courage, and the comforting clasp of his hand on her shoulder, but oh – for them to die like cornered rats in this foreign land would be so senseless!

'So don't die, then,' she muttered to herself. 'There must be some way out of this.'

Anvar wasn't giving up. He was still leaning out of the window, blowing shrilly on the whistle fit to burst his lungs. 'Come *on*, you misbegotten feathered freaks,' she heard him gasp between breaths.

'*You had better hurry.*' The Moldan's voice sounded grim as iron in her mind. '*They have broken through into the stairwell. They have only to clear your rockfall . . .*'

'Have they now?' Aurian replied grimly. 'Well, I hope you have plenty of rock to spare, Basileus, because if they clear that rockfall I can always provide another.'

'*Wizard, I warn you – I will not permit you to injure me again.*' It was the first time she had heard the Moldan sound angry.

'You said it wouldn't hurt you badly – and you know I'd never harm you if I had a choice,' Aurian interrupted. But even as she was pleading for his understanding, she was striding purposefully towards the door.

Anvar's triumphant yell halted her in mid-stride. 'Aurian – they're here. They're *here!*'

Whirling, the Mages ran back to the embrasure, where the heavy curtains were blowing inwards and the air was vibrating to the concussive thunder of great wings. In an excess of relief she hugged her soulmate. 'Well done, Anvar. If you hadn't been so persistent . . . Hurry, everyone. We're getting out and there's no time to lose . . .'

'Indeed there is not, if you wish our aid in your escape. There are only two of us left – the rest have returned to Aerillia.'

Aurian turned to see the figure of a single winged warrior perched precariously on the windowsill. Beyond him another figure hovered – but only one. Her heart sank. If they hurried, though, there might still be time – so long as these Skyfolk could still be trusted. 'I'm endlessly grateful for your loyalty,' she told the winged man. 'But why . . .?'

He raised an eyebrow. 'Why did we stay? Because we are loyal to Queen Raven, and we treat our acceptance of her command as a sacred oath.'

'And besides,' the other warrior – a female – added from beyond his shoulder, 'we are indebted to you groundling wizards for slaying Blacktalon and ending the winter, and not least for saving our queen.'

That was good enough for Aurian. It only took a second to get Iscalda in position on the windowsill. They could not take her far – only to a safe place on the mountain beyond the perilous ledges – for normally it took four of them with a net to maintain their flight with a burden as heavy as a human. But it would be far enough. Each of the Winged Folk took hold of one of her arms, and then they hoisted her up and away, their wings beating rapidly as they strove to gain height with their unaccustomed burden.

While they were gone, the other humans of the party drew lots with broken bits of the straw matting to solve the quarrel over who should be next to go. Aurian and Anvar insisted on remaining to the end, because, with their powers, they stood a chance of defending themselves if the Xandim should break through. None of the others wanted to abandon them. Chiamh was next, and could only be persuaded to go because he could defend the others and lead them to safety if anything happened to the Mages. Parric followed, fuming, and after him Yazour, Sangra, and Schiannath. By that time, the sound of the Xandim breaking through the rubble could clearly be heard.

Only the Magefolk remained. While Schiannath was being flown across, Anvar turned to Aurian. 'You're going next,' he told her. 'I don't want any argument.'

Aurian opened her mouth to protest, but he forestalled her. 'Three considerations. First, this started out as your fight against Miathan – not only should you be the one to finish it, but if what the Dragon said was true you are the only one who can, for no one else can wield the Sword. Second, Wolf needs his mother. Third –' He grinned. 'If they *should* break through, I can stop them by taking them out of time with the Harp.'

'Only so many of them,' Aurian argued, 'and only for so long. Even with the Harp to help you, it would be too great a drain on your powers.'

'I can manage for a short time, and with luck that's all I'll need. If you must wield the Sword, Aurian, we must keep you safe to do so. You know I'm right.'

Aurian grimaced. 'Damn it – I *hate* it when you're right.'

All too soon, the sound of wings presaged the arrival of the Skyfolk. As they hovered, waiting, by the window, Aurian noticed that their faces were haggard with weariness and white with strain. She only prayed they had the strength for two more trips. Turning back to Anvar she hugged him convulsively, and wondered how she would have the strength to ever let him go. She looked deep into his eyes, shining intensely blue through the black mask of soot and smoke that smeared his face, and kissed him deeply. 'You take care of yourself,' she muttered gruffly, 'or you'll have me to answer to.'

Anvar grinned crookedly. 'Don't worry. After waiting all this time, I'm not going to lose you now.'

He helped her up on to the windowsill, where the strong hands of the Skyfolk clamped around her wrists. 'Take special care of this one – she's precious,' he adjured them.

'We've never dropped anything yet,' the female warrior chuckled. Before Aurian had time for a tart reply, they launched themselves with a rush of wings – and the Mage's stomach leapt into her throat as she felt herself dangling by her hands over a fathomless drop, only two handclasps away from oblivion, and Anvar left far behind.

It was far worse than the net. There, at least, she'd felt enclosed, with some support between her and the empty air. This time, there was nothing but the void beneath her swinging feet, and the muscles of her arms were screaming in protest as they were forced to bear her entire weight. What it must be like for the two Skyfolk, who had valiantly performed this flight over and over, Aurian dared not imagine. They must be in agony – and certainly reaching the end of their strength. She tried not to think what would happen if that strength should suddenly fail. The cold wind blew into her eyes, making them water, and plastered whipping tendrils of hair across her face, and of course she had no hands free to push the strands aside, or wipe away the streaming tears. 'Where are they going?' she thought wildly, and would have asked the Winged Folk, had she dared to distract them. 'Surely we must be almost there by now!' Even more than she longed for the end of her own wild flight, she desperately wanted them to get back to rescue Anvar.

And then it was over. 'This is the place,' a voice yelled

247

shrilly above the rushing wind and drumming of wings, and suddenly Aurian found herself loosed, and falling . . . to land bruisingly on her hands and knees on an expanse of soaking turf, after a drop of several inches.

'Aurian – are you all right?' The voice belonged to Chiamh. In an instant he was beside her, trying to pull her upright.

Aurian wrenched her arm out of his grasp. 'Let go of me,' she muttered ungratefully, and buried her face in the wet, dawn-fragrant grass. Right now, she wanted to keep as much contact with the blessed, solid ground as she could get. For a luxurious moment she stretched there, until her worries drove her to her feet. Her companions surrounded her – she could see their drawn, soot-smirched faces quite clearly now. To her surprise – for she had kept her eyes firmly shut during the duration of the flight – the sky was brightening in the east. Already, the faintest blush of copper stroked the fangs of Steelclaw, giving the tortured peaks a weird, un-earthly glow against the sapphire sky.

Then all such thoughts were driven from Aurian's mind as a huge black shape arrowed down on her, and she found herself on the turf once more, flat on her back this time, with Shia wrapping strong paws around her body and rubbing a bristly black face against her own, all the while purring fit to shatter the fragile dawn. 'You're safe! I thought I'd lose you too!' Shia drew back and glared into Aurian's eyes with her fiery, golden gaze. 'Don't ever do that to me again – telling me to stay away while you were in danger!'

'I'll do my best,' Aurian promised breathlessly, and sus-pected that she lied. Struggling into a sitting position, she threw her arms around Shia's neck. 'I'm so glad to see you!'

The great cat pressed close to her, and Aurian knew that she was seeking comfort from her grief at Bohan's death. 'He was the first,' the great cat said softly. 'Excepting Anvar, you and he were the only remaining companions from the start of my freedom.'

'And he was your friend,' Aurian replied. 'I know how close you were. He was my friend too, Shia, and when we have a chance we'll mourn him fitly.' Now, however, she was more concerned with Anvar. There was nothing she could do for Bohan, but while there was a chance that her soulmate still lived . . .

He lived indeed. Because she had been preoccupied with Shia, she had missed the first distant thrum of wings, but Aurian could hear it now, and could see the black speck approaching in the northern skies. In another instant, they had dropped Anvar at her feet. He looked pale and haggard, but unhurt, and very much alive. Thanking all the gods, Aurian disentangled herself from the cat and pounced on him, in much the same way as Shia had pounced on her. 'You're here!' She knew how ridiculous it must have sounded, but she didn't care. 'You're all right!' She drew back and peered at him closely. 'You are all right, aren't you? The Xandim didn't get through?'

'No – but it was close.' Then Anvar's strained expression changed to a grin. 'I would like to have seen their faces when they discovered an empty room.'

'We'll let them work it out, but in the meantime we should be moving.' The voice came from Chiamh. 'When they discover my absence, the first place they will think to seek me is my vale.'

'But I thought you said they would be afraid to pass the standing stones,' Aurian protested.

'Yes – but if they can, they will try to stop me getting that far.'

'It's true.' Aurian looked up to see one of the Skyfolk standing beside her. 'Already, as we completed our last journey, we saw men and horses mustering, and heading for the cliff path.'

'Curse them!' Aurian cried. 'Will there never be an end to this?'

'Not yet,' Chiamh said softly. 'Not until dawn tomorrow, when there will be a challenge, and a new Herdlord elected. They must abide by that decision, Lady – and they will, so long as the victor is one of our folk. Until then, we have only to survive – and hope that the victor will be our friend.'

There was no more time to lose. It would be a race, now, to reach the Valley of the Dead before the Xandim could

249

block their way. Chiamh, Iscalda and Schiannath offered to change to their horse-shape; and it was decided that Iscalda would take Yazour, Chiamh would take his old friend Sangra, and Schiannath, being bigger and stronger than the Windeye, would bear the Mages, riding double, on his back. That only left Parric, and Aurian's heart bled for him, that he, a cavalry master and the Herdlord of the Xandim, should be forced to fly with the Skyfolk while the others rode. There was no time now, however, to worry about hurt feelings. All such considerations must be put aside in favour of survival. Though Aurian knew that Parric was enough of a soldier to appreciate the fact, the look on his face made her spine prickle with unease. Somehow she knew for a certainty that they had not heard the last of the matter.

Even as Aurian was worrying, the Skyfolk took off with Parric. Chiamh and Iscalda had already changed. A bay stallion and a white mare stood there, impatiently awaiting their riders. Schiannath looked at the Mage, his teeth flashing white in a grin. 'Get ready, Lady – I promise I'll give you the ride of your life.'

Before Aurian's eyes, he changed. His form blurred, shimmered and altered, and there stood a great, proud warhorse, shadow-etched in dark, dappled grey, with black legs and mane and tail. Schiannath arched his muscular, curving neck and tossed the midnight clouds of his mane. To Aurian, it was like a beckoning. She leapt astride his warm, broad back, and felt Anvar scramble up behind her. The others were already mounted.

With a bound they were away, Shia racing alongside like an extra shadow, keeping up with an effortless lope as the sun climbed over the horizon and flooded the plateau with a sea of misty amber light. On the crest of that golden wave they rode, with the thundering hooves of the Horsefolk throwing up diamond-sprays of dew from the glittering emerald grass and the silver spires of the mountains rising high above them, crowning the new day.

16

Out of Time

Zanna screamed, and dropped the candle. She fell to her knees, cringing like a hare beneath the shadow of the hawk, her mind blank with terror. For what seemed an endless time she huddled, cringing, with her eyes tight shut, awaiting the end. But when she felt a hand touch her shoulder, some buried instinct for survival made her fight. She leapt up with a shriek, flailing out blindly with her fists at her assailant.

'Stop that, you idiot. It's me. Zanna!'

Belatedly, Zanna recognized the voice. 'Dad?' she squeaked.

'It's all right now, love. I'm here.' Everything was still in darkness, but she felt his arms go round her. She leaned against his shoulder, shaking uncontrollably and trying to fight off the urge to burst into hysterical tears, while Vannor stroked her back with his uninjured hand, soothing her as he had done when she was a little girl awakening from childish nightmares. 'What happened, love?' he asked her gently. 'What did you see that scared you like that?'

Zanna clutched at him, all her fears reawakened. 'Dad, there was a man, in the alcove. I saw him . . .'

'Hush, lass. There's no one down here but us. If there had really been someone, don't you think we'd have heard him? And if he meant to do us harm we'd have known about it by now. I expect you saw a statue or something, that's all. I'm not surprised it gave you a shock. Had it been me, I'd still be running.' He chuckled, and Zanna felt her fears beginning to melt away.

'Come on,' said Vannor. 'Do you have the tinderbox in your pocket? You knocked my candle right out of my hand, but it should be down here on the floor somewhere. Let's have some light, and we'll take a look at this man of yours.'

251

Letting go of her, Vannor dropped down to grope for the lost candle, and Zanna delved in her pocket for the tinder-box. After a few minutes of scrabbling, fumbling, and a curse or two from Vannor, they managed to get the wick to catch alight, and Zanna blinked her eyes as the scene came into focus around her in an orb of spreading golden radiance that was dazzling after all the darkness.

'Now, then. Let's see this statue, or whatever it is.' Awkwardly and left-handed, Vannor drew the sword that he had taken from the dead guard in the Mages' Tower. (He had raised his eyebrows at the sight of the two fallen men, and given Zanna a long and thoughtful look; but as yet, thank providence, he had forborne to ask her any awkward questions concerning how they had come to be in that state).

'I'm sorry, love, but you'll have to hold the candle for me,' he told her. Zanna took it reluctantly, and held it high as he turned towards the shadowy alcove. Even though she was forced to follow him closely with the light, she made sure that he was between herself and whatever might be lurking in the niche. Though her good sense had accepted her father's explanation, the memory of her terror was still fresh enough to overcome her courage.

Unexpectedly, she ran into Vannor's back as he halted abruptly, standing stock-still as though he'd been turned to stone. 'Seven bloody demons!' he cried. 'It can't be!'

Zanna caught at the dangerously tilting candle as he staggered back against her, reeling and wide-eyed with shock. 'What is it, dad?' she gasped. 'You look as though you'd seen a ghost.'

'I have – or bloody nearly.' In his distress, Vannor seemed to have forgotten that he was talking to his daughter. He sheathed his sword, and rubbed a shaking hand across his eyes. 'I just don't believe it.' He shook his head. 'What the blazes is that bastard playing at?'

'Who?' Zanna demanded.

'The Archmage,' Vannor said angrily. Suddenly, his eyes focused on Zanna, and he seemed to collect himself. 'Sorry, love,' he sighed. 'It was just – well, it was such a shock. I was forgetting you didn't know . . .'

252

'Know what?' Zanna almost shrieked at him. 'Dad, what's going on? What did you see in there?'

'You'd better take a look.' Taking her hand, Vannor led her forward. 'Don't be scared, now – the poor beggar can't hurt you . . .'

The rest of his words were drowned by Zanna's cry of horror. In the niche a tall figure stood, stiff and lifeless as a statue, but unmistakably a man.

'It's all right, lass.' The firm clasp of Vannor's hand was a comfort, though the strained tone of his voice belied his words.

'Who is – who is he?' Zanna whispered. She saw what shock had driven from her mind the first time she saw him: that the strange man was surrounded by a faint, thin nimbus of shimmering silver-blue that could only be a spell. Strands of brighter blue, like tiny tongues of lightning, crawled in a fiery network across his body and long mane of silver-shot brown hair. Zanna looked at that face, twisted in its hideous rictus of terror, and thought she could discern, in the finely carved bone structure and the brilliance of the glazed, blue-grey eyes, a look of the Magefolk about him.

'It's Finbarr. Poor Finbarr. Of course, you never met him, did you? It was always a standing joke with Aurian that we could never pry him out of his archives.' Her father's voice was choked with what sounded suspiciously like tears, though when Zanna stole a glance at him his eyes were still dry. 'He saved our lives when the Wraiths attacked, and gave us time to flee, but . . .' He frowned in puzzlement. 'Aurian said he was killed – she felt him die. So why would Miathan waste magic to preserve his body like this? It would only make sense if Aurian was somehow wrong, and he isn't dead . . .' Abruptly, he turned to Zanna. 'Well, whatever the explanation is, there's nothing we can do about it. But the Lady Aurian should know about this, as soon as may be.'

'Do you want me to try to contact her again?' Zanna fished in her pocket for the precious crystal.

'Not now, love. We've delayed here long enough. I think we'd best get out of these tunnels while I still have the strength to manage it.' He groaned. 'Oh, for a warm bed, and a blazing fire, and a flask of good wine . . .'

Zanna took his arm. 'You'll have them all, dad, I promise, once we get you out of here.'

'Supposing I ever get out of here,' Vannor muttered grimly under his breath. The words sent a chill through Zanna, and mixed with the sinking fear she felt was a flash of scalding anger at him for frightening her so. It made her all the more determined to succeed. Damn it – she had rescued her dad against all the odds and brought him this far. Zanna gritted her teeth. I'll find a way out of here if it's the last thing I do, she thought fiercely. But she knew he had never meant her to hear his words, and so for his sake she pretended she had not.

Sadly, they said a last, silent farewell to Finbarr. Though she had never known him, and had no idea whether the archivist was alive or dead beyond the fetters of the spell, it wrenched Zanna's heart to leave him. It seemed wrong, somehow, to abandon the Mage to the lonely darkness once more.

Hours later, Zanna had no sympathy to spare for anyone save her father and herself. Famished, footsore and exhausted as she was, it had begun to feel as though she had spent her entire life blundering around in these cold, damp, endless catacombs, and that she would be doomed to continue until she died. As for her father, he had long ago reached the limits of his endurance, and was somehow keeping himself going only through sheer stubbornness and strength of will. For a long time now she had been tortured by the painful rasp of Vannor's ragged breathing, and the hesitant, scuffing sound of his dragging, stumbling footsteps.

Vannor tried to gather his faltering strength, though his injured hand throbbed now in a screaming mass of agony, and the dizzy faintness from shock and loss of blood was hard to fight. Zanna had been so brave, but he could see that her confidence was beginning to falter, and knew it wasn't only weariness and hunger that were the cause. From the set expression on her face; the determinedly cheerful look that was belied by the faint line like a pen stroke drawn between her brows – he knew that her courage was being eaten away by worry over his condition. Poor child – it wasn't fair.

She had gone through so much for him – had shown more courage and grit than he would have expected even from a son. Judging by the bodies he had seen outside his prison in the Mages' Tower, she had even killed for him – and her little more than a child, and a cosseted girlchild at that. He had to keep going, just to repay her bravery and loyalty.

The candle in Zanna's hand had burned down to a soft and guttering stub, scalding her fingers with hot wax. He saw her flinch, and flick the hardening drops away, but she bit her lip and said nothing. He had been half-amused, half-shocked, before by her futile attempts to curb her language, but it worried him more, now, that she was too weary to waste energy on a curse. 'Just a minute, dad.' Putting down her basket, which by this time was ominously light, she rummaged quickly inside for another candle by the waning glow of the one she held. She turned to him, her eyes wide with dismay. 'We're down to the last one.'

Suddenly Vannor was overcome by a dreadful vision of himself and his daughter wandering lost in the smothering darkness until these accursed tunnels became their tomb. Zanna had clearly been thinking along similar lines. Her voice broke on a sob of frustration. 'Oh, gods,' she wailed, 'we're never going to find our way out of here.'

'Here, Zanna – give it to me.' Quickly Vannor took the stub of candle from her unresisting fingers before it went out completely. 'Now, lass, just hold the new one – I can't manage with one hand.' Zanna, bless her, had so far shown a toughness that amazed him. He knew that having something to do would help her gain control of her impending hysteria. He was right. By the time Vannor had kindled a flame on the new wick she had managed to calm herself and swallow her tears, though she was still shivering with suppressed fear.

Vannor stuck the candle on a narrow projection in the rough-hewn wall of the passage and put his arms round her. 'Don't lose heart, love. Look how uneven these tunnels are. We've been going downwards for hours – we must be in the oldest part of the catacombs by now. Come on now; let's try to go on a little longer. Surely this must be the last lap.'

Sighing, Zanna scrambled awkwardly to her feet, but her

255

tired legs would barely support her and she stumbled, catching herself against a jutting spur in the tunnel wall to stop herself from falling. She paused there, just to catch her breath, and found herself coughing and gasping. From a narrow crack in the shadow of the spur came a cold and noisome draught. 'Dad?' Zanna's voice shook with excitement. 'Dad – come here and look at this!' After hours of searching, they had finally found the narrow crack in the wall of the catacombs that led down into the sewers.

The discovery gave them new heart. They organized themselves quickly, abandoning the now-useless basket and taking only the candle, tinderbox, and the bottle with their dwindling supply of water. The crevice was so narrow that Zanna was forced to turn sideways to squeeze through at all, and according to her father the drain beyond was narrower still. Though she did not want to, Vannor insisted that she go first, and she knew, with a sinking feeling of dread, that he was afraid of getting stuck, and blocking the way out for her. 'Look, lass, be sensible,' he said when she tried to argue. 'If worse comes to worst, at least you'll be able to go and fetch help.'

Zanna could only look at him helplessly, lost for words. If he should be trapped, how would she find her way out through the sewers? For that matter, whom did she know in the city who could, or would, come back and help her father, even supposing she'd be able to find him again? Vannor, however, would brook no refusal. She had no choice but to force herself through the narrow crack, holding her breath as much as possible against the stench that drifted up from the drain beyond.

The journey through the sloping drain proved to be a nightmare beyond Zanna's worst imaginings. It was such a tight fit for her body that the nameless slime which coated the inside of the pipe was a blessing, in that it helped her to squeeze through, though she could only manage to make any headway at all by inching herself along by her fingernails and pushing with her toes. To make matters worse, it was pitch black inside, for it was far too damp and draughty to keep a candle alight. When the narrow pipe bent to the side at an angle, Zanna simply wanted to lay her head down on her aching, outstretched arms and howl with frustration, but she gritted her teeth and reminded herself that when her dad had been hiding out here with the rebels Parric the cavalry master had used this route regularly. Well, if he could do it, so could she. She gritted her teeth, bent her tortured spine until she thought it would snap, and *pushed* . . .

Suddenly she felt herself sliding, faster and faster, and shot out of the drain mouth, skinning her elbows and scraping her shins on the edge of the pipe. She lay for a moment, breathless, and then burst into sobs of relief that ended just as quickly as they had begun when she remembered her father. Now, after she had made the terrible journey herself, she truly realized what a trial it would be for her dad. Only the fact that the stocky Vannor had lost a good deal of flesh during his imprisonment with the Magefolk might give him even the slightest chance of squeezing through, but he only had the one good hand to pull himself along. He would never do it . . . Surely it was impossible. Her heart beating fast with fear, Zanna found the mouth of the drain by dint of feverish groping in the darkness. She put her ear to it and listened. Echoing hollowly down the pipe came the sound of muffled grunts and curses. For a time Zanna listened in wretched silence, understanding the difficulties her father was experiencing and not wanting to distract him. Eventually, though, she could bear the waiting no longer. He should be out by now. Something must have gone wrong. When even the cursing stopped, she could bear it no longer. 'Dad?' she ventured hesitantly, her voice quavering with impending panic. 'Are you all right?'

'Of course I'm bloody not!' Then Vannor seemed to collect himself. 'Sorry lass. I'm having a bit of a problem here, where the pipe bends . . .'

Though he was trying to sound optimistic, Zanna could hear the harshness of strain in his voice. None the less, she found his response not entirely discouraging. As long as he still had the energy to curse, all was not lost. 'Listen, dad,' she said. 'You've reached the hardest part now. After that it's easy. If you can just angle yourself round that corner . . .'

'If wishes were diamonds,' Vannor snapped, 'you'd be the richest heiress in Nexis. I just can't seem to get any kind of purchase on this blasted slime.'

Not all the diamonds in Nexis – in fact nothing in the whole of creation – would have induced Zanna to go back into the drain. Nothing save her love for her father. 'Hold on, dad. I'm coming.' Without hesitation, Zanna wriggled back into the pipe.

'Don't you dare, girl. Damn it, don't be so bloody stupid! You get out of here. Save yourself.'

Zanna let him bellow. In truth, she had no breath for a reply. Getting back up the sloping part of the drain was far more difficult than sliding down it. Again and again she lost her hold through pure weariness, and slid back to the bottom. Again and again she picked herself up, swore heartily, and started the climb again. And at last the miracle happened. Her groping fingers touched the cold, clammy flesh of an outstretched hand that twitched weakly in her grasp.

Vannor's protests had long since ceased. Zanna had been praying that he was all right, but had little breath to spare for talk. 'When I say the word,' she gasped, 'try to bend yourself round the corner.'

'What . . . What the . . .'

'Now!' Zanna cried. Grabbing her dad's wrist in both hands, she deliberately relaxed the bracing pressure of her legs and feet and let herself dangle, with all her weight hanging from her father's arm. There was a startled yell from Vannor, and suddenly Zanna found herself sliding, faster and faster, hurtling down the pipe at a far greater speed than she had previously managed. She shot out of the drain like a cork from a bottle with her father on top of her, flailing his arms and legs, yelling fit to wake the dead, and knocking all the breath from her body with his weight. Though it was still pitch dark in the tunnels, exploding lights shot across Zanna's vision, and for a moment she knew no more.

'Seven bloody demons, girl – don't you ever try a trick like that again. You might have broken your neck!' were the first words that penetrated Zanna's inner darkness. Vannor was cradling her in his arms.

'But I didn't, did I?' she rallied pertly, wanting nothing more than to erase that ragged note of fear from her father's voice.

'No,' Vannor muttered, 'but the next time you scare me like that, you little wretch, I'll break it for you.' Then he laughed, and hugged her. 'Are you all right, lass? By the gods, but Dulsina was right when she kept saying how much you took after me. Your methods might be a bit extreme, but you saved my life then and no mistake! I thought I would be stuck in that pipe for good.'

After a time they collected themselves, and managed to find the candle again. It was much battered and cracked from having been fallen on, but still quite usable. In the light of the burgeoning flame Vannor and his daughter scarcely recognized one another, so begrimed were they from the slimy innards of the pipe. The candle also lit up the rusting stubs of the inspection ladder that would be their next challenge. They looked at one another, sighed, and climbed painfully to their feet to start again.

Though Vannor had to climb one-handed, which presented several dangerous moments, the ladder proved far less difficult than the pipe had been. Soon they squeezed up through another drain – mercifully, a very short one this time – and found themselves in the sewers at last. The very familiarity of his old haunts seemed to restore Vannor's energy and spirits, though, like his daughter, he was staggering with fatigue. He stood on the narrow, slippery ledge that overlooked the noisome channel, and took a deep breath – Zanna wondered how he could, the smell was so bad – looking around the dank, squalid, and rat-infested tunnel with the proprietary air of a landowner surveying his domain. For the first time during the whole of their escape, he looked genuinely cheerful. 'At last,' he sighed. 'A home from home. Now we'll be all right.'

Zanna was glad that one of them felt confident.

'What the blazes do you mean, he's gone?' the Archmage thundered. 'How did this happen?' He crashed his fists down on the table, and the gems that were his eyes flared with a

fiery crimson light. The very air of the chamber seemed to
ignite and throb beneath the burden of his rage. The Captain
of the Academy Guard, massive man and experienced cam-
paigner though he was, blanched and trembled, and the
wretched little scar-face who'd been guarding Vannor's
chamber the night before looked nothing like a killer now.
Cringing in terror, he was trying, unsuccessfully, to edge
himself behind the impassive figure of the Weather-Mage.

Eliseth alone seemed unmoved by Miathan's wrath –
probably, the captain thought sourly, because the scheming
bitch was letting the brunt of it fall on himself.

'Well, you needn't look at me,' she was saying coolly. 'I left
Vannor well guarded as always last night, though frankly, by
the time I'd finished with him, he was in no condition to
arrange his own escape, let alone get far. This whole business reeks of some kind of plot.' She shot the captain of the
guard a poisonous look from beneath her lowered eyelids.

'Well, I had him guarded as usual too, sir,' the captain
added hastily, deciding that her example was not a bad one to
follow. 'Both the top and lower gates were manned, and the
road up here was patrolled. How anyone could get past that
lot beats me.' He turned to glare at the shrinking scar-faced
guard. 'He was there. Why not ask him how those two block-
headed bastards managed to get themselves ambushed.'

'Let us find out.' Miathan's voice was steel wrapped in
silk. He turned the sinister gaze of his dispassionate, arach-
nid eyes on the unfortunate guard.

Only too glad to be dismissed, the captain hurried down
the tower stairs. He wasn't fast enough, however, to escape
the screams of excruciating torment that came from the room
above. Clapping his hands over his ears to shut out the gut-
wrenching howls, he abandoned all dignity and fled.

'It was my maid?' For once, even Eliseth's face betrayed
her shock.

'From what I wrenched out of the guard's mind' – the
Archmage glanced contemptuously at the twisted body on
the floor – 'there would seem to be no doubt.'

'But she was only a kitchen menial – scarcely more than a
child, and with barely wits enough about her to – '

'She had wits enough about her to plan and execute the escape of the most wanted man in Nexis – thanks to you!' Miathan snapped. Despite the crisis, he was enjoying the discomposure of the ice-cool Mage.

'And who was it that charged her with Vannor's care?' Eliseth retorted with a sneer. 'Not I. That was your idea, Archmage, and you put the little wretch in a perfect position to carry out her plan.'

Miathan's scant pleasure in the situation vanished abruptly. A vision of his hands squeezing Eliseth's throat flashed briefly through his mind, then he pulled himself together. 'Enough!' he barked. 'I admit, she duped us both. But the question remains – who is she? One of Vannor's rebels? Does he have other spies within the Academy?' It was an unpleasant thought, that the Magefolk might no longer be inviolate. He remembered the traitor Elewin, and clenched his fists.

'I'll soon find out,' Eliseth promised grimly, 'even if it means tearing apart the minds of every servant in the place. She had to have help, Miathan. How could a slip of a girl like that have managed to kill both Janok and a trained warrior three times her size?'

'That's not the only mystery to concern us.' The Archmage frowned. 'How did she get Vannor out of the Academy without being seen? And where are they now? If you had injured Vannor as badly as you described,' he scowled at her in displeasure, 'he couldn't have gone far.'

'Do you think they're still hiding somewhere in the Academy?' Eliseth suggested.

'It would seem the most likely option. And if they are, the gods themselves will not be able to help them. We'll seal the place off – no one goes in or out for any reason – and have it searched from top to bottom.'

'And what if they aren't here?' the Weather-Mage demanded. 'We can't search the entire city – we don't have sufficient men. And we can't offer a reward for Vannor's recapture, because that would mean admitting to the Mortals that he's still alive.'

'No – but we *can* offer a reward for the girl.' Miathan's

eyes glittered. 'We'll say that she stole something of value from the Magefolk – which is true enough,' he added wryly. 'My release of those provisions yesterday worked to our advantage – there are some in Nexis, at any rate, who are already blessing my name. We'll offer a large reward, both food and gold, to anyone who can lead us to the girl. Either Vannor will be with her, or' – he smiled with avid cruelty – 'we can soon extract the information as to his whereabouts. I intend to get Vannor back, no matter what it takes, and when I do I'll make both him and that wretched girl sorry they were ever born.'

Benziorn hurried through the streets of Nexis, losing himself among the early passers-by, and congratulated himself on giving his guardians the slip once more. Though Yanis, the young Nightrunner leader, was gradually recovering under his care – and, thanks to the skills that the physician had not forgotten, had lost neither his arm nor the use of it – it was becoming more and more difficult to escape the vigilance of Tarnal and Hebba, who seemed to have a totally unreasonable attitude to the idea of a man's taking a little drink every once in a while. Benziorn shrugged. Well, that was just too bad. Though he welcomed the amenities of Hebba's household – in fact, he admitted, after the privations he had suffered he welcomed the luxury of a stout roof and a fireside again, not to mention Hebba's cooking, when there was anything to cook – he was damned if he was going to let her dictate to him with regard to his drinking. Was there no respect for a physician in Nexis any more?

Luckily – for Hebba would not allow so much as the sight of a bottle in her house – Benziorn still had his own private cache of strong spirits hidden away in the old fulling mill: payment in kind for treating a vintner's warehouse guard, a mercenary who'd been suffering the inevitable results of spending too much time with the wharfside whores. Try as they might, Hebba and Tarnal had been unable to discover the source of his secret supply of drink.

Unfortunately, Tarnal had taken to following him in the

hope of unearthing the cache. Benziorn chuckled to himself. The lad still had a lot to learn. Hebba had gone out this morning to the Academy, to wait in an endless line for the rations that the Archmage, for some reason of his own, had seen fit to release, and the young smuggler, perforce, had gone with her to guard the precious food from robbery on the way home. Yanis had been asleep, which had given his physician the perfect opportunity to escape.

By the time the sun had reached its zenith, Benziorn was feeling more than mellow, and he had the rest of the day ahead of him. Given the number of hungry folk in Nexis, the food distribution was likely to take a good long while. Spring sunlight filtered down in dusty bars through the high, smeared windows of the old mill, warming the air and bleaching to near-invisibility the flames of the small fire he had kindled for his comfort. Seated on his folded cloak, with his back resting comfortably against one of the great dye vats and a bottle in his hand, Benziorn almost felt like singing – in fact, why not? It was a while since he'd had a respite from his responsibilities; it was almost like a holiday . . .

He awakened suddenly, shivering, and saw that the dusk was stretching shadowy fingers through the ruins of the old building. Benziorn groaned and rubbed his eyes. His head was beginning to throb, and his mouth felt as though someone had filled it with mud from the river bottom. The last thing he remembered was singing – he had no recollection of falling asleep – and he wondered blearily what had wakened him so abruptly. Then it came again – a tortured, grating squeal of metal on stone, loud enough to send a fresh burst of pain exploding through his pounding head.

What in the world . . .? Cursing under his breath, Benziorn scrambled quickly to his feet and kicked dirt over the smouldering ashes of his fire. Melting back into the shadows, he found a crumbling spot in the stonework of the wall and boosted himself up to lie flat on the broad rim of the massive dye vat – a vantage point from which he could scan most of the floor of the old mill. There came another grinding squeak, and the muffled sound of a man's voice cursing, followed by the crash of something heavy falling. The sound

seemed vaguely familiar. With a shock of belated recollection, the physician identified the noise. His mind went
back to the night when Jarvas's compound had been
attacked, and the Nightrunners had come up through the
grating in the floor of the fulling-mill.

Could it be someone seeking Yanis? Benziorn shifted his
position slightly, craning his neck to try to see around one of
the supporting pillars. A moment later, two figures stumbled
into sight, silhouetted against the fading light of the doorway.
They were reeling and tottering as though they were the ones
who were drunk, supporting one another briefly before they
sank down in a huddle on the millroom floor.

Benziorn waited, rigid with suspicion and suspense, for
another sign of movement, but the intruders did not stir. As
the light from the doorway faded, he wondered if he could
safely escape by slipping through the shadows. Yanis might
need him, and Tarnal would be hunting for him by now for
sure. Silent as a ghost, he slid down from the top of the vat –
at least, that had been the idea. In reality, the physician was
still suffering from the effects of all the spirits he had im-
bibed. He missed his footing and came down hard, landing
with a grunt and stumbling over one of his empty bottles,
which rolled and shattered against the side of the vat with a
crash that sounded deafening in the dusky silence of the
abandoned mill. Cursing under his breath, Benziorn froze.
He heard the soft, rustling scrape of someone stirring on the
other side of the vat.

'Dad? Did you hear that?'

'Shhh.'

There came the hissing, slithering sound of a sword being
quietly unsheathed, but Benziorn had already identified the
first voice as being that of a young girl, and coupled with the
drink still in his blood it gave him courage. The very fact that
these people seemed to be afraid and hiding too seemed to
imply that they would scarcely be a threat.

'Who's there?' he called. 'Whoever you are, there's no
need to be frightened. I mean you no ha –' His words were
cut off in a choked squeak as the keen steel of a swordblade
pressed an icy line across his throat.

'Move and you die. Call out, and the first word you utter will be your last. Is that clear?'

'Yes,' the physician whispered, trembling. He was seized with a desperate urge to look round to see the face of his attacker, though he knew it would be impossible to identify the assailant in the growing darkness, and such folly would certainly mean his death. He felt that his knees must give way at any moment through sheer terror, but if they did the sword would slice his throat. A trickle of rank sweat ran down his spine. Benziorn held his body rigid, concentrating very hard on facing forward and staying on his feet.

'Who are you?' the gruff voice demanded.

'B-Benziorn. A physician . . . well, a former physician.'

'What?'

'I don't mean you any harm – I'm not your enemy. Look, if you want I'll go away and not look back. I don't care who you are – I can't hurt anyone and I don't take sides. Please, good sir . . .' Even in the midst of his undignified babbling, Benziorn felt a flare of outraged pride. How could you sink so low? asked a small voice at the back of his mind, but with his life at stake he knew he would abase himself as much as necessary. Since the death of his wife and children he had often sworn to himself that he did not care whether he lived or died, yet now that the time had come to make good his vow he found, to his amazement, that he cared very much indeed. Life, which had been a burden to him for so long, had, in the space of an instant, and by the narrow margin of a sword's edge, become a very precious gift.

'Benziorn?' mused the voice. 'Gods, that name sounds familiar. Just a minute – aren't you the man who attended my wife in childbirth when the Magefolk healer wouldn't come?'

Terror knotted the physician's bowels. The owner of the sword could only be one man – the only Mortal in the city who might have expected to call upon the services of Meiriel. A frantic notion of temporizing further – of lying, even – raced through his mind and died abirthing – just as Vannor's wife had died. 'At least I saved the child,' he whispered. 'I would have saved his mother, too, had there been any way . . .'

'Damn you.'

The sword trembled against his unprotected throat, and a thin line of hot blood ran down into the collar of his tunic.

'Dad.' It was the young girl's voice again, urgent and pleading. 'Dad, don't do this. Dulsina told me the physician did his best. It wasn't his fault that the Lady Meiriel wouldn't come. Whatever you do, it won't bring mother back. After what we've just been through, how can you blame him for the actions of the Magefolk? If it's anyone's fault that mother didn't survive Antor's birth, the blame should lie with Lady Meiriel, but now she's dead –'

'She's *dead*?'

Benziorn felt the sword drop away from his throat. With a whimper, he sagged against the curving wall of the vat, too undone to even think of running away.

'I had no time to tell you,' the young girl went on, 'but they knew, in the Academy . . .'

Vannor gasped. 'But Parric was with her – and Elewin,' he cried in anguish. 'What happened to them? Are they dead too?'

At that moment, shadows leapt high into the rafters of the mill as the saffron light of a torch blazed in the doorway. The physician saw the faces of his assailants for the first time, and wondered how he could ever have been afraid. A familiar voice called: 'Benziorn? Benziorn, you drunken idiot! Are you there?'

'Tarnal!' the young girl cried. 'Thank the gods it's you!' To Benziorn's amused astonishment, she flew into the Nightrunner's arms – and a quick, sly glance at Tarnal's face proved that the young smuggler didn't object at all.

17

The Seeing

Aurian awakened, stiff and tired, with Wolf whimpering in her arms. Automatically she soothed the cub, as she opened her eyes to see an unfamiliar ceiling of silver-veined rock; much darker and rougher than that within the fastness. Is this a cavern? she wondered blearily, only half-awake yet. Where the blazes am I? Gripped with sudden anxiety, she turned to see Anvar asleep beside her, the smudges of smoke accentuating his pallor of weariness, and dark circles shadowing his closed eyes. Reassured, she was about to turn over and snuggle back into the warmth of the furs that were tucked around her when the memory hit her.

Bohan. Another friend lost in this senseless struggle. She had promised to help him find his voice again, but there had never been time. A memory surfaced from the previous hours, following their escape from the fastness; of warm, flickering firelight within this cavern, a hot drink, and Shia, greatly distressed, telling her that the eunuch had actually called out as he fell. *'Shia. My friend.'*

The Mage closed her eyes against the pain. Shia had always been Bohan's friend – and had proved a better one than Aurian, who had sent him to his death.

'No, you did not. You were trying to save him.' Though the voice had picked the thought from her mind, it was speaking aloud now. Aurian turned to see the Xandim Wind-eye sitting cross-legged beside the fire, not far from the shelf of rock that formed her bed. Chiamh looked worse than Anvar – and as bad as herself, she suspected. His face was so haggard with weariness that he seemed to have aged overnight. Aurian left Wolf in his nest of furs beside Anvar and, sighing, slid out of her warm refuge. Tired and heartsick as she was, there was too much to do to lie abed. She went to join the Windeye by the fire, trying vainly to straighten her creased and rumpled clothing as she went. She sat down beside him, gratefully accepting a steaming cup of fragrant herb tea. 'You're right about Bohan, I know,' she sighed. 'But it's hard not to feel responsible.' She felt her throat grow tight with unshed tears. 'We never even had a chance to bury him . . .'

Chiamh covered her hand with his own. 'If you must blame someone, Lady, blame the Xandim who attacked us. If they had only trusted me . . . Had they only waited a little longer, the matter of the succession would have been resolved in any case.' He sighed. 'Perhaps the fault is mine. Had I tried sooner to gain the respect I merited as their Windeye . . .' He shook his head, and she felt his grip tighten on her hand. 'In any case,' he went on, 'Bohan did have his burial. I asked Basileus . . .'

'And I loosened the rocks of the cliff to fall down upon the body of your departed friend. Fear not, wizard. No one will despoil his resting-place.'

Aurian frowned. 'Basileus? How can we still hear you in this place?'

'You rest at the foot of the Windeye's tower – but you are still upon the Wyndveil, are you not?' The Moldan chuckled. *'All this mountain is my body, and Chiamh's Chamber of Winds is wrested from my bones.'*

'Then why couldn't you have helped Bohan?' Aurian didn't hide her resentment. It would do no good, in the long run, to conceal her feelings from the Moldan. They might as well have it out now, for later there would be much else to concern her.

'Perhaps I might have helped him, wizard, had my attention not been occupied elsewhere,' Basileus answered sharply. *'But you were in danger too, as was the Windeye and your soulmate. There is a limit to what I can accomplish.'*

'I'm sorry. I'm sure you would have helped Bohan if you could. It's just so hard to lose a friend.'

'You think I do not know that?'

Aurian thought of the fate of Ghabal, the Moldan imprisoned beneath the Academy. She thought of the stark, tortured shape of Steelclaw Peak, and remembered Anvar's account of the death of the Moldan of Aerillia. Yes. Indeed, she did understand the losses that Basileus must have suffered. But now her own survival and that of her friends was at stake.

'What's happening now?' she asked the Windeye.

Chiamh shrugged. 'It is an hour or two past noon,' he told her. 'The Xandim have encamped beside the standing stones, at the mouth of the valley. Khanu is watching them. As I suspected, they are afraid to come any further. They await tomorrow's dawn and the challenge for a new Herdlord.'

Aurian sighed. 'We had better talk to Schiannath, then.' She grimaced ruefully. 'While we've been so busy hatching our plans, we've never actually asked him if he wants to do this.' And what, demanded a tiny, nagging voice in the back of her mind, if he does not?

'Lady,' Chiamh said hesitantly. 'What of the seeing?'

'The what?' Aurian frowned.

'You remember – the day after your child was stolen. We came up here and talked, and I promised you . . .'

'Oh. Of course.' The events of the last two days had driven the conversation from the Mage's mind. Chiamh had promised to search upon the winds, to see if he could locate the Sword of Flame . . .

'The seeing must be performed before the challenge takes place, if we do it at all,' the Windeye told her urgently. 'Who knows what may happen to any of us tonight, or at dawn tomorrow? If Phalihas should prevail, I can measure my life in minutes.'

'If Phalihas wants to harm you, he'll have to get past Anvar and me to do it,' Aurian vowed. 'Nevertheless, I think you're right. We ought to get it done as soon as possible. It's vital that I find the Sword. We've lingered in the south too long now, and the gods only know what Miathan is doing in Nexis.' With an effort, she broke off that train of thought. One worry at a time. She turned to the Windeye with a smile. 'Thank you, Chiamh – for everything. I don't know how we would have managed these last days without you.'

He was not the only one she had to thank, Aurian reflected. What about the two remaining, loyal Winged Folk, who had rescued herself and her companions from certain death? She asked Basileus where they were, and discovered that they were both fast asleep, perched up in a niche in the rugged walls of the great rock spire.

Thoughts of the Winged Folk gave her a moment of anxiety for the rest of her companions, but a quick check around the cavern proved that they had all arrived safely. All except Bohan had gained the sanctuary of the Windeye's refuge. Shia lay asleep at the foot of the bed that Aurian shared with Anvar. Wolf's foster-parents were nearby, curled together so tightly that it was nigh impossible to distinguish one from the other. Schiannath was sleeping in a nest of woollen blankets on the floor, while Yazour and Iscalda were rummaging through Chiamh's hoarded food supplies and putting together a sketchy meal for everyone. Sangra lay on the other rock-shelf bed beneath a mass of furs, one arm outstretched into a vacant indentation ... Aurian frowned. Where had Parric got to?

'Parric is outside,' Chiamh supplied. He frowned. 'For some reason, he is unhappy and angered over what happened last night, when you would not leave until Anvar was safe.'

'Oh, surely not,' Aurian protested.

She found the cavalry master not far from the great stone spire, where a slender cataract thundered down into a feeder pool for the stream that went tumbling down the vale. As she approached, the little man looked up at her bleakly.

'What's wrong?' Aurian sat down at his side.

The cavalry master scowled. 'Forral was my friend.' He was looking anywhere but at her. 'Have you no respect for his memory, that you replaced him so quickly?' he muttered resentfully. 'Couldn't you even wait a decent interval?'

'Wait for what?' Aurian flashed at him, anger igniting within her. 'The way things are, I don't even know if I *have* a decent interval! Don't you realize what I went through when Forral died? Don't you know how much I grieved? Forral himself warned me, long ago, that as a Mage I would outlive him – though neither of us suspected that the end would come so soon. He told me to find someone else and be happy.' She rubbed a hand across her eyes. 'I resisted Anvar's love at first,' she said softly, 'but in the end I had to admit that I loved him too.'

She glared at the cavalry master. 'Parric, you've been my friend for a long time now, but if you can't deal with this it's not my problem. I came to terms with Forral's death in my own time, and if that time isn't the same as yours, then I'm sorry, but it's not your life. It has nothing to do with you, or anyone else but myself and Anvar.'

'And if you truly cared about Aurian, you would rejoice that she'd found happiness again.' Aurian spun around, startled by another voice, and caught a glimpse, out of the corner of her eye, of Parric leaping to his feet.

Anvar stood behind them. 'As far as we know,' he went on softly to Parric, 'you're Aurian's oldest surviving friend. Whatever you may think of me, the time has come to prove that friendship.'

'You stay out of this,' Parric snarled. 'It has nothing to do with you.'

'You're wrong,' Anvar said levelly, never taking his eyes from the older man. 'Aurian's happiness has everything to do with me – and the sooner you get used to the fact, the easier it will be for all of us.'

For a moment the air was thick with tension between them, than Parric exploded in anger. 'I don't have to take that kind of talk from a former Magefolk drudge.' He elbowed Anvar roughly aside. 'Get out of my way!'

Anvar grabbed hold of his arm, his eyes flashing fire and ice. 'No – but you do have to take it from one who is Mageborn in his own right, and Aurian's soulmate besides.'

Parric tore himself away with an incoherent shout of anger, his hand on the hilt of his sword.

'Stop this madness, both of you!' Aurian leapt between them. She turned her cold gaze on the seething cavalry master. 'For shame, Parric,' she said softly but clearly. 'What would Forral think? This would sadden him more than anything that has happened since Miathan's evil began.'

She held out her hands to him, her grim expression

softening. 'Apart from Forral, you and Maya were the first Mortal friends I ever had. As a warrior, you know what it's like to lose loved ones in battle; but you also know that life must, and does, go on.' She took a deep breath. 'If you care about me at all, you should be thanking Anvar, not blaming him, for without him I would not be here today. Not only has he saved my life on countless occasions, but it was Anvar who gave me the will to live on after Forral's death.' She turned to her soulmate with a crooked grin. 'He was infuriatingly insistent about it, as a matter of fact – right from that very first night when we fled downriver, and he wouldn't let me drown us in the weir.'

Parric's hand dropped from his swordhilt. 'You were going to drown yourself?' He looked accusingly at the Mage. 'Is that true?'

Anvar shrugged. 'She had a bloody good try,' he admitted. 'And frankly, it wasn't the last time.' He smiled apologetically at his soulmate, but she was nodding in support.

'Half the time, I didn't even realize what I was doing when I behaved so rashly,' she said, 'but Anvar always took care of me. He knew me better than I did myself.'

Parric looked from one Mage to the other for a long moment, his face expressionless, but Aurian was relieved to see that the ugly flush of anger had vanished from his skin. Then, rubbing his hand across his face, he shrugged and sighed, and reached out to grasp the Mage's outstretched hands. 'I'm sorry, lass. I didn't realize it was so bad for you. Can you forgive such a daft old bugger?'

'Oh, Parric!' Aurian pulled him into a hug. 'You do yourself an injustice. I wouldn't say you were old,' she added with a sly chuckle.

The cavalry master's roar of laughter broke the last of the tension that had gripped them all. 'That's one thing about you that hasn't changed, at any rate,' he snorted. 'That wicked tongue of yours is as sharp as ever.'

'I don't think I've changed that much,' Aurian protested. 'I haven't really, have I?'

Parric shook his head. 'No, not at heart, lass – though it's taken me a long time to get that through my thick skull. You

272

just grew up, that's all, and you've grown so greatly in power that it frightened me, I suppose, though I couldn't admit that to myself. It was easier to get angry instead, and blame Anvar here. I never thought, until you just told me, that he might have made you want to keep on going after Forral was killed. What with everything that's happened, you never did have time to tell me the entire story.'

'Maybe I had better tell you,' Anvar put in with a grin. 'Some of her escapades would make your hair stand on end.'

'Do you mind?' the balding cavalry master exploded. 'Bloody Mages – you're as bad as she is!' He held out his hand to Anvar. 'I'm sorry, lad, for what I said to you. After the way the others behaved, especially that mad bitch Meiriel, I suppose I was a bit wary of suddenly finding another Mage on my hands. But I was impressed with the way you stood up to me. I never really got to know you in the old days, but Forral always said you were a good sort. I should have trusted his judgement – and Aurian's.'

'Yes, you should have,' Aurian said. 'But we've all been through a lot these last months, Parric. I'm sure we can let you off with one mistake,' she added with lofty condescension.

'Let me off? Why, you . . .' Parric spluttered indignantly, and saw her smirk at having baited him so successfully, in an echo of the old game they had played so long ago, back at the Nexis garrison.

Aurian raised an eyebrow. 'Got you, Parric. You owe me a beer,' she crowed.

'Not again,' Parric groaned. 'I'll have to remain in your debt until we get back to Nexis – if I haven't settled the score by then,' he threatened, and joined in the laugher of the Mages.

Chiamh, seeing the three of them walking back to his tower together, was relieved to see that they seemed to have settled their differences, whatever they had been. Sometimes the peculiar ways of these outlanders baffled him beyond belief, but he had grown very fond of them all in a short time.

'Ho, Chiamh,' Parric called. 'Have you got any of that wicked mead you brew? I think the occasion calls for a cup or two.'

Aurian laid a hand on his arm, her face suddenly sobering. 'Not now,' she warned. 'We have no time to spare for drinking – we're still in considerable trouble. Anvar and I have a task of our own to perform with Chiamh, and then you and he must go down to the valley gates and give our decision to the Elders of the Xandim.'

'Too true, alas,' Chiamh agreed. 'And worse – I must permit Phalihas to resume his human shape, so that he can undergo the trial of tonight's vigil. The risk of treachery will be greatest at that time.' He shuddered. 'Once Phalihas is changed back to human form, there will be no further need for the Xandim to spare me. Windeye or not, I will be lucky to escape with my life.'

'You'll be all right,' Anvar said firmly. 'Aurian and I will shield you.'

'Indeed we will,' Aurian agreed. 'But before we do anything else, we must have Schiannath's agreement. Suppose he doesn't want to be Herdlord?'

'I think you need have no fears on that score,' Chiamh said wryly. 'Nonetheless, it is time for us to ask him.'

'You want me to do what?' Schiannath looked at the four – Aurian, Anvar, Chiamh and Parric – who were ranged before him, and realized that his jaw was still hanging open in sheer disbelief. He closed his mouth quickly, but his mind was still reeling. 'You would really give me another chance to become Herdlord?' he repeated, unable to assimilate the incredible implications of such an opportunity. 'You can truly do this, and the Xandim will accept it?'

'If you are challenging as an elected substitute for the current Herdlord, it is within the law,' Chiamh assured. 'They must accept it, but they will not like it.'

'They don't have to bloody well like it,' Aurian snapped. 'I just want to be sure that Schiannath is happy with the decision. I won't have him pressured.' She turned to the Xandim warrior. 'Schiannath – are you absolutely sure you want to do this? Have you considered the risks involved? Chiamh says that last time . . .'

'Please, Lady, do not judge me by last time.' Schiannath's

face was set with determination. 'I have suffered much in the interim, but I have learned a very great deal since then. This time things will be different. Last time I fought through hatred, but this time I will fight through love.'

His words triggered a memory in the Mage of something Forral had said to her long ago, when he was teaching her to fight: *'Other factors being fairly even, a warrior who fights for a true cause that he believes in will always win over one whose motives are destructive. His passion will give him the intensity of focus he needs to prevail.'*

Aurian nodded her understanding. 'You're right, Schiannath. Very well, then – it's agreed.' She took his hand. 'I wish you the best of good fortune, my friend.'

'Schiannath – no! How could you let them persuade you into this folly?' Iscalda's eyes blazed with anger, and Schiannath flinched from the look of hurt and betrayal on her face.

'My dear Iscalda – only listen . . .' He tried to soothe her, putting an arm around her shoulders, but she tore herself away from him with an oath.

'How could you do this – to yourself – to *me*? Did you learn nothing at all from what happened last time? Phalihas will not exile you again, you fool. This time, he will take your life.'

'He will not.' Schiannath fought for calm. 'This time will be different, Iscalda. This time he will not prevail.'

'How can you know that?' Iscalda blazed at him. 'You put your life at stake . . .'

'Yes – for greater gain, in the end.'

'What greater gain?' Iscalda snapped. 'For power? For glory?' She spat contemptuously on the ground. 'How like a man, to –'

'Will you be still and listen?' Schiannath caught hold of his sister's shoulders, gripping hard enough to stem her torrent of angry words. 'Listen to me now,' he repeated, and took a deep breath. 'I confess that the first time I challenged, I did it for all the reasons that you so rightly decry. I was young, rebellious and foolish – and in truth, I was lucky to escape with my life. I care far more about the fact that I almost lost you yours, and put you through such suffering for my sake. Now, against all the odds, Parric had given me another chance to defeat Phalihas – but power and glory are my last considerations.'

He paused, and looked deep into her eyes. 'The last time I challenged for myself, Iscalda. This time I do it for you. If Phalihas is not stopped – and stopped for good – he has every right to make good his claim of betrothal upon you.'

Iscalda gasped, and turned pale.

'Yes,' Schiannath nodded. 'And he will make you suffer for his enmity with me. I will not – I can *not* allow that to happen. And so I must fight him, this one last time – for your safety, and your future.'

Tears flooded Iscalda's eyes, but the stubborn set of her jaw remained unaltered. 'I don't care,' she whispered. 'I would rather Phalihas subjected me to all manner of indignities than see him take your life.'

Schiannath put his arms around her. 'With luck,' he assured her, 'Phalihas will do neither. I intend to see to that'.

'Do we have to go up there?' Aurian groaned. 'Couldn't you just perform your seeing down in the vale?' She was standing at the bottom of the cliff path (if you could dignify that narrow, treacherous lip of rock – barely a slanting fault where the layers of stone had slipped and overlapped – with the name of path) that led up to the top of the spire, and Chiamh's Chamber of Winds.

The Windeye shook his head. 'There is not enough wind down here in the valley – and besides, for a seeing, highest is best. I can see much further and with greater accuracy up there at the top of the spire, where the air is so much clearer, and free to move.'

Aurian looked up at the cliff and shuddered. Unbidden, the horrific vision of Bohan's lethal plunge came into her mind. The world around her tilted dizzily, and she found herself trembling. In panic, she grabbed hold of Anvar's hand. 'I can't,' she whispered. 'I'll never get up there.'

'Surely it can't be the height that's bothering you,' Anvar encouraged her. 'Why, the cliff at Taibeth was far higher than this, and so was the tower of the Dragonfolk at Dhiam-mara. You managed both of those all right.' He put a comforting arm around her shoulder. 'Is it the manner of Bohan's death that's upset you so?'

The Mage nodded reluctantly, glad to look at her soul-mate instead of the crumbling cliff – and even more grateful that he should be so in tune with her thoughts. 'You're right – it's the ascent itself,' she told him. 'We've never climbed anything as precarious· or as difficult as that – and then there's the memory of what happened to Bohan last night . . .' Suddenly she stopped, gasped, and hugged him, laughing with relief. 'Of course!' she cried. 'Thank you, Anvar – you've just found me the solution. We don't have to climb.' Fishing in the pocket of her tunic, she brought out the slender whistle of carved bone that summoned the Sky-folk. ·

There came a shrill cry of acknowledgement from high above the Mages, followed by the drumming thunder of wings. From their lofty perches high among the crags of the spire the Winged Folk came spiralling down, to land in a swirling windstorm at Aurian's feet.

They were a mated pair, Aurian had discovered on her previous night's adventure, when they had transported her-self and her companions from the beleaguered tower of the fastness. Ibis, the male, was tall and gangling for a Skyman, with white plumage trimmed and edged in black and a serious, considered mien. Kestrel, his mate, was small, bright-eyed and quick, with speckled plumage in blending shades of brown. Though she smiled more often than her mate, and seemed to have a greater sense of playfulness and fun, the fierce intensity of her manner could be somewhat daunting. As they landed, the two Skyfolk spoke simulta-neously.

'Not trouble again,' said Ibis, with a worried frown.

'You need help?' Kestrel asked.

'It's not a crisis, but I'd be only too glad of your help,' the Mage told them. She pointed to the top of the spire. 'Can you take me up there?'

They could and did, grasping her arms as they had done

277

the night before and lifting her, with little effort over such a short distance, to the top of the spire and Chiamh's Chamber of Winds, where they set her down as delicately as a feather on the flat, wide, windswept platform of stone. The Windeye, following his normal route with the ease of long practice, was already partway up the cliff, and would soon be joining her. While the Winged Folk went down to pick up Anvar, who had also elected to come up by the easier method, Aurian, making sure to keep as close as possible to the centre of the platform, away from the perilous brink, looked curiously around at the peculiar structure.

The first thing that she noticed – because it was impossible to ignore – was the wind, which was much stronger up here on this platform between earth and sky. It wailed and whistled shrilly as it poured from the north like a swift-moving river, blowing her hair back from her face and making her jaws and ears ache with its chill as it coursed around her swaying body and ripped her flapping cloak back from her shoulders to gnaw into her very bones. It buffeted and worried at her as though she was being attacked by a living creature. Aurian felt its merciless, inexorable force, and shuddered. Who was Chiamh, that he could tame and harness such elemental wildness?

Annoyed that she had allowed herself to be so disquieted by plain moving air, Aurian took herself to task very sharply. 'Fancy a Mage succumbing to an attack of the vapours,' she muttered to herself, and chuckled dourly at her own poor joke. To distract herself from such foolishness, she forced herself to concentrate on her surroundings. In typical Moldan style, the edifice looked as though it had been grown rather than been constructed. The circular floor was flat and smooth, with a lustrous polish, and four sturdy pillars grew up at regular intervals around the periphery, supporting the arching roof that was the apex of the spire. The view was staggering, only blocked to the south by the cliffs and upper summit of the Wyndveil. To the west and east were the long, wooded spurs that formed the cradling arms of Chiamh's vale, with the snowy heads of other mountains beyond. Aurian, facing west, turned away with a shudder from the shattered peak of Steelclaw and looked north, down the length of the valley and the plateau beyond. The view there gave her even less comfort. A scattering of coloured dots strewed the sward beyond the mouth of the vale: the Xandim had arrived in force. Aurian shuddered, suddenly gripped by a formless fear for Schiannath and Chiamh, who would have to deal with these, their own people, on the morrow. She was so wrapped up in her worries that she did not hear the flurry of wings behind her, until she felt the reassuring touch of Anvar's hand. She gripped it tightly, and turned to face him with a rueful grimace. 'I know,' she sighed. 'We'll cope with it somehow.'

'Of course we will. Not just the two of us, but the rest of our allies. Now that we have Parric back on our side . . .' Anvar's grin betrayed his relief, but Aurian detected a slight tightening of pain around his eyes. 'He was the last person I would have expected to . . .'

'I should have guessed long ago that something was troubling him,' the Mage replied. 'He and Forral were always so close – he just needed time to accept that so much had changed. He'll be all right now.'

Their conversation was interrupted by the arrival of the Windeye, who was panting heavily from the strenuous climb. He hesitated when he saw the Mages, feeling like a clumsy intruder. They seemed so deeply engrossed in talk that he was reluctant to interrupt them.

Aurian, however, turned at the sound of his harsh breathing. 'Serves you right – you should come up the easy way, as we did,' she teased him, with a wicked grin.

'Thank you, no.' Chiamh shuddered. 'If the goddess had meant me to fly, she'd have given me wings of my own.'

'And if she'd meant me to climb, she'd have given me feet like a fly,' the Mage countered swiftly.

'Ah, but flies have wings too,' Anvar added, joining in their nonsense, 'so where does that leave us?'

'Maybe we had better forget the climbing and flying, and concentrate on gathering the winds.' Chiamh was reluctant to put an end to the good-natured camaraderie that was such a release after the dreadful happenings of the previous night, but he wanted to get the seeing over with as soon as possible. As always, the effort of such farsight would be a great strain on him, and he had many more trials ahead of him in the next few hours.

Aurian nodded gravely. 'What do you want us to do?'

'Little, I suspect,' Chiamh told her. 'I have no idea whether your powers can access this type of magic. With luck, you may be able to share the vision, but if not, then simply stay back, listen – and bear witness.' He smiled ruefully at the Magefolk. 'In truth, I welcome your presence and support more than anything. For me, a seeing has always been a lonely and terrifying experience.'

'A little like riding the winds used to be,' Aurian said softly, and Chiamh remembered the night at the Tower of Incondor when she had joined him on the winds to travel to Aerillia. No longer alone, he had discovered a glory and joy in his powers that he had never before experienced. His life had changed that night, and he was grateful to the Mage for her timely and encouraging reminder. His eyes met hers in understanding.

'Maybe it will be the same this time,' he told her. 'At any rate, we'll soon find out.'

Chiamh closed his eyes, and concentrated hard upon summoning the arcane, mysterious powers of the Windeye – and gasped, as though he had taken a breathless plunge into an icy stream. The melting chill of his Othersight enveloped his body, blurring his vision to shimmering silver as his eyes changed from their normal hue. As his sight cleared, he took command of himself, and peered out into the otherworld that was now revealed.

In sunlight, the images of his Othersight were somewhat different from those he saw when his surroundings were dark. The streaming currents of the winds showed less of their silvery brightness, but glowed instead with sparks and shimmers of moonstone, fiery opal and burnished, liquid gold. The stone that comprised the surrounding mountains and his Chamber of Winds had a crystalline, amethyst glitter, and the living auras of the Magefolk at his side shone with the blinding effulgence of two jewelled rainbows. Gritting his teeth, Chiamh tore his attention away from the perilous entrancement of such beauty. He steadied himself by taking long, deep breaths, and held out his hands, which blazed with a dazzling iridescence of their own. Squinting against the light that came from his inner self, he reached out and grasped two handfuls of the flowing strands of wind, formulating in his mind the question he wanted to ask as he did so.

Stretching the skeins of living air between his fingers, the Windeye controlled and shaped them, moulding them into a wide, reflective disc that shimmered like a swirling, opalescent web between his hands. As he looked deeply into it, surrendering his own will to the power of the seeing, he felt it drawing him down and in, further and further, into the maelstrom of light, until all knowledge of himself had been abandoned, left far behind, as his spirit went spinning away, beyond, in pursuit of the answers that he sought.

Chiamh came back to himself with a jolt, and immediately felt the difference. It was working! His heart leapt with elation. The mirror of air had turned into a living thing between his hands. He had given of himself – and now, in return, the wind was surrendering its powers of knowledge up to him. The Windeye looked deep into the mirror and watched, wide-eyed, as the images began to form within its fiery depths.

Two great stallions, one black, one clouded grey, fighting at dawn upon a windswept plateau. One stumbled – fell – great hooves struck down, and a swirl of crimson blood spiralled out to obscure his vision. Chiamh caught his breath. Which had fallen? *Which?*

But when the blood cleared, the vision had changed. The mirror darkened to a blackness so profound that the Windeye thought he had somehow lost the seeing – then an actinic flare of lighting split the sky, and he saw the brutal churning of storm-lashed waves, boiling white as they hurled themselves against the jagged rocks of a headland ... In the next flash, his Othersight pierced the black cauldron of the waves to reveal terrifyingly monstrous shapes, swimming beneath the waters; waiting ... Then all was dark once more until another lightning bolt revealed the Mage, standing poised upon the edge of the rocks. She dived, with the clean arc of a salmon's leap, launching herself right into the teeth of the ravenous waves . . .

Chiamh gasped in horror. Involuntarily he closed his eyes, and opened them again to a sight of such breathtaking beauty that the horror of the previous vision was forgotten. It was a unicorn: an unearthly creature translucent and ethereal, formed of all different kinds of light. She turned her exquisite head to look at him, and tossed a mane that was like sunrise on a swirl of morning mist. Then, kicking up sunbursts from her silver heels, she raced away into the darkness, his only guide the moonspun glimmer of her coat, and the starlight that streamed and sparkled like a comet tail from her spiral horn . . .

Chiamh followed, and burst out into the sunlight that lay thick as mead in the cup of a deeply forested green valley. The view shimmered as though seen through a heat-haze, beneath a web of the strongest magic he had ever encountered. Despite the unearthly beauty of the vision, the Windeye felt a pang of agonizing fear, like a sword thrust deep into his vitals, and had to steel and steady himself so as not to flee in terror. He looked down from above with the sight of an eagle, and saw the unicorn standing by a slender wooden bridge which led across to an island in the centre of a tranquil lake. On the island was a jewel – a massive, blood-red gem – and within it was the silhouetted shadow of a sword. The fierce blade, cradled in the pulsing light of the crystal's crimson heart, looked as though it had been drenched in blood. It hummed to itself, redolent with somnolent power, singing songs of victory and sacrifice that took shape and shot like spars of carmine light into the heavens. They reached out like bloody fingers to entrap and seize the Windeye, and in the power of their fell clutch he saw the fate that he had dreaded: the ending of the Xandim.

With a scream of anguish that was ripped from the very depths of his soul, Chiamh fled in terror, not knowing where he went, or how; only wanting to get away from the Sword and the two-edged fate it held. Darkness surrounded him and he plunged into it gladly, desperate for concealment, for succour . . .

'Chiamh – *Chiamh!* Wake up, damn you! Come back to us, please . . .'

Someone was slapping him, then fingers dug bruisingly into his shoulders, shaking him . . . The Windeye felt the firm grasp of a mind – no, two minds – clutching at his consciousness; holding him, supporting and comforting him, and gradually but firmly drawing him back towards the sane and normal light of day. For a moment he continued to fight them in blind, mindless panic, and then memory returned to him, and he recognized the familiar mind-touch of the Magefolk. Gladly, trustingly, he surrendered then, and let them bring him home.

18

Horncall and Sunrise

Chiamh's mouth was dry as he approached the two great standing stones that were known in the Xandim language as the Gates to the Vale of Death. Beyond them, in the narrow maw of the valley's entrance, he could see the colourful tents of the Xandim, encamped in profusion on the green turf to either side of the Gates, leaving the broad expanse of the plateau bare for tomorrow's challenge. Before the great stones, mocking the gay hues of the scattered dwellings, the red light of the sinking sun gleamed like fire and blood on a grim, bristling thicket of spearpoints and drawn swords.

Though he was still distant, they had seen him. An angry murmur went up from the hostile crowd. The ugly sound, like the wrathful drone of a shattered nest of hornets, echoed within the narrow ugly walls and rolled up the valley towards him like an overwhelming tidal wave of resentment and loathing. The Windeye paused in the spurious shelter of the last stand of trees, fighting his reluctance to approach any nearer to that wall of pulsing, bloodthirsty hatred. He suddenly felt extremely grateful that he had the Mages with him, and Aurian's friend the formidable great cat (whose male companion was back in the valley with the two Skyfolk, guarding Wolf and his foster-parents) – not to mention his other comrades, both outland and Xandim. He needed their support as he had never needed it before – he doubted that even his legendary Grandam could have dealt single-handedly with such a crisis as this – and Chiamh was already utterly spent, following the mind-wrenching efforts and nightmare terrors of the seeing he had performed for Aurian.

Had it not been the Time of Challenge, the Mage would not have allowed him to come at all. As it was, she had been furious with him, now that she had found out exactly what a

284

seeing entailed, for taking such a risk with himself – though, perversely, she had been more angry with herself for letting him do it in the first place, despite the fact that he had deliberately concealed the potential dangers from her. Fortunately, the Mages had been unable to follow his seeing with their own powers, and were forced to rely on what he told them of the vision, so Chiamh had been able to conceal that horrifying final image. He only wished he could so easily hide the memory from himself.

Now, as he made his way towards the Place of Challenge, the impact of his discovery was truly coming home to him, and the Windeye found himself faced with an anguishing dilemma; brutally torn between two loyalties. He could no longer pretend ignorance – the fate of the Xandim lay in his hands. How easy it would be to turn upon his new friends and betray them to the angry hordes. By simply performing the same binding spell on Schiannath as he had used upon Phalihas, Chiamh could vastly increase the likelihood that the Sword of Flame would never be found and his people would be safe. The Mages and their outland companions would almost certainly be killed, but was such a sacrifice truly too much to ask when compared to the life of an entire tribe?

And have you forgotten the Evil Powers so soon? he asked himself. Without Aurian and the Sword, they are sure to triumph, and what of the Xandim then? But the Evil Powers were strange to him, and far away, and had he not witnessed the very plain and immediate threat of the Sword with his own Othersight?

'Chiamh? Are you all right?' The Windeye came out of his reverie with a guilty start to see Aurian looking at him with a frown. 'I knew you should have rested longer,' she told him, putting a supportive hand beneath his elbow. 'You look dreadful. I wish you'd at least let me give you back some of the energy you lost in the seeing. You're in no fit state to do this, and you know it.' Her eyes were shadowed with worry and concern, but with her usual courage she tried to lighten the moment. 'We don't want to lose you, you know. I've soared with you over the mountains, and raced the wind with you across the plateau – I rather counted on being able to do both those things again.' She smiled at him – her own wry, expressive smile that held all the love of one friend for another, and was especially for him.

Chiamh could not meet her eyes. You want to betray her? his thoughts goaded him. You want to see her lying dead? How many true friends have you had in your life, save these who are with you now? He looked past the Mage at Anvar, who seemed similarly concerned, and at Sangra, who had helped him through the worst of his fears when they came down the mountain in the storm. He saw Parric, whom he had risked his life to more than once to aid – and Schiannath and Iscalda, whom he had already betrayed once, on the orders of his Herdlord. He could not do so again.

The Windeye straightened his sagging shoulders, and reached out to take Aurian's hand. 'I'll be all right,' he reassured her, with an effort. 'This is a time of heavy burdens for us all. I will rest tonight, I promise – though I ought not, while we keep vigil.'

'Bugger the vigil,' Aurian growled. 'I won't let Phalihas and his men see you sleeping, but sleep you will, my friend. I'll see to that. You deserve it, and you need it.'

'Just so long as you don't snore,' Parric threatened, with a grin.

'What?' Chiamh raised his eyebrows in mock horror. 'I'll have you know that the mighty Windeye of the Xandim never snores!' Though the burden was still his to bear, his heart felt immeasurably lighter now that his decision had been made. He answered Parric's comradely clap on the shoulder with a buffet of his own, and turned reluctantly away from the warmth of his friends towards the hostility of his enemies. 'We must be moving,' he told his companions. 'The sun is almost setting, and there is little time remaining to do what we must.'

It was as though an invisible line had been drawn between the standing stones across the mouth of the vale, from one tall and sinister monolith to the other. Beyond that impenetrable boundary of fear and superstition the Elders stood. Behind them, ranked in line, were the regional chieftains of the nomadic Xandim hunters, and the leaders of the

286

small family communities of fisherfolk, salt-panners and beachcombers who spent part of their year in residence down on the coast and traded their goods at regular gatherings with the inland tribes. Accompanying them was Phalihas, still trapped within his equine shape, that of a great black stallion. At the sight of Chiamh the former Herdlord tensed with rage, flattening his ears back against his skull while one huge hoof pounded restlessly at the ground, tearing the turf to shreds.

Ysalla, leader of the Elders, stepped forth; tall and gaunt and brittle as an ancient pine. Though her russet hair was more grey than chestnut now, and her weathered face was hollowed and lined with age, her manner was still haughty and imperious as she addressed the Windeye. 'Well, tergiversator? The dark of the moon is upon us again. What word have you for us, upon this Night of Challenge? Does that skulking outland scum that you have raised to power intend to keep his word to us this time? And what of your own promise? Will you free Phalihas? For we have ruled that under our ancient law he was unfairly challenged, and may contend again if he so wishes – but not under the geas of a foul traitor.'

Chiamh, though he shook inwardly, met her cold gaze without flinching. 'True to my vow, I will release Phalihas.' He paused to give the murmurs and cries of the assembled Xandim a chance to die away. 'And to meet him I bring forth another who would challenge. Though the present Herdlord keeps his word and will not fight again, under the law he may nominate another to stand in his place – '

'Another Xandim,' Ysalla snapped.

'He is another Xandim.' The Windeye's expression of impassive calm did not alter as he beckoned Schiannath to his side, though he was almost overwhelmed by the cries of anger and outrage that erupted all around him.

'Traitor!'

'Injustice!'

'It is forbidden!'

'He would foist an outlaw on us now!'

'Schiannath has already failed!'

287

'He may not fight again!'

Chiamh lifted his hand, and a blast of howling wind swept all their words away. Into the stunned and resentful silence that followed, he spoke again. 'May I remind you that Phalihas had also failed a challenge – yet you still call upon the law to let *him* fight again. The Herdlord, Parric, is willing to give up his position – but a resigning Herdlord has the right under our law to nominate a challenger – any challenger that he may choose, so long as it be one of the Xandim – to take his place. You cannot deny that it is so.'

For a long moment Ysalla hesitated, plainly desperate to refute his words, but she could not. At last, she dropped her eyes from Chiamh's unwavering gaze. 'It is so,' she admitted through gritted teeth, sounding as though each word had been dragged by force out of the very depths of her soul. 'If you restore Phalihas, then Schiannath may challenge, and we, the Xandim, will abide by the result. But hear me, Wind-eye – ' Her eyes smouldered with the intensity of her loathing. 'If Phalihas should prevail, then tomorrow's dawn will be the last that you and your accursed outland companions will ever see. By the light of the goddess I swear it.'

'Before you make such a rash vow, you should be sure you are able to enforce it,' the Windeye replied levelly. 'I, at least, can keep the promises I make.' With that, he lifted his hands, grasped the air that shimmered around Phalihas, and twisted. The horse-shape blurred and altered, and standing in its place was the tall, strong figure of the former Herdlord.

Phalihas hurled himself at Chiamh, his hands outstretched to grasp and maul. He fought the Xandim who held him back, all the while spitting out vile epithets and snarling like an animal in his rage. The Windeye stood unmoving, never taking his eyes from his would-be murderer.

Ysalla put an end to it. 'Stop this, you fool!' she roared. 'Do you want to ruin everything? If you cross into the Vale of Death – or if you shed blood upon the Eve of Challenge – you will be cursed, and may not fight tomorrow!'

Phalihas subsided immediately, though his eyes glinted with unsatiated rage. 'Count the hours, Chiamh,' he told the Windeye. 'You have not many left.'

288

Chiamh shrugged, a deliberate move designed to keep Phalihas angry and off-balance throughout the night. 'For certain, one of us has not.' He turned on his heel and walked away.

Aurian, watching, almost burst with pride.

The sun was dipping low behind the riven peaks of Steel-claw, streaking the gaunt and looming monoliths with crimson as the two camps of the challengers settled down by the stones for the night's uneasy vigil. There was little time left for talk before the darkness brought the rule of silence, and Parric hurried to catch the Windeye alone while Aurian and Anvar lit a fire, and the others were busy setting up their rough camp and arranging the watches between themselves so that two would always be there to guard Schiannath and one other would be on hand to feed the fire, and surreptitiously keep the challenger awake if he should falter. Chiamh was coaxing a reluctant, nervous Schiannath to eat the last meal he would have before his challenge, but when he felt the cavalry master's hand upon his shoulder he turned quickly.

Parric led him into the shadows behind the great stone. 'Look,' he began roughly, 'I'm just a soldier, and not much of a one for words, but if I didn't thank you before for all you've done for us I want to do it now. And, well, I wanted to thank you for what you did the other night. When I'm wrong I admit it – and you stopped me from making one of the worst mistakes of my life when I tried to get Aurian away from the fastness without Anvar. I'm sorry for what I tried to do – and I'm in your debt, because you never told Aurian I was such a bloody fool. The lass would never have forgiven me – I realize that now. You saved me from making a right old fist of things, and probably saved Anvar's life into the bargain. I'm truly grateful to you.'

At that moment the last shred of sunlight vanished, and the lonely wail of a horn rang out across the plateau, signalling that the hours of silent vigil had begun. Chiamh was prevented from making a reply, but his smile and his strong clasp of Parric's hand managed to convey both friendship and approval as they walked back together to the fire.

Though they had all arranged to take watches, none of Schiannath's companions save the chagrined Windeye – who insisted, afterwards, that Aurian had bespelled him – got any sleep that night. The thoughts of Sangra and Yazour were astonishingly similar, though their backgrounds were so disparate. Each of them was longing for home. Sangra was thinking wistfully of the busy, muddy streets of Nexis; the taverns, the training, and the rowdy, rough-and-tumble companionship of the garrison. Yazour sat shivering in his thick cloak, missing the shimmering, broiling heat; the rhythmic chirrings of the frogs beside the river that made each night less still and lonely; the sound of his mother tongue; and the endless, glittering horizons of the desert.

Parric had a good deal to think about since Aurian's revelations had led him to see her attachment to Anvar in a different light. He was not, however, much given to that kind of introspection, and his mind soon strayed back to the more immediate issue: Schiannath. The cavalry master's sympathies went out to the Xandim warrior who sat, pale and plainly ill at ease, on the other side of the fire; forced to fight a battle of nerves through the watches of the night with Phalihas – a wily and experienced opponent, as Parric knew to his cost. Having been through the same gruelling ritual, he didn't envy the lad in the least, and couldn't help but feel a twinge of concern. Schiannath was an unknown quantity save that he had lost to the former Herdlord once already, which didn't bode well at all to the cavalry master. He only hoped that the young Xandim would prove equal to the test.

Aurian, who always observed Forral's lessons about not looking at the fire while on night watch, sat tense and shivering a little with weariness and the damp chill of the mountain night, peering into the shadows beyond the massive standing stones. How could she possibly sleep? She had much on her mind following the revelations of Chiamh's seeing: how could that double-dratted Sword have turned up in her mother's Valley? Of all places? It seemed as though the fates were mocking her. And that was by no means the only matter to occupy her attention. Tomorrow would be vitally important not only to Schiannath and the Xandim people, but to the entire course of her future. Depending upon the outcome of this duel, she would either be making plans to head back north to find the Sword and confront Miathan at last – or fighting for her life, and very likely losing more of her beloved companions in the battle.

At her side, she felt Anvar's hand tighten on her own in response to the pain that had consumed her at the unexpected reminder of Bohan. 'I'm not dwelling on it, truly,' she assured him in the mental communion that was becoming increasingly easy now that they enjoyed a lovers' bond. 'I know that would serve no purpose. Besides, mourning is a luxury we can't allow ourselves just now.'

'You're right.' Anvar's reply came into her mind, and Aurian blessed the fact that they could speak without words on this night when they must remain silent. 'But that doesn't diminish our love for Bohan,' her soulmate added, 'and one day, if all goes well, we'll find a suitable way to honour him.'

'That's a lovely thought – and very fitting.' In echo of her words, Aurian sensed Shia's unspoken approval, and saw the great cat's golden eyes gleaming like gemstones in the firelight. Shia was also keeping watch tonight, though she was more concerned for the two Magefolk than the Xandim warrior. The Mage laid a hand on the cat's broad, sleek head, and leaned her head on Anvar's shoulder, enjoying the closeness of her two dearest companions. 'Can't you two sleep either?'

'Certainly not. I am watching over you,' Shia replied firmly.

'Not a chance.' Anvar's thought was rueful. 'Not with so much at stake. Do you think Schiannath can do it?'

'He'd damn well better do it,' Aurian replied fervently, 'or we really are in trouble.' She stretched out her long limbs with a sigh. 'It's this endless waiting that's the worst part.'

'Do you want me to do for you what you did for Chiamh?' Anvar asked her mischievously, indicating the slumbering Windeye.

'Don't you dare! He's going to murder me when he wakes up and finds out, but it's for the best. Poor man – he was worn out after what he did for us today. He desperately needed to sleep.'

'And he deserves to. I was very impressed with the way he handled the Xandim Elders.' His mental chuckle sobered, and she sensed his hesitation. 'But, Aurian . . . Didn't it seem to you as though he was keeping something from us after the seeing?'

'You caught that too?' Aurian frowned. 'I'd hoped it was only my imagination. But I trust him,' she added firmly. 'Anvar, I'm convinced that Chiamh wouldn't betray us. Do you doubt that?'

'Not I.' She felt the slight shake of Anvar's head. 'But what was he hiding, then?'

'I don't know – but it struck me that whatever it was, it terrified him.' Aurian fell silent as she pondered the possibilities. 'I think,' she went on slowly, 'that if we were in peril he would certainly have warned us. So the danger can only be to himself – and that worries me more than I can say.' She shivered. 'I couldn't bear to think of anything happening to Chiamh. I've grown very fond of him.'

'You mean I have a rival?' Anvar protested in mock alarm.

'Not that fond, you idiot!' Aurian responded to his attempt to lighten their mood. He was right – this was no time for gloomy, nebulous speculation. 'You don't have any rivals,' she promised him, 'and if we didn't have all these folk around us I'd prove it to you.'

Schiannath, alas, was denied the comfort of mental communication. He was forced to keep his vigil in silence – and he was spending an uneasy night, with Phalihas, only two spear-lengths away, glaring at him with an unremitting hatred far more intense than the usual attempt to unnerve an opponent. He shuddered, feeling the first uncomfortable stirrings of doubt. He dropped his eyes from the former Herdlord's black gaze, and knew, with a sinking feeling of shame, that he had already lost the first round. What if I can't do it? he thought wildly. If I should die tomorrow, what will become of my poor sister?

He looked up again to see Phalihas staring avidly not at himself, this time, but at Iscalda; with a sneering expression compounded of lust, calculation and such downright arrogance that Schiannath found himself grinding his teeth in thwarted fury. The former Herdlord was making it perfectly plain that he, at least, had no doubts whatsoever concerning the outcome of this challenge.

Schiannath's self-doubt vanished in a flare of incandescent rage that hardened just as quickly into icy resolution. Never! he vowed to himself. Never again will Phalihas lay a hand on my sister, for I *will* defeat him. I *must*. Setting his jaw, he sought again for his opponent's eyes – and this time, such was the strength of his desperate resolve, it was Phalihas's turn to falter and look away. Not once, after that, did Schiannath take the pressure of his gaze from the Herdlord throughout that long, long night.

Iscalda sat, rigid with apprehension, beside her brother, keeping his cold hand clasped tightly in her own. She missed the by-play between the two challengers, for she was not looking at them; was trying not to give way to her thoughts at all. If Schiannath should be vanquished on the morrow, she would not only lose the brother whom she loved more than life itself, but her own subsequent fate at the hands of Phalihas did not bear thinking about. With her free hand, she fingered her dagger in its sheath, and vowed to herself that if Schiannath died she would follow him into the arms of the goddess.

The blast of a horn shrieked a single, warning note across the plateau. Aurian had been wrapped in thought, in that uncertain limbo between sleep and waking, and had not noticed that the sky was growing light. The clarion call brought her back with a start to a shivering body whose limbs were locked in stiffness. Just in time, she stopped herself from uttering a heartfelt curse.

'It's all right now – in the moments between horncall and sunrise you may speak.' It was the voice of the Windeye. he struggled out of the blanket she had laid over him, and glared at her. 'Was this your revenge, Lady, for the time I drugged your wine?'

'You needed the rest,' Aurian told him unrepentantly, and was glad that he had no chance to reply.

The companions gathered around Schiannath, who was stamping his feet and swinging his arms to move the sluggish blood in his cold limbs. The Xandim warrior looked deathly pale in the crepuscular light, but his haggard face was set with determination. Chiamh handed him the water-flask, and he took a quick drink before dousing his face and head with the remainder. There was no time for more: a faint golden aura was already appearing above the eastern slopes, and he must be in position before the first rays of sunlight hit the plateau, or forfeit the challenge.

Quickly, Iscalda embraced her beloved brother. 'May the goddess be with you,' she whispered, and tore herself away from him before her brittle mask of courage could shatter.

'And with you, my sister.' Schiannath swallowed hard and started forward, then paused to lay a hand on the Mage's arm. His eyes held a desperate plea. 'If – if anything should happen to me,' he whispered quickly, 'I beg you – protect her from Phalihas.'

'I will, I promise,' Aurian assured him. Then he was gone.

The world was utterly silent in that moment before sunrise, as the two opponents stepped out upon the plateau. Then, where two men stood locked eye to eye in the tension that preceded combat . . .

Aurian gasped. Two mighty stallions, one midnight black, one a darkly dappled grey, faced each other across the stretch of shadowed turf; tails streaming, manes flying in the wind as the great arched necks flexed and the finely sculpted heads were lifted proudly. Muscles moved with fluid power in deep chests and strong haunches as lethal hooves tore up the turf.

The third call of the horn was the triumphant cry of the rising sun. As its light blazed up on the horizon, the grey turf turned to dazzling green, save where the long shadow of Phalihas stretched out to engulf his opponent in a swathe of darkness. Schiannath shrilled a strident challenge and reared, pawing at the air, lifting himself high into the sunlight above the black stain of his enemy's shade. The glittering dew cast sprays of fire beneath pounding hooves as the stallions screamed and charged.

As the two great horses hurtled towards one another, Schiannath lost all vestiges of human consciousness to the white-hot ecstasy of pure animal rage. He thundered towards Phalihas, intending to dodge and smash into him from the side – but the other had had the same idea. Both beasts veered in the same direction – but Phalihas was older, and reacted more quickly to the new development. Wrenching himself round on his powerful haunches, he bore down on the grey stallion, teeth snapping, and drove his head into Schiannath's belly, winding him and knocking him off his feet.

With unexpected agility, Schiannath rolled over and scrambled upright, trembling from that instant of panic when his feet had left the ground. Phalihas' hooves came pounding down on the place where his opponent had been, but they had missed their target. Schiannath's head snaked out: the black stallion screamed in pain and outrage as a line of white fire ripped across his flank where the other's teeth had slashed him. He whirled away, jolted back to cold sanity by the shock; for he had not expected Schiannath to take first blood.

Schiannath came at him again and reared, his sharp hooves lashing dangerously close to Phalihas's skull. Phalihas ducked beneath the flailing bludgeons, went for his enemy's throat, but missed his hold. One of Schiannath's hooves struck bruisingly against his shoulder as his teeth met in the deeply muscled chest and tore out a lump of flesh. Now it was Schiannath's turn to scream and stagger backwards, bleeding. His rolling eye held a new respect for his opponent, and the steely glint of a grim determination to succeed at all costs against his foe.

Again and again the stallions charged each other, plunging and biting, kicking and slashing. Blood stained the trampled turf and the air rang with screams of rage and pain as first one and then the other penetrated his opponent's guard. The two were evenly matched: Phalihas a little heavier; Schiannath slightly taller. The older stallion's cunning and experience was offset by the greater endurance of the younger beast. Both were maimed and bleeding; both were streaked with a froth of white sweat and staggering with exhaustion; yet neither would give ground, and neither would give in.

To the companions, standing in an anxious huddle by the massive stones, the fight was an unbearable agony. Iscalda had never felt so helpless. She could scarcely bear to watch her brother being torn apart before her eyes; yet watch she must, though her vision blurred again and again with tears that she angrily dashed away. In her mind she was out there on that bloody field with Schiannath – she felt the pain of every wound inflicted, and her heart bled as did his ravaged flesh. As the stallions' battle took them further away from where she stood she strained to follow them, squinting her eyes to try to penetrate the intervening distance. If watching them had been a torture, not being able to see was infinitely worse. She felt a hand grip her own and hold on tightly and was grateful for the support it offered, yet could not spare a glance to see who was trying to help her.

It must end soon – it must! Schiannath almost dodged a lunge from Phalihas, but not quite. The other's teeth met with a click in his ear, and pain lanced through his head. He shook himself free with a squeal, blood running down his ragged forelock into his eyes, and staggered aside; his re-actions and movements slower now, his thinking dulled and blurred by pain. His sides were heaving with exertion, and blood-streaked foam dripped from his open jaws. Catching a glimpse of his foe, Schiannath whirled stiffly and kicked out, his hind feet smacking into the other's ribs with a thud that almost drowned the crack of bone. Phalihas tottered and nearly fell, the breath going out of him in an agonized whistle, but Schiannath stumbled, unbalanced by the kick. A wrenching pain stabbed up his left foreleg. He recovered himself with all his weight on the other, for the hoof of the injured limb could barely touch the ground.

The fight broke off as the two stallions stood, heads drooping; each of them desperately trying to summon the energy to finish his opponent. None of the Xandim would interfere from the sidelines – this battle must be fought out to settle the succession. The last challenger left standing would become the Herdlord; the other would die.

Schiannath knew that he had reached the end of his endurance. With his foreleg crippled, he had lost mobility;

worse, he could not kick. The injury had robbed him of a major weapon – it could only be a matter of time, now, before Phalihas outmanoeuvred him. Schiannath's heart sank beneath a weight of black despair. He had tried, but he had lost . . .

Then, through the grey haze of bloodloss and fatigue that fogged his brain, Schiannath's sensitive equine hearing registered the sound of muffled weeping. Iscalda! With a jolt, he remembered his sister, and the Lady Aurian and her companions, who had saved him from his dreadful exile. Their lives rested on his success. And Iscalda: he was fighting this battle not for himself, but for her. What right had he to give in so easily? A thought came to him with this renewed determination: if he was in this woeful state, then his older opponent must be in even worse case. That spark of hope, faint as it was, buoyed his flagging spirits, and he felt one last reserve of strength trickle into his weary limbs. Shaking his head to clear his vision he took a good look at his foe for the first time in what seemed to have been an endless age. Phalihas stood trembling in all his limbs, wheezing and choking with the effort to draw air into his lungs. Blood was streaming from his mouth and nostrils, and his eyes were dull and glazed.

Schiannath stiffened to a thrill of hope. With the pain of his own injury, he had forgotten that last kick into Phalihas's ribs. Had it done more damage than he'd thought? There was only one way to find out – but he must expose himself. If Phalihas was only feigning, and saw that limp . . .

Setting his teeth against both fear and pain, he took a hesitant, hobbling step forward, and another . . . His enemy's head swung up sharply; a new fire kindled in the depths of his dull eyes. Schiannath froze, heart pounding. Phalihas gathered himself and charged. That was what Schiannath had been waiting for. As the black stallion came lumbering towards him he sidestepped clumsily, and reared with a shrill scream of triumph that changed to choking terror as Phalihas' head whipped round to close great slablike teeth around his throat. Schiannath felt himself toppling, dragged down by the other's weight. In the final second, he lashed out with one last desperate effort. His uninjured hoof came smashing down upon Phalihas's skull, and the two of them crashed together into darkness.

Iscalda screamed as she saw the stallions fall. She ran forward, tearing herself away from the strong hands that tried to hold her back. As she broke free she was peripherally aware of others beginning to follow, streaming out behind her with shouts of excitement or concern; but her anguish for her brother lent wings to her feet, and with the start she had she easily outdistanced them all. With an effort she stifled her sobs to keep her breath for running – but she kept her eyes fixed, through a haze of tears, on those two dark shapes that lay so ominously still on the blood-soaked ground. The final stages of the battle had taken the stallions a long way out across the plateau. Iscalda pounded on with sweat trickling down into her stinging eyes, trying to ignore the catch in her side and her shortness of breath. *Schiannath!* Though she had no breath to speak, the cry was wrenched in agony from her heart. Would she never reach him? It was like trying to run through water; like her childhood nightmare, when she'd fled in terror to evade pursuers, but for all her running had stayed stranded in the exact same place.

Ahead of her, one of the dark humps stirred. She stumbled; looked again. Surely she must have imagined that feeble movement? The low, slanting sun was in her eyes, obscuring all detail. No! She was not mistaken! One of the stallions was struggling weakly, trying in vain to rise. With a gasp, Iscalda redoubled her speed. One of them was still alive – but which one was it. *Which?*

Then she heard it, ringing raw and shrill across the plateau – a stallion's scream of victory. Iscalda would have known that voice anywhere. Schiannath! Unstrung with relief, her legs collapsed beneath her and she fell to the crisp, cool turf weeping tears of gratitude.

For all that, Iscalda was still one of the first to reach him. Just as she was struggling to her feet, Aurian came thundering up on Chiamh, with Shia racing alongside. The Windeye had kept his wits about him, and taken a moment to change to his equine form.

'Come on, Iscalda! Quick!' The Mage reached down a hand and all but yanked the exhausted girl up behind her. Then they were off again with such speed that in less than a minute they were at Schiannath's side. The stallion was in too much distress to recognize them. He was floundering, struggling and plunging and slipping in a pool of churned up mud and blood, trying in vain to get to his feet. His dark grey flanks were unrecognizable beneath a thickly plastered coat of blood and clay, and his rolling, white-rimmed eyes were glazed with pain and panic.

Muttering a shocked imprecation, Aurian swung herself off Chiamh's back and ran towards the stallion, Iscalda at her heels. 'Hurry,' the Mage yelled. 'He's so terrified, he doesn't know what he's doing. We've got to try to get him up before those idiots arrive.'

He would not let them approach him, despite the fact that the great cat was keeping well back out of his sight. When they tried, he struck out wildly with teeth and an awkwardly held forelimb that was plainly injured. 'Schiannath, it's me – Iscalda,' his sister cried, but her words were lost in the sound of his angry screams. If she could only get him to see her . . . She turned quickly to the Mage. 'Aurian, if you can distract him, I'll try to reach his head.

Aurian nodded. 'Be careful,' she said briefly, and ran towards the horse from one side, waving her arms and screaming like a banshee. Schiannath flattened his ears and turned towards her. Quick as a flash, Iscalda darted in and grabbed hold of his muzzle before the snapping teeth could reach her. Already she was conscious that the Xandim were starting to arrive. If she couldn't reach him soon, she'd never do it with a lot of people crowding around. He plunged, trying to shake her off, but she hung on grimly, refusing to be dislodged. Putting her mouth close to his ear, she yelled: 'Schiannath! Schiannath! It's Iscalda! It's all right – you're safe now. You're safe with us. Come back to us, please. You won, you're safe . . .'

As her soothing litany penetrated the stallion's terrified consciousness, his struggles ceased. Beckoned in by Aurian, the other companions arrived, gasping for breath, and helped the exhausted beast to find his footing, while Chiamh and Yazour kept back the crowds with the aid of a snarling Shia. Once up, he stood there trembling with weakness, his head hanging low, but slowly, to Iscalda's vast relief, the light of intelligence began to creep back into his eyes.

In the meantime, Aurian had been examining Schiannath with her healer's senses. When she had finished, she spoke to him quickly. 'Schiannath, listen to me. You'll be all right, and I'll help you – but don't try to change back yet. You're too exhausted. Do you understand? Let me heal you first, and then you can think about changing.'

Chiamh, in the interim, was addressing the crowd. 'O Xandim, I give you your new Herdlord: Schiannath, victor of the challenge. May the goddess grant that he govern you wisely and well – and may her curse fall swiftly on any who dispute his rule, which was decided fairly under Xandim law.'

There was not much cheering. Judging from the expression of the Xandim, some disappointed, some angry, Aurian knew that they had all been counting on Schiannath to lose. She wanted to spit in their faces. Ysalla came forward for the Elders, her face set like stone. 'And what is the will of the Herdlord?' The savage mockery in her voice was like the lash of a whip.

In her mind, Aurian caught Chiamh's anguished tones. 'Can you help him, Lady? Schiannath must address them soon, or it bodes ill.'

'I can, but it'll take a while,' the Mage replied in the same silent fashion.

'I doubt that we *have* a while,' the Windeye pleaded. Already, a restive murmur was beginning to spread through the crowd.

Aurian felt the raw power of their hostile anger, and came to a decision. 'All right. Anvar, you shield our own folk as best you can. This bloody lot have energy to dissipate – I'm going to borrow it.'

'Aurian – you can't! The Mages' Code . . .'

'Oh, bugger the Mages' Code, just this once. It's in a good cause. I've done this before, in the Nexis riot, and the Khazalim arena – they'll take no hurt at all.' Even as she was

300

reassuring him, she was readying herself. Surreptitiously, she took hold of the Staff of Earth that was tucked, as always, into her belt. Laying the other hand on Schiannath's drooping head, she reached out with her will to the aura of smouldering rage that hung over the crowd and took it into herself, forming a channel through which the purloined energy could be passed to the grey stallion by way of her hand. As she had promised Anvar, it took very little, and the crowd had more than enough to spare. And the exchange had an unexpected benefit. As she drained away the energy that fuelled their anger, Aurian noticed a change come over the assembled Xandim. They seemed more relaxed: less uncertain, less unhappy, and definitely far less hostile. Fleetingly, she found herself wondering if the happy outcome to the Nexis riot had been entirely due to the coming of the rain, then put the thought aside to ponder later.

As the transfer came to completion, Aurian felt Schiannath's trembling cease. His head came up alertly from beneath her outstretched hand. Though it still remained for her to heal him, his ears were pricked and his eyes were bright as he looked around the encircling Xandim and snorted sharply.

'All right,' Aurian told him softly. 'Now you have the energy, you can transform yourself. Go to it, Herdlord – we're all so very proud of you.'

Aurian stepped back a little to give him room to change. The great grey stallion set himself, his dark eyes clouded with concentration – then his outline seemed to waver and shrink upon itself, until in its place stood Schiannath the warrior. His left arm dangled uselessly at his side. He was white-faced, bruised and battered, his clothing was ripped to shreds, and there were bloody wounds all over his body – yet there was a regal dignity and power in his bearing that marked him indisputably as Herdlord. Lifting his head with weary pride, he took a deep breath to address his people, wondering, for a panic-stricken instant, what he was going to say. Then, as he caught sight of Iscalda and his new companions, the answer came to him.

'Last year, a very wild, rebellious and foolish young man

lost a challenge on this plateau, and was banished into the mountains as an outlaw. You all knew that wretch – you all, alas, can remember his errors and escapades.' He grimaced wryly, and a tentative chuckle trickled through the ranks of watching Xandim.

Schiannath caught Iscalda's eye. 'That man is dead.' At his words the laughter ceased abruptly. Suddenly everyone was listening as Schiannath went on more quietly but clearly: 'The Schiannath that you knew died in those mountains, as surely as if he had stepped over a precipice, or fallen prey to the Black Ghosts.' He bowed apologetically to Shia, who was rumbling fiercely, and heard a gasp of amazement from the crowd as the snarling instantly ceased.

Schiannath made the most of their awe. 'It was I who bested Phalihas today, but I am not that misguided, feckless youth who was exiled from his tribe. Your new Herdlord has learned the hard lessons of patience and courage; honour, love and responsibility for others. I ask only the chance to prove myself – as the Xandim must prove themselves in these difficult perilous times. Under my rule, we need no longer fear our neighbours, the Black Ghosts and the Skyfolk. There will be peace between us, so that our peoples may flourish, and support one another against evil – for evil is coming. For too long, we have kept ourselves from the world, guarding our secret – but now the world is reaching out to us, and unless we fight it will overwhelm us. In the north, a great storm is rising – a dire malevolence from which my outland companions once fled. Even now it reaches out towards us, and were it not for the warnings of our brave and faithful Windeye we would be caught unprepared. But for our own sakes, we *must* prepare. There must be no strife amongst ourselves now. Even as the new age dawns, you have been given a new Herdlord – a man whose nature has been forged anew in the fires of pain and adversity. Once I knew nothing but to take from my tribe. Now I want nothing but to give myself and serve my people. O Xandim – will you accept me?'

There was an instant of breathless silence, and then Schiannath was overwhelmed by the cheers. Stamping their

302

feet and rattling their swords upon their shields, they cried his name again and again as they flocked round him. Iscalda ran to her brother, her face shining like the sun with relief and pride.

'Well I'm buggered,' Parric muttered to the Mage. 'I wish I had made a speech like that.'

'You would have, if they'd given you enough mead first,' she chuckled. Sobering, she turned to Anvar. 'Well, wasn't that amazing? I'm so proud of Schiannath.'

Her soulmate nodded. 'He's quite a man – and it's been quite a day! It certainly looks as though there'll be no obstacle to our plans now.'

'You're right.' Even as she said it, Aurian suddenly felt a premonitory prickle of unease. Looking around, she realized that someone was missing from the throng of celebrating companions. Chiamh stood apart, watching the Xandim honour their new Herdlord, his face grey and twisted with a look of utter despair. At the sight of him, Aurian shuddered. 'At least I hope not,' she added, so quietly that no one heard her.

19

The Infiltrator

Hebba turned pale, and let out a little shriek. 'Gods save us –
it's the master!' She sank down weakly in the chair beside the
fire, fanning herself with her apron. Zanna, recognizing an
attack of Hebba's vapours, ran to comfort her old friend the
cook. It was almost like being back home.

From somewhere, Vannor found the strength to chuckle.
'It's all right, Hebba – I'm not a ghost.'

'No – but with all respect, you look like one, sir.' With his
shoulder under Vannor's arm, Tarnal guided him across to
the other soft chair, supporting the merchant as he had supported him all the long, weary and nerve-racking way up
through the city. 'Pull yourself together, Hebba,' the young
Nightrunner went on sharply, as Vannor sank down with a
sigh of relief and closed his eyes. 'Stop flapping and give that
chair to poor Zanna – she needs it more than you. We need
hot water – and have you got some taillin? We've got to sober
up that idiot Benziorn as quick as we can. Vannor's hurt.'

'Hurt? The master? And half-starved too, by the look of it
– him and the poor little lass.' The mere thought was enough
to restore the old cook's wits. Vacating her chair as though it
had suddenly turned red hot, she helped Zanna into it, settling her with a rug across her knees and then finding
another for Vannor. She began to bustle about the kitchen in
a businesslike manner, setting water to boil and rummaging
in cupboards for food and utensils and linen for bandages,
clucking like an old hen all the while to conceal her distress.
'That Benziorn. The good-for-nothing. Why I even give him
house-room, I don't know. Why, the wretch is no more use
than a hat in a hurricane!'

She turned to glower at the physician, who was still hovering sheepishly in the doorway, unsure of his welcome, as well

he might be. 'Get in, if you're coming,' she snapped at him, banging a pot down on the table to punctuate her words. 'And shut that door – the master's in a draught. Call yourself a physician? You should know better.'

Vannor relaxed and let her nattering flow over him, concentrating on the delicious warmth of the fire that was seeping into his chilled bones. Though he was filthy and aching, thirsty, starving and exhausted; though his injured hand was throbbing unbearably as the feeling flooded back into his limbs, he was overcome with an incredible sense of euphoria, and a gratitude for his deliverance so intense that it brought tears to his eyes. What unutterable and unhoped-for luxury, to find himself and Zanna safe, and alive, and back among friends again.

Zanna, too, was feeling as though she had ventured into a dream. First dear Tarnal, and now Hebba – and she had rescued her dad. Though common sense told her that the blissful interlude must of necessity be brief, for they'd be hunting for her father, she put the thought firmly away from her. Tomorrow would take care of itself. Damn it, she had earned this respite, and she was going to make the most of it.

Hebba came to her with a cup of taillin. 'There, my lovey, this will tide you over – I'm making you some soup right now . . .'

Zanna sipped the hot drink appreciatively. Surely nothing in her life had ever tasted so good. It was sweetened liberally with honey, and as she drank it she could feel the warmth spreading right down to her achingly empty stomach. When she glanced up through the fragrant steam, she saw that her dad also held a cup in his hand. He winked at her across the hearth, and lifted his drink to her in a silent, heartfelt toast.

Tarnal was walking a staggering Benziorn up and down the room, muttering imprecations under his breath. He had a cup on the table, and one on the shelf by the door, and was feeding the spluttering physician with strong taillin at every turn. Zanna smiled as she watched him, so intent and angry; with his brows drawn down over his grey eyes in a scowl at Benziorn's intransigence, and his hair glowing burnished gold in the lamplight. He caught her eye, and his angry frown changed to a reassuring grin. 'Don't worry, Zanna,' he told her. 'I'll have this wastrel sobered up soon. He's a good physician when he's not in his cups, and he'll fix up your dad in no time, you'll see.'

It was so good to see him again. Although they had only been apart for a matter of months, he seemed to have matured in her absence, and strikingly so. *I wonder if I seem the same to him?* Zanna mused. Had she been meeting him now for the first time, she would be thinking of him as a man, not a lad. She noticed that he was tall and strong enough to haul the struggling physician along behind him as he paced grimly back and forth. Suddenly, Zanna wondered what he was doing in Nexis. Because of the urgency of getting Vannor to a place of refuge, there had been no time for explanations as they had come up through the town. And where was Yanis? What was *he* doing now? Thinking of the handsome, dark-haired leader of the Nightrunners, Zanna lapsed into a dream . . .

She must have dozed, because the next thing she knew the kitchen was filled with a delicious aroma, her stomach was growling, and Hebba was shaking her gently by the shoulder. 'Come on, lass – I know you need to sleep, but you'll do it all the better for some good hot soup inside you. That Benziorn's gone to look at your dad, and so you just eat up then we'll make you up a proper bed, though the good gods only know where or what with . . .'

As she had done so often at home, Zanna shut out Hebba's flutterings, concentrating instead on filling her empty stomach with the wonderful soup – until the name of Yanis fell upon her ears like a thunderbolt. *'What?'*

Perversely, the old cook stopped talking at once. 'What did you say,' Zanna repeated carefully, 'about Yanis?'

Hebba looked at her as though she had just fallen out of the skies. 'Why, his fever's up again, poor lad, and what with that no-good physician nowhere to be found all day – '

'Just a minute,' Zanna interrupted her sharply. 'You mean, Yanis is here?'

'Why yes – tucked up in the spare room next door, poor lamb, and – ' This time, she was interrupted by the crash of splintering pottery, and the banging of the door. Hebba looked down at the shards of her best bowl amid the puddle of soup that was spreading across the hearth, and planted her fists on her ample hips. 'Well,' she said to the empty room at large. 'That young lass has been learning her manners from them smuggler lads and no mistake.'

Yanis stared wide-eyed at Zanna without a trace of recognition. His limp dark hair clung to a face that was flushed and sheened with sweat, and the bedclothes were twisted about his body from his restless movements. The stained bandage around his arm gave her the reason for his fever. Zanna felt a chill go through her. She couldn't lose him – not Yanis! Her fear was abruptly replaced by a flare of anger. Surely Tarnal had said that Benziorn was a good physician? If he was really any good, how could he have let his patient get into this state? And that useless, drunken sot was at this very minute treating her father? Zanna's blood turned cold at the thought, and she had to steel herself not to rush from the room and demand an accounting of Benziorn.

Calm down, she told herself firmly. Think. We're fugitives now, my dad needs help urgently, and good or bad Benziorn is the only physician we've got. We're lucky to have him, at that. Once she'd thought things through, she realized that Yanis had only been neglected this long because of herself and her father. Even Hebba had been too busy to make him comfortable. Well, at least Zanna could do something about that.

Carefully, she straightened the Nightrunner's twisted sheets and rearranged his pillows, trying to disturb him as little as possible, firmly keeping in check her desire, made possible at long last, to hold him, to touch his face, to stroke his hair. She found water in a jug on the table beside the bed, and a cloth to bathe his face. She tipped some of the water into a mug and managed to get him to swallow a little, though most went down his chin. Having made up the fire, and filled and trimmed the lamp, she thought she had reached the limit of what she could do for him at present. He certainly seemed to be resting more comfortably now. With a guilty start, Zanna remembered her father. Benziorn should have finished with him by now. She ought to go and see how he fared. She was just heading towards the door when Yanis began to murmur. Zanna turned back, her heart lifting with hope. Was he coming out of his delirium?

Apparently not. Yanis was restless again, rolling from one side to the other, undoing her efforts to straighten his bedding and muttering fretfully all the while in slurred, unintelligible tones. Her efforts to soothe and reassure him were of no avail, and she began to grow frightened. She was about to go and fetch Benziorn or Hebba when, to her relief, he seemed to grow calmer again. As his speech became more clear, Zanna leaned closer to listen. What was he saying?

Yanis's eyes flew open, and he stared uncomprehendingly into Zanna's face. 'Emmie?' he called weakly. 'Fire, climb down . . . Safe journey, beautiful sad Emmie . . .'

Zanna shot bolt upright. Who the bloody blazes was Emmie? Some woman – that was clear enough. Maybe it was just some old granny he'd helped downstairs to the kitchen fireside – or one of the smugglers, perhaps. No. She knew perfectly well that there was no Nightrunner with that name. And he had called her beautiful. Suddenly, Zanna felt cold all over, then flushed hot with furious humiliation. What had this idiot been doing in her absence? He hadn't the sense of a newborn babe. Well, she told herself very firmly, she was much too sensible to worry about the escapades of a stupid smuggler. She had much more important things – like her dad – to look after; and she'd be willing to wager that this Emmie, whoever she was, couldn't have single-handedly rescued Vannor from the clutches of the Magefolk!

Yanis had fallen silent now, but he was still thrashing about in his covers, turning his neatly made bed back into a jumble of twisted linen. Zanna looked coldly at the mess and its fevered perpetrator. Let this Emmie come and straighten it for him, if she was so bloody wonderful – *she* had wasted quite enough time on Yanis. She turned her back and forced herself to walk away without a backward look. She needed her rest – she had only just realized how unutterably weary she was – and she had to find her father. *He* needed her, at least. Only when she couldn't find the door handle did she stop to wipe her eyes.

'The fire must be smoking,' she muttered to herself, and left the room, closing the door firmly behind her.

Benziorn and Tarnal were waiting for her in the kitchen. Zanna took one look at their grave faces and all thoughts of Yanis fled her mind. 'Dad?' she whispered. Tarnal, his eyes shadowed with concern, got up and took her arm, leading her gently to the chair. Perversely, Zanna wanted to hit him. She wrenched her arm from his grasp and leapt back to her feet. 'What is it?' she shouted. *'What's wrong?'*

Tarnal opened his mouth and shut it again with a helpless shrug, and for the first time Zanna saw the shimmer of tears in his eyes. He looked expectantly at the physician.

Benziorn leaned across the hearth and took hold of Zanna's hand. 'Your dad was telling me how you got him out of the Academy,' he began conversationally.

Zanna stared at him in disbelief. Something bad had happened to Vannor – she knew it – and this lunatic wanted to waste her time with idle chatter? Yet, to be fair, he did not seem like such an idiot now that he was sober. He seemed fatherly and sensible: someone who respected her. Someone she could trust. 'What's wrong with my dad?' she demanded through gritted teeth.

'I was astounded,' the physician went on as though he had not heard her, 'that such a little lass had the courage to accomplish so much for her father when he needed her. But it's not over yet, Zanna. Vannor needs your courage and assistance again.' She felt his strong fingers squeeze her own. 'His hand is too badly damaged for me to save it,' he told her bluntly. 'It'll have to come off.'

'No!' Zanna gasped. Her strong, vigorous father, maimed and crippled? It was unthinkable. Though her eyes burned with tears, she managed to keep her voice steady. 'Are you really sure? Is there nothing you can do to give him a chance?'

'I'm sorry,' Benziorn told her. 'I know what you're thinking. He's only a hopeless drunk – what can he know? Surely someone who has the faintest notion of what he's doing could save that hand. But you'd be wrong. Whatever else I am, girl, I'm a damn good physician who already saved the

309

arm of your young smuggler friend in there – you ask Tarnal. I used to be the foremost Mortal healer in Nexis before the Wraiths took my family and I lost myself in the bottle. You're not the sort of person who can be fobbed off with a few soft words. You'd rather have the truth, so you can know what you're facing – and that's what I'm giving you. That hand is nothing more than a lump of mangled meat. The bones are smashed and splintered, the muscles pounded to oblivion, and where the tendons are the gods only know. After your little jaunt through the sewers, infection has set in, and is spreading rapidly. Vannor had to make a decision – his hand or his life – and he had the sense not to mess about. We were only waiting for you, to begin. Vannor needs you with him in there, girl – he asked for you – but if you don't think you can cope with it – if you'll be sick, or faint, or get all emotional on us – you'd be better staying away. Your father needs you strong now.' Benziorn raised his eyebrows challengingly. 'Well? What is it to be?'

'I'll come, of course,' Zanna replied without hesitation. 'Just tell me what you want me to do.'

The moors at night were a cold and eerie place. The low, black, barren humps of the hills stretched endlessly in all directions, and there was nothing to break the force of the thin, cold wind that whistled mournfully across the slope. Bern shivered, and pulled the hood of his cloak up around his face to hide the vast dark spaces that surrounded him. This accursed wilderness was no place for a city man. The baker, who had never taken an interest in horsemanship, wished now that he had not left all the errands involving riding to his older brother in their youth. He shifted uncomfortably in his saddle, trying to find a bit of his backside that had not already been rubbed raw, and wished that he knew where he was. Once he'd left the road, he had usually camped by night, but this time, just as the sun was setting, he had seen a smudge of darkness on a distant ridge that looked as though it might be the trees the Lady had told him to watch for. Foolishly, he had thought he could reach it before the darkness fell. He'd been wrong.

Not for the first time, Bern wished he had never agreed to undertake the Lady Eliseth's mission – until he thought about the cellar of his bakery, packed to the doorway with all that wonderful grain. He smiled to himself. The thought of the men and women he was about to betray perturbed him not at all. He had only to get through this, and when he got home he'd be the only working baker in Nexis. Why, he could ask whatever price he liked for his bread, and no one could object. Just thinking of the riches that could be his on his return helped stiffen his resolve. Besides, he must be almost there by now. On the horse that the Lady had provided for him, and following her directions, he had made good time. If he turned back at this late stage, he would have much further to travel, and nothing to show for it at the end – and though he would rather die than admit it, even to himself, the mere idea of crossing the cold-eyed Magewoman turned his bowels to water.

What was that? The distant wailing was low and eerie, raising prickling gooseflesh on his skin and transporting his mind back to childhood tales of the ghosts and demons that haunted the moor by night. Bern's fingers tightened on the reins. Then the sound came again, much closer now, and suddenly ghosts would have been a comfort. Wolves! This time, Bern had no difficulty in recognizing the sound. Neither did his horse. Uttering a shrill neigh of fear, it took off with a bound that almost unseated its unwary rider, and bolted.

All thoughts of wolves fled from the baker's head – he was too preoccupied with simply staying in the saddle. Clinging desperately to the horse's mane and jolted about with every stride, he was borne helplessly onward, galloping blindly, at breakneck speed, across the rough terrain. His hood blew back from his face and the cold wind pierced his clothing as his cloak flapped uselessly behind him. He plucked up his courage to let go of the mane and hauled desperately on the reins until he thought his arms would tear free from his shoulders, but it had not the slightest effect on his terrified mount. He lost one stirrup, then the other, and began to slip inexorably sideways. Suddenly the horse lurched forward over some hidden obstacle, and pitched head over heels. Bern went flying, and landed hard. He remembered nothing more.

When he opened his eyes, he was dazzled by daylight. For a moment, he wondered where he was. He was freezing cold and drenched with dew; he ached all over, and his head was throbbing abominably. Another man might have wondered what he had been drinking the night before, but Bern was far too tightfisted with his money to waste it on ale as his father had done, and too surly and singleminded about his work to seek comradeship and conviviality. Besides, he had no friends, and viewed them as an unnecessary luxury.

With a groan he rolled over, and the first thing he saw was the body of the horse lying nearby, cold and stiff, its neck skewed at an angle so grotesque that it brought his stomach into his throat. It was only then that Bern remembered the previous night, and the wolves. The wolves! In panic, he tried to struggle to his feet – and then realized that if they hadn't got him last night, while they were hunting and he was unconscious, there was little danger now.

Even that brief but frantic effort had exhausted him. The baker sat for a while with his eyes closed, until his head stopped spinning. When he opened them and looked around, he saw to his surprise that he had almost reached the forest after all. It was there ahead of him, on top of the next rise. He had no idea whether horses could see in the dark – his obviously hadn't been able to, he thought sourly, glaring at his fallen mount – but it had probably smelled the trees, or whatever horses did, and had been making for their dubious shelter when it had fallen.

Well, at least the stupid creature had almost got him where he wanted to go, Bern thought. He pulled himself stiffly to his feet and limped over to the body, unfastening his blanket and pack from behind the saddle with numb fingers. He threw the blanket around his shoulders as an extra cloak, and rummaged in his pack until he found some cheese and a heel of hard, stale bread. He washed down the unpalatable breakfast with water from his bottle, thinking wistfully of porridge and bacon, though the latter had not been seen in Nexis for a long, long time. But these accursed rebels must have some food – and the sooner he found them, the sooner he could eat. Refastening his pack, he slung it across his shoulder, and after a bad-tempered kick at the dead horse he was on his way.

Three hours later, he was still outside the forest. It simply would not let him pass. Bruised, begrimed, and bleeding, Bern threw himself down on a hummock with his back to the impenetrable wall of trees and swore horribly for several minutes. What the bloody blazes was going on? At first he had tried simply pushing his way through the tangled thicket, but the interwoven branches, all seemingly armed with sharp, hooked thorns, had blocked his path. When he tried hacking a way through them with his sword, they sprang back into his face, clawing at his eyes – and once, a heavy branch had fallen, narrowly missing his head. In desperation, he had tried fire, but as soon as he had kindled a small blaze, a freak gust of wind had blown it out, whirling smoke and sparks into his eyes. By now, Bern was at his wits' end. What in the world was going on? Anyone would think that the bloody forest was alive!

All at once, an arrow came zinging through the air. Almost parting Bern's hair, it planted itself in the turf beyond the hummock. 'Ho, stranger!' called a voice. 'What's your business here? Get to your feet and turn round slowly – and keep your hands well away from your sword.'

Shaking, Bern did as he was told. To his utter astonishment, the tangled undergrowth had vanished, and a narrow path arched over with leafy branches had opened in the ranks of trees. (But where had all the leaves come from? It was too early yet, and there was no sign of them from the outside of the forest.) In the opening stood a tall, bearded young man clad all in green and brown, wielding a bow that was almost as tall as himself. He held another arrow nocked to the string, aimed at Bern and ready to fire.

'I said, state your business,' the archer shouted impatiently.

Bern pulled himself together. 'I come with news from Nexis,' he blurted. 'News of Vannor.'

313

The arrow dipped and wavered for an instant. Fional pulled it quickly back into line, and squinted at the stranger down the long, straight shaft. His heart had leapt to hear Vannor's name, but he tried hard to keep his emotions in check. This could be an ambush, or a trap. 'Who are you, and what do you know of Vannor?' he demanded.

'He's alive, but he's in dreadful danger. My name is Bern. I was a servant at the Academy, and as soon as I found out what had happened I came to warn you. I barely escaped the Magefolk with my life . . . Please let me in. They know who I am now, and I daren't go back to Nexis.'

Fional frowned. The man seemed genuinely terrified, but . . . 'How did you know where to find us?' he demanded.

The stranger was sweating visibly now. 'There's talk all over the city about how Angos' mercenaries went to the Lady's Vale and never came back. I thought it had to be you. Who else could it have been?'

The archer cursed softly to himself. This did not bode well. But if this man now knew the whereabouts of the rebels, it would be safer in any case to have him under their eye. And his news seemed urgent. Dulsina had been going out of her mind with worry ever since Vannor had failed to return, with or without his daughter.

Fional made his mind up. 'Put your weapons down at the edge of the trees and come with me,' he told the stranger. 'For the time being, until you prove you can be trusted, you must consider yourself my prisoner.' But even though the man was weaponless, the archer was not foolish enough to trust Bern completely. He whistled, on a shrill, high note, and a dozen wolves came melting out of the forest's shadows. Snarling menacingly, they surrounded the captive. 'Make one false move,' Fional warned him, 'and they will tear you to pieces.'

The stranger turned pale and shuddered. 'I won't, I promise,' he vowed.

'After you.' The archer gestured with his bow and the man walked on obediently, surrounded by his guard of wolves, along the path that opened up ahead of him between the trees. Fional followed, keeping his arrow at the ready.

'What is that idiot doing?' D'arvan muttered to Maya. From the shelter of the trees he had watched the stranger's approach, and it had taken him little time to decide that he didn't like the look of the man at all. The Mage had used every trick he knew to bar his entry to the forest, and had almost discouraged him sufficiently to make him go away when Fional had arrived and ruined everything.

D'arvan sighed. 'The trouble is,' he told the unicorn, 'that I can't really keep him out now without killing him, and that wouldn't be wise at present – not if he really knows what has happened to Vannor. Besides, we know no real harm of him.'

The unicorn tossed her head, seemingly in agreement, and whinnied softly. D'arvan wished she could talk to him. Not only did he miss Maya desperately, but he could use her common sense right now. This was the first time, in his role as Forest Guardian, that he had found himself at a loss, and it worried him. So far, friends and foes had been easily recognizable, but this man was an enigma.

D'arvan rested an arm across the unicorn's withers. 'I don't like this at all,' he told her. 'There's something about that man . . .' He shook his head. 'He will bear watching – closely.' So saying, he suited word to deed, and made his way towards the rebel camp, the unicorn following at his heels.

20

A Queen in Waiting

'What do you mean, they decided to come back?' snapped Raven, her voice echoing sharply among the rafters of the great throne room. 'Who told them they could do that? How dare they! And what has happened to the Mages?'

Cygnus flinched, and he was not the only one. All of the queen's council of advisers, with the exception of Elster, who seemed calm as always, and Aguila, Captain of the Royal Guard, whose impassive face rarely betrayed his emotions, looked decidedly uncomfortable, if not distinctly nervous.

'Your Majesty, I'm sure that you distress yourself needlessly,' said Sunfeather, his suave demeanour only belied by the haste with which he spoke. 'As Wingmarshal of the Syntagma, I took it upon myself to question the couriers myself on their return, and – '

'Did you now?' Queen Raven glared at him. 'Then you have taken too much upon yourself. Where are the couriers? Why were they not brought to me at once?'

'My – my Lady, I did not wish to disturb you with such trifles . . .' For once, Sunfeather seemed at a loss. Since the departure of the groundling Wizards, the queen had seemed much more malleable, and he had been growing increasingly confident of his power over her. He'd thought that he had charmed her with his handsome looks and courtier's manners, but suddenly he had the sinking feeling that he might have miscalculated.

'This is not a trifle!' Raven shouted, hammering her fists down on the table in front of her. 'Bring them to me at once!'

'But, Majesty, they are sleeping after their long journey . . .'

'At once, I said!' The queen locked eyes with Sunfeather – and she was not the first to look away.

'Very well, Majesty. If that is your wish, I will have them sent for,' the Wingmarshal replied with cold dignity.

'No, Sunfeather.' Raven spoke quietly now, but her voice had an edge of steel. 'I told you to fetch them. This council will await your return – with the couriers.'

Sunfeather opened his mouth as if to protest, but closed it rapidly when he saw Aguila half-rise, his hand upon his sword. Though his expression remained as impassive as ever, the Captain of the Royal Guard's eyes were sparkling with malicious amusement.

Tight-lipped and fuming with anger, Sunfeather stalked out of the chamber. In the awkward silence that followed his departure, Elster gestured for a servant to refill the wine cups. When the youngster had finished her task and gone, Aguila turned to the acting High Priest. 'Did you know about this business?'

Skua shrugged. 'Sunfeather did mention it when the couriers returned, but I had to oversee some matters concerning the rebuilding of the temple, so I left him to deal with the situation as he saw fit. Even as *acting* High Priest' – he glared resentfully at Raven, who still had not confirmed his position – 'I have responsibilities. My time is not my own . . .'

'Really,' Aguila drawled. 'Well, at least you did better than I. The first I heard of it was just before this meeting, when I asked Sunfeather if he knew why her Majesty had called us together. And what of you, Cygnus? You are Wingmarshal's friend. Was he keeping you equally in the dark?'

Raven glared at him. It was typical of him – of all of them – to start talking across her, taking over the meeting and ignoring her as though she wasn't even there. 'That's not the point,' she cut in, wanting somehow to take back control. 'What I want to know is –' She was interrupted by two things: a sharp kick on the ankle from Elster, and the return of Sunfeather, with the four winged couriers behind him.

Raven rose to her feet. 'Well?' she demanded sternly. 'What have you to say for yourselves? Why did you disobey my orders and abandon the Magefolk and their companions?'

The culprits fidgeted uncomfortably under her harsh gaze.

Raven gritted her teeth. 'You may begin,' she told them, 'by telling me what happened to the Mages after they left me, until you left them.'

The couriers looked at one another, then one of the winged men stepped forth. 'The world is a fearsome, hostile place, your Majesty, beyond the boundary of our mountains. You would do well to hearken to what we say . . .'

Raven listened as he recounted what had taken place after the Mages had left Aerillia. As the tale unwound, her heart grew heavier and colder with dread for her former companions, until it seemed as though it was sinking to her very feet. When the winged man's story ended with the attack in the Xandim fastness, she could not believe it was over.

'And you just abandoned them?' she demanded. 'You don't even know if they survived? You offered them no help at all, despite the orders you were given?'

The winged couriers looked at the ground and shuffled their feet.

'Speak up,' Aguila barked. 'The queen asked you a question.'

One of the Winged Folk looked up, her expression sullen. 'If it please your Majesty,' she began, 'no, one mentioned anything about orders when we went with the groundlings. We were given to understand that we were volunteers.'

'That's right,' another winged man chimed in. 'And no one mentioned anything, when we volunteered, about fighting with the great cats, our lifelong foes; or getting caught up in wizardly battles; or risking our lives in some attempt by the Horsefolk to overthrow their leader. With the greatest respect, these matters are not the concern of the Skyfolk. And as for being cursed out by that female demon of a Wizard . . . Well, your Majesty, it was just too much.'

'I notice it doesn't seem to have been too much for your two *loyal* companions, who elected to remain behind,' Aguila growled. 'The blood of the Skyfolk runs thin these days, if that is all the extent of your courage.'

'Sir, that is scarcely just,' the winged woman protested. 'We are loyal warriors of the Syntagma. But when we volunteered Wingmarshal Sunfeather told us that if ever we wanted to come home, it would be permitted . . .'

318

'He told you that you could leave the Mages whenever you liked?' Raven demanded furiously. 'Those were not my orders.'

'Upon my honour, Majesty, I told them no such thing,' Sunfeather protested loudly. 'Full well I knew what your orders were. These cowards must have wilfully misunderstood me.'

'Perhaps you didn't explain it to them clearly enough,' Aguila drawled. 'Are you sure you understood her Majesty's orders yourself?'

Sunfeather flushed scarlet with rage. 'Of course I understood . . .' His words tailed off and he shut his mouth hurriedly when he realized how neatly Aguila had trapped him.

'That is all very well,' Cygnus cut in quickly, rescuing Sunfeather from his floundering, 'but it brings us no nearer to deciding the punishment of these miscreants.'

'Punishment for the couriers?' Aguila lifted a sardonic brow. 'Since the confusion seems to have stemmed from the Wingmarshal's orders, perhaps he should, in all decency, share their fate.'

Sunfeather's hand went to his sword. 'Are we to act upon the words of a lowborn piece of dung who has risen much too far above his natural state?' he snarled. 'Your Majesty, I ask permission to make Aguila pay for these insults with his own base blood.'

Aguila grinned mirthlessly. 'Any time – if you think you're up to it.'

'Be quiet, both of you!' Raven thundered. 'How dare you bicker and trade insults in my throne room like a pair of quarrelling fledgelings!' Following her outburst, she realized that everyone was looking at her expectantly, and suddenly she found herself blushing and floundering for words.

'Lady?' Skua seized the initiative. 'May I make a suggestion? Why not make these couriers pay for their defection by making atonement to Yinze himself? Because so many of our folk have been pressed into duty in the fields, I am desperately short of help to rebuild the temple . . .'

Raven jumped at the opportunity to get out of this interminable wrangle. Her head ached, and she was sick to death of the very sight of her advisers. All she could think about was whether Aurian and her companions were safe. At least Skua had given her the chance to make a decision at last, even though her conscience told her it was not the right one. 'Yes, yes,' she said hastily. 'I thank the acting High Priest for his timely words of wisdom. It shall be as he advises. I deliver the miscreants into his charge, and once the new temple has been completed they can return to the Syntagma. Whether they resume their former ranks or not depends on how they behave in the interim. That is my decree.' Letting her breath out in a sigh of relief, she sank back into her seat.

Aguila's mouth had tightened into a thin, hard line. He was glaring at her so angrily that she looked away, unable to meet his accusing eyes. Behind the cover of his hand, Sunfeather was smirking. Raven bit her lip. She had got it all wrong in some way, that was plain – but how?

Cygnus was relieved that his friend had escaped the queen's censure for his part in the affair. Who'd have thought that Raven would have proved so difficult? Thank Yinze that she lacked sufficient experience to see what was going on. And as for that Aguila – he was truly to blame, stirring matters up as he had. The time was fast approaching when the Captain of the Royal Guard would have to be put back in his lowly place.

The sudden realization that the queen was still speaking brought Cygnus out of his reflections with a jolt.

'Whatever you may think about my association with the Mages, I have made a promise I must keep,' Raven was saying, 'so someone else must be sent to see if the Lady Aurian is safe, and to help her if he can. Someone who can be trusted, this time, to send back proper messages, and not to desert his post at the first sign of trouble. Can anyone think whom we may fitly send?'

Cygnus's heart leapt within him. At last, beyond all hope, his chance had come! He had been livid when the queen had named him as her taster, thus ruining for good any chance he might have of winning the position of High Priest. Since then, he had found his greedy thoughts fixing again and again upon the Harp of Winds. If the Artefact were only his . . .

'Your Majesty – for the love and loyalty I bear you, I will go.' The words were out of Cygnus's mouth before he even knew what he was doing, and for an instant he felt the clutch of panic. But his instincts had not played him false.

Raven's face lit up with her smile before she hesitated. He could see her lips tug down at the corners, and knew she was hating herself for that moment of indecision. 'Loyal Cygnus, you are such a good friend to me. But are you sure? I can ill spare you.'

Cygnus inclined his white head in a bow. 'Majesty, it would be my privilege. And as one who already knows and is friendly with the Mages, who better could you send?'

The Queen of the Winged Folk nodded. 'You have my eternal gratitude – and when you return from your mission you will be rewarded as you deserve.'

I will indeed, thought Cygnus – but not in the way you imagine, if all goes well . . .

When the meeting of the council finally ended and the winged men had departed, Elster lagged behind. 'Your Majesty,' she said gravely, 'may I speak privately with you?' Without waiting for an answer, the master physician took hold of Raven's wrist and practically yanked her from the chamber. Instead of going out on to the vast covered porch and flying the quick route to the queen's rooms, as they were wont to do, Elster shepherded her young charge through the labyrinth of little-used corridors within the palace, never once letting go of her arm.

When they were finally alone in Raven's sumptuous chambers, and a servant had poured wine for them both and been dismissed, leaving the flask behind at Elster's behest, Raven turned to her mentor. 'All right,' she muttered. 'By the expression on your face, I can tell that you have something to say.'

Elster took a long draught of her wine, shook her head and sighed. 'What am I going to do with you?'

'What do you mean?' Raven demanded. 'What have I done wrong now?'

'You mean you really don't know?' The physician raised an

eyebrow. 'Foolish girl – did you have to antagonize Sunfeather like that?'

Wine spilled on the inlaid surface of the ebony table as Raven slammed down her cup in temper. 'And just what was I supposed to do?' she exploded. 'Sit there meekly and smile at all his veiled insolence? Yinze take it, Elster – how am I supposed to rule if I can't antagonize Sunfeather, not to mention those other arrogant, smug, manipulative bullies on the council?'

'Wipe up that wine, your Majesty,' said Elster mildly, 'before it stains the table. It's not that you must never cross them, but what counts is the way you do it. Today you were right to put Sunfeather in his place – he was trying to conceal important information from you, and that you must never allow. But you didn't have to humiliate him at the same time. You only needed to be firm. Once he saw that you wouldn't let him get away with such tactics, it would have been enough. He wouldn't have liked it, but he could respect such a move on your part. Sending the Wingmarshal of the Syntagma out on a mere servant's errand, however, was inexcusable. Believe me, Raven – if you set out to alarm the council with such high-handed behaviour, you will have the shortest reign in the history of the Skyfolk.'

Raven looked at the old physician in silence, her mouth set in a stubborn line. 'It's not fair,' she muttered at last. 'The way they act towards me, no one would ever think I was the queen – and you're not much better. You treat me like a baby.' Her eyes flashed with a spark of anger.

'If you act like one, that's all you can expect,' Elster responded swiftly. 'Now heed me, Raven. Until today, Sunfeather and the others thought you were nothing more than a spoiled child who could be manipulated. Therein lay your power. When men are off their guard, they usually can be defeated, and not even realize what has happened until it is too late. You would do well to take your example from Aguila instead of hackling at him all the time – that one has his wits about him.'

The queen made a small noise of derision. 'Aguila? Wits? Why, he's nothing but a boorish, lowborn –'

322

'And that's my point.' Elster leaned across the table, interrupting the girl in the midst of her tirade. 'You see?' she said quietly. 'He has you fooled as well as the rest of them.'

Raven stared at the physician, open-mouthed.

'Close your mouth, dear. Queens definitely do not gape.' Elster took a sip of her wine. 'Now, instead of sitting there glaring at me, think back to that meeting, after you sent Sunfeather away. With one simple, seemingly casual question, Aguila managed both to establish his own innocence in this affair, and put Skua in a very awkward position – at least that would have been the case had you been paying attention. Had you not interrupted when you did, he might also have discovered for you whether Cygnus was part of this plot to conceal the truth from his queen.'

'Oh.' Raven blushed crimson. 'I didn't think . . .'

'But you must think, if you want to rule.' The physician rapped the table with the base of her goblet for emphasis, then reached for the flask to refill it. 'The trouble is,' she mused, as she poured, 'you need time to learn how to rule – and time is just what you don't have, with those vultures surrounding you. You need someone strong enough and wise enough – and with sufficient authority – to support you until you find your feet. Yinze blast it to perdition – now look what I've done!' Suddenly realizing that she had flooded her cup, she put the flask down with another muttered oath.

'You should wipe that up,' Raven told her with a pert grin, 'before it stains the table.'

Elster chuckled. 'You see, you can be sharp enough when you want to – that's plain by the way you always keep acting like a dizzy girl so you can put Skua off from assuming the position of High Priest officially.' Fishing a very businesslike kerchief from a pocket in her robe, she began to mop up the spilled wine. 'While he's still only acting High Priest, you have him nicely in you power.'

'Oh, Aguila told me to do that.'

The physician glanced up sharply. 'Did he indeed?' She frowned thoughtfully. 'Anyway, girl, stop trying to put me off. Before I was interrupted,' she looked seriously at Raven, 'I was saying that you can't keep on alone like this. Apart from anything else, you'll need an heir, you know. You must stop prevaricating, and take a consort.'

'What?' Raven shrieked. 'How could you, Elster? How could you even suggest such a thing after what happened with Harihn . . .' Her voice tailed off in distress.

Elster leaned across the table and took hold of the young queen's hand. 'You must put that dreadful business behind you, Raven,' she said firmly. 'You are still young . . .'

'How can I take a consort now, you old fool? The Winged Folk mate for life! I'm ruined . . .'

'Utter nonsense!' Elster retorted bracingly. 'In that respect, at least, Blacktalon was right. Groundlings cannot be said to count . . . Or do you want to ruin your life and lose your kingdom over one stupid mistake?'

Tears overflowed Raven's eyes and ran down her face. 'But I could never love again,' she whispered tragically.

The physician sighed, and raised her eyes heavenwards. 'You youngsters! Who said anything about love? Find someone you can like, and respect, and work with – that's all you need. Queens have no business even thinking about love.'

'Fine words, coming from someone who never took a mate at all,' Raven sneered. 'So who have you decided I should choose? I presume you had someone in mind before you even started this conversation. Someone else, no doubt, who will manipulate me, with you the chief puppetmaster of them all . . .'

'If you have any sense at all, you'll choose Aguila.'

Elster's words cut like a swordstroke through the young queen's ranting. Raven stared at her, her eyes wide with dismay; too thunderstruck even to protest.

'Think.' The physician pressed her advantage. 'You like him – you've admitted as much to me on several occasions. He's very fond of you, and what's more he's loyal, and commands the loyalty of the Royal Guard in turn. He's intelligent, and he won't take any nonsense from those other backstabbers who advise you – especially not once he outranks them as royal consort.'

Raven burst out laughing. 'Elster, you can't be serious. This is a jest – go on, admit it. Why, he's nothing but a low-born commoner. And he's so old!'

The physician raised an eyebrow. 'Aguila? Old? *I'm* old, you little idiot. He may be a few years older than you, my girl, but that doesn't make him ancient. And as for his birth – well, anyone who could rise from his beginnings to become Captain of the Royal Guard is truly a man to be reckoned with. You couldn't have anyone better on your side – and what's more, you could always trust him to *be* on your side.'

She looked at the young queen gravely. 'Listen, Raven. While we are speaking of age, I must remind you that I won't be here for ever to help and advise you. Being queen is the loneliest business in the world, my child – and while I'm still around to plague you I want to make certain that you'll have someone to lean on when I'm gone.' Seeing Raven's stricken face, she smiled to lighten the moment. 'Besides,' she added mischievously, 'I have no fledgelings of my own. How will I have my just memorial if you don't have a little princess to name after me?'

'Oh, Elster!' With a sob, Raven flung her arms around the old physician. 'You're not going to die.'

'Not for a good while yet, I hope – unless your aim gets better with those winecups you fling at me in temper, when I tell you things you don't want to hear.' Elster chuckled. 'No, but seriously, child – do as I advise you. Take Aguila as your consort. It will be the best decision you'll ever make. I promise you, you won't regret it.'

'But, Elster –' Raven bit her lip. 'After that business with Harihn . . . What if Aguila doesn't want to marry me?'

The physician laughed out loud. 'Not want to marry you? My dear child, of course he'll want to! Why, any one of that nest of vipers who advise you would cut off his wings to become your consort. Out of the lot of them, however, Aguila is the only one who loves you.'

When Elster finally departed, she had left Raven with a good deal to think about. The winged girl went to the window and stood, deep in contemplation, staring blindly out at the city she ruled. Should she do as the physician advised? After Harihn's betrayal, she had abandoned the idea of ever taking a consort. She'd had far too much to occupy her mind in these first, difficult days of settling into her rule to even consider the matter of an heir. But Elster, as usual, had spoken wisely. Raven bit her lip, struggling with her feelings. That was all very well, but, after Harihn, could she bear to take another man to her side – to her bed? The words of Flamewing, her mother, spoken in anger so long ago, came back to her: *'You were brought up to recognize that you have responsibilities to your people and to the throne, one of them being that you must marry to advantage.'*

The ruler of the Winged Folk sighed. Elster had also told her that queens had no business thinking about love. Well, so be it. They were right – both of them – and it was time she grew up and faced the facts. It could have been much worse, Raven reminded herself. Not long ago, she had been faced with the unthinkable prospect of having the cruel High Priest Blacktalon forced upon her as her consort. Then, she had had no choice, but now it was different. And Aguila had been kind to her, cheering the lonely young queen almost as much as Elster had in these last, difficult days ... Elster had even said that he loved her, which had come as a shock – but she wasn't ready to think about that yet. He was certainly the only one who didn't seem to want to use her, though.

Raven realized that she had made her decision. She would do it. Suddenly, she thought about the reactions of Sunfeather and Skua when they heard the news, and a malicious grin spread itself across her face. Those two were going to be so sick ... She chuckled to herself, feeling more cheerful than she had in days. Elster, as usual, had been right.

21
Just Like the Old Days . . .

In a very different city, far to the south, another queen was contemplating her future.

Sara awakened with a jolt, torn out of the nightmare by the sound of her own screaming. Her eyes flew open, blind to everything, for a moment, but the closing scenes of the dream that were still imprinted on her inner eye. As full consciousness crept back to her, she realized that she was looking through a mist of gauzy white hangings that hung limp in the stifling heat, diffusing the bars of strong afternoon sunlight that invaded the chamber through the lattice of the shutters. Sara rolled over on the wide bed, almost weeping with relief, clutching the tangled silken sheet to herself for additional security. She was home. She was safe. It had only been a dream.

She pushed aside the light coverlet and reached for the loose white robe of gold-embroidered silk that lay across the bottom of the bed. Slipping it over her head and smoothing the clinging fabric down over her sweating skin, Sara swung her legs off the low couch, enjoying the comparative coolness of the blue and white tiles against her bare feet. Fighting her way through the layers of white gauze that hung down from the canopy above, she emerged into the stifling gloom of the shuttered chamber.

Standing on tiptoe, Sara raised her arms above her head and stretched until her joints cracked in complaint. Ah . . . that felt better. She twisted the thick, heavy mantle of her golden hair into a rough knot at the nape of her neck and pulled the clinging robe away from her sticky shoulders, before padding across to the low table. As always there was water there, and a pitcher of fruit juice that had been cool when she had gone to sleep; for like the Khazalim, she had learned better than to drink wine or spirits in the heat of the day. On this particular day, however, Sara felt the need for something stronger. Taking a flask from a nearby cabinet, she filled a goblet to the brim with wine, before crossing the room to the great windows that stretched from floor to ceiling, taking up half the wall.

As she folded back the shutters, dazzling sunlight poured into the chamber in a flood of molten gold. Sara blinked, and shaded her eyes until her vision had adjusted to the stronger light. The air that had entered the room was no cooler than the stifling air within – if anything, it was hotter – but she had grown used to that by now. Feeling a need for space, as though the four walls of her chamber still held the echoes of her nightmare trapped within, Sara went out on the balcony and leaned against the rounded top of the marble railing.

The maze of white buildings, courtyards, gardens and low towers that formed the Khisu Xiang's seraglio were still and deserted in the afternoon's oppressive heat. The soft, silvery patter of fountains, the rhythmic rasp of cicadas and the chirruping of a drowsy bird were the only sounds that invaded the heavy silence. Beyond the walls of Xiang's vast palace, dropping down tier after tier into the shadowed, red-walled canyon of the river, stretched the city of Taibeth, of which she was now Khisihn – the queen. Some queen, she thought bitterly. Why, I may be the royal wife of the Khisu, but I'm as much a prisoner here as – her glance flicked back into the shadowed room where her bright-hued finches slumbered in the heat, within their golden cage.

Don't be stupid! Suddenly, Sara was furious at her own weakness. She thought of her clothes, her jewels – the power that was hers within the constrained, unnatural little world of women that was hidden behind these high white walls. Would you rather be back in Nexis, she demanded scornfully of herself, dressed in rags and sewing and scrubbing and trailing all the way to market for your father? Would you rather still be married to that dolt Vannor, with his sly little sneak of a daughter and his endless demands that you share his bed? Would you rather have been married to Anvar?

A shiver ran down her spine. Clutching the goblet in both

hands, she took a long swallow of wine to steady hands that had suddenly begun to shake. She had dreamed about Anvar. The remainder was enough to disturb her all over again. For a long time now, Sara had succeeded in putting him out of her mind entirely, ever since he and that red-haired harridan of a Mage had stolen the ferocious Black Demon from the Khisu's arena, befriended Xiang's rebellious son, the Prince Harihn, and thrown the entire city of Taibeth into utter turmoil before making their escape into the desert. Why did he come back to haunt her now, of all times – just when she needed her wits about her to survive these next few months?

With a shudder she forced herself to remember the dream, in the hope that once she had confronted it she could expunge it from her mind. She had been in Nexis, with Anvar, in the shop of his father Torl in the Grand Arcade. The events had been those that had led up to the death of Anvar's mother Ria in the fire – but this time Sara herself had been the victim of the blaze. She remembered screaming and screaming as the flames leapt up around her, catching greedily at her clothes and hair – and instead of extinguishing the fire, it was Anvar who had started it, and Anvar who was burning her. He was standing over her, gloating, a ball of Magefire in his hand. *'Now you will never have a child . . .'*

With an anguished cry, Sara dropped her face into her hands.

'Lady, what in the Reaper's name are you about? Come away from there at once! Have your wits been stolen by the desert winds, that you stand thus for all the world to see?' The reedy, piping voice that broke through her meditations was snappish with alarm. Sara gasped, and whirled – but it was the voice itself that had startled her, not the identity of the owner.

There was no mistaking the shrill, lisping tones of Zalid, chief eunuch of the seraglio, procurer of women for the Khisu – and, in this place, the only person she could trust. Just at this moment, Sara couldn't have been more pleased to see him, though it looked as if he was far from returning the

329

compliment. The swirling designs in gold paint that adorned his bald head were blurring at the edges in the heat, and the many sparkling necklaces that adorned his neck were jingling with his agitation. His chubby, frowning face was creased with anxiety.

'Come inside at once, Lady,' he scolded. 'Where is your veil? Have you already forgotten how ill you were last time from the sun? And for shame, to stand brazen and barefaced before the world like a harlot on your balcony. Is this the behaviour of a queen?'

When Sara turned to face him he gave a yelp of dismay; so agitated that he abandoned all pretence at courtesy. 'The padding! You fool – how could you have forgotten? In your heedlessness you will kill us all.'

'Be still, Zalid!' Sara snapped. 'Don't be such an old woman. I don't need the padding yet. And who is there to see me, you imbecile? The entire seraglio is asleep.'

Zalid's blow caught her completely by surprise. His hand flashed out, striking her so hard across the face that she staggered back against the marble railing. While she was still unbalanced, he grabbed her arm and spun her back inside the room. Sara fell, only a last-minute reflex saving her from striking her face on the hard tiled floor. She pulled herself shakily to her feet, her head still spinning from the force of the blow. She was blazing with an anger which nevertheless had a cold, pulsing seed of fear at its core. 'How dare you strike your Khisihn?' she snapped. 'When Xiang gets back – '

'When Xiang returns and the spies that infest this palace tell him what they saw on your balcony, he will have you tied in a sack and dropped in the river to feed the great lizards.'

The cold implacability of the chief eunuch's words stopped her ranting as effectively as though he had hit her again. Zalid advanced on her, his dark face pale with anger. 'Just because the Khisu is away, you may not allow yourself to grow careless – not even for a moment. This plot was your idea. I warned you before we started of the difficulties involved, and constraints that would be upon you – and now that we *have* started there is no going back. I have no intention of losing my life through your stupidity. You may no longer sleep unclothed, and walk naked through these apartments like a brazen northern whore. You must become accustomed to that padding now, before it becomes essential. You will wear it *at all times*, no matter how it inconveniences you and galls you. Now go and put it on – immediately.'

When Sara hesitated, he advanced upon her menacingly, spitting out the words in his anger. 'You should bear in mind,' he hissed, 'that though you might be queen, in the king's absence I am in charge of his women. There are many ways you can be beaten without scarring – and the marks will long have healed ere Xiang returns. Now go – and if I ever again see you on that balcony without proper robes, and padding, and decent veils, I will punish you until your screams can be heard all the way to that godless northern cesspit from whence you came.'

Sara stared at him, appalled. He meant it – and in fact, she realized, with cold, sinking fear in the pit of her stomach, on the flimsiest of excuses he would beat her anyway. She had dragged Zalid into this plot of hers, and now that he was in too deep to back out again he was terrified, and wanted to take it out on her. Shaking with fear, she rushed into her robing room and found the tangle of straps that held the thinly stuffed and slightly weighted sack securely to her stomach. She fastened it on, already hating the unwieldiness and trying not to think about the next five months, when the weight and padding must be markedly increased. Once it was hidden beneath her loose robe, she stared at her silhouette in the tall mirror of polished silver and scowled, wondering how in the name of all the gods she'd thought she could get away with this. And yet what choice did I have? she thought despairingly.

When she had manoeuvred and plotted to become queen, she had never considered the fact that she could not have children. But neither had she reckoned on the Khisu's desperate desire for another son, another heir, to replace the luckless and despised Harihn. As each month passed without a hint that the long-for child had been started, Xiang had begun to turn colder towards her; less patient and more careless and cruel. When he started to neglect her, and turn

331

back once more to the beauties of his harem, Sara knew that
she would have to act quickly to preserve her position – and
Zalid, with his power and influence within the harem, was
the only one who could help her. Luckily, because he had
been the one who'd brought her to Xiang in the first place,
his fortunes were very much tied up with her own. Being the
discoverer of the new queen had brought him riches and
prestige; but Xiang had no use for those who failed or disappointed him, and if that queen should be found wanting
Zalid would lose not only his livelihood but quite possibly his
life.

Between Sara and the eunuch, the plot had gradually been
hatched. Zalid had found the queen her own personal, and
very bribable, physician, and was squandering much of his
own gold and her jewels upon the man in the happy knowledge that the wretch would not live many more months to
enjoy the benefit. Sara only had to pretend to turn moody, as
pregnant women often did, and Xiang happily acceded to her
request that her body servants be replaced by a single mute
slave-girl. The odd custom of this land, where women were
sequestered during pregnancy, had worked in their favour, as
had other, unexpected events.

Xiang had been overjoyed by Sara's false announcement,
but swiftly following his first rush of triumph came the ran-
kling awareness that the other, older heir still lived. Though
Harihn had vowed never to return, the Khisu brooded
blackly upon his son's continued existence, and the threat it
posed to the unborn prince – for, of course, in the manner of
those who always got their own way, he was convinced the
child would be a boy. Enough time had passed now for Xiang
to forget the fear that Aurian had instilled in him. For days
after her departure the city had been a bloodbath, while his
soldiers quelled the uprising of the slaves that the Mage had
freed and got things back on a proper footing – but once this
had been accomplished, and with none of the dire re-
percussions that Aurian had promised, he had dismissed her
as a threat. When the sudden ending of the sandstorms had
opened up the desert route to the north, he had decided to
take his army and put paid to Harihn once and for all.

Xiang's departure had come as a considerable relief to the queen and her fellow-conspirator. Aman, the vizier, who had taken charge in the Khisu's absence, knew what was good for him and kept away from the seraglio. When it came to his women, Xiang had a well deserved reputation for jealousy. That left Sara and Zalid free to act – and it was much easier to keep up the subterfuge. The eunuch had agents among the poor, in the lower quarters of the city, who were keeping an eye on several girls due to give birth at about the right time. As soon as one dropped a son . . . Sara smiled to herself. What a joke on Xiang, that the next ruler of the Khazalim would be a beggar's brat. By the gods, if she could bring this off it would be worth everything!

Heartened by the thought, she washed her face and collected herself before going back into the other room to confront the eunuch. She must not let him see how badly he had frightened her. As she passed the mirror she caught a glimpse of the bruise that was darkening on one side of her face, and scowled. One day she would make him pay for that. As the beloved mother of Xiang's heir she would have far more power than she possessed now. In the meantime – Sara grimaced. Zalid had certainly found a way to ensure that she wore those accursed veils.

The other chamber felt much more pleasant now, with the approaching cool of evening. The eunuch was standing looking out over the very balcony that he had forbidden her to use. Anger dissipated the last traces of Sara's lingering fear. She drew herself up to her full height and looked at him coldly. 'Have you no duties to perform?' she snapped. 'I want cooled wine, a light meal, and my slave girl to draw my bath . . .'

Zalid turned to her with an insolent bow that was hardly worth the name. 'Your will, my queen. And do you not want the news I came to bring you? News of your beloved Khisu?' His smile was mocking – he had no illusions about Sara's true opinion of her royal husband. Sara's heart leapt into her throat.

'There's news? What is it? Why didn't you tell me sooner?'

'Pray do not distress yourself, Lady – not in your delicate

condition.' His manner was so falsely unctuous that she wanted to strike him.

'Get on with it!' she shrieked.

'As you wish. A homing bird arrived today with a message that Xiang had reached the far side of the desert. Not only did they find signs of Harihn's occupancy at Dhiammara, but there are clear indications on the edge of the forest that the prince and his companions survived the crossing. That being the case, the Khisu is determined to follow his trail further northward.' The eunuch bowed again, not making an effort to hide his smile. 'Alas, my Lady, it seems we must steel ourselves to bear sad tidings. The absence of our beloved Lord must be extended.'

Sara sat down on the edge of the bed, weak-kneed with relief. No matter what abuse she had to put up with from Zalid, it seemed that the gods were still smiling on her plan. Companions, the eunuch had said. So when Xiang finally caught up with the runaway prince, he would have Aurian to contend with. She wondered what would suit her best – to have Xiang return to indulge her for giving him an heir, or to have him dead, and be the mother of the newborn Khisu of the Khazalim, with all the power attendant on such a position. Either way, she stood to win. Sara smiled to herself. It looked as though the next few weeks would be very interesting indeed.

Xiang was unnerved by the forest. This place was like nothing in his experience. He was used to the open spaces and endless horizons of his barren land, where the only sounds were the chirring of the cicadas and the susurration of the shifting desert wind. Here, the trees pressed in on him, surrounding him with gloom and cutting off the warmth of the sun. On all sides there were shifting shadows – swift flickers of movement that startled the horses and made the Khisu jump and whirl, hand on swordhilt, to face a threat that turned out to be nothing more than a branch that was tossing in the wind.

That same wind in the trees was like the distant whisper of surf, creating a constant background sound that drowned out the warning of any approaching dangers, as did the unfamiliar chuckling chatter of the rushing streams. Strange beasts and birds rustled the undergrowth and cried shrilly from the treetops overhead. The hooves of the horses were muffled by soft loam that concealed hazardous holes and roots and fallen branches. The way ahead was blocked time and again by tree trunks, deadfalls, and patches of thorny, impenetrable brush, so that the band of Khazalim warriors were forced to turn aside from their chosen path. Before long, they had lost all sense of direction and were wandering blindly through a thick green maze.

The Khisu was a worried man. His troops were wearied from the gruelling race across the desert, as unnerved by this alien place as himself. From time to time, he was certain he had heard distant shouts and screams coming from other parts of the forest. Three times now he had sent messengers to locate the remainder of the forces. None of them had returned. With regrets that were growing greater by the minute, Xiang pushed grimly on, surrounded by only a handful of his men. Of the two hundred soldiers he had brought with him, these scant few were all that were visible through the rustling, screening foliage. The Khisu suppressed a shudder. Never in his life had he felt so alone; so hemmed-in, yet conversely so exposed.

By this time, the Khazalim forces had penetrated deep into the forest. All sight of the blessed limitless expanses of the desert had long been left behind them. When they came at last to a broad clearing Xiang relaxed a little. How good it was to see the sun again, and have open space around him! Without warning, an arrow came whirring through the trees and struck with deadly accuracy through the eye of the guard who was riding beside him.

'Down!' Before the echoes of his warning had time to die away, Xiang was off his horse and lying flat on the forest floor. For a moment all was chaos: confused and shouting men, horses hurtling in every direction with shrill neighs of terror, trampling the hapless warriors who were trying in vain to conceal themselves from the deadly bolts that rained down from the trees. The sounds of the forest were drowned by

335

the screams of dying men, and the loam underfoot ran red with blood.

Xiang, cringing on the ground with a mouthful of leaf-mould, was beside himself with fear and fury. In all his life, no one had dared to do this to him. No one! Except that wretched woman – but that was not a thought to dwell on, especially now. An arrow came thudding into the ground inches from his face, and shock and outrage made him gather his wits. Quickly, he loosened the brooch at the neck of the sumptuous cloak that marked him out among his men and slipped from under the dangerous garment. Praying that he would be unseen in the confusion of running horses and falling men, he rolled towards the edge of the clearing with its thick fringe of bushes. The undergrowth that he'd been cursing a moment before he blessed now, as he squirmed deeper into its concealing shade.

Eliizar was pleased. The day was going well. The plans over which he had laboured through so many sleepless nights seemed to be working perfectly, and he was infinitely grateful for Anvar's warning. His little community, which consisted of Harihn's surviving warriors and the household staff that the prince had abandoned in the forest, had been well prepared and organized in the defence of their newfound home. Though Eliizar had hated to take men from the all-important tasks of building the new settlement and clearing and cultivating hidden pockets of land within the forest, today had proved that the sacrifice had not been in vain. Lookouts had informed them in ample time when the Khisu had left the desert. Once Xiang and his men had entered the thick woodland it had been easy for the settlers to split up the invading forces, luring the scattered groups apart and ever deeper into the labyrinth of trees. Then the Khazalim interlopers had turned swiftly from predators to prey.

Small groups of warriors had been concealed beneath a camouflage of woven branches, so that they could spring up beneath the very feet of Xiang's soldiers and gain the inestimable advantage of surprise. A few pit traps had been dug and covered, although they were expensive in labour and besides, Eliizar wanted to save as many of the Khazalim horses as he could for his little community. Settlers lurked up in the branches with weighted nets to drop down on the riders, and slender ropes had been strung between the trees at neck-height for a mounted man and trip-height for a horse. Eliizar had hand-picked the most skilled of the bowmen and placed them at strategic points.

Even the women had their role to play in the defence of the forest – Eliizar, having been forcibly given the example of Nereni's courage and fortitude, had learned his lesson. Not only had they aided the diggers by carrying away the loose, betraying soil and disguising the traps and their approaches with fallen leaves, but they had woven ropes and nets and the camouflage for hidden warriors. The younger and more nimble girls, made agile by months of foraging in the woods while their men were at Incondor's tower, were among those who waited in the treetops with their nets and ropes.

A band of older women led by the redoubtable Nereni lurked in concealment with blowpipes armed with stinging darts that maddened the horses so that men were thrown to the ground, at the mercy of Eliizar's waiting warriors. The secret of making these had been given to Nereni by Finch and Petrel, the two winged couriers whom Raven had sent with the little band of settlers. They were the self-same pair of Skyfolk who had conveyed Nereni to Aerillia on that fateful day, and who by now had been so thoroughly pampered by her cooking and her care that they would do virtually anything for her. Another group of the more timid women, who had no stomach for fighting, were back at the camp, boiling water, preparing salves and making bandages for when the wounded should come home.

Not, Eliizar fervently hoped, that there would be many of those. As it was, the numbers of his settlers were pitifully few to found a new community, but that was what he intended to do. He had had enough of cruel tyrants, treacherous princes and magical adversaries. He wanted to live out his years in peace, and those who had joined him felt the same. If they had to fight to establish that freedom, then so be it – and this was a battle that Eliizar intended to win.

Though they were outnumbered, the settlers had several advantages over the marauding Khazalim. They were fore-warned and prepared; they were not coming to the fight at the end of a long journey; and they knew the terrain, which was favourable for ambushes and traps. They were fighting for their land and their freedom, and they had one additional advantage that the Khazalim could not even imagine. The two winged couriers, though they took no part in the fighting, soared above the forest, hovering over the treetops to fix the positions of the invaders and bring word of the battle to Elii-zar. Thus it was that the leader of the settlers could pinpoint the location of the king, instantly recognizable in his robes of royal purple that stood out so well against the forest green-ery. When the Winged Folk brought him the news of Xiang's ambush, Eliizar stiffened. 'What of the Khisu?' he demanded.

Finch shook his head. 'We did not see him. We only found his cloak, abandoned in the clearing.'

Eliizar cursed. If the Xiang should escape, then the forest community would sooner or later be destroyed. The Khisu would not rest until every man and woman had been annihi-lated. 'You had better take me there at once,' he told the Skyfolk.

By the time the winged couriers landed with Eliizar, the battle in the clearing was over. Bodies strewed the pine-mast across the sweep of open space, some alive and groaning from the pain of their wounds; others lying still and twisted, never to move again. Eliizar's archers, led by Jharav, moved among the bodies, collecting weaponry and distinguishing the living from the dead. The one-eyed swordmaster frowned. In all his planning, he had given no consideration to the fact that some of Xiang's men would inevitably survive the battle. He supposed that those who lived should be given the chance to join the settlers – but what of those who demurred? They certainly could not be permitted to return to their homes. Eliizar shuddered. The idea of executing his countrymen and fellow-soldiers in cold blood was not a plea-sant one. Well, there'd be time enough to worry about that later. For now, he would have his hands full finding Xiang.

338

Jharav was standing at the edge of the clearing with the Khisu's purple cloak in his hand, scanning the surrounding earth in search of any tracks or other clues to his enemy's whereabouts. His frown rivalled Eliizar's own, for he was one of the Prince Harihn's ex-troopers, and Xiang had been his enemy long before he had joined the settlers. As the swordmaster approached, the grizzled warrior looked up from his contemplation of the ground. 'My sorrow,' he said heavily, 'that I let this viper escape. In the thick of the fighting, he seems to have crept off through the undergrowth.'

'We will find him,' Eliizar reassured the man. 'The men must search –'

He was interrupted by the return of the Skyfolk. 'Eliizar,' Finch was shouting, even before he had landed. 'Help is needed. A large group of the invaders have broken through our defences over to the east, and are heading towards the settlement!'

'Reaper's curse!' Eliizar snarled. 'The women there are undefended. Everyone – leave the fallen. Back to the settlement!'

Within an instant, the clearing was deserted once more as the settlers raced for home. Eliizar commandeered a captured Khazalim mount and leapt astride. The animal squealed and sidestepped, terrified by the Skyfolk, and he wrenched its head round, holding it in tightly. 'Petrel, Finch – gather our other warriors from the forest and send them back to the settlement. Make sure they bring all the women!' Then he released his frantic mount and was off like an arrow, spurring away through the trees.

The settlement, as yet, was barely deserving of the name. It was nothing but a cluster of woven shelters that huddled in a broad clearing near a stream, with other, more sturdy timber dwellings in various early stages of construction. So far, only one permanent building had been completed, which was currently used as a meeting-place and a retreat for everyone in bad weather. Today, it was doubling as an infirmary.

The women who had remained behind were attending to the first few wounded who had already been brought in.

Those outside tending the fire looked up in surprise and consternation when Eliizar galloped into the clearing with Jharav and a handful of other mounted warriors hot on his heels. The swordmaster leapt from his lathered mount and flung the reins into the hands of the nearest man. 'Hide the horses!' He turned to the knot of startled women by the fire. 'The enemy is coming. Take what you need and get inside the longhouse. No matter what happens, I want absolute silence from everyone in there. Keep the wounded quiet in any way you can. Now go!' The women scurried to obey him.

By this time, groups of warriors and the women who had been taking part in various ambushes were running back into the clearing, warned by the Winged Folk. Eliizar gathered them together. During his wild race through the forest he had been thinking quickly. Summoning Jharav to his side, he began to explain his plan. By the time he had finished most of his warriors had returned. He looked quickly from one to another, expecting questions, but none came. All of them understood. Eliizar's heart swelled with pride. Every one of them was more than ready to lay down his life for ... Suddenly Eliizar realized that one familiar, beloved face was missing. His heart froze within him. 'Nereni!' he gasped. 'We must find her!'

Jharav laid a restraining hand on his arm. 'It is too late, Eliizar – we must take our places. Already the enemy approach.'

Nereni, her little band of three women and the two young soldiers who guarded them had concealed themselves so well in the undergrowth near one of the forest trails that they had been missed in the general panic of the call to return. So they stayed in position, according to their orders, waiting for other victims to happen along, or for word that it was safe to disperse. At first the waiting was easy, for they were buoyed by their success, and understandably proud of the role they had played in the defence of their settlement.

The mixture of herbs and tree sap with which they had coated their darts had worked perfectly, itching and burning in the tiny wounds until the horses of the invaders had become frantic, throwing and trampling their riders or bearing them helplessly away to fall prey to the warriors who waited further along the track. Although the young women – who had hitherto occupied all their lives with gentle, feminine tasks in the service of the Prince Harihn – had turned pale and sick at the sight of the ensuing gore and violence, they soon overcame their revulsion in the knowledge that they were defending their men and their homes. Nereni, who could sympathize with their distress, having seen far worse in her travels with the Magefolk, was proud of the courage they had shown.

As time went on, however, the women began to grow restive. A long time had passed since any victims had come their way, and there had been no sight or sound of their own folk. Had they been forgotten? And what should they do now? The two young soldiers, with scant experience between them of warfare, were little help. Eventually, after a long and intense debate conducted in whispers, the ambushers decided that they must have been overlooked and should head for home. After all, there had been no sign of life in their part of the forest for ages. Surely it must be safe to emerge from their refuge?

For a time, all went well. Nervously at first, they pushed their way with difficulty through the tangled underbrush to one side of the track. Thin branches snagged them with thorns, tearing their skin and catching in their hair and clothing. The going was dreadful underfoot, with nettles and briars, roots to trip them and concealed, uneven hummocks and hollows in the ground to turn an unsuspecting ankle. They had soon had enough. After all, they had seen nothing on the trail to alarm them. Scratched, begrimed and sweating, they abandoned the slow and difficult route with relief, and came out on to the open track itself. Nereni was beginning to relax, convinced they had made the right decision. It had worried her, for a time, that they were disobeying orders, and she had found herself at a loss without the support and experience of her former comrades. How she missed them – especially now. Still, it seemed that she could manage on her own after all . . .

Rounding a sharp bend in the trail where two paths joined, they walked right into a dozen Khazalim warriors. It was hard to tell who got the biggest shock. For an instant, the two groups stood looking at each other, Nereni's group transfixed in horror, the invaders suspecting some kind of trick. Then it dawned on them that their opponents were really no more than they seemed: two callow youths and a handful of women. As one, they charged.

Shrieking, the women scattered into the bushes that bordered the track as one of the young soldiers was cut down where he stood. The invaders' horses could not penetrate the undergrowth, and the Khazalim wasted precious seconds having to dismount. Her heart hammering in panic, Nereni forced her way through the bushes, careless now of thorns and whipping branches, dragging Ustila – at barely fifteen the youngest of the girls – behind her, the surviving soldier at their heels. Piercing screams came from somewhere off to their left, and Nereni's stomach knotted in terror and revulsion. One of the women, at least, had been caught. Ustila broke into sobs and stumbled, and the older woman yanked her savagely to her feet. 'Come on! Do you want to share her fate?' Mercilessly, she pulled the girl onward.

The sounds of pursuit were growing louder behind them now. The girl was dragging with exhaustion, and Nereni herself was in little better case. She ran on blindly, lacking the energy to push back the sweat-soaked hair out of her eyes. Her legs were weak and aching, and her face and limbs bled freely from a hundred scratches. Each breath was a gasping torment. But unless she wanted to share the other poor woman's fate she had no recourse but to run, and run she did. One thing she had learned from Aurian – to keep on going, no matter what.

Suddenly the earth dropped away beneath Nereni's feet. Flailing in panic, she found herself sliding down a steep bank – then rolling, as her feet went out from under her. She could hear Ustila shrieking as the others tumbled down behind her. Then something hit her, hard, and the next thing she knew the girl and the soldier were both on top of her. Fighting for breath, Nereni struggled to slide out from under the tangle of bodies. As rough bark scraped her shoulder, she looked up into the towering branches of the immense old tree that had broken her fall. Now that the others were beginning to pick themselves up, she finally managed to get free of them, using a low branch to pull herself to her feet, and discovered that they were at the bottom of a broad, steep-sided dell – a trap if ever there was one.

'Hurry!' She bent down to help the girl, but triumphant cries from above froze her in position. Even as she straightened, four Khazalim warriors came sliding down the bank. Nereni used a word she had learned from Aurian and backed against the tree, pulling Ustila to her side. She drew the knife from her belt, hiding the hand that held it in a fold of her skirt. The young soldier – though her heart went out to him, she could not, in that black moment, remember his name – scrambled to his feet and drew his sword, placing himself between the women and the enemy – a futile gesture, but brave. Nereni heard his death scream but did not see him fall; for by that time, the other Khazalim had surrounded her.

The warriors of the Khisu stopped dead at the edge of the great clearing and stared at the settlement in amazement. This cluster of woven huts, the women working around the fire and all the other signs of a young but burgeoning community was the last thing they had expected to find in the forest. The wily, scarred old veteran who had been Xiang's second-in-command for years reined in his horse. He held up his hand and gestured, and the forty-odd soldiers he had managed to collect together melted back into the forest, awaiting his signal to advance. Yet something made him hesitate. He had not survived and kept his command for so long by rushing blindly into any situation.

He frowned and played absently with his long moustaches, as he often did when he was thinking. Just what was going on here? In all his years of venturing north to raid the Horse-folk, the forest had been deserted. He was amazed that the pampered Harihn had elected to settle here, of all Reaper-forsaken places, yet the men who had ambushed his troops –

and done it very well, he was forced to admit – were certainly Khazalim.

In all the ambushes, however, there had been no sign of the prince. The spineless puppy was probably skulking here, the warrior thought scornfully, as usual letting his men take all the risks. For a long moment he watched the women, decorously veiled in the Khazalim manner, going calmly about their homely tasks, guarded only by two sleepy men who stood with drawn swords on the steps of the large wooden building. Clearly, Harihn had never expected any of the enemy to penetrate this far. The fool must have been confident indeed. The veteran captain grinned mirthlessly to himself. Well, the prince was in for a big shock. Dropping his hand, he gave the signal to advance and spurred his mount, charging into the clearing with his soldiers swarming at his heels.

In a flash, the women at the fire shed their skirts and veils to reveal themselves as men and warriors. Even as their swords flashed in the sunlight, there came a hail of arrows from the smaller woven shelters that mowed down the charging soldiers as soon as they were in the open. Those left standing found themselves divided from each other and fighting for their lives against groups of stern-faced warriors who used to be their countrymen. The captain's horse screamed and went down, an arrow in its neck. The veteran rolled clear of his thrashing mount and scrambled back up to his feet, his sabre still in his hand, and only to come to face with a ghost from his past – Eliizar, the one-eyed swordsman who had once been his commanding officer. 'You!' the captain gasped.

Eliizar nodded. 'I am glad that you remember me,' he said grimly. His sword flashed down so quickly that the veteran barely defended himself in time. He parried clumsily and scrambled backwards, almost tripping over a fallen body. Eliizar followed, his sword a whirling blur of light, the other responding with the speed of pure desperation. To his dismay, the captain discovered that despite the lack of an eye the swordmaster had lost none of his old skills. White-hot agony ripped through his guts, and a flood of weakness overwhelmed him. Through a darkening fog of pain he saw

Eliizar's sword dripping crimson. The veteran staggered but kept his footing.

Eliizar stepped back and looked at him consideringly. 'It need not be a mortal wound,' he said. 'You always were one of the best, and we need good men for the new life we are making. Yield, and I will spare you. Join us, here in the forest.'

The veteran spat in his face. He raised his wavering blade again, determined to sell his life dearly. 'Betray the Khisu? Never!'

Eliizar shook his head sadly. His sword swept down again, and the captain saw no more.

Briefly, the swordmaster leaned panting on his blade. I'm not as young as I was, he thought ruefully. Catching his breath, he turned to survey the progress of the battle, and found that it was over. Bodies were strewn about the clearing, most of them wearing the uniform of the Khisu. A group of survivors were being held at swordpoint by the settlers, and the women were emerging cautiously from the longhouse to tend the groaning wounded. One of them stooped over a still form and stiffened in shock. 'Eliizar,' she called urgently.

The wounded man was Jharav. His face was grey, and he breathed in wheezing, bubbling gasps. The front of his leather jerkin was stained with crimson. As Eliizar leant over him, he opened his eyes. 'Good fight,' he whispered. 'Just like the old days . . .'

Eliizar cursed under his breath. Jharav needed help quickly. He needed Nereni . . . The swordmaster froze. *Where was Nereni?*

They had not counted on a woman fighting. The first of the Khazalim to lay hands on Nereni got the knife between his ribs, but two others, one with his arms stained crimson to the elbows with the young lad's blood, laid hold of her and dragged her down, raining blows upon her and tearing at her clothing. The other warrior must have caught Ustila. Even as she fought her assailants, Nereni could hear the girl shrieking. The tearing cries gave her the anger-driven courage to fight all the harder. Aurian had taught her a trick or two in the time they had spent imprisoned together. She managed to wrench an arm free, and jabbed her rigid fingers into the eyes of one of her attackers. Bile rose in her throat as she felt his eyeballs yield. He reeled backwards howling, his hands clasped to his face as gory fluids leaked between them. Wild with rage, his companion drove a fist into Nereni's jaw, and she choked on the blood that flooded her mouth. Holding her down, he was too close to draw his sword, but suddenly a knife was glittering in his hand.

Nereni had known from the start that it was hopeless. Even if they had raped her, they would have killed her afterwards. At least she had spared herself that pain and humiliation. Eliizar would have been proud of her . . .

The knife rose, flashing blood-red in the sunset light – and dropped from convulsing fingers as the man choked, eyes bulging, clawing vainly at the thin cord that was looped around his throat. Even as he was jerked away from her, a wiry hand pulled Nereni to her feet, and she found herself looking up into Petrel's storm-dark eyes. She doubled over his arm, retching and spitting out blood and a tooth that had been knocked loose by her attacker's fist. When she straightened, blotting her streaming eyes with a rag of her torn skirt, she saw Finch removing his foot from the Khazalim's back as he wound up the bloody cord. Ustila, her clothing torn, was huddled sobbing among the roots of the great tree. Her assailant lay beside her, a Skyfolk dagger with its distinctive carved bone haft protruding from his back. Not far away, the man Nereni had blinded lay dead, his skull smashed by a large stone. Petrel spread his great wings, blotting out the horrors from her sight. 'Come, brave Lady,' he said gently. 'The worst is over now. We will take you home.'

A frantic Eliizar was organizing search-parties when he heard the sound of wings in the distance and saw the Skyfolk swooping towards the clearing, dipping dangerously near the treetops with their human burdens. As Petrel landed with Nereni he rushed forward, his heart turning to ice at the

346

sight of her tattered, bloodstained clothing and her bruised and swollen face.

'Nereni!' As he took her in his arms he could feel her shaking, but she lifted her chin proudly and scrubbed the tears from her eyes with her sleeve in an impatient gesture that was oddly reminiscent of Aurian. 'I'm all right,' she said thickly through swollen lips. 'The Skyfolk saved us, just in . . .' Over his shoulder, she caught sight of Jharav. 'Eliizar, no! He isn't . . .'

'No, but he is badly wounded,' Eliizar told her gently.

'I must help him!' Brushing aside his protests that she was also in need of care, Nereni rushed to the side of the wounded man.

The swordmaster turned to the Winged Folk. 'I can't thank you enough,' he began, but Petrel forestalled him.

'Think no more of it,' he told Eliizar. 'Today, for the first time in centuries, the Skyfolk have actively joined in the affairs of a groundling race. Finch and I have discovered that we can care – and fight – for someone not of our own kind, and that felt good to us. If it please you, we would like to bring our mates here, and any others that we can persuade to come, and settle in the mountains at the edge of the forest, to be your friends, and to join in your endeavours; the two communities, in the sky and on the ground, acting to help and support each other.'

Eliizar's jaw dropped open. Not only was this the longest speech he had heard one of the Winged Folk make, but its content astounded and delighted him. Smiling, he held out his hands to the two winged warriors. 'Join us and be welcome,' he told them. 'I can think of nothing that would please me more.'

An hour later, the clearing had been transformed, as the exhausted settlers hurried to clear the aftermath of the battle from their homes and from their lives. Food was being cooked on several fires, and savoury smells were beginning to drift on the darkening evening air. The wounded had been settled in the longhouse under the devoted care of the women, and Nereni had reported that Jharav was still clinging to his life. 'If we can get him through tonight,' she had

347

told Eliizar, 'I believe he has every chance of recovery. The Reaper knows, the old fool is tough enough – and stubborn enough – to pull through.'

The remainder of the evening's work had left Eliizar far less happy. Plumes of greasy smoke arose from a nearby clearing, where the bodies of friend and foe were being burned on separate pyres. Despite his misgivings about the wisdom of the move, he had offered the captured survivors of Xiang's forces a chance to join the settlers; but he need not have worried. All had remained unswervably loyal to Xiang, and had refused to break their oath of allegiance. To a man, they had taken the only honourable way out that he'd been able to leave them, and had fallen on their blades. Eliizar was sickened by the waste of so many good men. Once again, he blessed Aurian for giving him the opportunity to leave the land that had been responsible for such atrocities. The events of this day would haunt him to the end of his life.

But these were no thoughts for a day of victory. The swordmaster had walked apart from his people to the edge of the clearing, hoping that the solitude would help settle his mind, when, to his relief, he heard the sound of the Winged Folk coming home. They had offered to do one last sweep of the forest before the light was gone, to make sure that none of the invaders had slipped through the net, but they had been gone far longer than necessary for that, and as darkness had fallen Eliizar had begun to grow worried.

'Good news,' cried the impatient Finch, speaking, as was his habit, before he'd even reached the ground. 'We have located your missing king!'

'At least we believe so,' added the more cautious Petrel as he landed. 'If the fool had been less impatient and waited until moonset, we might never have found him. But we could see him in the gem-glow, riding off across the desert as though demons were on his tail.'

Eliizar stiffened. 'How far has he gone?' he demanded. 'Can you take me to him?'

'Of course!' said Petrel. The less robust Finch flexed his wings and sighed.

'For you, we will contrive – but this had better be today's

last errand. I could sleep until the seasons turn and spring comes round again.'

From the air, the Glittering Desert was an amazing sight. Across the rippling sea of gem-dust, the light of the new-risen crescent moon ignited sparks of fire in ruby, sapphire, emerald and diamond-brilliant radiance. Spars of dazzling light were reflected up into the air to dim the glory of the heavens – and Eliizar, dangling beneath the labouring Winged Folk, could descry, far out across the sand, the dark blot of a swiftly moving figure. The Skyfolk, with their raptor's vision, had already seen it. The swordmaster felt the change of pressure in his ears as they swooped down on their prey.

Xiang, intent on his escape, never thought to look up at the skies. Eliizar waited until he was above the Khisu, the weary Winged Folk making one last valiant effort to match their victim speed for speed. Then he took his knife and sliced the bottom of the net, dropping down upon the fleeing king and knocking him from his saddle.

They both fell hard, but the swordmaster had been expecting it and his dagger was already in his hand. He wasted no time on duelling with Xiang – with a fighter of his calibre it was the first stroke, and the first stroke only, that counted. The Khisu was a killer born, and besides, Eliizar had seen too much death for one day to indulge in unnecessary heroics. As the two men hit the ground, still entangled, he slashed at Xiang's throat with his dagger, hoping to get in a mortal blow on the first strike, but his arm was jarred by the fall and the blade missed its mark. Cursing, Eliizar loosed his hold and sprang to his feet, his sword coming out of its scabbard even before he was fully upright.

Xiang's eyes widened as he recognized his attacker. Quick as a striking snake he scrambled to his feet in a spray of incandescent sand, roaring: 'I should have killed you when I had the chance!' He was almost as quick as Eliizar – almost. Before his sword had fully cleared his scabbard, Eliizar's blade bit into his neck. His head came to a rolling halt in the gem-dust a dozen feet away.

Eliizar leaned on his sword and shook his head as he

looked upon his vanquished king and foe. 'I always used to tell you not to waste time talking in battle,' he muttered. There came a thunder of wings from above and Finch and Petrel landed beside him, the backsweep of their wings raising a whirl of glittering sand that drifted down to cover the Khisu's body.

'Thank Yinze that's over,' said the irrepressible Finch. 'Now can we go home?'

Petrel glared at him, and touched a hand to his forehead, in homage to Eliizar. 'All is well, O Master of the Forest Lands. The battle for our new home has been won.'

Eliizar looked down at the mortal remains of Xiang the Tyrant. 'Yes.' He smiled grimly. 'Now it truly has.'

22

The River Run

Since Benziorn had amputated, the days had passed for Vannor in an inescapable labyrinth of agony and anguish. The worst of it was that he could feel the hand as though it still existed, even though he could see the bound and ugly stump that lay on top of the covers. If he closed his eyes, or looked away, he could feel his fingers clenching and unclenching. And for something that wasn't there it hurt like perdition, despite the concoctions that Benziorn gave him, which were meant to dull the pain.

Though he knew full well that the physical injury would heal given time, Vannor's mind was shattered by the loss. Gone were his days as leader of the rebels. What use could he be to anyone now, crippled and maimed as he was? How could he continue to fight against the Magefolk when he couldn't even use a sword.

Why me? was the litany that kept repeating itself over and over again in his mind. Why did this have to happen to me? Why couldn't it have happened to a cutthroat or one of those thieving human dregs from the waterfront – or to those damned Mages themselves?

Vannor could bear to see no one – not even his beloved Zanna, though she insisted on coming anyway. The hurt in her eyes when he railed against her pierced his heart, yet he couldn't help it. He didn't want anyone, and especially his beloved daughter, to see him like this. He could no longer perceive a future for himself, only darkness. His only surcease was sleep, but sleep was slow in coming, despite the soporifics that Benziorn gave him. If he was honest with himself, what he really wanted was to die – but the core of stubbornness that was so much a part of his nature would not permit him to seek death.

351

So here he lay, on another day much like the rest; drowning in the depths of self-pity; lying awake with the agony of his hand and the greater agony of his thoughts, and wondering if there would ever be a way out of this torment. For a long time the merchant had been dimly aware of the soft murmur of talk in the kitchen below his room, but suddenly, as the voices were raised in furious argument, they intruded on his notice and he began to make out what they were saying.

'Leave the city?' Zanna shouted. 'You can't possibly be serious. My dad is in no fit state to make such a journey!'

Benziorn sighed patiently. 'I'm his physician, lass – do you think I don't know that? Moving him now is not what I would choose, but we're no longer safe here. Do you want your father to be captured again by the Magefolk?'

'Damn you!' Zanna snapped. 'You're not being fair. I don't have an answer to that, and well you know it. Look,' she begged, 'it's scarcely three weeks since you performed the amputation. He still needs rest, and time . . . How the blazes do you expect him to clamber around in the sewers with only one hand?'

'Why, the little lass is right,' came Hebba's querulous tones. 'The poor master, bless him, is still sick abed. How can you think of sending him down them dirty, stinking drains?'

Vannor half-smiled to himself – the first time he had smiled in days. Clearly, the others had told the cook she must come with them for her own safety – and there was no way in the world that the timid, nervous woman would take kindly to a journey through the sewers.

'We'll help him,' Yanis volunteered. 'Don't worry, Hebba – he'll manage. We all will. Why, even though my own arm is only just healing . . .'

'So how can you help someone else, you idiot?' cried Zanna in exasperation.

'It'll be all right, Zanna, you'll see.' It was Tarnal's voice. Vannor could just imagine the serious, solicitous young man putting a comforting hand on his daughter's arm. 'I will help him,' he said softly. 'We both will. If we meet with any difficulties on the way, you and I can help Vannor, and Benziorn

352

will assist Yanis. But Benziorn is right. We can't risk remaining in Nexis any longer. You and your father are fugitives, and with every day that passes Miathan's net is tightening. Already the soldiers are searching houses on any excuse, and we know that there's a reward out on your head. Hebba's neighbours must have realized by now that she's no longer living alone here. How long do you think it will be before the gossip begins to spread, and folk start putting two and two together?'

'But what about infection?' Zanna pleaded. 'In the sewers . . .'

'Zanna, let's not pretend any longer.' Benziorn's voice was soft with concern. 'Admit it – it's not Vannor's body you're worried about, it's his mind. Though we'll help him in every way we can, to a certain extent he'll have to cooperate, and at the moment he's so lost in self-pity –'

His words were broken off in the sharp impact of flesh on flesh. 'How dare you say that,' Zanna yelled, 'about my dad! Why, he's the bravest man I know. No one else could have undertaken that journey through the catacombs and sewers the way he did, wounded as he was, and made it through. He'll be fine – he just needs time . . .' The words tailed off, swallowed in a sob. A door slammed sharply, and there was a thunder of feet on the stairs. Then Vannor heard the sound of brokenhearted weeping in the adjacent room.

Suddenly, the merchant was deeply ashamed. In all this time he had been thinking only about himself, and had never considered how deeply he must have been worrying Zanna. Poor lass – her mother already dead, and her dad worse than useless to her. Like a thunderbolt, it struck him that he was not useless after all: that someone still needed him; still depended on him to be brave and strong – and still believed, with utter faith, that he could do just that.

'Get up, you bloody selfish old fool,' Vannor muttered wrathfully to himself. 'This is no time to be lying in bed feeling sorry for yourself and whining about the harshness of the world. Your daughter needs you.'

Getting out of bed was far more difficult to accomplish than the merchant could ever have imagined. The gruelling underground journey to escape the Mages was as nothing compared to the problem of simply hauling himself upright on legs that had turned, it seemed, to two limp strings, while the room spun dizzily around him. Inwardly, Vannor railed against his weakness, and found that the anger helped, not only to impel him towards his goal, but to scour away so many of the all-consuming doubts and fears that had so unmanned him in these last few dreadful days.

Vannor clung with his one hand to the post at the foot of the bed and cursed vilely, wondering how he was ever going to manage to let go without falling over. How the bloody blazes could he make it all the way to the next room? He shuffled as far as he could reach while still holding on to the bed, and suddenly the door did not seem so very far away. Taking a deep breath, he let go and lurched across the room, only his staggering momentum keeping him from falling flat on his face. He reached the door only just in time, and leaned against the blessed, solid wood, hanging on to the handle like a drowning man and breathing heavily as sweat trickled down his forehead.

Why, by all the gods – he was almost halfway there already. He had only to get across the tiny landing ... Suddenly, Vannor realized that his phantom hand was no longer troubling him.

In the darkness of the cramped little bedroom, Zanna lay on the bed, muffling the sound of her weeping in the pillow. She had reached the end of her endurance. She had been brave for so long now, for her dad's sake, but it seemed that she just couldn't hold up her courage any longer. What will we do now? she thought despairingly. Oh, if only there was some way I could help him. Suddenly, she heard the door open behind her. 'Go away,' she snapped without lifting her face from the pillow. 'Leave me alone, can't you?'

She felt a weight settle on the edge of the bed, and then a gentle, familiar hand ruffled her tangled hair. 'It's me, love. Don't cry any more.'

'Dad!' Zanna shot upright and flung her arms around him.

One-handed, Vannor hugged her. 'Everything's going to be all right, lass – don't you worry. Just give me a day or so to get my legs back under me again, and then we'll be on our way.'

Getting out of Nexis was not going to be easy. The patrols of guards in the streets had been markedly increased since Vannor's escape, particularly at night, and Zanna's description had been circulated all around the city with a large enough reward to ensure that folk would be looking twice at every girl her age. To that problem, at least, it was Yanis, of all people, who found the solution. 'Then why does she have to be a girl?' he said. 'Why can't she go disguised as a lad?'

'What?' exclaimed Hebba, scandalized. 'And cut off her lovely hair and all? Why, the very idea!'

'Well,' said Benziorn, with an apologetic smile in Zanna's direction. 'It does seem to be the only solution.'

'Don't worry, Hebba,' Zanna said stoutly. 'I can always grow it again.'

But later, when her thick mane of shorn curls was lying on the kitchen floor, and she looked at herself in Hebba's tiny mirror, she felt far less brave about the scheme – in fact, she was utterly aghast. Dear gods! she thought. That can't be me. I look like a scarecrow. With the defensiveness of a young girl who had always known she wasn't pretty, she had long ago stopped worrying about her appearance, but now that her hair had been hacked off – badly – by Hebba the plainness of her features seemed more pronounced than ever. What would Yanis, so handsome himself, think of her now, compared to the girl Emmie, whom he had called for in his sleep? He'd said that the stranger was beautiful ...

And Hebba was no help – even now, she was fluttering around Zanna, clucking with dismay.

'Poor little lass, what have we done to you? All your poor hair – what a dreadful thing to happen, and at your age too. Why, what young man would look at you now – you look just like a lad yourself, and no mistake. How the master could have allowed it ... I told him, I did. Oh, if only he had listened to me.'

Zanna could bear it no longer. 'Shut up, you stupid old

355

woman! It was necessary. Better this than being recaptured by the Magefolk.'

'Well, I'm sorry, I'm sure,' snapped Hebba. 'Still, you're bound to be upset, I expect.' She flounced out of the kitchen in a huff, banging the door behind her.

The hated reflection in the mirror suddenly blurred as Zanna felt her throat grow tight with tears. She swallowed hard, not wanting to betray herself to the menfolk when they came back into the kitchen. You fool! she told herself angrily. What you told Hebba was right – it *was* necessary. Fancy getting so upset over such a little thing after all you've been through these last few weeks. If your face isn't good enough for the so-called leader of the Nightrunners, then that's his loss. But even common sense was little comfort, and she dreaded what she would see in the faces of the others when they returned.

Vannor was the first to enter, and from the cautious way he put his head round the door Zanna knew that Hebba had been telling tales. The very notion made her seethe. 'Well?' she snapped. 'Go on – have a good laugh and get it over with.'

Gravely, Vannor shook his head. 'I don't see anything to laugh at. I never could understand this notion of yours that you weren't pretty – there's more to beauty than looking spectacular, like your sister and Sara . . .' A slight frown crossed his face at the memory of his lost young wife. 'Anyway,' he went on, 'don't let Hebba upset you. She's all heart and no brains, as Dulsina used to say. You look just fine, love – and if it really bothers you, remember that your hair is something that you can grow back in no time . . .'

As his voice tailed away, Zanna's eyes went guiltily to the bandaged stump of his hand. Though he tried to hide it from her, she knew he was still suffering a good deal of pain from the injury. Her own resolution hardened, which was just as well, because she needed it when she saw Yanis's mouth twitch in ill suppressed amusement. Tarnal, however, cheered her a little. 'Why, I never noticed what lovely eyes you have, under all that hair,' he exclaimed. Zanna could have kissed him.

The escape from Nexis was set for the following day, and the fugitives sat up late that night around the kitchen fire making plans. Hebba, with Zanna in her lad's disguise and Tarnal – who insisted on accompanying the women in case of trouble – would leave early in the morning, when folk were out in search of food and the streets were at their busiest, in the hope that they could lose themselves in the crowds. Tarnal was to convey them safely to the fulling mill and leave them hidden in the sewers to wait there until nightfall, when Benziorn would come down with Yanis and Vannor. In the meantime, Tarnal would make his way out of the city via the sewers to the few outlying merchant mansions that had been built too far out of Nexis to be enclosed by Miathan's great wall. Once there, he would scout their little riverside boathouses in search of a pleasure craft to steal.

'And let's hope he finds one,' Vannor put in at this point, 'otherwise it'll be a bloody long walk all the way to Wyvernesse.' He had reluctantly allowed the others to talk him into heading for the smugglers' hideout rather than the rebel camp because it could be reached by water, sparing him the hardship of a long trek across the moors. It was the only workable solution, but that didn't mean he had to like it. Not only did he want to be back with his own folk, but the thought of what could happen to a small boat on the open sea, even hugging the coastline, made his blood run cold.

Zanna made no reply. She was busy worrying about Tarnal. His would be by far the most dangerous role in their escape, having to creep through the grounds of the well guarded mansions – especially in broad daylight.

However, the following morning, when Vannor shook her awake in the dimness before dawn. Zanna was far too tired to worry about anything. Shivering and reluctant, she climbed into the mismatched selection of lad's clothing that Hebba had been able to scrounge together for her. It felt strange, not having skirts to swirl around her legs – very free, yet at the same time oddly constricting. It was lucky, she thought ruefully, as she fastened a band of fabric tightly across her breasts and pulled on a loose, ragged tunic to hide the evidence, that she didn't have much there to conceal.

When she left the cramped little room she had shared with the cook and came downstairs the others were already in the kitchen, huddled round the fire drinking taillin and speaking in subdued voices. Hebba, who was bustling about trying to get breakfast, kept dissolving into tears at the thought of leaving her beloved home. On that score, however, Vannor had been very firm. If the Magefolk should ever find out that she had harboured the fugitives, her life would instantly be forfeit. Whether she liked it or not, he was determined to have her safe.

When he saw his daughter, Vannor's eyebrows went up in surprise. 'By the gods, lass – I never would have recognized you.' He pulled her roughly into a hug. 'Do you know,' he said softly, for her ears alone, 'when you and your sister were born, I was young and daft enough in those days to wish for a son. Well, I want to tell you now that you're far braver and more clever, and more precious to me, than any son could be. I couldn't be more proud of you.'

Zanna held his words in her heart, and they helped boost her courage when, for the first time in three weeks, she stepped over Hebba's threshold and into the perilous and hostile streets. Suddenly she felt utterly naked, and not simply because of her unaccustomed clothing. Surely her very thoughts must be transparent to the eyes of every passer-by. Then Tarnal winked at her. 'You're a lad, re-member – just keep thinking of that. And a very convincing one you are too – though I like you much better as a girl.'

Zanna grinned back at him, and concentrated on her role as they threaded their way down through the city streets. She was a lad, she told herself firmly, out with her brother, she supposed Tarnal would be, helping their granny get safely to the market. Solicitously, she took Hebba's heavy basket, and hooked her hand through the old cook's arm. Beneath her cloak Hebba was trembling, and Zanna was suddenly very glad of the shawl that draped the woman's head, hiding her face in shadow. They had made her wear it to hide her eyes, which had been red from weeping; though the gods only knew, grieving widows were a common enough sight in the streets of Nexis, after the hardships of the unnatural winter.

Nonetheless, Vannor's daughter realized that her dad had been right to insist on Hebba's wearing the shawl. Not only did it conceal her bloodshot eyes, it would also hide the look of terror that was doubtless on her face at this very minute.

Zanna was so lost in her thoughts that at first she didn't hear the tramp of booted feet, until Tarnal's elbow poked her sharply in the ribs. 'Soldiers!' he hissed at her. 'Act normal – remember the lad has nothing to fear.'

She was glad of the timely warning – it gave her time to compose her features into what she hoped was an expression of amiable stupidity. Zanna gaped at the patrol in admiration as they marched past, wishing, as would any lad her age, that *he* could be a soldier, and wear a shiny sword.

By the time they were safely past she longed to be wearing skirts, so that she could let her knees knock, as they were trying to do, without anyone seeing. Tarnal gave her a heartening grin. 'Well done,' he whispered. 'They didn't suspect a thing.'

They passed two more patrols before reaching the waterside and by that time Zanna, elated with the success of her disguise, was very glad that she had not let vanity prevent her from cutting her hair. But when they reached the fulling mill and Tarnal lifted the grating to let them descend into the noisome, dripping, slime-coated drains, her elation vanished abruptly at the thought of descending into the sewers again. The memory of that last nightmare journey, dragging her wounded dad through the cramped and stinking tunnels, was still too recent. In coping with Hebba's fears and hesitations, however, she forgot her own. Somehow, between them, she and Tarnal managed to get the rotund old cook down into the tunnel, Hebba weeping, wailing and protesting every inch of the way until Zanna wanted to slap her.

Then, all too quickly, it was time for the young Nightrunner to leave them. Zanna walked with him as far as the dim light that filtered through the grating would reach, and when it was time for him to leave her Zanna's fears for him returned in an overwhelming rush. Impulsively, she flung her arms around him and hugged him hard. 'You be careful,' she told him fiercely.

Tarnal grinned and hugged her back. 'Don't worry – I will. I'll see you tonight.' Then he was gone, leaving a kiss upon her brow. Absently touching the place on her forehead where she could still feel the imprint of his lips, Zanna watched his light until it disappeared around the next bend in the tunnel, then went back with reluctant, dragging steps to comfort Hebba.

Taking thankful gulps of blessed, sweet fresh air, Tarnal emerged at last from the outlet of the drain, a short distance downstream from the great barred arch of the river gate in Miathan's newly constructed city wall. He slithered as quickly as he could down the steep bank of the river's edge, and vanished into the dappled shadow beneath the willows that dipped into the water. From there he made his way swiftly downriver, pausing only long enough to wash the slime from his boots.

Though he was worried about his companions and grimly aware of the dangers that awaited him, Tarnal felt an unaccountable lightness of heart to be free of the city at last, free of the grime and smoke and crowds; to see the sunlit sparkle of the water; to hear the birds calling, and the cheerful lapping song of the river. It might not be the open sea, which he'd been missing so badly that he even dreamed about it, but at least it was moving water – and that was something!

Tarnal crept on cautiously, not allowing the pleasures of the open air to distract him from his task. As the hours went by, however, he became more and more disheartened. The first boathouse he encountered was open to the river, but proved to be empty. When Tarnal peered cautiously over the low stone wall that bordered the grounds of the second mansion, he saw a gardener working close by the boathouse, trimming the ornamental hedges in a desultory fashion. From the scant progress the idler had already made, he looked as if he'd be there all day. Ducking down behind the wall and keeping low, the Nightrunner sneaked past and continued what seemed to be turning into an endless trek – especially when the third boathouse, which he'd climbed an almost unscalable wall to reach and then spent a nerve-racking hour trying to break into, proved also to be empty.

Keeping well within the cover of the trees that thronged the waterside, Tarnal made his way downriver, trying to ignore his sinking heart and his growling belly, until he caught a glimpse through the bushes at the top of the bank of a high brick wall mounted with iron spikes, which guarded the last of the outlying mansions from his thieving kind. Despite his weariness and hunger, the Nightrunner grinned. He would see about that. Such elaborate precautions were a good omen – they usually indicated that there was something within worth stealing. He ran along the bank, skirting the wall, until, as he had expected, it turned in his path, down towards the river itself, where it gave way to high black iron railings that guarded shallow steps down to a little wooden jetty, on the far side of which was an ostentatiously constructed boathouse; built, no doubt, of the same stone as the house and with scrolled iron water gates to match the railings.

Damn! The blasted thing would have to be on the far side of the jetty, necessitating a hazardous trip across an open space. Tarnal sighed. Well, nobody had said that this was going to be easy. Divesting himself of his cloak and then the rest of his clothing, including his boots and sword, he rolled them into a bundle and thrust them safely between the roots of a tree, high up the bank where the earth was dry. Shivering a little in the cool spring wind, he looked doubtfully again at the stretch of open space along the railing, and wished he could have waited until after dark. But Vannor had warned him that many of the merchants kept huge and savage dogs which were let loose when dusk closed in, to roam the grounds by night. No. Risky though it was, the boat would have to be stolen during the daylight hours, or not at all.

Silent and stealthy as an otter, the Nightrunner slipped from the bank and into the river, clad only in a loincloth and a thong about his neck that carried a slender lockpick. The water was icy cold against his shrinking skin, and the current tugged at him strongly but, having lived all his life beside the sea, Tarnal was a powerful swimmer and accustomed to cold water. Swimming below the surface, he let the current take him down along the iron-fenced bank until he saw the shadowy wooden piles of the jetty through the murky water. There he came up, gasping but safely sheltered from hostile eyes, to take a few deep breaths before diving again to complete his swim towards the boathouse.

Due to the unexpected swiftness of the current, Tarnal all but overshot his mark. At the very last minute, he spotted the iron bars of the water gates, and shot out a hand to grab one, practically drowning himself in the process. Finally he managed to get his other hand to the bars and hauled himself up until his head was out of the water. Clinging to the gate for dear life, he hung there choking, spitting out water and trying desperately to muffle the noise of his coughing and spluttering. At last he got his breath back, and rubbed his head against his arm to push the dripping hair out of his eyes.

Peering through the bars into the gloom within the boathouse, Tarnal spat out a vicious and heartfelt curse. After all his efforts, *this* blasted place was empty too. Groaning, he sank back into the water to the full reach of his aching arms. Now he would have to swim all the way back again, and return damp and weary to the sewer in the chill of evening. And how could he break the news to the others – especially Zanna – that he had failed them? Worse still, how would they manage to get Vannor and Hebba all the way to Wyvernesse now?

For a long, hopeless moment, Tarnal simply hung there, resting his head on his arms and lacking the heart to go on, though the freezing water was rapidly sucking the last of the energy from his body. The sun was sinking towards evening now, slanting low through the trees and turning the river into a rippling path of beaten copper. His spirit darkened with defeat, the Nightrunner was oblivious of the lambent beauty of the evening, but common sense finally triumphed over his black mood, and told him he'd better get out of the water – and fast. As he raised his head, he noticed that the sunlight on the river was now striking a dappled reflection right into the boathouse. Tarnal blinked, unable to believe the evidence of his eyes. There, on the walkway at the very back of the building, was a rowing boat laid upside down on trestles, fresh-caulked and painted. It had been taken out of the water for winter, and was ready to be launched.

'Thank you, gods – oh, thank you,' the Nightrunner whispered aloud. Almost weeping with relief, he reached up to pick the sturdy padlock that held the chained gates shut. More than once he had cause to be thankful that his burglar's tool was fastened to the thong, as it slipped again and again from his numb fingers until he was swearing with frustration. Eventually, however, his perseverance was rewarded. The chain and lock fell with a soft splash into the water, and the gates swung open on oiled and soundless hinges.

Single-handed, it was a struggle to get the boat into the water, but Tarnal worked with desperate haste. Dusk was falling now, and the dogs would be out at any minute. Even though they could not get into the boathouse from the land side, they would certainly know that he was there. Once he had the little craft afloat, with its oars inside it, he looked around and found a coil of rope and an old tarpaulin, both of which would come in handy. Perhaps, using one of the oars, they could even jury-rig a little sail when they reached the open sea . . .

His weariness forgotten in the surge of hope renewed, Tarnal sculled quietly out of the boathouse in the gathering twilight. Once he reached the concealing shelter of the trees on the other side of the jetty, he ran the boat aground and moored it securely before scrambling up the bank to grope for his clothes. Getting into the warm, dry garments was a luxury akin to ecstasy. It gave him the final reserve of strength he needed to row back upriver to await his friends.

For Zanna, cold and uncomfortable on the slippery walkway of the damp and stinking sewer, the hours stretched on and on in an endless agony of waiting. Though after a time she was both thirsty and hungry, and Hebba had plenty of food packed in her basket, the mere idea of eating in this foul and filthy place was enough to make her gorge rise. Frantic as she was with worry over the dangers of her father's journey through the perilous night streets, and the risks that Tarnal was running trying to steal a boat in broad daylight, Hebba's doom-laden whining soon drove her to distraction. Eventually, she decided that the only way to shut the wretched woman up was to pretend to go to sleep.

'Hebba, I'm sorry, but I can't keep my eyes open any longer,' she interrupted the older woman's complaints. 'You should try to get some rest, too – we've a long night ahead of us.' Yawning hugely for the benefit of the cook, she snuggled as best she could into her cloak, and pillowed her head on her arms. Almost as soon as she closed her eyes, her late night and early rising had turned pretence into reality.

She was jerked awake by the clutch of Hebba's fingers, digging bruisingly into her arm in the darkness. Gods, she thought fuzzily. How long have I slept?

'Listen,' Hebba hissed. Zanna could feel her trembling violently. 'There's someone coming!'

Now that she was properly awake, the girl could hear the sound of dragging footsteps coming from above. 'It'll only be dad and the others,' she said, but nevertheless she drew the knife that Tarnal had left with her, glad that the darkness masked her actions from Hebba. The woman was scared enough already. Further down the tunnel, she heard the tortured scrape of the grating being shifted.

'Zanna – it's us!' a hoarse voice whispered, and suddenly she felt unutterably foolish for letting herself become infected by Hebba's fears.

'Dad,' she whispered joyfully, 'we're just along the walkway.'

'Light the lantern, love, will you? We daren't risk a light up here, and we can't see a thing – especially not the ladder. It's blacker than Miathan's heart inside these blasted tunnels, and I can't climb down one-handed in the dark.'

Even with the aid of the light, and the assistance of Benziorn below him and Yanis above, Vannor still had a difficult time getting down the ladder. In the end he gave it up and dropped the last few feet, cursing as the impact jolted the bound stump of his arm. Zanna noticed that he was wearing the leather gauntlets they had prepared especially for him, the right one bound securely in place and stuffed to the fingertips with rags. They had been Benziorn's idea – to help protect Vannor's injury from the infections that proliferated in the sewers, and to disguise from any prying eyes the fact that he lacked a hand. If word of such a man should get back to the Magefolk, the consequences would be dire indeed.

'Stand clear!' Yanis called softly from above, breaking into Zanna's train of thought. She barely had time to step back quickly before two heavy packs (much to his indignation, they had refused to let Vannor carry one) came hurtling down to be caught by Benziorn. The Nightrunner leader followed, easing the grating back into place before scrambling swiftly down the ladder.

'Done it!' he said cheerfully. 'It wasn't so bad after all, getting here – though I must admit that my heart was in my mouth when that patrol came by and you pretended to be drunk, Vannor, and we made out that we were carrying you home.' As Yanis spoke, Zanna caught the flash of his smile in the lamplight, and was consumed by a surge of irritation. How could the idiot be so complacent? They had to get through the sewers yet – and in the meantime what about poor Tarnal, who'd been risking his life out in the open? What if he hadn't been able to find a boat? What if he was lying out there somewhere in the darkness, hurt – or even dead? With a shudder, Zanna turned her mind away from such appalling thoughts. He'd be all right, she told herself firmly. Tarnal, at least, had sense.

Wearied as Vannor was from his long journey through the city streets, he had no desire to linger in the sewers a minute longer than he had to. On they went, with Zanna lending a supporting arm to Hebba and carrying her basket while Benziorn helped the merchant. Yanis, who was most familiar with the route, took both of the packs and went ahead with the lantern down the dank and dripping tunnel.

How Zanna hated those sewers. Though her second long journey beneath the city was proving less difficult than the first, she still had to deal with the stench, the slime, and the scuttling, squeaking rats – not to mention Hebba's hysterics on account of the latter, which nearly plunged the pair of them, more than once, from the slippery walkway into the slurry-filled channel. Since they were already at the level of the river, there was no climbing to be done, though there were some tricky places to negotiate where the walkway narrowed at the junction of tunnels. None the less, their progress seemed painfully slow to Zanna, for Vannor was reaching the end of his endurance and had to stop and rest more and more frequently as time went on.

Just as she was beginning to give up hope of ever seeing daylight again, she caught a waft of fresher air, fragrant with the pungent mixture of wet grass and wild garlic. Zanna's tired heart lifted within her. At last, they were coming to the end of this dreadful place. Within moments they had reached the sewer outlet, and she had time for one deep breath and a rapid glimpse of jewelled stars caught in a black net of tree-tops before Yanis pulled her quickly down the bank and into the shelter of the willows. In the darkness beneath the trees she could hear her father cursing softly, with a desperate edge of worry to his voice. Immediately, Zanna realized what had happened, and her blood turned to ice within her veins. Tarnal was not there to meet them.

By the time she turned her attention back to her surroundings, Yanis was speaking. 'Well, it's no good us waiting this close to the city walls. Trust Tarnal to go and mess things up. I should have gone myself. Vannor, can you carry on a little further tonight? Maybe, if we can somehow make it down to Norberth in easy stages, we can steal a boat from the port . . .'

Already his voice was fading as he led his way along the slippery bank in the darkness, the others close behind him. Even Hebba was trailing obediently after him, too tired by far now to complain. Zanna gritted her teeth and followed, quietly seething. How could Yanis be so heartless? In her own distress, she had missed the anxiety in his voice, which he'd masked with anger. It's a good thing the beast is so far ahead, she fumed. Why, for two pins, I'd push him in the river.

Lost in her angry thoughts, she followed blindly. The going was difficult, with tussocks and roots to trip over in the darkness, and patches of slippery mud. Before too long, Zanna's knees were scraped and bruised from falling over so many times, her hands wore dripping gauntlets of black mud, and both her feet were soaked from straying too near the river's edge. She didn't care about any of it – she was too frantic over Tarnal's fate to worry about such trifles.

Then, from the darkness ahead, she heard a low, delighted cry from Yanis. 'By all the gods – there's a boat here under the trees!'

By now the moon was rising, and as Zanna hurried forward she saw the Nightrunner leader silhouetted against the silvery water as he reached out to pull on the rope that moored the little boat. Suddenly a dark shape rose up in the bows, causing Yanis to drop the rope with a cry of alarm and reach for his sword.

'Yanis? Is that you?' The sleepy voice made Zanna's heart leap for joy, for it belonged to Tarnal.

A minute later, a happy reunion was taking place on the riverbank – at least, Zanna was happy. 'What do you mean, you fell asleep?' Yanis was demanding indignantly of his friend. 'What kind of a stupid trick is that? Here's us trailing all this way in the dark while you lie there snoring like a pig … And is this little washtub all that you could get? I didn't expect to row all the way to Wyvernesse.'

Tarnal's grey eyes flashed dangerously in the moonlight. Without saying a word, he grasped Yanis by the shirtfront and hurled him bodily into the river. 'Swim, then, you ungrateful bastard,' he told his spluttering leader, as he extended a hand to help the dripping Yanis out of the shallows. Zanna had to stuff her cloak into her mouth to muffle the sound of her laughter.

After that, things went more easily, though they had to struggle to lift their craft down the narrow portage-way that bypassed the weir. 'I'll wager you're glad I didn't get a bigger one now,' Tarnal goaded the panting Yanis as they staggered beneath the boat's ungainly weight. They managed to sneak through the port of Norberth before the sun rose, and laid up through the hours of daylight in one of the little coves along the coast. Though they were hungry and damp they dared not risk a fire, but they were all far too weary to pay much heed to such hardships. Besides, the weather seemed unseasonably warm. Rolled in their blankets in a hollow of the sheltering dunes, they slept most of the day, trading watches, before setting out again on a still and stifling evening in the fading light of a lurid, purple sunset.

Luckily the coastal current had been with them and so far the sea had stayed calm enough not to swamp the little boat, though Hebba had remained rigid with terror throughout the entire trip. Now, however, just before they were due to set out once more from the sandy cove, Zanna noticed Yanis and Tarnal looking at the sea and frowning, before going off into a huddle to talk in low, worried voices. 'What's wrong?' she asked them, looking at the ocean in puzzlement. It seemed fine to her – there was barely a ripple to disturb the sluggish, oily swell. 'Surely it's calm enough?'

'Aye – for now,' Yanis muttered. 'But it's setting itself to blow up into the mother of all storms before this night's out. The question is, do we risk going now, and pray we can get there before the stormfront reaches us, or do we stay here and wait until it's over? By the look of the sea and sky, it's going to be a bad blow; and even when the worst of it's done, it could take days for the sea to calm itself again.'

Zanna could have wept. Not now – not when they were so close! At that moment Vannor joined them. 'Do my eyes deceive me or does that sky have a particularly ominous look to it?'

Yanis nodded. 'There'll be a storm all right – but what shall we do? Stay here, or risk it and go on?'

'You and Tarnal are the seamen.' Vannor shrugged. 'We'll abide by your decision. But if we stay here we'll have no food and no shelter. I'd say it might be best to set off now and try to make it to Wyvernesse before the storm hits. After all, we can always put in further up the coast if things get too dangerous – and we'll be all the closer to our destination.'

Quickly, they got into the boat and set off again, doing their best to hide their worry from Hebba. To speed the journey, the able-bodied divided themselves into pairs, taking an oar each: Yanis with Benziorn, and Zanna, who had become at home in boats during her stay with the Nightrunners, rowing with Tarnal. Zanna felt a surge of pity for

368

her father, who remained at the tiller. She could tell from his glowering, abstracted expression that his inability to help the rowers only reminded him of his disability. Though it made her back and arms ache, and she was sweating and gasping for breath in the heavy, stifling air, she was glad when it was her turn to row. That way, she did not have to look at the ominous mass of heavy, bruised-looking clouds that were filling the sky to the west.

The first sign of change came with a freshening of the wind. Though it was more comfortable to row now, Zanna felt a shiver of dread race down her spine. Soon the sea was becoming increasingly choppy, and the little craft began to rock and pitch in the heaving swell, making it difficult to handle the oars. Waves began to slap against the bows, splashing spray over the sides of the boat. All of them now except for Tarnal and Yanis, the two experienced sailors, were beginning to feel queasy. The two nightrunners took over the rowing, for they knew better than the landsman and women how to handle the pitching craft. Hebba began to moan and whimper in fear. Zanna handed her the bailer, and soon the old cook was far too busy scooping water out of the bottom of the boat to complain.

The wind was increasing with every moment now. In the sudden darkness they could barely see each other, for the clouds had spread from horizon to horizon, blotting out the stars. In the distance they heard the first low grumble of thunder. Vannor tugged at Yanis's arm. 'Don't you think we had better put in?'

Yanis shook his head. 'We've left it too long now. It's all reefs along here – there's nowhere to land.' He took a brief glance over his shoulder. 'That's the last headland, up ahead – see the standing stone?' he panted. 'If we can only make it round there, we'll be all right.'

'Give Zanna the tiller now,' Tarnal told Vannor, his voice jerky with the exertion of rowing. 'She's more experienced than you, and she's sailed these waters before. She knows the way in through the rocks. Put your hand over hers – that's right. She'll need your strength to steer.'

Zanna blessed him for the last suggestion. She had heard

her dad's sharp, hurt intake of breath when Tarnal had suggested he give up the tiller, and knew he would be feeling more of a burden than ever. But even in their extremity the Nightrunner had been considerate of Vannor's pride.

They made it round the headland before the full force of the storm hit them, though they floundered for a terrifying moment in the crashing seas that hammered the rocky point. Zanna clung desperately to the tiller as the small boat crested the side of a mountainous breaker, and braced herself against her father, grateful for his strength to help her keep the craft on its heading. Hebba's shriek drowned the whistling of the wind as they dropped down the other side, hitting the water with a gigantic splash. Yanis and Tarnal, their faces taut with strain, pulled desperately on the oars to keep them from the jagged rocks as another and yet another great wave lifted and hurled the frail shell that was all that stood between them and the hungry seas.

And then, with shocking suddenness, they were round the point and into calmer water that had subsided to a rolling swell. Zanna knuckled the stinging seawater from her eyes and steered as she had never done before through the treacherous maze of rocks that sheltered and concealed the entrance to the secret cavern of the Nightrunners; straining her mind to recall the positions of the rocks before the cavern, and her eyes to catch the white flashes of foam that marked the locations of those rocks in the darkness. Once she cursed as she heard the keel grate on a rock – and then, when they were almost safely through, the boat leapt to a shuddering halt that threw all of them into a heap. There was the sharp, brutal splintering sound of a cracking plank, and even as she picked herself up Zanna felt the icy swirl of water round her feet.

'Keep steering,' Tarnal yelled, as he pushed the boat off the rock with his oar. 'We're almost there. She'll make it yet!'

And so it proved. As the weary voyagers paddled their foundering craft into the cavern, the entire smuggler community, with Remana weeping tears of joy at the safe return of her son, turned out to meet them on the curving, silvery beach within the vast and echoing cave. Willing arms reached out to pull the wallowing, leaking boat to the shore and welcome back the wanderers.

Yanis had his eyes fixed on the beautiful, flaxen-haired stranger who stood with Remana on the beach, a huge white dog by her side, but Zanna didn't notice. She was looking at Tarnal. 'You did bloody well to get us through,' he told her. 'In darkness, and a sea like that, I couldn't have steered better myself. Now you can truly call yourself a Nightrunner.'

Zanna grinned happily, her heart swelling with pride. 'It's good to be home,' she said softly. Smiling, Tarnal extended a hand to help her to the shore.

23

Stormfront

The elements were in turmoil. The slick black rocks of the Xandim coastline were lost between the grinding white fangs of the breakers. Swelling, steel-grey waves hurled themselves against the obdurate stones of the shore. The gale whined shrill counterpoint to the surf's thundering boom and the roar and hiss of the vanquished waves. Salt mist from the wind-whipped spume laid a sheen of moisture on Aurian's skin and stung Anvar's icy face as he squinted into the gloom. The Mage licked the taste of the sea from her lips and pulled the hood of her cloak more closely around her ears.

'I suppose it had to happen sooner or later,' she shouted, augmenting her words with mental speech so that Anvar could hear her above the howl of the tempest. The two Mages had walked apart from Chiamh and the great cats to discuss this new problem that faced them. 'It was only to be expected after Eliseth forced her winter on the world for so long, then we created an unseasonal spring . . . it'll take some time for the elements to settle down.'

'I only hope we haven't done too much damage – this is quite a storm. It's already been blowing for two days and nights.' Anvar bit his lip, frowning out across the heaving ocean. He wondered how his soulmate could sound so calm.

Aurian shrugged. 'Eliseth started this. I doubt we could cause much more harm in trying to correct what she had done. In the end, the world is far greater than we can encompass, even with our magic. The weather is simply settling back to its proper pattern. Only . . . I wish it hadn't decided to do it now. This couldn't have happened at a worse time for us.' She glanced back over her shoulder at the expectant crowd of wet, chilled and bedraggled Xandim who had been

372

unable to pitch their tents in the gale, and now thronged the headland behind the Mages. Anvar understood her concern. The last days had not been easy for any of the companions. As Herdlord, Schiannath had persuaded many of the Horse-folk to accompany himself and Chiamh north to help Aurian in her quest, but there had been many dissenting voices. If there was too long a delay in finding transportation across the sea, even the volunteers might easily have second thoughts.

'Want me to get rid of it?' Anvar's hand crept inside his cloak to touch the Harp of Winds, slung across his back on cunning straps wrought by the skilled Xandim leatherwork-ers. A thrill of starsong in the back of his mind sent pleasurable shivers through his body as he touched the crys-talline frame, and he gritted his teeth to resist its allure. Because he had not, as yet, completely tamed the power of the Artefact, the Harp was always trying to tempt him with its siren music into unleashing its magic upon the world.

'Anvar – wait!' Aurian captured his hand in her own. She was aware, from her own early experiences with the Staff of Earth, of his difficulties in controlling the Harp, and had helped him tremendously in recent days. Hearing him sigh, she squeezed his hand sympathetically. 'Don't worry – you'll get your chance shortly. But since this blasted storm has been blowing two solid days already, who knows who much longer it may last? If we can get Parric's Nightrunner friends to send their ships for us, we may need you to calm the ocean so that they can get across. Too much tampering at this stage might bring us worse problems later.'

'Then how will you reach the Leviathan?' Anvar protested. He had a feeling that he didn't want to know the answer.

'I'm going to go find him now.' Aurian's mental tones brooked no argument. Already, she was reaching up to un-fasten her cloak. 'I'm damned if I'm going to wait around any longer.'

'Aurian, don't be stupid!' Anvar snatched at her hands. 'You'll kill yourself.' His old terror of deep water rushed back to overwhelm him.

'I won't.' Gently, Aurian pushed his hands away. 'If I really thought so, I wouldn't even consider this, believe me –

373

not now that I have you and Wolf.' Her mental tones were
softened with a smile for him. 'It's impossible to drown a
Mage, remember? Besides, the storm was worse than this on
the night of the shipwreck, and we both survived that with
the help of the Leviathan. All I have to do is avoid getting
dashed to pieces, and if you look down there on the eastern
side of the headland you'll see a kind of inlet where the water
swirls around. If I enter the water in the right place, the current should be pulling me away from the rocks.'

'What?' Anvar demanded. 'Have you lost your mind?'

'No – just my patience,' Aurian retorted, scraping her wet,
windblown hair out of her eyes for what seemed to be the
hundredth time. 'Judging from my last meeting with the
Leviathan, it may take them a while to make their minds up
to help us. If I can make contact now and state our case, we
can all go back to that fishing settlement we passed to wait in
comfort; and all being well, the messengers can be on their
way just as soon as the storm blows out.'

Anvar sighed. He recognized the obdurate glint in his
soulmate's eye, and knew that no matter how long he
attempted to dissuade her the result would be the same in
the end. It would save a lot of time if he simply bowed to the
inevitable, trusted her judgement, and let her get it over with.
'Go on, then – but for the sake of all the gods, be careful.'

Aurian kissed him. 'For the sake of you and Wolf, I will.'
Then she was gone, running along the headland down the
narrow track worn by the Xandim fisherfolk. By the time he
caught up with her, delayed by the puzzled queries of
Chiamh and Shia, she was already on the rocky shore of the
inlet, shedding her clothes. 'Ugh!' she muttered through
chattering teeth. 'Me and my bright ideas.'

'Serves you right,' said Anvar callously, taking her cloak
and the linen shirt and leather tunic and breeches, Xandim
garments all, from her before they could blow away. He
weighted them down with her sword and boots but thrust the
Staff of Earth, which she gave him carefully into his hands,
into his own belt, where its proximity to the Harp made both
Artefacts combine their energies in a blaze of joyful radiance,
setting the very air thrumming and sparkling with their con-
joined and augmented power.

'Stop that!' Anvar muttered irritably, wanting to keep all his concentration for Aurian. As he extended his will to damp the surge of power, the incandescent green-white blaze died away, leaving only a soft, defiant humming. When he looked up, Aurian was already a pale and distant figure, picking her cautious, barefoot way along the jutting reef of rocks that protruded out into the little bay.

'You might have waited.' Anvar sent his mental message in injured tones.

'Why? To freeze to death?' came the abstracted reply. 'I can talk to you just as well from – ouch! These blasted rocks are sharp!'

The next minute she was gone, diving out over the end of the rocks into the churning waves. Anvar sighed and, clutching her bundled clothing to his chest, sat down on a nearby boulder to await her return. She was right, he thought, shifting uncomfortably. The blasted rocks were very sharp indeed. After a time Shia and Chiamh joined him, having sent the others back towards the fishing settlement Aurian had mentioned. As the shrouded sky darkened towards night, they waited together on the stormswept beach.

As Aurian had struggled, shivering, along the wicked knife-edged rocks, she had wondered how she was going to find the courage to take that first, agonizing lungful of water that would adapt her breathing to survive beneath the sea. As it turned out, she need not have worried. When she entered the water the sea was so cold that she gasped involuntarily, and after a moment's frantic thrashing in pain and panic she found herself breathing quite naturally beneath the ocean.

It was as well that the struggle had been brief. Already, the current was changing, trying to pull her back to be battered against the cruel rocks of the reef. Staying underwater, out of reach of the crashing waves above, Aurian began to swim outward, fighting the current with all her strength. Because she didn't have to surface into the teeth of the storm, the going was easier than she had expected, and soon she began to settle into a rhythm. Had it not been for the thick murkiness of the water, cloudy with sand churned up from the bottom by the waves above, and the unrelenting coldness of the northern ocean, she would have quite enjoyed the swim.

When the Mage had travelled further out from the shore, she found that the deeper water was much more clear, and the conflicting currents no longer tugged her this way and that. She could dive down deeper now, to calmer water where the fury of the storm above was little more than a distant memory. At last she decided she had gone far enough, and settled in the water to call the Leviathan.

Reaching out with both her voice and her mind, Aurian began to sing the poignant, plangent, swirling song that would travel for leagues through the storm-tossed waters, summoning the Whalefolk from their far wanderings. Especially, she called to Ithalasa, the old friend who had rescued her from the shipwreck and had given her sage counsel and a great deal of additional help besides.

For a long time she sung, and then she listened, praying that she would hear a distant reply. But there was nothing. Aurian suppressed a stab of impatience, remembering that the fierce emotions of the land-dwellers were anathema to the Leviathan race. But it was so hard to have to wait. While she knew that part of her water-breathing adaptation would let her survive in the freezing sea far longer than she would otherwise have done, there was still a limit to the time she could spend submerged before the deadly cold took its toll – and her life. And as well as needing Ithalasa's assistance once more, she was simply looking forward to seeing him again. She had much to tell him concerning the finding of the Staff and the Harp, and her search for the Sword of Flame.

Aurian rested a little, for the singing of the high, plaintive whalesong had drained her both physically and emotionally. Then she began again, starting over at the beginning of the lengthy cycle of song – and this time, about halfway through the pattern, she received an answer.

The distant call was so faint that as yet she could hear it only with her mind, not her ears. Aurian waited for the singer to come nearer, changing her own song now to one of welcome. Soon, the dimly-heard voice became more distinct.

'Mage? O Mage?' It was Ithalasa.

'Ithalasa! Oh, how glad I am to hear you again,' Aurian cried joyfully. 'How incredibly fortunate that it should be you.'

'Not fortunate, Mage – but it explains our long delay in answering you,' the Leviathan replied. *'A pod of my sisters heard your song far out in the ocean and decided that, once again, I should be the one to represent our kind, for I had talked with you before. They called me – and I came.'*

Within minutes he was with her, surfacing briefly to blow and take another mighty breath before diving back down to her. His massive, streamlined body hung motionless in the current save for the sweeping notion of his curving flukes. His vast bulk dwarfed the Mage as she swam, holding herself in position as he did, beneath the gaze of a deep, wise, twinkling eye.

'Now,' said Ithalasa, with great good humour, *'what is your need this time, little one? I see no shipwreck here.'*

'You wouldn't – I swam out from the Xandim coast to find you,' Aurian explained.

'Did you so? And in this storm?' The Leviathan's tones were tinged with surprise, and not a little respect. *'Then your need must be pressing indeed.'*

'It certainly is – but more immediately pressing is my need to get out of the water before I perish with cold,' Aurian told him. She could only see him now through her Mage's vision, for already the waters had darkened with the onset of night. Her extremities were numb and white, and she could feel her thought processes growing gradually more sluggish. 'I don't think I can stay here much longer, Ithalasa. Would you mind taking me back to the shore, so I can talk to you from there?'

'It will be my pleasure. It will be good to swim with you again, little one.' Helpfully, the Leviathan extended a great, curved fluke. *'Can you climb up on my back, as you did before?'*

Weakened by the cold as she was, Aurian would have found it a struggle to do what once she had accomplished so easily, had it not been for the buoyancy of the water. Pushing herself off from the extended fluke, she swam upwards until she saw his broad, grey back beneath her. The Leviathan swam slowly towards the surface, pushing her up with him; making a slow ascent so that her body could become accustomed to the change in pressure. At last he broke through into the open air, and the Mage found herself lying on his back, choking, retching and coughing out water as her lungs made the change back to breathing air.

Now I know what a drowned rat must feel like, Aurian thought. She lay there limply, lacking the energy to move, gasping and shivering; for in the cold wind she felt no warmer than she had in the sea. Waves broke over her as Ithalasa forged his powerful way back to land through the heaving waters, and time and again she almost found herself washed back into the ocean, for there was little to hold on to on his expanse of mottle, barnacle-covered back save the slight ridge of his dorsal fin, which was so pronounced in other clans of the Leviathan race.

Out of consideration for her wretched state, Ithalasa refrained from asking the Mage any questions as he took her to shore, though she could feel the undercurrents of avid curiosity bubbling beneath the calmness of his surface thoughts. Soon – though she could have wished it had been sooner – a vivid sheet of lightning lit up the sea for miles around, and Aurian could make out the dark smudge of the Xandim coastline in stark relief on the horizon. When the next flash came, the land had grown very much closer.

The water was deep enough to allow Ithalasa to come partway into the inlet, and Aurian only had a few yards to swim to reach the outthrust reef from which she had started. She was glad it was no further. Anvar, waiting at the end of the rocks, reached down a strong hand to grasp her arm and pull her out of the water, and without his help she would never have managed. Dimly, she heard his voice in her mind as he greeted the Leviathan; then she became aware of a blissful warmth as he wrapped her cloak around her. He picked her up and carried her safely back across the slippery, sharp-edged rocks to the beach, where she saw Shia, Chiamh and, to her great delight, a massive driftwood bonfire that blazed bravely in the teeth of the storm, kept alight through Anvar's magic.

Anvar put her down beside the fire and began to towel her roughly with the cloak, restoring circulation to her bloodless limbs before wrapping his own, dryer, cloak around her. Aurian's joy became complete when the Windeye handed her a mug of his steaming herb tea, lavishly laced with honey and strong, rough Xandim spirits. Anvar steadied it in her shaking hands, and she forced the mug between her chattering teeth and took a swallow, feeling the warmth spreading all the way down through her chilled body. Within a few minutes she was feeling very much better, though drowsy, and wondering if she would ever truly be warm again.

Sleep, however, would have to wait, for the patient Leviathan had been neglected long enough. With Anvar's help she struggled back into her clothes, not resisting when his assistance turned into a quick embrace. 'I'm so glad to see you again,' she murmured, 'and grateful that you didn't tell me you warned me this would happen.'

'Well, I did – but at least you succeeded, so I'll let you off this time.' He grinned at her. 'Feeling better now?'

Aurian nodded. 'It's time we went to talk to Ithalasa.'

'I am happy to see you with your mate again, after all your quarrels and mishaps in the south,' was the Leviathan's opening comment to Aurian. He listened to the tale of how they had found each other, and showed no surprise whatsoever to learn that Anvar was also a Mage. Ithalasa rejoiced to hear of the safe delivery of the Mage's child, who was currently back in the fishing settlement with his lupine guardians. (Sangra had been left to keep an eye on them, muttering darkly all the while that she was a warrior, not a bloody nursemaid.)

Since both Shia and Chiamh were adept at mental talk, the Mages were able to introduce their companions to the Leviathan, and he greeted them graciously; and with a great deal of curiosity – especially as to the unusual nature of the Windeye's powers. But when Aurian and Anvar, standing together out on the storm-lashed rocks, told him how they had won the Staff of Earth and the Harp of Winds, all other concerns were forgotten. They could feel Ithalasa's growing excitement, tinged none the less with an undercurrent of concern, beating strong in their minds.

379

'I thought I could feel the power of High Magic!' he exclaimed. 'And what of the Sword of Flame?'

'That's why we need your help.' Quickly, Aurian explained their predicament.

'I see . . .' Ithalasa mused. 'So you must get a message to your friends across the northern ocean, and then they can send ships to fetch you?'

'That's right,' Anvar said. 'You couldn't take all of us – not the cats and the Xandim too. And Wolf is far too small to attempt such a journey.'

'But how can I convey a message? I can only communicate with you Magefolk.'

'Well,' said Aurian, 'we hoped that you might take one or two of us to Wyvernesse, then they could tell the Nightrunners.' Immediately, she felt the Leviathan's hesitation and her heart sank, although she'd been expecting something of the kind.

'Yes, little one,' the great voice echoed in her mind. 'As you have guessed, such an act on my part will constitute another interference by the Leviathan in wars of power. After the Cataclysm, we vowed never again to become involved in the affairs of the Magefolk – and already we have done so, for without our help you would never have gained the first two Artefacts. Before I can take you to find the Sword, I must consult again with my people.'

'I thought so,' Aurian sighed. 'But, Ithalasa – are you sure that you want to become involved again?'

'Little one, I am sure. For my part, I trust you to use the Weapons wisely. Whether my brethren will do so remains to be seen . . .' He hesitated, but when he spoke again his voice was decisive. 'No – already I know what their answer will be. Last time, they permitted me to help you because they did not believe that you could truly find the lost Artefacts. This time it will be different, for already you have the Harp and the Staff, and the dangers of another Cataclysm have become very real. They will not let me intervene again – and so they must not know. Return to this place as soon as the storm blows out, and I will convey your messenger.'

'But wait,' Aurian objected. 'If they find out what you've done, will they not punish you? Ithalasa, I can't let you take that kind of risk for us!'

'You are right,' said Ithalasa. 'If they find out, I must certainly pay the penalty – but the risk is mine to take. Come, little one – what choice have you, other than to accept? How else will you get back across the ocean?'

Aurian knew he was right – there was no choice – but that didn't make her feel any better about the business. None the less, she accepted his brave offer with all the gratitude that he deserved, before the Magefolk made their farewells. Through the blowing curtains of rain, they saw the mighty Leviathan erupt gracefully from the water as he leapt high in answer. Falling back into the waves with a splash of fountaining foam that was loud enough to be heard above the keening of the storm, Ithalasa was gone, racing swiftly for the open seas.

Both Mages were soaked and shivering by this time, and Aurian was glad of Chiamh's offer of a ride back to the home of the fisherfolk, who welcomed the companions of their Herdlord lavishly with hot food and blazing fires. The largest house was given entirely over to their use, for Schiannath's father had been born of this coastal clan, and they had taken his victory in the challenge as their own. When they finally managed to escape the effusive hospitality of the fisherfolk, the Mage had never been more grateful in her life to climb into a warm, soft bed with Anvar – but when she got there, she couldn't sleep all night for worrying about the Leviathan, and the risk that he was willingly taking to help her in her quest.

The storm continued to rage all through the next day and into the following night, whistling in the dripping thatch and battering the sturdy stone-built dwellings of the Xandim fisherfolk. Living on the coast with its capricious weather, the fishing community did not favour tents except during summer – a fact for which Aurian was extremely grateful. Though she chafed at the delay, it gave her time to appraise her companions of what had resulted from the talk with Ithalasa. The Mages, Aurian with Wolf upon her lap, gathered with Chiamh, Shia and Khanu around the great central firepit that warmed the communal living space of the large stone house, together with Parric, Sangra, Yazour, and the Xandim Herdlord and his sister. Sharing a flask of mead between them, they began to make their plans.

Since there would be some delay while the Xandim were brought across, Aurian and Anvar were reluctant to travel to the north too soon, lest Miathan and Eliseth should sense the presence of the Artefacts and strike at the Mages while they had no companions to support them. Though they were sorry to miss the journey with Ithalasa, it was decided that Parric and Sangra would go in their stead, for they had already stayed with the Nightrunners, and had a claim on their friendship. Chiamh would go with them, to communicate with the Leviathan. His powers as a Windeye might also be needed if the weather turned bad again during the crossing.

Once everyone had reached the north, however, they were to make for Eilin's Valley with all possible speed. Aurian wanted to waste no time in her attempt to claim the Sword. What would happen afterwards was still a matter for conjecture. They discussed the possibilities long into the night, before finally deciding that they must leave the future to take care of itself.

The following morning, the companions awoke to find that the storm had broken at last, and they emerged into a sodden landscape of dune and marram-grass that had been battered mercilessly by the fury of the elements. After a hasty breakfast, they walked down to the headland in cool and hazy sunlight that was frequently obscured by a high, thin scum of scudding clouds. The Windeye glanced up with a frown at the uneasy sky. 'I fear this run of evil weather has not finished with us yet – but so long as the Leviathan swims as fast as you say, we should have time to make the crossing before the next storm comes.'

'I hope so,' Aurian replied with a shudder.

'If it starts to blow again before you reach Wyvernesse, try to make contact with us,' Anvar told Chiamh. 'I'll do my best to hold it back with the Harp until you're safely across.'

When they reached the bay they found that the massive breakers had vanished, though the sea was still choppy, with a tumbling mane of white foam upon the crest of each swiftly-running wave. 'Storm or no storm, it looks like we're in for a bloody wet crossing,' said Parric gloomily – and then his words tailed off as he caught his first glimpse of the long, dark shape of Ithalasa, waiting patiently in the sparkling sea beyond the rocky point. 'Balls of Chathak!' the little cavalry master muttered. 'I didn't realize it would be so big!' Sangra, too, was suddenly looking rather pale, and Aurian chuckled at their discomfiture.

'Don't worry,' she assured them. 'He can't bite you – he doesn't have any teeth.'

'He doesn't have to,' retorted Sangra. 'He could swallow us in a single gulp.'

Aurian sighed, and gave it up. Some people would never understand that Ithalasa, for all his vast size and alien appearance, was a wise and gentle intelligent being. Sadly, she thought of the sacrifice that Ithalasa was making to help these ungrateful land-dwellers. She thanked the gods that Chiamh had been willing to undertake the journey with the warriors. If they could converse with the Leviathan, she was confident that they would soon lose their fears.

'Little one, are your companions ready?' Ithalasa prompted her gently. Suddenly Aurian realized that he was as anxious as Parric and Sangra to get this journey over.

'They are,' she told him.

Though the fisherfolk had provided a small wooden boat to row the voyagers out to the Leviathan, so that they could at least start their journey dry, she herself swam out to commune with him one last time before he left. Even Anvar had no idea of what passed between them in those final moments, but when the Mage emerged from the ocean to wave farewell to her departing friends he suspected that the redness of her eyes was not entirely due to the salt water. Picking up her cloak from the rocks where she'd left it, he draped it round her shivering shoulders and hugged her close to him. 'You know, if you keep on doing this, you're going to catch your death of cold,' he told her gently.

Aurian looked out wistfully across the water to the sleek, departing shape of the Leviathan. 'It would be worth it,' she said softly.

24

Southpaw

Zanna settled back into the old routines and friendships of the Nightrunner hideout as though the months of her absence had never happened. At first Remana had been very cool with her, but her anger had been mostly due to worry over the fact that she had run away. When the matriarch of the smugglers discovered Zanna's role in Vannor's rescue, her manner thawed abruptly and the two of them became fast friends again, with Remana treating her, once more, as the daughter she'd never had. There were many friendships to be renewed – the chief and most delightful of which was her reunion with her pony, Piper. Just now all the smugglers' ponies were down in the cavern, sheltering from the wicked weather, and so he had been on hand to renew their acquaintance.

Zanna spent a good deal of time with Piper – as much as she could spare from her dad, whose recovery had been set back by the gruelling encounter with the storm. He had taken a chill from the icy soaking he had received, but under Remana's cosseting, and the constant care of Benziorn and the blonde girl Emmie, he was gradually growing stronger, and Zanna hoped to be able to take up Tarnal's offer to go riding with her as soon as the weather cleared.

At least it would get her away from Yanis, Zanna thought sourly. He was driving her to distraction, hanging around Vannor's chamber all day making sheep's eyes at Emmie – who, to be fair, seemed completely oblivious of his attentions. Zanna felt a curious ambivalence towards the serious, sad-eyed girl who, according to Remana, was older than she looked, and had lost her husband and both her children to Miathan's depredations. Zanna felt sorry for her after that, and also deeply appreciated what Emmie was doing for her father – yet she knew that she ought to resent the older woman for her beauty, and for taking Yanis's attentions away from herself.

Yet during the time they had spent cooped up together in Hebba's house, Zanna had found herself becoming more and more irritated by the thoughtless, self-centred behaviour of the Nightrunner leader. Besides, he wasn't very bright – she had known that anyway, but it had never bothered her before. Zanna blushed to remember that casual announcement made months ago to her father, that she intended to marry Yanis. What an idiot she had been! Without a mother to advise her, there was no one to tell her that she was simply growing up, with all the trials and contradictions that entailed, and so Zanna was left to puzzle out her difficulties on her own.

In all her confusion, Tarnal was the solid anchor in her life. He always seemed to be there when she felt most in need of a friend, and she was always glad to see him. It also meant a lot to Zanna that the young smuggler was so considerate of her father, whom he held in great respect. Tired of the awkward atmosphere between Emmie and the Nightrunner leader, she looked forward to having Tarnal's company all to herself as a relief from Yanis's foolishness, and waited impatiently for the weather to change. On the day after the storm had broken at last, she was glad to accept his invitation to go riding on the cliffs.

Wrapped up warmly against the bite of the wind that stung her glowing cheeks and ruffled her short-cropped hair, Zanna galloped her pony along the clifftop, racing Tarnal to the distant landmark of the solitary standing stone. Oh, but it was wonderful to be out in the fresh air again! Piper seemed to think so too – the pony was full of energy after his long confinement in the caverns, and needed this run to calm his fidgets. It seemed to be having the same effect on Zanna, for by the time she had reached the bottom of the mound on which the great stone stood – as near as she dared to approach on horseback, for the ponies were afraid of the sinister megalith – she was feeling happier and more free than she had felt for months.

Laughing, she turned to Tarnal, who had come galloping up behind her. 'I won!' she crowed. 'That fat slug of yours will have to pick up his hooves if he wants to beat my Piper . . .' Zanna's words tailed off as something – a long, dark, unfamiliar shape far out at sea – caught her attention. It certainly wasn't a ship, though it was big enough, and from the way it moved it seemed to be alive. 'Tarnal, what on earth is that?' she cried, pointing.

'It looks like a whale.' The Nightrunner was frowning in puzzlement. 'But they never come into these waters. What the blazes is it dong here? Why is it all alone? And why is it staying on the surface all the time? Do you think it's sick?'

Together they sat and waited on the clifftop, dismounting to let their ponies crop the grass as they watched the behemoth approach the coast. At one point in their vigil Zanna noticed that Tarnal had taken hold of her hand, but it felt so pleasant that she made no effort to pull away. Suddenly, she felt his fingers tighten on her own. 'Zanna . . .' His voice was little more than a hoarse whisper. 'Please tell me I'm not imagining things. I'm sure I can see people riding on that whale.'

His eyes were keener than hers, but after a few minutes Zanna could see them too. 'They *are* people! But who could command such power over a creature of the deep?' She turned to the Nightrunner in sudden panic. 'Tarnal – do you think it's the Archmage? What if he's found us?'

Cursing, Tarnal pulled her to her feet. 'Quick! We must get back to the caverns. We've got to warn them.'

Zanna flung herself up on Piper's back, wrenching at the reins as he reared in startlement. Then they were racing back towards the Nightrunner hideout, both she and Tarnal praying that they could make it in time, before the speeding Leviathan reached the shore.

It was Sangra, whose turn it had been to keep a lookout, who first spotted the distinctive shape of the clifftop megalith that marked the location, for those privileged few who knew of its existence, of the smugglers' secret home. 'There it is!' she cried. Parric awakened blearily and rolled over, only just saving himself from sliding off the Leviathan's curving back. Sangra put out a hand to steady him and he scrambled back to safety, muttering epithets, before sitting up to look in the direction of her pointing finger.

'You're right,' he cried. 'Who'd have thought this beast could swim so fast? This is one up on that miserable bastard Idris who took us south, and that leaky old washtub he calls a ship.' Turning, he began to shake the Windeye into wakefulness – which took some doing, because Chiamh had spent most of the night sitting up in delighted conversation with Ithalasa.

'Chiamh? Chiamh, wake up, you idiot. We're here.'

'What? Already?' Chiamh mumbled, sounding disappointed. Parric ignored that. The Windeye, though a pleasant lad and harmless enough, had always been a strange one. For his own part, the cavalry master couldn't wait for this wretched, miserable, wet, uncomfortable, *boring* journey to be over. Suddenly remembering where he was, he put a guilty damper on such thoughts, lest the Leviathan should somehow hear him. Parric was still very much in awe of the immense creature.

'Can you ask our friend to make for that standing stone on the cliffs?' he asked the Windeye quickly, and with unusual politeness.

'What cliffs?' asked Chiamh, squinting shortsightedly at the horizon. Parric sighed. This was a problem he hadn't considered.

'You know,' Sangra said gently, for she was fond of the Windeye, 'you should ask the Lady Aurian if she couldn't use her healing powers to help you see properly.'

'We did talk about it,' Chiamh said, 'and she offered – but I'm afraid that if she gives me normal vision I might lose my Othersight. I just daren't risk it.'

'Never mind that for now,' Parric interrupted impatiently. Already, he could see that the Leviathan was veering off course. 'What are we going to do about getting to the Nightrunners?'

'Well, since neither the Leviathan nor I can see this stone

of yours, you're going to have to guide us,' Chiamh told him good-naturedly. 'Just tell me whether we should head right or left, and when to go straight on, and I'll pass the message to Ithalasa.'

It wasn't the perfect solution, but they managed – and before very much longer Parric could make out the deep bay in the cliffs, with its scattered guardian reefs, that concealed the Nightrunner caverns from prying eyes. 'Thank the gods we're home at last,' he said feelingly, 'not meaning any offence to your southern lands,' he added hastily to the Windeye, 'but home is – well, home, if you know what I mean.'

Chiamh sighed. An outcast among the Xandim, he had never really felt as though he belonged anywhere – not until these new outland companions had arrived from the north. Suddenly he wondered what would happen if Aurian should defeat her foes and complete her quest. What would he do then? There was no going back to what he'd been before. For the Windeye, the future looked unbearably lonely.

'You will contrive,' the kindly voice of Ithalasa intruded into Chiamh's bleak thoughts. *'Who knows what fate will hold for you? But whatever happens, and wherever you go, there will always be a welcome for you with Aurian and Anvar. Besides . . .'* and Ithalasa chuckled, *'through some freak of interbreeding in the past, you seem to hold some of the powers of the Magefolk, and after this sad business there will be few of that race left indeed. Will it not be your duty to find a mate, and father children, to carry those powers on into the future?'*

Abruptly, the Leviathan changed the subject – and just as well, for Chiamh's mind was reeling at his unexpected suggestion. *'Windeye, I cannot pass those reefs that guard your destination. Will you ask the humans what they want me to do?'*

Parric cursed when Chiamh passed on the news. 'It looks as though we'll have to swim for it.'

'Never mind,' said Sangra, 'we're wet enough already – another soaking won't make any difference.'

'I know that – but arriving like washed-up piece of flotsam in the Nightrunner cavern isn't exactly the triumphal entry I'd expected,' the cavalry master grumbled. 'Besides, it's going to take days to dry my gear out – this bloody seawater is playing havoc with all my knives.'

Sadly, Chiamh said goodbye to Ithalasa, and passed on the farewells and thanks of the others. Then he slid, for the last time, down the Leviathan's curving sides, and joined Parric and Sangra in the icy water. As soon as they were clear Ithalasa turned and headed back towards the open sea, diving swiftly and striking the surface with his elegant, curving tail in farewell. The Windeye watched him go, treading water until the Leviathan vanished completely beneath the waves. He only prayed that Ithalasa would not be called to account by his own people for assisting Aurian and her companions. But Chiamh had little time to think of such matters, for as soon as the weary travellers swam into the maze of rocks that filled the little bay they were met with a hail of arrows that came hurtling down with increasing accuracy from the cliffs above.

'Gods!' Sangra cried, and dived beneath the water. Parric saw Chiamh flounder in panic, getting a mouthful of sea. Keeping his wits about him, the cavalry master dodged into a narrow space between two rocks to protect himself from the deadly bolts that rained down on all sides. Rashly, he stuck his head out, and an arrow whistled past his ear, too close for comfort. They were getting the range now. 'Hoy!' he bawled, in his best parade-ground bellow. 'Don't shoot, you bloody idiots! It's me – Parric!'

The barrage of arrows faltered, and then stopped completely. The cavalry master heaved a sigh of relief, then looked around anxiously for his companions. They seemed to be all right, save that Sangra was holding Chiamh's head above the surface while he spluttered and coughed up water. Then Parric heard the creak of oars, and a small boat emerged into the sunlight from the shadows of the narrow cavern entrance. At the tiller was a blond-haired smuggler lad he vaguely recognized – and to his delight it was Vannor's young daughter, her hair cut short like that of a boy, who rowed the boat, wielding the oars with an expert flourish.

Giving her entire attention to the business in hand, the girl held the small craft steadily in place while the lad reached down to help Chiamh and Sangra clamber in. Parric swam towards them, knowing that there was very little space for a boat to manoeuvre between the submerged reefs, and clambered carefully aboard.

Only then did Zanna give her oars to her companion. 'Parric!' she exclaimed delightedly, squirming round to hug him. 'I'm so glad you've come back safely.'

'And I'm glad to see you, lass.' He ruffled her cropped hair affectionately. 'I see that you've become a warrior, as you always wanted. A lot of women cut their hair short on campaign. It's the mark of a true professional.' He chuckled at Sangra's indignant exclamation. 'Saves a lot of messing about,' he continued blithely. 'By the gods, lass, but you're a sight for sore eyes after only having Sangra and a bunch of foreigners to look at for months.' He glanced at his companions with a teasing twinkle in his eye. 'Zanna, this is Chiamh, but I'll introduce you properly when we've landed.' As they passed into the narrow, echoing tunnel that led into the cavern, his expression darkened with a scowl. 'And where the blazes is that bloody idiot Yanis?'

'Waiting on the beach,' Zanna told him. 'He said he wanted to give you a fitting leader's welcome.'

'I'll give him a welcome he won't forget in a hurry,' Parric growled. 'Has the fool forgotten how to use his eyes?'

Zanna chuckled as they emerged from the tunnel into the vastness of the cavern. 'I'm afraid that was our fault.' She glanced at the young smuggler, with an expression in her eyes that made Parric wonder. 'We were out riding on the cliffs,' she went on, 'and when we saw you on the whale – well, we thought it must be the Archmage.' Her voice sank to a haunted whisper, and there was a shadow of terror in her eyes that the cavalry master could not account for. But there was no time to enquire further, for at that moment a familiar voice came booming out from the shore.

'Parric, you old bastard! Have the southerners had enough of you, then?'

'That's Vannor!' The cavalry master's eyes widened in amazement. 'What are you doing here, you fat old moneygrabber?' he bawled across the water, and then his words tailed off at the sight of the merchant's missing hand.

'Parric, be careful, please,' Zanna whispered urgently. 'He still can't accept it. He feels so useless now.'

'By all the gods,' Parric growled, his eyes bright with pain and anger. 'Who did this to him? I'll string the bastard up with his own guts.'

'I don't think so.' Zanna's voice was grim. 'It was Eliseth.'

As the boat scrunched on to the shingle, Parric leapt out, brushing aside the Nightrunner leader who had stepped down to meet him. He went straight to Vannor and clasped him in a rough embrace, pounding the merchant on the back until Vannor yelled in protest.

'I never thought I'd be so glad to see your ugly face,' the cavalry master said, and stepped back, his eyes going deliberately to his friend's right arm. 'Well, of all the bloody nerve,' he grumbled in injured tones. 'Just because I'm a southpaw, suddenly everyone wants to get in on the act. The next thing we know, you'll be wanting to me to teach you all my tricks of fighting left-handed.'

In the horrified silence that followed, Vannor's expression was a mixture of rage and utter shock – until suddenly his face broke into a grin. 'Well, since I did have the nerve to copy you, you foulmouthed little runt, perhaps you'd better teach me some of those tricks you mentioned – if you have any, that is.'

'Oh, I have them, all right,' the cavalry master promised. 'The dirtiest tricks that never got into the book. And I'll teach you them all, my friend – but it can wait until after we've done some serious drinking!' Putting his arm around Vannor's shoulders, he was about to lead him out of the cavern when Sangra called him back.

'Hold on a minute, Parric. Your serious drinking is a fine idea, and I'm all for it, but it'll have to wait until we've talked to Yanis.'

'Bugger!' Parric muttered, turning back. 'You can see why I never made commander. For a minute there I'd forgotten why we came.'

25

The Cauldron

The headland looked very different in the sunshine, Aurian thought. She stood there watching, as she had done every day since Parric left, for a sight of distant sails. After a while Shia came up to join her. 'You know this is folly,' the great cat remarked. 'You must give them time to get here, my friend. Why not come back down and join us in the settlement? Wolf is missing you, and even Anvar has got tired of watching.'

Aurian sighed. 'I suppose you're right,' she admitted grudgingly. 'I just hate this endless waiting. I want to get back to the north . . .'

'And you are worried about Ithalasa,' Shia added with her usual perception. 'But all was well with him when he returned to tell you that he had delivered your companions safely. And by standing here to do your worrying you do him no service. So far, he has kept his mission secret, but if another of the Leviathan should be passing, and pick up your thoughts . . .'

'All right, all right,' Aurian muttered resignedly. 'Let's go back to the settlement.'

As she turned away from the headland, the air was rent by the thunder of wings, and a cry of greeting came from the skies above her. Aurian looked up, startled. After Schiannath had become Herdlord, she had sent the two winged couriers back to Raven, with her blessings and her thanks. Crossing the ocean to an unfamiliar land had been too much to ask of them. She had sensed their reluctance, and had sadly let them go. They had already done enough for her, though she could have used their assistance where she was going.

But now, to Aurian's astonishment, Cygnus was landing beside her in a blur of white wings. 'Greetings, Mage. I come from the queen,' he told her, 'with an offer to accompany you to the north, if you will have me.'

'Why, I would be delighted to have you join us,' Aurian told him, much cheered by the sudden appearance of the winged man. *Maybe everything is going right for a change,* she thought.

She still thought so two days later, when three lean Nightrunner vessels appeared on the horizon, their sails glowing bravely in the fading sunset light. Aurian watched their slow approach in a fever of anticipation, thinking that soon they would be carrying herself, her companions, and the Xandim, back to the north. To complete her pleasure in the moment, she recognized the thoughts of Chiamh reaching out across the ocean in greeting.

As the three ships finally dropped anchor in the gathering twilight, she ran down with Anvar to meet the Windeye, who introduced them to Yanis, the Nightrunner leader.

'We missed you,' Aurian told Chiamh sincerely, releasing him from a hug. 'But you didn't have to trail all the way back again to fetch us.'

'I did,' said Chiamh, smiling. 'I was missing you Magefolk, and someone was needed to guide the ships. Parric and Sangra said they had had enough of the sea to last them a lifetime – you understand, of course, that I've left out all their curse words,' he added with a grin. 'But there is someone else here, who did want to come to meet you.'

He beckoned, and Aurian turned to see Vannor's daughter rowing across from the adjacent ship with a young blond Nightrunner.

'Ho – Zanna!' The Mage ran down the beach to meet the boat, marvelling as she did so at how much more mature and independent the young girl seemed since they last had met in the solstice market in Nexis. 'What happened to that crystal of yours?' Aurian asked as she helped pull the boat up on to the shingle. 'Ever since you spoke to me that night, I've been wondering if you escaped the Magefolk safely.'

'I lost it in the catacombs,' Zanna apologized, scrambling from the grounded craft with the ease of long practice. She'd been looking forward to meeting the Mage again. When she saw that Aurian had also cut off her hair – it was growing out now, but the fiery mane still only just reached past her shoulders – the girl's mouth opened in an O of delighted amazement. She did not have to worry about her own short hair when she was keeping such honourable company!

The ships were to sail on the dawn tide, but no one got any sleep that night. The communal room of the fisherfolk dwelling was filled with talk, as Yanis's crew conversed with the local Xandim (Aurian had a feeling that the Nightrunner was extending his markets, and would soon be back) and the Mages told their own tales, and were brought up to date with the news from the north.

When at last the ships embarked in the soft blue light of dawn, Aurian stood in the bows with Anvar. 'Do you remember the last time we voyaged like this together?' said Anvar softly. 'Little did we think, when we fled Nexis, that such incredible things would happen to us.'

'Or that we'd meet such wonderful friends.' Aurian looked at the Windeye, who was peering shortsightedly over the stern at the receding Xandim coastline; and at Shia and Khanu, who were curled up asleep on a tarpaulin nearby with Wolf and his foster-parents. The Mage noticed, with some amusement, that despite her reassurances the Nightrunner sailors were giving that particular area a wide berth. 'I hope we get the chance to come back some day,' she went on, 'especially to see Hreeza – but right now I'm looking forward to going home.'

'It's not over yet,' Anvar reminded her with a frown.

'No,' agreed Aurian, 'but at least it feels as if we're making progress. And once we find the Sword, who knows what will happen?'

Her words, though spoken in all innocence, sent a premonitory prickle of dread sheeting across Anvar's skin.

Eliseth shrieked curses, and threw the crystal away from her across the room. 'She's back! I don't believe it!' But there was no room for doubt. She had seen it in the crystal – and with increasing practice her scrying was becoming very accurate nowadays. The Weather-Mage began to pace back and forth across her chamber, thinking furiously. It had been humiliating enough when Vannor and his daughter had escaped her. Her face now bore the ravages of an extra ten years – the mark of Miathan's rage. She intended to pay him back for that; but now that Aurian had returned her time was running out.

Eliseth had lost all faith in Miathan's effectiveness as Archmage. More than once, he'd had a perfect chance to end Aurian's life, but had always refused. And look what had happened. The accursed renegade and her half-blooded abomination of a paramour were practically knocking on the very door of the Mages' Tower!

If only I possessed the Cauldron, Eliseth thought desperately. After his dreadful error that had resulted in the Night of the Wraiths, Miathan had always seemed afraid to use the Artefact again. If he had only learned to control it, as she would have done, had the Cauldron been hers . . . If only he had taken the trouble to spend as many hours in the dusty, freezing archives as she had done, poring over ancient, half-decipherable scrolls to research the Cauldron's powers . . . Abruptly, the Weather-Mage stopped pacing. Well, why not? she thought. Why shouldn't I possess it? Have I not earned it? Would I not make better use of it? It's wasted on that doddering old fool.

But here common sense asserted itself. That fool was not so old and feeble that he couldn't snuff out her life like a candle if he caught her crossing him. Eliseth resumed her pacing. After a time, her eye lit on the pile of scrolls on the table, which she had brought from the library to continue her researches in comfort. The glimmerings of a plan began to form in her mind . . .

Miathan looked up in some surprise and annoyance as the Weather-Mage entered his chambers without knocking. What on earth was she thinking of? It was still a disgustingly early hour of the morning – in fact he had not been to bed yet, for as was his wont these days he'd spent the night thinking in the restful solitude of his garden. He had just been contemplating going to bed now, and here she was, interrupting him.

'Yes?' he demanded testily. 'What the blazes do you want at this hour, Eliseth?'

'I'm sorry to disturb you, Archmage...' Smouldering beneath her civility, he could sense a blaze of suppressed excitement. 'It's this old document,' she went on, waving a scroll under his nose. 'I found it last evening in the library, and I've been up all night trying to decipher it. It relates to the Cauldron – it should help you to control its powers, and use it in safety.'

'What?' Suddenly Miathan was wide awake. 'Let me look at that!'

'Certainly.' The Weather-Mage handed the scroll to him, but when he unrolled it he found it was written in a language so ancient, with an ink so faded, that he could barely decipher a word of it. Little did he guess that Eliseth had made certain he could not.

'Don't worry.' She slipped the document from his fingers. 'I can only understand it myself because I've been studying Finbarr's notes over the last months, hoping to find a way to help you...'

Very likely! Miathan thought. Trying to help herself, if he knew anything about it. Yet she had brought the scroll to him...

'It says that there's writing, hidden on the side of the grail,' Eliseth was saying, 'that describes the Spells of Power to control the Cauldron...'

'Sounds like a lot of nonsense to me!' Miathan snorted. 'Hidden spells, indeed!'

'If you fetch the grail,' Eliseth prompted, 'I can try to use the scroll to bring out the secret writing. Surely it's worth a try.'

'Now, just a minute.' At this point, Miathan's suspicions definitely were stirring. He temporized. 'Why don't you make a translation for me and then I'll see how well it works?'

'That's just like you!' Eliseth flared, losing her temper completely. 'You never trust me – you want to keep me out of everything! It was *my* hard work that found the scroll; *my* eyes that got strained translating the accursed thing. And now you want me just to hand it over to you without as much as a please or thank you. Well, you can go to perdition, Miathan. If you won't let me be a part of this, you can whistle for your scroll – and the priceless knowledge it contains.' Taking the brittle parchment in both hands, she made as if to tear it across.

'Wait – wait!' Miathan shouted hastily. 'All right, have it your own way.' He went into the adjoining chamber, and Eliseth heard the grate of shifting furniture, followed by a soft but distinctive click. She raised her eyebrows. So the Archmage had a hidden panel in there, did he? Well, she'd investigate that later. Who knew what other secrets it might hold? Then she put the thought out of her mind as Miathan came back into the room, carrying the blackened, tarnished grail.

As he placed the Artefact on the table between them Eliseth could feel the power that thrummed through it, belying its sorry condition. Without touching it, she examined it closely. 'Couldn't you have cleaned it up a little?' she complained.

'I tried,' Miathan said with a sigh. 'I've tried many times, but since that night it stays as black as ever.'

'Well, there's no trace of secret writing that I can see – but then there wouldn't be. Let's see what our document says ...' Eliseth turned away, as if looking for the scroll – and suddenly whirled back, her fingers extended and pointing at Miathan as she threw all her powers behind the spell that would take him out of time.

Miathan had been expecting an attack on the Cauldron, not on himself, and had prepared his defences accordingly, as Eliseth had hoped. As the Archmage froze in position, taken out of time by her spell, the grail flared with a brief white light and then went dark again. She extended a cautious hand towards the Artefact, all her sense attuned to the slightest hint of more defensive magic – but there was nothing there now save its own, thrumming power.

As the realization of what she had done came home to her, Eliseth laughed aloud in triumph. 'As for you,' she told the frozen Archmage, 'you can go down into the catacombs and keep Finbarr company, until I decide how to dispose of you.'

She knew, with a chilling certainty, that Miathan must never be unbound from the spell. Her life depended on it.

But now there was other work to be done. These next few days would be busy, for she must keep an eye out with her crystal for any sign of her enemy's movements while also working with the grail, to wrest its powers to her will. Eliseth smiled to herself. She was looking forward to it all immensely.

The next few days were also busy ones for Aurian. Now that she had returned, she wanted to put her search for the Sword in motion, and she had no time to waste. Thanks to the generosity of the Nightrunners, she arranged for the provisioning of her little band during the crossing of the moors. With Vannor, however, she had less success. He insisted on joining her, and would not be dissuaded. 'I'm fine now,' he argued. 'Getting my strength back by the day, and Parric is teaching me to fight left-handed. I wouldn't be a burden to you.' From the tacit plea in his voice, she knew the latter was his greatest fear, now that he had lost his hand. There was more here at stake than his safety – he needed desperately to prove himself. Sighing, she gave in, praying she'd made the right decision, though Parric consoled her greatly by promising never to leave the merchant's side. After that, of course, Zanna wanted to come too, but this time the Mage put her foot down firmly, as did the girl's father.

'What?' Aurian had teased him afterwards. 'You want to stop her from being as big a fool as you?'

Yanis, Tarnal and a dozen other smugglers volunteered to join her, but Aurian reasoned that if the Sword was truly in the Vale, her success in finding it would not depend on numbers. Her Xandim were enough for her – and if things were to go wrong it was vital that some of Miathan's opponents should survive. Besides, she particularly wanted Tarnal to stay behind, as he was clearly the best person to console Zanna.

At last – after what seemed an endless round of discussion, preparation, and debate – Aurian and her band were ready to leave the Nightrunners. The Mage said a reluctant farewell to her son, for Wolf and his foster-parents were staying behind in safety, though the wolves were clearly not at home in the crowded caverns of strange humans. Remana had promised to try to find them somewhere more quiet, and to keep an eye on them.

Then, at last, it was time to go.

As she rode out across the cold, dark moors, Aurian felt incredibly relieved to be moving at last. She would have been far less happy some hours later, if she could have looked back to the Nightrunner haven. In the silent hour before dawn, two grey wolves, one of them carrying a cub, emerged stealthily from the hidden entrance to the ponies' cavern. After casting around for a time to find the scent, they loped off across the bleak expanse of heathland, following the Mage's trail.

But other eyes, hostile eyes, saw Aurian set forth towards the Vale. In the Mages' Tower in Nexis, Eliseth put down her crystal thoughtfully, then summoned the captain of her mercenaries to prepare his troops.

26

Lightning-Strike

Dawn was gilding the curled fronds of the new green bracken and the skylarks were climbing in dizzily spirals to shower the earth with song. The early sun shone unchallenged in the east, its splendour defying the heaviness of the air, unusual for spring, and the dark, forbidding stormclouds that were massing on the western horizon. As Aurian crested the final rising swell of moorland, and looked down across the last mile towards the home of her childhood, Schiannath, who was carrying her in his horse-form, hesitated on the brow of the hill and came to an uncertain halt as he felt her body grow tense with doubt and dismay.

'Now what's wrong?' Shia demanded. Khanu, who had also been running at the Mage's side, looked up questioningly.

Aurian stared in disbelief at the dark, impenetrable tangle of trees that surrounded the Valley and filled the bottom of the great bowl of obsidian stone. 'I just don't believe this – I would hardly have known the place. Anvar – what can have happened here? It all looks so different!' The Mage turned to her soulmate who had been riding at her side, borne by Esselnath, the Xandim warrior who had volunteered to carry him; in his horse-shape, a magnificent chestnut stallion who glowed like fire in the golden early light, his coat as deep a burnished red as Aurian's hair.

Anvar rubbed at eyes that felt hot and gritty from a long night's riding with no sleep. 'It was the Phaerie who brought the Wildwood in to guard your mother's Vale – I remember telling you, ages ago, after Hellorin and Eilin rescued me from the Aerillian Moldan, and sent me to find the Harp.' His face darkened in a frown. 'You know, they told me that D'arvan and Maya had been left here as guardians – but I thought they only meant guardians of the Valley. Why the blazes didn't they tell me the Sword was here? Think of all the trouble it would have saved if we had known.'

'I suppose they couldn't – I think the location of the Sword was something I had to discover for myself,' Aurian said thoughtfully. 'Besides, we would still have been forced to pass through the lands of the Xandim.' She glanced cautiously around to make sure that Cygnus was out of earshot. 'You remember how the Skyfolk behaved towards us. They weren't capable of carrying us all the way across the sea in any case, but even had it been possible they would never have consented to do it.'

'I suppose you're right,' Anvar said. 'At least if D'arvan and Maya are the guardians, we should have no difficulty getting through the forest.'

'I hope not, but . . .' A shiver of unease ran up Aurian's spine and she clenched her hands in Schiannath's crow-black mane until he shook his head in protest. 'Anvar, what if D'arvan and Maya were put there to guard the Sword itself? I couldn't bear to think I would have to fight my friends.'

Anvar looked grave – then his jaw tightened with determination. 'Well, there's only one way to find out.'

'Yes,' Shia added tartly, 'and it isn't standing out here in the open in broad daylight like a pack of fools. Come, Aurian – this is no time for hesitation . . .'

Her words tailed off as she was distracted by a rush of wingbeats overhead. Cygnus, who had been scouting ahead, came hurtling down from the skies. 'Move!' the winged man shouted. 'Run! An army approaches, led by a silver-haired woman. They are heading this way at a gallop round the southern side of the forest. If you do not hurry, they will cut you off.'

'Damn!' Aurian cried. 'Eliseth! Come on!' With a bound, Schiannath was racing downhill at a breakneck pace, with Anvar and Esselnath but a pace behind. Together they thundered towards the shelter of the forest, their hair, fiery red and burnished gold, streaming behind them like bright banners in the early morning sun. Behind them galloped their companions and the Xandim, while Cygnus circled like a vulture overhead. Already, coming into the open beyond the dark mass of trees, Aurian could see Eliseth's army, speeding towards them from the west like a wave of darkness, with the storm following fast upon their heels.

D'arvan and Maya, as was their custom, were watching the sun rise over the lake, seeking comfort in one another's company and the peace of the fresh new morning. They had taken to avoiding the rebel encampment lately, unable to bear the grief of Vannor's friends at the news, brought by Bern, of their leader's suffering at the hands of the Magefolk. D'arvan sighed, wishing his worries wouldn't intrude themselves upon this magical moment of the day. It seemed that the heart had gone out of the rebels when they heard of the merchant's capture. The Mage wanted to help them, but how could he? They could neither see him nor hear him – and even if they could, what words of his would be sufficient to allay their grief?

Suddenly the unicorn stiffened, her silver ears pricked forward, as D'arvan caught the sound of an agitated murmuring among the ranks of trees behind him. The word was being passed back through the forest of an armed and mounted troop circling the Wildwood from the west. A moment later came the word of another wave of invaders, riding down like the wind out of the east.

'From the east?' the Mage muttered to Maya, frowning in puzzlement. 'But there's nothing that way but fishing settlements. Where can they be coming from – and who in the name of all the gods can they be?' He felt a stab of anxiety. Eliseth and the Archmage had been quiet far too long – he had been half-expecting something of this kind for a while. 'This has surely got to be some kind of trick.' Leaving the unicorn to guard the bridge according to her task, he hastened away towards the eastern side of the Vale.

Neck and neck, the two Horsefolk carrying the Mages came bounding to an abrupt halt, almost beneath the very eaves of the forest; their companions racing up behind them. There was a moment's hesitation. There was no obvious way into the Wildwood through the dense and tangled growth, and the sinister darkness of the forest was bristling with threat. Anvar looked at Aurian. 'What do we do now?' She dared not use the Staff of Earth yet, lest she betray her possession of the Artefact to Eliseth.

Aurian shrugged helplessly. 'You were the one who met the Forest Lord – I was hoping you might know.'

They could hear the thunder of hoofbeats growing louder as the enemy drew ever closer. Already they were near enough for the Mages to make out the flash of sunlight on naked steel, and to recognize the tall figure that rode at the head of the advancing foes, her silver hair streaming behind her in the wind.

Vannor shouldered his way to the front of the crowding Xandim. 'Don't worry – if the forest remembers me, I'm sure it'll let us in. It had better.' He stepped forward. 'Hey,' he yelled, sending a flock of startled birds rocketing out of the treetops with shrill cries and a reverberant clatter of wings. 'It's me – Vannor. Let me pass!'

Even as he hurried towards the edge of the forest, D'arvan stopped, his mind reeling in shock at the sound of Vannor's voice. But Vannor was captive – or was he? The Mage had harboured suspicions about Bern when the man had first arrived. Had the wretch been lying all along? Or was this simply a ruse of the Archmage's devising, to trick his way into the Wildwood and try to seize the Sword? D'arvan broke into a run. He would have to find out – and quickly.

The companions stood at the bay at the edge of the forest as Eliseth and her cohorts hurtled down upon them. Parric leapt from his mount and positioned himself at Vannor's vulnerable right side. Half of the Xandim, most of whom had been in horse-shape to travel more speedily, began to change quickly back to human form, taking bows and swords from the packs they had been carrying strapped to their backs. Grim-faced, they leapt astride their equine companions and turned to face the foe. Iscalda, in horse-shape with Yazour on her back, took up a position close to Aurian and her brother. Shia snarled and flexed her claws, positioning her self in front of the Mages. Aurian, on the plunging Schiannath, drew her sword. 'Don't use the Artefacts yet – not until we have no choice,' she called to Anvar. 'Wherever Miathan is, it's better if he doesn't know we've got them.' She turned to the merchant. 'Vannor – whatever happens, you stay here. Keep trying to get us into the forest, no matter what.'

The Windeye, who had been carrying Sangra, whinnied shrilly and tossed his head. As the woman slid from his back, he resumed his human shape. 'Lady – let me . . .' Stepping out into the path of Eliseth's approaching warriors, he moved his hands rapidly in the air. The foremost horses reared and screamed, dislodging their terrified riders as the shape of Chiamh's demon materialized in front of them. The charge disintegrated into a rout as horses hurtled into one another and men fled screaming in terror.

Only Eliseth was unmoved by the vision. 'Come back, you fools,' she shrieked, wrenching the head of her plunging horse and holding in the panic-stricken beast so mercilessly that blood dripped from its torn mouth. 'There's nothing there! It's only an illusion!' Suddenly she looked past Chiamh and caught sight of Vannor, and her face turned white with rage. 'How?' she hissed. 'How did you escape me, Mortal? Well, you shall not escape me again!'

Lifting her hand, she reached up to the gathering cloud and launched a sizzling bolt of lightning through the air at the unprotected Windeye. Aurian, moving more quickly than she had ever moved before, flung up a magical shield to surround him and the bolt impacted against the barrier, dissipating in a shower of spitting sparks. But because the shield was also blocking Chiamh's powers the demon vanished abruptly, and the attackers began to take heart once more.

Anvar, in the meantime, had launched his own bolt of force at the Weather-Mage, forcing her to abandon her attack and shield herself, until the captain of the mercenaries picked himself up off the ground, unslung his bow from his back and fired arrow after arrow into the ranks of his companions, who stood at bay, trapped by the forest's wall. Two, three, four of the Xandim screamed and fell. Urged on by their commander's shouted orders, his remaining troops followed his example, and in moments a deadly hail of arrows was streaking down upon the Xandim, forcing the Mages to extend their shields to protect their companions.

Now that both Aurian and Anvar were on the defensive, the Weather-Mage was free to act once more. Again and again, she launched her deadly bolts at the fragile barrier of the shielding, while the arrows kept on raining down. Schiannath and Esselnath displayed their own remarkable brand of courage, standing firm with the Mages on their backs, though they rolled their eyes and trembled at the barrage of magic that was so terrifying to them while they were in equine form. The white mare Iscalda, stalwart as ever, remained firmly beside her brother.

Though she was warmed by her companions' courage, Aurian's heart was sinking. Despite the fact that they were two to Eliseth's one, she and Anvar were hampered by the need to protect so many. They were forced to spread their powers so thinly to cover everyone that gradually, inexorably, their magical barrier began to waver and fade beneath the repeated onslaughts of their foe.

Grimly, Aurian and Anvar held firm until, to their horror, they realized that Eliseth was drawing on more and more power to oppose them. Where is she getting it from? Aurian thought desperately – and then she recognized the surging, barely controllable power of the High Magic. 'Anvar,' she whispered, her voice cracking in horror. 'She's got the Cauldron!'

'Why don't you just give up?' Eliseth taunted, her eyes ablaze with triumph and her flawless face disfigured by a gloating sneer. 'You pathetic, soft-hearted, spineless fools! You can't keep this up much longer. If you surrender now I may spare the miserable lives of the rabble that follow you. Miathan can always use more Mortal slaves.'

'Eat dung, you stinking, verminous sack of bones!' Shia snarled, projecting her mental voice towards the Weather-Mage. 'May maggots gnaw what passes for your brain!'

Eliseth jumped as the cat's abuse echoed unexpectedly in her mind. Her magical attack faltered for a moment as she

405

scanned the ranks of her foes, puzzled as to who had sent the message. Aurian, who had been far too busy concentrating on her shield to formulate a suitable reply herself, glanced at Shia. 'Very nice,' she muttered. 'I couldn't have put it better.' It was all she had time for before Eliseth, white with anger at the insult, renewed her attack with redoubled force, sending white flares of energy rippling across the magical barrier, which was beginning to smoke and spark.

Anvar turned to Aurian, his face taut with strain. 'We can't keep this up much longer – not against the Cauldron.' He spoke through gritted teeth. 'Soon we'll be forced to use the Artefacts.'

'I know.' Somehow, Aurian managed to force the words out. 'But not until the shield goes . . .' But the shield was already beginning to buckle. With a sinking heart, Aurian realized they had only a few more minutes . . .

As he reached the edge of the forest, D'arvan could hear the whistle of arrows through the air. He was almost knocked from his feet by the reek of evil magic. Gasping, he took in the scene before him. Aurian – it was Aurian, returned, and with her Anvar and Parric . . . And, by all the gods, there was Vannor; definitely the merchant and not some illusion. He was very much alive, and screaming curses at the unyielding forest that denied him entry. But who were the strangers with them? No matter. The Mage's eyes went to Eliseth, her eyes ablaze with hate and triumph, attacking Aurian's crumbling shield . . .

D'arvan acted quickly, calling to the Wildwood. The trees, uneasy about the battle that was waging at their feet, resisted him. Grasping the Lady Eilin's staff tightly, the Mage put forth all his power until, slowly and reluctantly, he felt the forest yielding to his will.

Vannor, incredulous, saw the widening gap in the ranks of trees. His heart leapt fiercely within him. 'Come on,' he called to the huddled, beleaguered Xandim. 'This way – hurry!' They needed no second telling. Vannor was forced to jump quickly to one side as they rushed past him into the shelter of the forest, until only Parric, the cats, Chiamh, Yazour and Iscalda remained. Eliseth's face turned ugly with rage as she saw how she was being thwarted. Fuelled and impelled by her wrath, the force of her bolts increased against the disintegrating shield. Vannor, realizing that the Mages and their two Horsefolk could not retreat until everyone was safe, urged the remaining companions after the fleeing Xandim. 'Move, you bloody idiots,' he roared. 'Don't just stand there – you're holding everyone up!'

Luckily they saw the sense in what he was saying, and reluctantly obeyed him. Shia stopped beside him to wait for Aurian, fixing him with a baleful glare that froze his blood. Chiamh also waited. 'When I change, get on my back quickly,' he told the merchant. 'I will bear you swiftly away from our foes.' Once everyone else had scurried to safety, Vannor mounted Chiamh, who turned back from the edge of the forest. 'Aurian, Anvar – now!' the merchant shouted. 'Everyone's safe. Get out of there!'

Schiannath and Esselnath wheeled as one, and came hurtling back towards the safety of the trees. Behind them, the shield collapsed in a final shower of sparks, and a scorching bolt of lightning ripped up the turf at their heels. Eliseth gave a scream of rage when she saw her prey escaping. She spurred her horse to follow, hurling thunderbolts and curses, but it was already too late. The trees of the forest closed ranks quickly, their branches entwining and a bristling barrier of thorns and briars springing up around them as the way snapped shut before Eliseth's face. Cursing, the Weather-Mage turned away, and did not see the two wolves, a bowshot away from where she stood as they ran from behind the cover of a gorse-bush. Dangling securely from the female's mouth by the loose skin on its neck was a very young cub. Soundlessly, they slipped into the forest, following Aurian's trail – and the trees parted swiftly to let them pass, and closed again behind them.

Still shaky from the narrowness of their escape, the companions went on into the shadowy depths of the Wildwood; too weary to talk, not daring to stop; following the easy path that had opened up ahead of them. At the brink of the Vale itself, where a beck from the moorland threaded its way between the trees to tumble down the black walls of the crater in a shimmering cascade, D'arvan arranged a clearing for the fugitives, so that they could regroup and rest a little before making the final descent into the Valley. He stood back from the edge of the open space, invisible to the clustered Xandim, and waited, fidgeting with impatience and consumed with curiosity, for the Mages to arrive.

When they reached the clearing, on Horsefolk who were stumbling with fatigue, Aurian and Anvar slid down from their mounts to let Schiannath and Esselnath change back to their human shapes. 'Thank the goddess for that!' Schiannath pushed back a straggle of dark, curling hair from his sweating forehead. 'I must confess that there were times, back there, when I thought I'd never get the chance to wear my human form again.'

'Herdlord, you were a true hero.' Aurian embraced him. 'Had it not been for the courage of yourself and Esselnath, standing firm despite all that Eliseth could throw at you, Anvar and I could never have kept up our shields. We would all have perished. We owe you our lives.'

'As we owe you ours, Lady – for without your shields we would have stood no chance,' Schiannath replied gravely. 'Having only known you and Anvar, not to mention the Windeye, I never realized how potent a force magic could be when turned to evil. I came to help you willingly, but today, for the first time, I truly understand how vital our quest is to the fate of the world.'

As the Horsefolk went off to the stream to drink, Aurian and Anvar hugged each other in wordless relief, but they knew the reprieve could only be temporary. 'How long do you think we have?' Anvar asked the Mage.

Aurian shrugged. 'Who can say? The forest seemed pretty determined to keep her out, but we're dealing with Eliseth here – and now she possesses the Cauldron, too. Knowing her, I don't think it will daunt her for long.'

'There's one thing that puzzles me,' Anvar muttered, with a frown. 'If Eliseth has the Cauldron, what has become of

Miathan? He wouldn't voluntarily give such power into her hands, so what has she done with him? And how did she manage it? He must still be alive, for we never felt him die.' He grimaced. 'It would be the ultimate irony if we ended up having to rescue the Archmage from Eliseth.'

'If we do,' said his soulmate grimly, 'Miathan had better pray for someone to rescue him from us.'

Quickly, Aurian healed the wounded who had been hit by the first of the enemy arrows, and thought sadly of the three who were no longer with them. But this was no time to dwell on sorrowful thoughts. As soon as everyone had been attended to, she and Anvar gathered their companions together. 'Time is pressing, and we can't stay here any longer,' Aurian told them, raising her voice over a chorus of curses and groans. 'Vannor, Parric and Sangra – you take half our forces and go to the rebel encampment. Gather them as quickly as you can and head for the lake – we'll meet you there. If Eliseth does manage to get into the forest, we don't want her anywhere near the Sword – especially not when I'm trying to claim it. Anvar and I will go directly to the island with Chiamh, Yazour and the cats and the remaining Horse-folk. Cygnus, I want you circling over the forest to bring us news of the enemy, and keep up communications between the two groups in case anyone runs into trouble. Now sort yourselves quickly, everyone, and let's get on with this.'

Parric, hearing an echo of Forral in every word she said, caught Vannor's eye and shared a smile as they went to pick out the troops that would go with them.

D'arvan, watching from the shadows of the trees, felt his heart falter when Aurian spoke of the Sword of Flame. Dear gods – then she must be the One! But in order to claim it, she must fight Maya, who, in the shape of the invisible unicorn, was bound by Hellorin's geas to defend the island and its bridges against anyone who approached. And he had no way to warn Aurian of the identity of her assailant.

The Mage of the Forest felt himself beginning to tremble. This was dreadful news – that two close friends should be thrown into such peril and contention for the sake of the

Sword. For the first time, he began to appreciate the two-edged nature of this terrible Artefact, and he had a dire suspicion that it had further secrets to unfold. Not for the first time, D'arvan found himself wondering if it would not have been better if the Sword had never come to light.

At least he could be with them – perhaps when the battle started there would be some way he could intervene. He was just beginning to follow Aurian and her companions as they picked their careful way down the steep, rocky walls of the crater when he heard the first sinister growls of thunder, and perceived the rapidly increasing agitation of the nearby trees. As he became attuned to their agony and anger, D'arvan went cold all over with horror. Eliseth had found a way to break into the Wildwood! His assistance was needed on the eastern border of the forest, lest all be lost. For a moment, D'arvan hesitated, impossibly torn between two agonizing choices: should he go to help Maya and Aurian, or rush to the defence of the Wildwood? But, he realized, he had no choice at all. It was doubtful that he'd be permitted to interfere in the claiming of the Sword – events would weave themselves as they must. But Eliseth could not be allowed to intervene. With a muttered oath, D'arvan turned away from the drama that was about to play itself out within the crater, and rushed back to help defend the eastern border.

Eliseth, seething with frustration at being thwarted by Aurian and this accursed forest, had reacted initially by taking out her temper on her troops, cursing and shouting abuse as she urged them to greater efforts in their fruitless attempts to hack a way into the thorny tangle of undergrowth. After a time, when she realized that her ranting and railing was accomplishing nothing but to alienate her followers, she had calmed down a little, and begun to think the situation through.

Clearly these trees must be protected by some magical force from within the Vale, for axes and swords had no effect on them and she had already been losing her men: several had been either throttled or blinded by thorny briars; not a few felled into unconsciousness by branches that had broken off and dropped down on them; and one who had unwisely tried to kindle a fire against the dry bark of a dying old beech, and had been crushed by the weight when the entire tree had seemingly uprooted itself and fallen on him. Eliseth thought she had guessed the identity of the forest's protector: Eilin, Aurian's mother. That accursed rebel Earth-Mage who had turned her back on the Magefolk long ago would naturally be doing her best to protect her daughter.

'Damn her!' the Weather-Mage snarled. Suddenly this battle had taken a far more personal turn, for it must also have been Eilin who had caused the death of Davorshan, who'd been Eliseth's lover at the time. 'I'll show her.' She turned to the mercenaries. 'Stand back,' she ordered. 'I intend to break a way into this accursed forest if I have to blast every tree to cinders!'

An angry rustle passed through the branches of the Wildwood, as though the trees had heard and accepted her challenge. Their mistake, thought Eliseth grimly. She did not intend to be kept from her goal by this pile of kindling! Standing well back from the trees, the Mage reached out to the lowering stormclouds above, and the dull, booming echoes of thunder began to roll around the Valley. With a cry of triumph, Eliseth extended her fingers into claws and pulled splintering forks of lightning down from the skies.

The bolts came sizzling down to earth, striking the trees near the edge of the forest, exploding them into flying splinters and igniting them in roaring gouts of flame. Eliseth's Magefolk senses could pick up their high, thin shrieks of agony as the fire began to catch and spread from bough to shrivelling bough. Smiling a cold smile that none the less held great satisfaction, she continued to pull down bolt after bolt of lightning from the tortured skies, kindling the trees like torches. As though she was back at her own fireside, Eliseth held out her hand to the shimmering heat of the flames. Since she had not felt the death pangs of a Mage, she must assume that Aurian had escaped the fire, but it didn't matter. Very soon now she would be in the Valley – and then it would be time to settle old scores.

27

The Sword of Flame

Finding the rebel encampment was simplicity itself to Vannor. Just as they had done for him when he had last been here, the trees simply opened up a path in the direction he wanted to take. The rebel leader looked around him, suddenly feeling happy despite the peril they were in and the ominous grumble of the storm above. He was not useless after all; his life had not been over when he'd lost his hand. Parric had been teaching him to fight left-handed and, though he had more sense than to trust his life yet to these new-learned skills, he had come through his first battle without dishonour and still in one piece. Apart from which, the expression of thwarted rage on Eliseth's face when she had seen him had been well worth waiting for.

Vannor was also glad to be back in the Valley, which had been such a haven for himself and his little band of rebels. How he was looking forward to seeing them all – especially Dulsina, who must be worried sick about him by now. No doubt he'd better steel himself for a tongue-lashing from her the like of which he'd never known. Vannor grinned. He'd let her have her say, and then hug the breath from her before she could scold him any further.

His eyes twinkling in anticipation, the rebel leader turned to Parric, who had elected to ride next to him, insisting on sticking to Vannor's vulnerable right side. 'It's a pity that you missed all this before, through going south. What do you think of the forest, then?'

The cavalry master scowled darkly. 'Frankly, I don't like it one little bit,' he retorted, to Vannor's great surprise. 'I hate these bloody trees – they give me the creeps. Trees should stick in one place if you ask me, not go roaming about dropping branches on people, no matter that it did save our skins

412

back there. Who is behind all this – have you ever wondered? And how can we be sure they'll stay on our side?'

'Oh, come on, Parric,' Vannor protested. 'Of course the forest is on our side – it always has been, since first I brought the rebels here, and the wolves and trees killed Angos and his mercenaries.'

'Well, even if it is,' the cavalry master argued stubbornly, 'there's no guarantee that it can protect us against Eliseth. If you don't believe me, why don't you look behind you?'

Obediently, Vannor glanced back over his shoulder. Far away on the eastern borders, a thick, black column of smoke was rising to mingle with the brooding skies.

'Thara's curse upon her! What is that bitch Eliseth doing to my poor Valley?' In the unearthly realm of the Phaerie, Eilin sat in the Forest Lord's strange palace, her face pressed to the mysterious window that looked out upon the Mortal world. Her attention was torn away from the dreadful events that were taking place in the forest by the sound of hasty footfalls behind her.

'You sent for me, Lady?' Hellorin's voice held a faint edge of irritation. Doubtless he was not accustomed to being so peremptorily summoned in his own land. Eilin, however, was not impressed, for her Mage's temper was hasty enough to match the worst of his rages. Running to take his arm she all but dragged him up the steps towards the great circular window.

'Look at that!' she demanded, her voice breaking with anger and grief. 'Just look at what is happening out there! After all my years of labour to make the Valley fruitful again, Eliseth is destroying the forest. Oh, hear the trees screaming! I heard their cries of agony in my very dreams, and when I woke and came to look . . . And where is D'arvan? Why is he letting her do this? My Lord, she must be stopped.'

'Courage, Lady.' Hellorin's fingers closed on her shoulder. There was a grim edge to the Forest Lord's voice. 'There is nothing we can do to stop her. We Phaerie are imprisoned here, helpless – unless . . .' Suddenly a strange, wild light kindled within the fathomless depths of his eyes. 'Why

is the renegade Magewoman attacking the forest? My Lady –
have you thought to search for your daughter?'

'Aurian? Here?' Eilin cried, whirling back towards the
window. She concentrated her will upon the thought of her
daughter, and the image of the burning forest wavered and
vanished in mist. When it cleared, the window showed her
. . . 'Dear gods – she is! She's heading for my island, with
Anvar and a lot of strangers.'

Suddenly Eilin was roughly thrust aside as the Forest
Lord flattened his face to the crystal panes, and gave a roar
of delight. 'The horses! O Phaerie, in this glad hour, our
steeds have returned!' He turned to the Magewoman, his
eyes gleaming in a face alight with excitement and a savage
joy. 'Eilin – this can only mean one thing! Your daughter has
come to claim the Sword of Fire, as was foretold – and, when
she takes it, at long last the Phaerie will be free!'

'If she can take it, you mean,' Eilin murmured, in a voice
too low for him to hear. She turned away from Hellorin so
that he would not see her frown. She was thinking, not about
the Phaerie, but about those poor Horsefolk out there who
would suddenly turn back to simple beasts if Aurian claimed
the sword. More than that, she was worrying about D'arvan,
under attack in the beleaguered forest. Had Hellorin forgotten that his only son was out there, under attack? And what
of Maya, who must fight her daughter, though the women
were the closest of friends? But most of all, her heart was
filled with fear for Aurian, who must undertake the perilous
task of claiming the Sword of Flame. Shutting her ears to the
glad cries of Phaerie voices, Eilin turned back to the window
and began to pray.

D'arvan ran through the storm-darkened Wildwood in the
bottom of the bowl towards the rising column of smoke upon
the eastern rim of the Valley, the death screams of the forest
ringing in his ears. Even as he ran, he knew he was too late.
The Mage's thoughts were bitter. His father and the Lady
Eilin had trusted him, but he, D'arvan, had already failed of
his guardianship. To wreak such destruction, Eliseth must
possess a power far beyond his own. It seemed that Aurian

had been right – the Weather-Mage must have somehow stolen the Cauldron of Rebirth from Miathan. And what can I do, he thought wildly, to counter one of the ancient Artefacts of the High Magic?

He knew he could do nothing. His only hope must lie in Aurian claiming the Sword of Flame. He must go back to the island at once, where he should have gone in the first place. It seemed that he was under an evil star today, for all his choices were turning out to be wrong. Cursing, he took one last, despairing look at the blazing rim of the Vale before turning back towards the lake – and froze, a cry of horror on his lips. The conflagration had reached the upper edge of the cliffs, where he had counted on it to be stopped by the steep stone walls, but even as he watched the burning trees began to topple, crashing over the precipice like comets trailing tails of flame. New smoke rose up to darken the skies as the trees below began to catch, and now another horror intruded itself upon D'arvan's ravaged consciousness – for the Valley was home and haven to many creatures of the wild.

The very air groaned beneath the burden of a host of birds who had taken abruptly to the skies, swooping and piping piteously, and colliding with one another in confusion. The undergrowth began to stir and rustle as mouse and vole scampered for safety and snakes shot out into the open, their forked tongues flicking in and out to taste the smoke. Squirrels swung shrieking through the branches overhead. The first terrified animals began to stream past the Mage, fleeing for their lives from the spreading fire. Wild-eyed deer leapt past him down the forest trails, their white tails flagged high in alarm. Wolves streamed after them like a grey mist curling through the trees. Sleepy badgers, confused by this new-made night, blundered through the bushes. Hare and rabbit bounded between the trees in perfect safety, for their enemies, the sinuous stoat and weasel and the elegant bold-brushed fox, were also occupied in fleeing for their lives. D'arvan gathered his scattered wits and called to all the terrified creatures. 'Head for the lakes, O forest-dwellers! Seek out the water – there is safety there!'

He was turning hastily to follow his own advice when he

heard a pitiful whimper coming from the nearby bushes. D'arvan ran forward into the thickening smoke, following the tiny thread of sound. Plunging his hand into a tangle of briars without a thought for his own skin, he groped, touched fur – and brought out a young wolf-cub, little more than two moons old. It seemed to have been in the fire already, for patches of its dark-grey fur were singed darker from smouldering sparks. 'How did you get there?' D'arvan muttered in surprise. 'Did your parents get frightened by the fire and forget you?' But there was no time to wonder. Thrusting the squirming wolf-child into the pocket of his robe, he fled towards the lake.

As Aurian and her companions picked their cautious way down to the floor of the crater, events seemed to have come full circle in the Mage's life, and she was transported back to the time when, as a tangle-haired and grubby-kneed urchin, she had first guided Forral down into the Valley. She seemed to feel him very near her, on this dark day.

Impatiently, Aurian shook her head. And if he *was* here, she thought to herself, the first thing he'd tell you would be to stop this woolgathering! There was too much at stake, now, for that. Aurian glanced worriedly behind her, towards the eastern border of the Vale, and the pall of smoke that hung over it. 'Hurry!' she urged the others in a low voice. 'It looks as though Eliseth is gaining on us!'

Willingly, Schiannath quickened his pace, but there was no clear trail through the tangled forest, and there was too much undergrowth and too many twining roots for the horses to gallop. Aurian swore. It seemed that the trees were too perturbed now to open up a proper path for the companions. Thinking quickly, she laid a hand on the Staff of Earth, and reached out her will towards the Wildwood.

No sooner had she touched the Staff than the Mage was almost knocked from Schiannath's back as the full rage and agony of the trees came blasting into her mind. The Valley itself was burning! Frantically, she put forth her powers to soothe the forest, begging the trees to clear a way and let her through. 'Don't fight the Evil One,' she told them. 'Protect

yourselves. If you flee from your burning brethren and surround them with a barren, open space, the fire will claim no
more of you. Let Eliseth come to the lake if she must. Open
up a path for her by all means – but let it be a long one.'

Suddenly, Aurian grinned to herself. 'She does not know
the Valley. Lead her around by circuitous routes, and delay
her as long as you can – but as soon as she becomes impatient let her through to the lake, and I will deal with her.
Many of you were my childhood companions. I played
among you and you sheltered me with your branches. I
would lose no more of you today.'

From the trees came a rustling murmur of assent, like a
soft breeze in the branches. The Mage heard her companions gasp as a broad avenue appeared before them. As
Aurian rode into it at the head of her little column, the trees
of the Valley bowed down their branches in homage and in
thanks. 'Follow!' Aurian cried. 'To the lake!' Schiannath
neighed shrilly and reared, then broke into a bounding gallop
as they raced towards the centre of the Vale.

The rebel camp was in chaos and utter turmoil as its inhabitants raced about, packing up their slender goods and
preparing to flee the burning Valley. Dulsina seemed to be
needed everywhere at once; to calm, to help, to organize and
advise. Fional and Hargorn were assisting her in the evacu-
ation – at least, the young archer was doing his best, but he
seemed to be best at getting under her feet, she thought impatiently. Hargorn's battle-trained bellow, however, was
proving extremely useful, and she was glad that the veteran
had left the Nightrunners as soon as his wound had healed,
leading back the group of Nexian fugitives who had elected
to join the rebels.

Vannor heard the shouted orders in the distance as he
hurried through the trees at the head of his Xandim warriors.
'Why, I know that voice,' he exclaimed. 'It's – '

'It's Hargorn!' Parric yelled delightedly, attempting to spur
his mount to greater speed before remembering, belatedly,
that he was riding one of the Xandim. 'Sorry,' he apologized

hastily. The horse whinnied and shook its head in irritation, but obligingly picked up its pace.

When they reached the edge of the trees, they found that the clearing of the rebel encampment was filled with a mass of panic-stricken folk running, lifting, shoving, tripping, and generally trying to do everything at once. It seemed impossible that he could pick one single figure out of the seething mass, but Vannor's eyes went unerringly to the tall, dark-haired figure of Dulsina.

'Dulsina!' he bellowed, his face breaking into a grin. 'I'm back!'

The result was not what he had expected. Utter silence descended on the clearing as everyone turned to stare at him, open-mouthed. And Dulsina – his brave, level-headed, sensible housekeeper – whirled to look at him, her face stark-white and blank with shock. 'Vannor!' she whispered, and crumpled to the ground in a dead faint.

'Don't just stand there.' Vannor roared. 'Somebody help her!' Leaping down from his horse, he ran to her side, with Parric close behind him. When he reached her, she was already opening her eyes, with Hargorn helping her struggle up into a sitting position. But the veteran was looking at Vannor, and his eyes were suspiciously bright.

'I thought you must be dead,' he gasped. 'Bern said that the Magefolk meant to kill you.'

'You thoughtless, boneheaded idiot,' Dulsina interrupted furiously, her eyes sparkling with her anger. 'Did you ever find Zanna? Where in all perdition have you been these last few months? Didn't you care about the anguish you were putting us through?'

Abruptly, Vannor decided to forgo the tongue-lashing after all. Throwing his arms around Dulsina, he hugged her tightly until she squeaked in protest. 'Yes, I found the lass,' he told her, 'or she found me, at any rate. She's safe with your sister now.'

Letting go of her reluctantly, he turned to the waiting rebels. 'Come on,' he told them. 'Explanations will have to wait – we've got to get to the lake as quickly as possible. Just take all the weapons you can come by and leave the rest of this stuff where it is. Fetch the horses – those who don't have mounts will ride double with the rest of us. Don't stand there gaping – move!'

As they scurried to obey him, something that Hargorn had said nudged its way into Vannor's memory. He grabbed the veteran by the arm, detaining him. 'Hargorn, who the blazes is this Bern?'

Hargorn shrugged. 'Just some fugitive from Nexis who came to us a while ago. He said you'd sent him with a message, but he thought they intended to kill you.' His brows knitted in a scowl as he realized how badly the rebels had been duped.

'Come to think of it,' Dulsina added, her voice sharp with anger, 'I haven't seen him since the fire started.'

'It's not surprising,' Vannor replied, but he had an uneasy feeling that, whoever this Bern might be, they hadn't seen the last of him.

Beside the bridge the unicorn waited. For those with eyes to see her, she shone more brightly than the evenstar itself in the shadowed murk of the beleaguered Vale. But no one could see her beauty save D'arvan, and she sensed that he was far away, though returning to her swiftly. But still more swiftly came another – the One with whose fate she was so closely entwined. The unicorn pricked up her ears, and turned her lovely head towards the east with a toss of her silver mane. In the distance, far around the lakeside, she could see a group of riders emerging from the trees. Two figures rode together at their head, both blazing bright with power. Maya would have recognized them, but the unicorn saw them only as invaders, trespassing on forbidden ground that she must defend. But – and she pawed the ground in puzzlement, scattering sunbursts from her gleaming hooves – there shouldn't be two powers. Which of them was the One – who, in claiming the Sword, could set her free at last – or send her to her death? Until she could find out, she would have to fight them both.

Aurian's heart twisted within her as she emerged from the

forest on to the open turf of the lakeside, and saw that the island was bare now of the tower where she had spent her early years with her mother and Forral. She turned to Anvar, who was riding by her side. 'The tower!' she cried. 'It's gone. Why didn't Chiamh warn me when he performed his seeing?' She knew she was being irrational, but it seemed as though someone had wrenched her childhood away from her. Though she had rarely visited the tower in recent years, she had always felt secure in the knowledge that it was there.

Anvar glanced back at the Windeye, who was in his human form and riding Iscalda, who had refused to be parted from her brother. 'How could he have warned you, when he didn't know there was a tower here in the first place?' he asked her reasonably. 'Hellorin told me, but I forgot,' he added in apology. 'It was destroyed when Davorshan came here to kill your mother. The Lady Eilin knows about it,' he added, trying to comfort her. 'She didn't seem upset.'

Aurian made no reply. She was still staring at the little isle, denuded of its tower. 'I don't see any sign of the Sword,' she muttered worriedly. As they rode closer, however, he saw her eyes widen, and her gaze become intense. 'Anvar,' she whispered, her voice rising with excitement. 'It *is* there. Chiamh was right – the Sword is on the island! Can't you feel it?'

'I can't feel anything,' Anvar answered, frowning. 'Perhaps only you can sense its presence, because you're the One for whom it was created.' He stamped firmly on the small green snake of jealousy that stirred in the back of his mind. They couldn't both wield the Artefact, after all, and this had been Aurian's quest from the beginning. Besides, from the way that Hellorin had talked about it, the Sword, of all the Artefacts of Power, seemed more a burden than a blessing.

While they talked they had rounded the lakeshore, and at last the slender wooden bridge came into sight. 'I'm glad the bridge survived, at any rate,' Aurian said, suddenly practical again. 'We'd have had problems getting across without it – the lake is very deep there.'

Her words were drowned in a thunder of approaching hoofbeats. She looked around wildly – there was no one there. But the hoofbeats kept coming, growing louder and

420

louder. "Ware!' Aurian shouted, pulling the Staff of Earth from her belt, but it was too late. Suddenly Schiannath stumbled, as though pushed aside by some unseen force. Aurian threw her weight back to help him keep his footing – and as he recovered she heard the sound of screaming: a horse in mortal torment. Esselnath, the Xandim who had carried Anvar, was rolling in agony on the ground, his gleaming chestnut coat dyed with the deeper red of his blood; the loops of his gut bulging out of a long wound in his belly that looked as though it had been ripped open by a sword.

Anvar, who had rolled clear of the thrashing mount, was just picking himself up when the sounds of the hoofbeats bore down on them again. 'Schiannath!' Aurian screamed, and the great horse wheeled and sped towards her soulmate. She grabbed Anvar's wrist and yanked him up behind her as some unseen thing whistled past them, blowing her hair back with the wind of its speed.

Aurian glanced over her shoulder, hardly daring to look, but Anvar was safe on Schiannath's back behind her, gaping at the ragged rent that had appeared in his sleeve. 'Gods!' he cried. 'What is it?'

Whatever it was, it was heading back towards them. The remaining Xandim scattered in all directions. One of them fell, pierced through the chest, and its rider did not get up again. Shia leapt towards the sound of the hoofbeats, and was hurled backwards, yowling. Khanu ran to her side, snarling fiercely, as the great cat staggered to her feet. Chiamh galloped towards the Magefolk on Iscalda's back. His eyes were blazing with the silver of his Othersight.

As the pounding grew louder, Schiannath waited until the very last second and wrenched himself aside – but the weight of two riders slowed him, and he squealed as a thin red line of blood sprang out of nowhere across his shoulder. The hoofbeats hesitated, veered towards the Windeye, then –

'I see it!' Chiamh yelled. 'I see it – it's a unicorn!'

And suddenly there were no more hoofbeats. Only the slender, leather-clad figure of Maya, standing dazed upon the grass.

Aurian let out a whoop and hurled herself from Schiannath's back.

'Wait!' Anvar reached down to grab her arm. 'It might be some kind of trick!'

'It's not a trick.' Maya seemed unsure of her own voice. 'I was the guardian.' Her brow creased with the effort to remember. 'In the shape of the unicorn, I didn't recognize you.' She looked regretfully at the bodies of the Xandim in the grass, and Shia, who glanced up from licking her bruised side to glare at her. 'I'm so very sorry about all this, but I couldn't help it. I had no choice but to attack you. Hellorin told me I was to defend the Sword, but if I became visible to anyone save D'arvan my guardianship would end, and I could return to human form. He said that the One would find a way to see me.' She turned to Chiamh. 'Are you the One?'

'Certainly not,' said the Windeye decisively. 'Aurian is – the Dragon told her so. I was only the means that she used to see you.'

'But how did you see me?' Maya demanded. 'No one could!'

Aurian had been wondering much the same thing.

'Oh, I can see all sorts of things with my Othersight,' said the Windeye cheerfully. 'If I can perceive the wind itself, then a unicorn made up of light shouldn't present too much of a problem. If only I wasn't so shortsighted, I would have seen you sooner, and saved a lot of trouble.' He sighed wistfully. 'I'm sorry the others couldn't see you, though. You were so very beautiful . . .'

'Meaning that I'm not now, I suppose,' snapped Maya. 'Well, things are certainly back to normal.' She held out her hands to Aurian. 'I'm very glad to see *you*, though.'

And Aurian ran to embrace her friend.

'Just how far is it to this blasted lake?' Eliseth muttered irritably. Having once gained entry, she seemed to have been wandering around in this benighted forest for ever. Her stupid escort seemed to have lost themselves, too, but that didn't matter now. They had served their purpose, and after her victory over the Wildwood the Weather-Mage felt quite invincible. With the refashioned Cauldron, she had such power at her command . . .

Eliseth pulled the tarnished chalice from the pocket of her robe and looked at it thoughtfully. Who would have thought that so small a thing could hold so much power? And now something was calling it, pulling it towards the lake. Could another of the Artefacts be hidden there? It would certainly explain how that wretched Eilin had gained enough power to murder Davorshan. Eliseth scowled. Well, soon she would see for herself. She had taken one of the Artefacts from its rightful owner; it shouldn't be difficult to steal another, especially not from Eilin. At least, it wouldn't, if she could only find that accursed lake . . .

She had not ridden much further down the narrow, twisting trail when she heard the cries for help. Spurring her lathered horse to greater speed, she rounded a corner to see a familiar figure, suspended and writhing in the branches of a tree that seemed to be tightening around him.

'Bern!' snapped the Weather-Mage. 'What the blazes are you doing here? You were told to stick with the rebels.'

'I did,' Bern wailed. 'But when they saw the fire they started to move camp, and I knew it must be you and came to warn you. Please get me down, Lady.'

'You should have gone with them, you fool,' said Eliseth. 'Now how will I know where they were heading?'

None the less, she turned to face the tree and lifted her hand in a threatening gesture. 'Let him down,' she snarled, 'or . . .'

There was a thud as Bern fell to the ground, almost weeping with relief. 'Oh, thank you, Lady!' He picked himself up, wincing, and seemed suddenly at a loss. 'What shall we do now?'

'Well, I am going to the lake, you wretched Mortal,' Eliseth told him. 'If you want to come with me, you'll have to keep up – I'm not waiting for you. I've had enough of wandering around this accursed forest.' She scowled. 'If the trees don't let me through, I'll burn them, as I did the others.'

'But you don't need to, Lady,' Bern protested. 'Look – the track's right there.'

The Weather-Mage turned to follow his pointing finger

and cursed vilely. 'That wasn't there before. Are you sure it's the right trail?'

'It's heading in the right direction, Lady. If you follow me, I'll set you right.'

Eliseth shrugged. Well, it was better than wandering round in circles, as she seemed to have been doing.

'Go on then,' she told Bern, 'and hurry up about it. And remember – if you lead me wrongly, I'll make you sorry you were ever born.'

'Don't worry, Lady – I know the way.' And off he went, scrambling ahead of her along the forest trail. Eliseth shrugged again, and followed.

Aurian was walking slowly across the bridge, her footsteps echoing hollowly on the wooden planks. D'arvan saw her from the lakeshore, where he had set the little wolf-cub safely down a moment ago, and his heart leapt in relief to see also, among the knot of people gathered at the mainland end of the bridge, his Maya, safe and sound – and human again. So far, then, Aurian had succeeded. He might have guessed she would. But the next part – the winning of the Sword itself – would prove more difficult. Anxiously, he hurried off to join them – and suddenly remembered that they should be able to see him now. Gods – it had been so long . . . Stifling a cry of joy, he broke into a run, forgetting all about the cub, who had wandered off into the bushes.

Cygnus soared over the lake, and caught sight of the little group of watchers by the bridge. There was Aurian, crossing to the island on her own – and there was Anvar, standing a little apart from the others at the very edge of the wooden span, his eyes fixed on the retreating figure of the Mage. He was alone now, and distracted . . . Cygnus smiled to himself. His chance had come at last, to seize the Harp of Winds! Banking into a steep turn, the winged man swooped towards his unsuspecting victim.

Vannor led his rebels out of the forest and saw the tableau by the bridge, around the curving sweep of the lake. What in the

424

world were the Magefolk doing? Was the Sword hidden somewhere on the island? Then Parric nudged him sharply in the ribs. 'Vannor – over there!'

The merchant looked across the lake and saw Eliseth emerging from the trees on the opposite side. She seemed about as far from the bridge as he was. Vannor cursed. There was no sense in shouting a warning – they probably wouldn't hear him from this distance, and besides, at this point, it might be fatal to interrupt Aurian's concentration. 'Come on – we've got to warn Anvar,' he told the Xandim he was riding, and it took off with him into a gallop, with the rest of the rebels following. Eliseth, on the other side of the lake, had seen them now, and had also spurred her horse into a run. But which of them would get there first?

As Aurian crossed the bridge she was oblivious of the dramas that were going on around her. The Sword of Flame was calling to her now; holding all her attention in thrall. But she knew that winning it would not be easy. There was bound to be some kind of test or trial – there had been with the other Artefacts. Suddenly, she was glad she had made Anvar stay behind, despite his protests. This could get dangerous, and she would need all her concentration on the task ahead.

Stepping off the bridge, Aurian caught sight of a great grey boulder where the tower had once stood. She frowned. Where had that come from? It had certainly not been there before. Its granite was a different stone entirely from the black basalt of the Valley, from which the base of Eilin's tower had been constructed. The Mage approached it cautiously, the warsong of the Sword ringing louder in her mind. Carefully, she put a hand out to touch the massive rock – and it changed under her fingers to a giant crystal that pulsed with a light that was the crimson of new blood. Within the dully glowing facets of the gem she could discern the gleaming outline of a Sword, created for her hand alone, that called out to her in its harsh metallic voice to free it form its prison.

Aurian grinned, but a warning voice was sounding in the

back of her mind. Surely it couldn't be this easy? The winning of the Staff had been so difficult . . .

None the less, the Mage reached out and laid her hands upon the crystal, searching with her healer's senses for any weaknesses within the lattice of the stone as she had done once, long ago, in the tunnels beneath Dhiammara. Swiftly she found the spot and jabbed at it with all her powers, shattering the crystalline structure. With a sighing whisper, the great gem crumbled away to sparkling dust, and the Sword of Flame leapt out into Aurian's hand.

Aurian sank to her knees as a surge of fiery power consumed her in agonizing ecstasy. The world faded away into a pulsing crimson haze as the song of the Sword rang loudly in her mind.

'You are the One, as was foretold, and you have found me – but before you can wield my powers I must first be claimed, as you claimed the Staff of Earth. There must be a bloodbond between us, Warrior – a sacrifice. The first blood I drink must be the lifeblood of someone you love. Then, and only then, will I be yours to command.'

The world returned to Aurian with a jolt as she recoiled in horror. 'What?' she snapped reflexively. 'I'll do no such thing!' The warning of the Leviathan came flooding back to her. 'How can I use you for good,' she demanded, 'if I begin my ownership with such an unspeakable act?'

'Then I am forfeit, and you have failed.'

And suddenly everything began to go wrong at once.

With the sound of a thunderclap, the ranks of the Phaerie appeared to throng the lakeshore, led by the towering figure of Hellorin, the Forest Lord. 'Free,' he cried. 'After all these long ages, we are free at last. The One has failed to claim the Sword, therefore we no longer need to pledge allegiance to her. Come, my followers – we must ride!'

Eilin cried out in protest at his side, but he ignored her.

As Aurian looked on in horror, the Xandim who had followed her so faithfully changed into their equine shapes, their screams of anguish ringing in her ears. One by one, the Phaerie seized them – all but Schiannath and the Windeye, who were closest to the bridge. They galloped at breakneck

426

speed across the wooden span, knowing that across the water they would be safe from the powers of the Phaerie Lord.

'No!' D'arvan shouted, his voice cracking with anguish. 'Leave them alone, father!'

Hellorin gave a howl of thwarted rage, then swung up on to Iscalda, who seemed to have grown to giant proportions to match his own. 'We ride!' he shouted. 'Let the world tremble – for the Phaerie ride at last!' And then they were gone, racing up into the looming clouds, leaving only the sound of Eilin's weeping.

And even as Aurian was reeling in horror, Cygnus came hurtling from the skies and fell upon Anvar, slicing at the thongs that held the Harp in place. The Mage cried out in anger and ran across the bridge to her soulmate's aid, lifting the Sword to smite the winged man – and dropping it in horror as she realized what she had almost done. Drawing her own blade, she struck at the white-winged figure, and he fell away from his victim, writhing in agony as his lifeblood stained the grass around the Harp of Winds.

Aurian reached out to Anvar, who lay unconscious on the ground, an ugly bruise darkening his forehead. But Eliseth was there before her, the Sword of Flame clutched triumphantly in her hand, clinging to it grimly though her fingers were black and smoking, and her face was twisted into a rictus of agony. 'I may not wield it,' she screamed, 'but neither will you!'

The blaze of the Sword's power drove Aurian back. Standing over Anvar, Eliseth took out the grail that was the Cauldron and brought the two Great Weapons together with a resounding clash. 'Slay her, O Powers,' she shrieked, but she had scant control over either of the Artefacts, and the result was not what she had expected. Aurian caught a glimpse of her face, twisted with horror, as with a soundless explosion a great rent ripped open in the fabric of time itself, as though the world had been painted on a sheet of fabric that had been suddenly rent asunder. Shrieking, Eliseth was sucked into the gap, and Anvar with her.

With a cry of anguish, Aurian snatched up the Harp of Winds and hurled herself into the closing rent, the great cats leaping at her heels. Neighing shrilly, Schiannath and Chiamh followed. Maya and D'arvan came out of their frozen horror and exchanged a single glance. Clasping hands, they ran towards the narrowing gap in time – and disappeared, as it snapped shut behind them.

Vannor and Parric came panting to a halt beside Yazour, who had been too late to follow, and the horrified Eilin. For a time they stood in silence, aghast at the enormity of what had taken place. 'Well,' said the merchant finally, 'at least she didn't go alone.'

'What good will that serve?' Eilin flared. 'We don't even know if they survived to emerge into another time.'

'Aurian will survive,' said Vannor firmly. 'I'll lay money on it. And since we'd have certainly known about it if she had gone into the past, that can only mean she'll be turning up again in the future.'

Smiling wryly, he looked at the place from which Aurian had disappeared. 'I only hope I'm still alive to see it.'